PRESERVING
Peaches

Books by Pamela Burford

Jane Delaney Mysteries
Undertaking Irene
Uprooting Ernie
Perforating Pierre
Icing Allison
Preserving Peaches
Simmering Stu
Liquidating Larry
Scrapping Scarlett
Jane Delaney Humorous Mystery Series: Books 1-3 Box Set

Romantic Suspense
Snatched
Going Commando
Storming Meg
A Case of You
Twice Burned (Double Dare book 2)

Contemporary Romance
Rags to Bitches
In the Dark
Snowed
Too Darn Hot
The Boss's Runaway Bride (a novella)

The Wedding Ring matchmaking series:
Love's Funny That Way
I Do, But Here's the Catch
One Eager Bride To Go
Fiancé for Hire
The Wedding Ring Matchmaker Series: Complete Four-Book Romantic Comedy Box Set

PRESERVING
Peaches

A Jane Delaney Mystery
Book 5

Pamela Burford

Paperback edition published 2019 by Radical Poodle Press
Copyright © 2019 by Pamela Burford

ISBN 978-1-944922-70-2
Ebook ISBN 978-1-939215-75-8

Interior design by BB eBooks
Cover design copyright © 2019 Patricia Ryan
Author photograph copyright © Jeff Loeser

www.pamelaburford.com

Acknowledgments

I want to take this opportunity to recognize my small but mighty crew of Jane Delaney first readers: Jeff Loeser, Patricia Ryan (aka P.B. Ryan), Meara Platt, and Neal Roberts. I value their sharp eyes, pithy insights, and steadfast encouragement more than they can know.

Though all the books in this series take place in quaint Crystal Harbor, Long Island (don't bother looking for it on a map), your intrepid author has recently made the big leap from Long Island to Austin, Texas. Austinites who make it as far as Chapter Six in this book might detect an eerie resemblance between that chapter's fictional setting—a piano bar I call Dawn's Depot—and the delightfully eclectic Donn's Depot on 5th Street. (See what I did with the names there? Fiendishly clever, no?) I took a few liberties for the sake of the story, not the least of which was relocating the bar eighteen hundred miles north, but trust me, the real and wonderful Donn's Depot is well worth going out of your way for. Many thanks to my new neighbor Craig Calvert for introducing me to this historic Austin night spot, where he occupies the stage on Thursday nights. Thanks, too, to Marji Calvert, who introduced me to the historic town of Gärlichnott, one of the first communities established by the German immigrants who settled in the Texas Hill Country. That's our story and we're stickin' to it.

1

All Talk and No Action

I SHOULDN'T HAVE been surprised. Even though that's, you know, the point of a surprise party. My fortieth birthday had come and gone two days earlier, on Thursday, March 27, with barely a blip of recognition from my nearest and dearest.

Which should have been the first clue that something was in the works, but I was too busy feeling sorry for myself to make the mental leap from *Nobody loves me* to *I'll bet those sneaky SOBs are planning a party.*

So there I stood, Slow Learner of the Year, inside the doorway of the Crystal Harbor Historical Society, wondering why the dark entrance hall was suddenly blazing with lights and everyone I knew was hollering, *"Surprise!"*

And yeah, I glanced behind me to see who they were yelling at while Sexy Beast, lounging in the straw bucket tote hanging from my shoulder, gave me a look of studied exasperation.

Poodles can, too, look exasperated! That includes high-maintenance (otherwise known as slightly neurotic) seven-pound apricot poodles with prominent buckfangs and an air of princely entitlement.

Okay, that's unfair to Sexy Beast. His buckfang isn't *that* prominent.

"Look at her," Sophie Halperin cackled to the assembled guests, while gesturing at my gobsmacked expression with her beer bottle. "Think we can safely say she never saw it coming."

I think I can safely say that if I *had* seen it coming, I'd have applied a dab of makeup, done something with my strawberry-blonde hair besides corralling it into a messy ponytail (not chic messy, mind you, more sad and scary messy), and chosen an outfit that didn't involve saggy turquoise-and-white track pants and an ancient, once-purple sweatshirt that advertised a local tattoo and piercing shop.

That's right, I'd once plunked down cash money for the privilege of turning myself into a walking billboard for flaming skulls and nipple rings. And before you ask: No, I personally have no body modifications, if you don't count a couple of dental fillings and a bullet scar on my left butt cheek. If neuroscientists ever decide to map my brain, they'll find a huge chunk of gray matter devoted to *It Seemed Like a Good Idea at the Time*.

The sweatshirt, that is, not getting shot in the butt, which had not, in fact, been my idea, good or otherwise. It hadn't even been the idea of the person doing the shooting, who had not, you will be unsurprised to learn, been aiming for my posterior. That particular mishap had occurred two months earlier, in late January, and resulted, fortunately, in nothing more alarming than a grazing wound. That said, I can now state with authority that there is little in life more alarming than getting shot, no matter the location or degree of injury.

Sophie was having altogether too much fun at my expense. She was the one who'd snookered me into hauling my disheveled self to the venerable Historical Society building at eight p.m. ("on the dot, Jane!") for what was supposed to have been a planning meeting for the town's upcoming annual poker tournament.

A squat, graying woman in her mid-fifties, Sophie had more energy and attitude than most people half her age. I shot her a grumpy look that asked how she could do this dastardly thing to me, which she answered with a big, jolly belly laugh.

In truth, I was happy to see her enjoying herself. Not only was Sophie my closest pal, but just the day before, she'd lost her bid to remain Crystal Harbor's mayor. It had been a tight election following a campaign marred by dirty tricks and mudslinging—by the opposition, natch. Mayor Sophie Halperin was now a civilian, or would be once Nina Wallace was sworn in a few weeks from now.

That's right, Nina Wallace—chic, pretty, ruthless Nina Wallace—would soon be *Mayor* Nina Wallace. It was too depressing to contemplate, so instead I concentrated on greeting all the folks who'd shown up on that frigid March evening to help me celebrate my nosedive into middle age. Speaking of things that are, ahem, too depressing to contemplate.

A couple of dozen people had crowded into the large entrance hall, intent on bestowing hugs, birthday wishes, and absolutely *hilarious* barbs regarding my advancing decrepitude. As a childless divorcee of a certain age, I was tempted to cup my ear and shout, "Could you repeat that? I can't hear you over the thunderous ticking of my biological clock."

My parents relieved me of my jacket and my dog. Sexy Beast—SB for short—had no complaints as he was passed from person to person. He licked every face he could reach, tail wagging. And why not? Almost all the partygoers were, if not part of his immediate pack, certainly part of his extended pack. Do dogs have those, like we have extended family? In any event, they weren't strangers and they weren't dogs, so he was happy.

I proceeded from the entrance hall to the front parlor, then on to the dining and drawing rooms, swept along by the human tide of All My Friends in the World. The mingled aromas of savory finger foods competed with ladies' perfumes and woodsmoke from the fireplaces. Clusters of colorful flowers spilled from an eclectic assortment of vases, bowls, and jars throughout the house. An antique sideboard supported mounds of wrapped gifts. Whoever had been put in charge of the music had done a commendable job. At the moment it was Billy Joel in a live recording of "New York State of Mind."

I chatted with Poppy and Beau Battle, the sweet young couple who owned the local pottery studio, then with my old friend Sten Jakobsen, who'd been practicing law in Crystal Harbor for nearly five decades.

Maia Armstrong grabbed me next. I complimented her flowing silk tunic in a bold geometric pattern of garnet and ivory. She'd recently grown out her extravagant froth of Afro curls so they just brushed her shoulders. "Hmm… no chef's jacket," I observed. "No apron. Does this mean you didn't cater this shindig?"

"Sophie tried to hire me," she said, "but I turned her down. I was determined to be a civilian tonight. I recommended someone else. He'll do a good job."

"But not *too* good a job, am I right?" I teased, and she winked.

The Historical Society might seem a strange place to throw a party, but the nineteenth-century stone farmhouse—restored to its original landmark-status elegance, complete with gleaming woodwork, leaded-glass windows, and exquisitely carved fireplaces mantels—was actually a charming venue for all sorts of private affairs, including the Death Diva's surprise fortieth birthday party.

What, you have a problem with "Death Diva"? A tad morbid, is it? I'll have you know I *earned* that nickname. And yeah, I didn't much care for it at first, but it's kind of grown on me.

My name is Jane Delaney, and let's just say I operate a somewhat unique freelance business. I'm one of those creative entrepreneurs you read about who saw an unmet need and devised a clever way to monetize it.

Okay, that's not strictly accurate. If I'm being honest, I sort of stumbled into this gig more than two decades ago when I was still in high school, first as a pet sitter for the late Irene McAuliffe, then as a sort of errand girl delivering floral arrangements to the graves of her deceased poodles at the Best Friend Pet Cemetery. The ex-dogs' names were Annie Hall, Dr. Strangelove, and Jaws. Can you tell she was a film buff? Sexy Beast had belonged to Irene, too, until her sudden demise a year earlier when I became his legal guardian.

Here's where it gets a little weird. Irene bequeathed her big, fancy house to Sexy Beast. No, seriously. Her multimillion-dollar home now belongs to a pampered toy poodle. Well, technically, she left it to me, but he holds a life estate in the property, so during his lifetime, he's the owner. I know, it's a little confusing. Bottom line: As his guardian, I get to live there with him. It sure beats the crummy basement apartment I called home until a year ago. Eventually the house will be mine, free and clear, but I don't want to think about that since it means Sexy Beast will no longer be around to share it with me.

Anyway, Irene recommended me to her friends, and before I knew it, I was delivering similar floral arrangements to human graves at the Whispering Willows Cemetery, on behalf of clients who'd moved out of the area or were really busy or, well, just too darn lazy to do it themselves. Hiring me assuaged their consciences, and it's not as if they couldn't afford my services. Crystal Harbor is an affluent community on the North Shore of Long Island about an hour and a half from Manhattan. I was a lower-middle-class kid from a working-class town on the South Shore, and to me, it seemed Irene and her pals had money to burn.

Before long I was doing other odd jobs of the deathy persuasion, such as scattering ashes, donating the deceased's belongings to charity, and helping to serve and clean up during funeral receptions. Over time the scope of my assignments expanded as clients requested services that you, or any sane person for that matter, might consider somewhat eccentric. Which is a polite way of saying ghoulish.

You'd be surprised what people will ask you to do, once they realize you're not going to swoon at the sight of a stiff. Well, maybe you wouldn't be surprised, but I was, at first anyway. Nowadays very little fazes me. Not that I do everything I'm asked. There's no end to the list of prospective assignments that are illegal, immoral, or too gruesome to consider. I have no problem turning those down.

Want me to disarticulate a loved one so he fits neatly into the more economical burial vessel you've chosen, aka the carton your Swedish bookcase arrived in? Sorry, no can do. Looking for someone to secretly mix Granny's ashes into your bridesmaids' face powder so the old gal can still be part of the wedding? Keep looking. This Death Diva isn't interested. And yes, I'd recently been asked to do both of those.

A waitress floated over with a tray of hors d'oeuvres,

complex constructions involving slices of filet mignon and melted cheese and other yummy stuff piled onto little rounds of garlic toast. When my mouth was crammed good and full, I heard, "Happy birthday, Jane."

It was Bonnie Hernandez, Crystal Harbor's chief of police, looking sleek and sophisticated as always, not to mention annoyingly young. She wore a form-fitting fuchsia dress, a polite smile, and a four-carat diamond which had been placed on her slender ring finger by my ex-husband, Dominic Faso. That's right, Dom is stinking rich, not that it does me any good since he was the exact opposite of rich back when we split.

Bonnie made no move to hug me or kiss my cheek. Ours was not a huggy-kissy sort of friendship. Let's face it, it wasn't any sort of friendship. Not only was she engaged to the man I'd spent far too long struggling to get over, but Bonnie and I had had our run-ins. We tolerated each other.

Her judgmental gaze flicked over me, lingering for an extra beat on my footwear. Don't ask.

Didn't I just say, don't ask? Oh, all right, since you seem to think it's *so important*. My feet were shod in plush orange bedroom slippers shaped like webbed penguin feet.

No, I did not wear them out of the house on purpose! I was in such a rush to get to Sophie's fictional poker-tournament meeting at eight p.m. "on the dot" that I forgot to change into actual shoes before jumping into my nowhere-near-new Mazda and racing to the Historical Society.

I discovered my blunder halfway there (penguin feet have a way of catching on the brake pedal), but saw no need to run back home and change. I'd known the other members of the tournament committee forever. They might rib me about wearing slippers out of the house—again—but were unlikely to be scandalized by it. Well, except for Nina, but scandalizing that miserable woman was one of my most rewarding hobbies, so it was all good.

Now, however, the expression on Bonnie's lovely face caused me to choke on my hors d'oeuvre and spray greasy crumbs all over her tasteful outfit. Did she know the Heimlich? More to the point, would she feel moved to perform it on me?

After what seemed an eternity of eye-bulging, tear-squirting, nose-dripping terror during which Bonnie gave my back a couple of anemic pats—what the heck was that supposed to do?—I finally managed to bully the thing down my gullet. I mumbled a tepid apology and swabbed my face with my little cocktail napkin, whereupon the two of us stood staring at each other for an excruciating half minute until Dom joined us, all smiles.

Well, he's almost always smiling—that's Dom—but this was the smile that said he hoped ex – Mrs. Faso Number One (that would be me) and future Mrs. Faso Number Four (you read that right) would become best buds.

And why not? After all, I got along fine with his two other ex-wives, not to mention the three kids he'd had with them. Surely Bonnie and I would hit it off eventually.

That's one thing I'd always treasured about Dom, his sunny optimism in the face of *when hell freezes over* odds.

Dom had dark, wavy hair and bottomless espresso eyes, and stood a couple of inches over six feet. While not classically handsome, he nevertheless exuded a potent sex appeal. At least I'd always thought so, since the first time I set eyes on him in Mr. Bender's eighth-grade Spanish class.

Dom gave me an enthusiastic birthday hug, which, unrepentant troublemaker that I am, I managed to prolong just past the outer edge of propriety, even treating those nice wide shoulders to a lingering caress.

What? I never claimed to be mature, so you can just zip it right now.

"So," he said, extricating himself and pointedly avoiding his fiancée's gaze—probably because he'd seen that stony expression before and it scared the bejesus out of him. "What were you two girls chatting about? Not me, I hope, heh heh."

Oh, Dom, I wanted to tell him, *just give it up.*

His smile abruptly fell away, his attention snagged by something behind me. Before I had a chance to turn around, a masculine arm snaked around me, proffering a small snifter half-filled with a golden liquid. The ambrosial aroma informed me it was my favorite sipping tequila, the expensive añejo brand I coveted but rarely splurged on. That arm could belong to only one person.

"Thanks, Padre." I accepted the glass and took a sip, savoring the luscious warmth that shimmied down my throat.

"Happy birthday, Jane." Smoothly slipping between me and Dom, he pressed a chaste kiss to my cheek. I say *chaste* because that's what it no doubt looked like to the casual observer. However, I'm not the only rascal who knows how to linger just a bit too long, and judging by Dom's narrow-eyed glare, he was not all that casual an observer. I suspected the padre's attentions toward me were motivated more by a desire to tweak Dom than any serious attraction to yours truly.

And before you get all snippy wondering how I could even think of a man of the cloth in those terms, let me assure you "Padre" is just a nickname, one I personally bestowed on Martin McAuliffe. You see, the first time I met Martin, he happened to be impersonating a priest.

Hey, I never said the guy was a candidate for sainthood. I

knew precious little about the padre's background, but I was fairly certain he possessed one of those pasts normally associated with the word *mysterious*. Maybe *checkered*. Okay, probably closer to *felonious*. The fact is, I didn't want to know. Knowing might place me in the position of having to choose between my personal code of honor and my friendship with someone I'd come to care for.

Now, don't get all excited. I mean *care for* in the sense that Martin and I had been through some intense stuff during the twelve short months we'd known each other. We'd even faced a pretty dangerous situation together. More than dangerous if you want to know the truth. We'd come darn close to buying the farm, not far from where we stood at that moment, as a matter of fact.

Well, a thing like that is bound to bring two people closer together, right? In a purely, you know, friendly way. It's only natural. I certainly didn't harbor girlish fantasies about the padre or lie in bed thinking about him or wondering how good a kisser he was or anything like that.

Are you buying any of this?

Martin and Dom exchanged curt nods. From the way Dom frowned at my glass of tequila, I could tell he wished he'd thought of it first.

And yeah, he was engaged to be married to Bonnie, but as you can probably tell, our relationship was complicated. And no, I don't mean *that* kind of relationship, which ended eighteen years ago when we signed our divorce papers, a divorce I'd regretted almost immediately. Dom and I had remained platonic friends while he married those other women and had the kids I couldn't help feeling should have been mine.

The complicated part was our lingering feelings for each

other. At least that's what I would have said a year ago—heck, even six months ago. Lately, however… not so much. As far as I was concerned, Bonnie could have him with my blessings. And he knew it.

At the moment, Dom's fiancée was scowling at him the way he was scowling at my tequila. Reading his mind. I couldn't help but notice she wasn't holding a drink.

Martin turned to her. "Chief Hernandez, you're looking particularly fetching this evening."

Her brow furrowed for a split second before she schooled her expression and murmured a barely audible, "Um, thanks." Like her fiancé, Bonnie had no use for the padre. For the past year she'd been looking for an opportunity to catch him red-handed at something—I don't think she much cared what, as long as he ended up in the pokey. I just prayed he didn't get careless or underestimate her.

He didn't say anything about *my* outfit, for which I silently thanked him.

Bonnie said, "I'm going to get a glass of wine." She turned on her heel and marched off, leaving Dom to figure it out and hurry after her.

Martin did not look sad to see them go. "Have those two cute kids set a wedding date yet?"

"Not to my knowledge," I said.

"They've been engaged for, what, a year?"

"Fifteen months," I said. "With a brief break in the middle."

"What are they waiting for?"

Good question. I suspected Dom was the one dragging his feet, and wondered how long it would take his fiancée to run out of patience. I shrugged. "I don't know and I couldn't care less."

"Uh-huh," he said. "So tell me. How does it feel to be middle-aged?"

"I'm not—"

He stopped me with a raised palm. "I seem to recall you mentioning that middle age begins at forty. Does this ring a bell?"

It did, darn it. "That's right, rub it in," I said, painfully aware that my ex-husband's fiancée was seven years younger than I. "And anyway, you have three years on me in case you forgot, Padre. Or are you going to claim it's different for men?" I finished my shot of tequila and looked around for somewhere to deposit the empty snifter.

"It's different, all right." He eyed me appreciatively as he took the glass from me and set it on an antique piecrust table. "From what I can tell, women age better than men."

"Huh. Good save." I felt my face heat even as I reached up and yanked out my hair elastic, releasing the bedraggled ponytail and trying in vain to finger-comb the tangled mess. Martin nudged my hand away and set to work fluffing my hair, running his fingers over my scalp and pretending not to notice my shivery response. He didn't seem to care who saw him playing hairdresser, either.

Yep, that's right, this Harley-riding, priest-impersonating, no doubt criminally connected bad boy had a gentlemanly streak.

For the record, there was nothing wrong with the way Martin was aging. He was athletically built, his sandy hair was all present and accounted for, and those blue eyes… well, let's just say if I didn't know he was the bastard child of one of Irene's stepsons, I'd wonder what Paul Newman had been up to the night he was conceived.

"There are advantages to being a decrepit forty-three year-old," he said. "Such as being called Grandpa."

He left that hanging there until my brain caught up with his words. "Wait, what? *Grandpa?*" I said, loud enough to turn heads. "Do you mean what I think you mean?"

I'd never seen him grin like that. "Lexie's due in September."

Lexie, as you might have guessed, was Martin's daughter, the product of a brief high school romance. I'd attended her wedding the previous May. I suppose I should have anticipated the prospect of her making Martin a granddaddy, but when you're a single woman—okay, a single middle-aged woman— still pining for a baby of your own, you don't tend to think of your age peers as grandparent material.

I threw myself at the padre and treated him to a rib-cracking hug, squealing with delight. "You're going to be a grandpa! I can't believe it." I pulled back and took in his euphoric expression. "I'm so happy for you, for all of you. How's Lexie feeling?"

"She's fine," he said. "Well, mostly fine. A little queasy once in a while."

"Boy? Girl? Do they know yet?"

He shook his head. "Not for a few more weeks. They're talking about doing it the old-fashioned way, waiting until the birth to find out."

I punched his shoulder. "This is such great news."

I flashed on Martin McAuliffe cradling an infant, a mental picture that should have appeared totally incongruous. Instead it seemed like the most natural thing in the world, and not just because I knew he'd done his share of burping and diaper changing as a teen dad—a surprising revelation that had come directly from Lexie's mom—but because I knew Martin. I knew there were dimensions to him I never would have imagined when we first met.

All around us, the party was in full swing. A waiter paused to offer us mini crab cakes perched on little squares of fried cornbread and adorned with avocado cream and pickled onions. I knew Maia wasn't responsible for the food tonight, but I hoped she was taking notes. The chow at this soiree was to die for.

The padre's smile was pure silk. "That's a sound I usually associate with something else."

It took me a moment to realize he was referring to the ecstatic groan I emitted after popping the delicacy into my mouth. I was accustomed to his suggestive remarks, which could reliably be counted on to make me blush like a schoolgirl. This seemed to be his sole purpose in saying them, considering he never took the flirtation any further. My flustered reaction was a source of entertainment, nothing more.

This time, however, I did not blush. Nor did I avert my gaze or roll my eyes in embarrassment. In fact, I never broke eye contact with Martin as I masticated my crab cake in thoughtful (an astute observer might have said *dangerous*) silence, swallowed, and daintily patted my lips with my colorful cocktail napkin, which I'd just noticed was emblazoned with the words *The Big Four-Uh-Oh!*

To hell with these men who seemed incapable of figuring out what they wanted. First Dom and now Martin. Enough was enough. I was in no mood.

I snatched a glass of champagne from a passing tray, downed the contents in one long pull, and shoved the empty flute at the startled waiter. Not that I needed Dutch courage to give voice to my exasperation, but, well… maybe I did, just a little.

I got in Martin's face. "You're all talk."

His eyebrows jerked up. "What's that supposed to mean?"

I lowered my voice, having no desire to fuel the indefatigable

Crystal Harbor rumor mill. I gave his chest a nice hard poke. "Just what I said, Padre. You are all talk and no action."

He glanced around and murmured, "What prompted this?"

"Oh gee, it couldn't possibly be the fact that here I've reached the big *four-uh-oh*—" I flung my wrinkled cocktail napkin at him "—and the only men in my life are clueless dolts who can't even figure out what they want, much less how to go after it."

Martin leaned down and spoke in a near whisper. "And it *couldn't possibly* have anything to do with the fact that you've reached the big four-uh-oh still hung up on a guy you divorced eighteen years ago."

I couldn't help noticing that he was the one getting flushed, for a change. Interesting. "I'm not talking about Dom," I said. "Well, not only about Dom. And I am *not* still hung up on him."

"Tell me another one," he said. "You've been mooning over the guy nearly half your life, Jane. You still have all his old love letters, every birthday card he gave you since middle school. I mean, what self-respecting divorced woman keeps her freeze-dried bridal bouquet in a glass display dome?"

Okay, for the record, yes, I'd held on to the bouquet, but it's not like I'd built a shrine to the thing in my living room. I'd kept it securely boxed up in a corner of the attic. And as for how the padre knew about the existence of all this pitiful memorabilia, it goes back to that mysterious past I mentioned earlier. The most advanced locks and security systems did little to slow him down. Believe me, I've tried. I didn't doubt Martin McAuliffe knew the contents of my house better than I did.

"Obviously it's been a while since you last snooped around my place," I said. "All that stuff is long gone. Flowers, letters, everything. I put it out at the curb."

Which, believe it or not, was true. I didn't blame the padre for looking dubious, considering my history.

No, not my history of abusing the truth, my history of pining for my ex-husband. Which I'm not sure is any better, but whatever. Give me some credit.

People around us began to take note of our heated conversation. Before Martin could challenge my claim, I seized his arm and carved a path through the throng of partygoers.

"Where are we going?" he asked, as I propelled him back toward the entrance hall.

"Upstairs, where we can get a little privacy."

I recognized the impish light in those too-blue eyes. I was in no mood.

Have I mentioned that? That I was in no damn mood?

"To *talk*," I barked. "And I advise you to think long and hard before you utter whatever naughty remark just popped into your head, because I guarantee you, you will regret it."

"This is a new and intriguing side of you, Jane," he said, as I forcefully hauled him past a grinning Sophie, my goggle-eyed parents, and Norman Butterwick, a tall, dapper fellow well into his nineties. The padre managed a quick hand-shake with the old man. "How's it going, Norman?"

"I'm delighted to be here," Norman said, "simply delighted. My word, wherever is Jane taking you?"

"Upstairs," Martin said, in a voice that carried. "For privacy, she says. To 'talk,' she says." And yes, he added jaunty air quotes.

I gaped at him. "You just can't help yourself, can you?" I was past caring who heard, which was just as well because I'm pretty sure everyone in the whole dang building heard.

Howie Werker, a detective buddy of mine, called out, "It's

about time!" This statement was met with enthusiastic applause. Well, from everyone but Dom, whose sullen glower was anything but enthusiastic.

"Amen to that." Sophie toasted us with her drink. She'd graduated from beer to something amber-colored on the rocks.

Sexy Beast was nestled in the crook of her other arm. He squirmed now, demanding to be set down. The instant she complied, he raced after the padre and me as we headed up the carpeted stairs.

The ground floor was the Historical Society's public face, reserved for meetings and the occasional private celebration. The onetime bedrooms on the second floor had long since been converted into the Society's utilitarian offices. I'd planned to drag Martin into one of them, close the door, and have a long-overdue conversation sprinkled with antiquated but perfectly serviceable words such as *intention* and *commitment*.

Once we stepped into the upstairs hallway, I realized the flaw in my plan. I'd expected the offices to be deserted on a Saturday evening. However, from a nearby open doorway I heard the unmistakable voice of the mayor-elect and current president of the Historical Society, Nina Wallace. She appeared to be talking on the phone. I lifted SB and held him close, hoping to keep him quiet. He gave my ear a thorough licking.

"Oh, well, that's so sweet of you to say," Nina gushed. "I'd be lying if I claimed I was surprised by the outcome of the election. The good people of Crystal Harbor were more than ready for a change."

Sure they were, once Nina had poisoned their minds with lies, exaggerations, and innuendoes calculated to turn them against Sophie Halperin, who'd fulfilled her mayoral duties with honor and distinction.

I felt the padre's warning touch on my shoulder. What did he think, that I was going to storm in there and give her what for? Did he have so little regard for my impulse control? For my ability to respond to toxic individuals in a mature and reasonable manner?

You can stop snickering.

He needn't have worried. I had no desire to explain to Nina why I was skulking around the administrative floor, but more than that, I had no desire to talk to her. Period. I'd promised Sophie I wouldn't cause a fuss about the dirty campaign her opponent had waged, and I kind of almost always keep my promises.

As much as it irked me, I conceded defeat and turned back toward the stairs. My cathartic confrontation with the padre would have to wait.

Martin halted my retreat, touched a finger to his lips, and cautiously peeked around the doorframe of Nina's office. He gave a thumbs-up and yanked me down the hall. As I hurried past her office, I glanced inside and saw she had her back to us but had begun turning toward the doorway, perhaps alerted by the squeaky old floorboards. If so, she declined to investigate.

She continued to bend the ear of whoever was on the other end of the line. "My first official act will be to redecorate the mayor's office. I mean, have you *seen* the place? Sophie deserved to be booted out for her decorating taste alone." Her trilling laughter spiked my blood pressure.

Good grief, when Sophie had become mayor, she'd declined to spend a nickel of the town's money redecorating her office, which was already pleasingly outfitted in pale earth tones with brass and marble accents. I could only wonder what changes Nina had in mind and how much they were going to cost. This was a woman with expensive tastes.

The doors to the other offices were closed. There was no way to tell whether any of them were occupied. I caught Martin's eye and shook my head, indicating it was a lost cause.

Naturally he failed to take my lead, instead casting a critical eye at our surroundings. Clearly, his burglar's instincts had been aroused.

And no, I can't say with absolute certainty that the padre's professional résumé included a section on breaking and entering. Call it an educated—and we're talking PhD level here—guess.

I trailed him down the hallway, hissing, "Let's get out of here, Padre. I don't want her to—"

He shushed me and approached a door at the end of the hallway that looked different from the others. Its lower edge was about six inches higher than the carpeted floor and rested on what appeared to be the first riser of a stairway.

It made sense that this old house would have an attic. The wealthy farmer who'd built it two centuries earlier no doubt employed a live-in servant or two, and they would have slept up there.

Martin tried the doorknob. Locked.

"Come on." I tugged on his arm, peering down the hall toward the open doorway of Nina's office, willing her to remain inside. "Let's go."

He produced his wallet and extracted a credit card, whispering, "Since when are you afraid of Nina Wallace?"

"I'm not afraid of her, I'd just rather not—*Padre! No!*" Suddenly I realized what he was up to. I'd seen that so-called credit card before. It was a cunning fake. I watched him slide it open to expose a set of little lock picks. "You're going to get us arrested."

"Did you really throw away all that stuff?" In the time it took him to whisper this, he'd picked the ancient lock and opened the door, which squeaked on its hinges. Before I had a chance to object, he pulled me onto the staircase and shut the door behind us.

Utter darkness enveloped us, disorienting me and making it difficult to get my bearings. The two drinks I'd had didn't help. Sexy Beast yelped and I realized I was squeezing him too tightly. I relaxed my grip.

I heard the jingle of keys. A second later, a small, bright light skidded off the walls, and I realized Martin had turned on the tiny flashlight he kept attached to his key ring.

The enclosed staircase was narrow, with a curve that amplified the claustrophobic feel. The walls sported ancient, peeling paint, and the stair treads were well worn. Clearly the house's restoration had not included the attic.

"Answer the question." The padre started up the stairs. "Did you?"

I snatched at the hem of his black sweater, trying in vain to halt his progress. "You're not going up there, are you?" I whispered. "Why are you going up there?"

"Just giving the lady what she wants." He'd reached the top. The light jittered around. "A private place to chat."

Sexy Beast didn't like this any better than I did. He began to gripe, forming his little mouth around sounds that were clearly meant to mimic the cadence of human speech. Whenever he did that, I was always tempted to say, "Enunciate!"

Good luck shutting up SB when he was in a complaining mood. Anyone passing in the hallway was likely to hear him. Reluctantly I followed the padre up the stairs and stepped onto the attic's wide floorboards. The flashlight barely illuminated our immediate area, leaving both ends of the huge room cloaked in impenetrable darkness. I spied a brick chimney stack and a scarred wooden trunk. And cobwebs. Lots of thick, dust-choked cobwebs festooning the rafters.

I scooted closer to Martin. "There must be a light switch."

"None that I could find."

My nose wrinkled. "It's so musty."

"More like something crawled in here and died."

"Ew, you think so?" I said. "I don't know, the smell's not *that* strong."

"A rat maybe. Raccoon." The padre swept his flashlight around, but the light failed to penetrate the edges of the room. Which was just as well. I had no desire to see an ex-raccoon. "Could've been here for weeks," he said, "months even. Smells fade over time."

"That must be what's freaking SB out," I said. "With his high-powered schnoz, he could probably tell us the poor critter's species, age, gender, and cause of death."

"Not to mention its precise location." Martin started to wander, aiming the light at the sides of the room, revealing a dilapidated chest of drawers and a stuffed armchair furry with dust and cobwebs.

"This must be where the maids slept." I nodded toward a pair of rusted iron bedsteads pushed against opposite walls, sporting sunken mattresses and mismatched spreads.

"Cozy." His tone was arid.

I pushed up the sleeves of my sweatshirt. "What I want to know is, why do they keep it so warm up here? It must be over eighty degrees."

He shrugged. "It's cold out."

I stuck close to him. "But why heat the attic when it's not, you know, being used for anything? I mean, it's obvious no one's been up here for ages. SB, will you please give it a break?" His grumbling had turned to sharp whines that skewered my brain like an icepick.

Martin tipped the flashlight under his own chin to spookily illuminate his face, which elicited a shriek of alarm from Sexy Beast and did nothing to calm my own abraded nerves. "We're getting off-topic," he said. "Answer the question."

"What question?" I asked.

"Did you really throw away all those mementos from your marriage?"

"Yes! You know very well that I'm over Dom. Give me that." I grabbed the flashlight from him and aimed it straight into his face.

"How am I supposed to know that?" he asked.

"Because you overheard us talking about it, me and Dom." I cut Martin off as he started to respond. "Don't you dare deny it. I know you were lurking outside my bedroom doorway that day, eavesdropping. It was back in January, right after I took a bullet in the butt and nearly drowned."

Specifically what he'd overheard was me telling Dom, *If breaking up with Bonnie is right for you, then that's what you should do. But don't assume I'll be waiting to take her place.* I'd accused my ex of hedging his bets, of trying to secure a commitment from me before breaking it off with Bonnie. Which I suppose made sense from the perspective of a man who couldn't abide being alone. Dom Faso was Mr. Serial Monogamy, never remaining single for long.

Martin studied me for long moments that were punctuated only by SB's increasingly frantic whining. Finally he said, "You were in an emotionally fragile state that day, Jane. I'm sure Dom won't hold you to your words."

Imagine my frustration when all I had to whack him with were a two-inch flashlight and a small dog in the throes of a minor meltdown.

I forced nonchalance into my tone. "I admit it took me too long to get over Dom, but I did. That chapter of my life is done. *Finito.* It's time to cut my losses and move on."

"To what?"

"To *who*, I think you mean." I kept the light aimed at his handsome mug, third degree – style, as I said, "I'm expecting a birthday call from Victor. Did you know he asked me to move in with him in Paris?"

The padre's gaze sharpened. He went very still. Victor Dewatre was a certifiable French hottie, the brother of a local Crystal Harbor chef who was murdered in his restaurant last fall. Victor had bunked at my place for a month during the investigation, and we'd grown quite fond of each other. Not that we'd done anything about it—anything, you know, physical— but Victor had indeed asked me to move to Paris, or at least go for an extended visit. And once I did, well, it was anyone's guess what might happen then.

Thank you for your guess, Captain Obvious. I was trying to be coy.

As flattered as I was by the persistent attentions of my French hottie, I was still hoping a certain American hottie would step up to the plate.

The hottie in question plucked the flashlight from my fingers and turned it off. I found my eyes had adjusted to the dark. I could now make out a small window set into the far wall about ten yards behind him. There was no moon that night. The faint glow through the grimy glass came from streetlights and nearby buildings.

The padre's voice was tight. "I think that would be a mistake."

"What?"

"You know what," he said. "Moving to Paris. That's just… You don't even really know the guy."

As diverting as it was to finally have Martin on the ropes, I found it impossible to give him my full attention. Vague shapes had begun to take form in the shadowed recesses near the window.

"I can't see you doing that," he continued, "pulling up stakes and abandoning everything, your whole life here, on a whim."

I squinted, struggling to identify what I was looking at. Some sort of small desk if my guess was right, facing the window. With a chair in front of it.

"So… what?" he said. "Some French guy crooks a finger and you come running?"

I knew I wasn't seeing what I thought I was seeing, because that was just nuts.

"Jane?"

"Huh?"

The padre spread his arms. "Am I talking to myself here?"

"Yeah. I mean no, just… give me that." I took the flashlight from him again, turned it on, and started making my way toward the window. The beam of light didn't reach that far. It quivered over the rafters, the scarred floor. I passed a broken teacup, a pile of disintegrating newspapers, a white enameled vessel I assumed was a chamber pot.

"What is it?" Martin's hand settled on my back, grounding me. Now he was the one squinting into the gloom. "What do you see?"

I swallowed hard. "I don't know. Nothing, probably."

Sexy Beast didn't think it was nothing. He scrabbled up my shoulder, clinging to my neck and giving me an earful of his displeasure.

"Okay, we're leaving this nasty place," I assured him in a quavering voice. "Jane just has to check something out first."

The circle of light finally reached the desk and chair.

"Whoa," Martin said.

"What is that?" I whispered. He didn't answer.

Something sat in the chair. It had a human shape, but it wasn't human, it couldn't be. We were facing the back of the thing, which wore a peach-colored dress. A scarf encircled its neck. A navy-blue jacket was draped over the chairback.

"Some sort of, um, mannequin," I said. It's funny what you can convince yourself of when your brain refuses to register what all your senses are screaming at you.

Numbly I moved around the chair to take in the silhouette, and gasped. "There's some—some sort of—of animal on its—its face." I raised a shaky hand to point to the front of the thing's bald, cobweb-draped head, which was tipped forward. A pale, furry something was perched there.

Martin commandeered the flashlight. Scanning the immediate area, he located a rusty fireplace poker, which he used to lift the furry object and fling it to the floor. We watched it land. It wasn't an animal, we now saw, but a wig. A blonde wig with wavy, chin-length hair.

The beam of light returned to the "mannequin." The padre and I groaned in unison and took a giant step back.

It was a human face, all right, the flesh now leathery, the features sunken and shriveled, as were the hands and exposed forearms. The head wasn't bald as I'd first thought. The corpse's dark hair was compressed under a close-fitting, beige wig cap.

Yellow rope encircled the body's torso, securing it to the chair. The wrists were tied to the chair arms, and the ankles to the front chair legs.

The source of the room's excessive heat became evident when I spied one of those portable oil-filled radiators, plugged into a nearby socket and cranked to high.

"Come on." Martin took my arm. "Let's get the hell out of here."

Sexy Beast seconded that suggestion with a warbling howl that was all too easy to translate. *I tried to warn you, but would you listen?*

2

That's Why They Call You the Death Dame

"YOU GOTTA HELP SEAN!" Cheyenne O'Rourke leaned across the counter and seized my wrist with more force than I'd have thought the lazy teenager capable of.

"What? Ow." I'd just stepped into Janey's Place, the vegetarian café on Main Street owned by Dom. Actually, this was the flagship location of a health-food empire that had begun as a lowly food truck way back when we were dating.

That's right, he named it after me. How astute of you.

I didn't have much use for ninety-nine percent of the offerings at Janey's Place—I mean, my ideal meal is Buffalo chicken pizza, orange soda, and a chocolate croissant—but this joint made a smoothie that was as yummy as any milkshake, with papaya and ginger and who knew what else. Despite my aversion to most of its menu items, Janey's Place always smelled heavenly, like Grandma's house if Grandma had been a master chef in a previous life. And a hippie in another.

It was around noon on Monday and I was already running late for a meeting with a prospective client, but my empty stomach was squealing like the geriatric brakes on my Mazda, thus the decision to suck down a quick smoothie on the way.

The potential client, Betsy van Heel, was considering hiring me to get in touch with her husband, Harvey, whom she hadn't heard from in a long time. I hear you thinking, But, Jane, you're the Death Diva. Isn't that a job for a private investigator? Not when the husband in question, owner of a successful chain of liquor stores, had been marked permanently out of stock fourteen years earlier.

I informed Betsy that although I had over two decades of experience in my admittedly bizarre chosen profession, my skill set did not include chatting up the deceased—whereupon she informed me she was willing to shell out a thousand bucks if I made a sincere effort to do so, plus a whopping twenty thou in the event I actually succeeded. She'd already spent far more than that on mediums, psychics, and assorted charlatans, and wanted to see what a "real professional" could do. Using, you know, science and stuff.

I had no hope of earning the eye-popping bonus, but a cool grand just for giving it the old college try? Couldn't hurt to hear the lady out, right?

Which I'd never get a chance to do if Cheyenne didn't relinquish her death grip on my wrist. The lunchtime rush was getting under way and hungry customers were lining up behind me.

"Cheyenne, I just want to order a—"

"He didn't do it!" she shrieked. "You gotta help him."

That's when I noticed that the tattoo she'd been sporting on the side of her neck for the past couple of months—an inexpert rendition of the name *Brian* in script—had been crossed out with a large *X*. A new name now adorned the other side of her neck: *Sean.* This tattoo was as amateurishly executed as the Brian tat. Both it and the *X* had that raw, scalded look that told me they were recently inked.

From somewhere in the grumbling queue behind me I heard Beau Battle call out, "Is anyone else working here? I've got to get back to the gallery."

Cheyenne abandoned her post, emitting an ear-splitting *"Daddy!"* as she tottered around the counter on her mile-high platform boots and yanked me out of line. Patrick O'Rourke, the manager, emerged from the back office, looking annoyed if not particularly surprised. His daughter's work ethic, or lack thereof, was not exactly news to him.

I struggled in vain to reclaim my arm as she hauled me away from the food-service area into a section of the café that served as a natural-foods grocery store, deserted at the moment except for us. Here, those who were so inclined could purchase all manner of fair-trade this, locally sourced that, and gluten-free everything. Sorry. Until Janey's Place began stocking Fruity Pebbles and Cherry Garcia, I'd continue to purchase my vittles at the huge, brightly lit Super Stop & Shop.

"Cheyenne, whatever this is about, I can't discuss it now. I have a meeting that's supposed to start—" I glanced at the wall clock and muttered a naughty word "—this very instant."

Despite Cheyenne's well-nourished figure, she wore her usual work uniform of an apple-green Janey's Place tee knotted at her pillowy midriff over a pair of skintight striped leggings in shades of purple, pink, and yellow.

"Sean didn't do it," she sobbed, as I finally wrenched my arm free.

"Is he your new boyfriend?"

Her eyes grew wide. "How did you know?"

I gestured toward the fresh tat, which she was vigorously

scratching with long fingernails painted toothpaste-green.

"Huh?" she said. "Oh. Yeah."

"What happened to Brian?" I asked.

"Who?"

Through a valiant effort I managed not to smack my forehead. I pointed to the other side of her neck.

Cheyenne offered a dismissive flap of her hand. "Oh, I, like, dumped that loser."

Hence the permanent *X* tattooed over his name. Cheaper and quicker than laser removal, I supposed. If it was true that she was the dumper rather than the dumpee, I could only wonder just how much of a loser a guy had to be to earn a dumping by the likes of Cheyenne O'Rourke—someone who'd willingly had his name permanently affixed to her body in a highly visible location. This, after knowing the guy for maybe a week and a half. I hoped for her sake this Sean was ink-worthy. She didn't have that much neck space left.

"So what's the deal with Sean?" I'd given up hope of snagging a smoothie. My sole mission at this point was to hightail it out of there in time to salvage my meeting. "Make it quick."

"They *arrested* him!" she screamed, turning the heads of everyone waiting on line for lunch. "It's, like, totally *unfair!*"

"Keep your voice down, Cheyenne." I steered her to the back wall, which was lined with self-serve hoppers filled with organic foods in bulk: exotic teas, dried fruits, nuts, beans, grains, granolas, and assorted so-called snack foods. I mean, quinoa-matcha protein balls? I couldn't imagine being that hungry.

"What was Sean arrested for?" I asked.

"Murder!" she howled. "They think he killed his mom."

It took me a couple of seconds, but eventually my distracted brain caught up. Gertrude Gillespey, the deceased individual Martin and I had discovered in the attic of the Crystal Harbor Historical Society two days earlier, had been the victim of foul play, according to the authorities.

What gave it away? you ask. Hmm… Could it have been the stout ropes binding her to the chair? How about the silk scarf knotted tightly enough around her neck to cut off air flow?

The scarf was printed with a lovely, Asian-looking watercolor image: ripe peaches hanging on a tree. Gertrude's nickname had been "Peaches," a lifelong moniker she'd embraced and encouraged. According to one rumor I'd heard, the last person to call her Gertrude had ended up quitting his job, selling his house, and moving to Lithuania to get away from her. You might think that's an exaggeration, but no one who'd known Peaches doubted it for an instant. When folks were feeling polite, they called her a "character." You probably don't want to know what they called her most of the time.

Peaches had managed to monetize that irascible attitude in the form of "Peaches Preaches," the advice column she'd penned for the past decade. It was published in print and online in *You Know It*, a slick pop-culture monthly with a readership in the hundred-million range. Readers wrote in asking for counsel on subjects ranging from domestic squabbles to workplace problems to the ever-popular sex and romance. Peaches's responses fell into three categories: Insulting, Outrageously Insulting, and I Can't Believe They Let Her Print That.

Everyone in town knew Peaches had been missing since shortly after Thanksgiving. Her family had filed a missing-person report. The police had investigated and come up empty.

And all that time her corpse had been sitting up there in the attic of the Crystal Harbor Historical Society. It was a case of natural mummification, according to the medical examiner. Turns out that can happen in dry environments like that overheated attic. The bacteria that cause decomposition need moisture to do their necessary but admittedly icky work. Peaches's body underwent a rapid drying process which retarded bacterial activity and turned her into the equivalent of human jerky.

I recalled now that Peaches did indeed have a son named Sean. A grown daughter, too, if I wasn't mistaken. Peaches had never married their father, and I'd heard that not long before her disappearance, the two had broken up after a decades-long cohabitation.

This was the first I was hearing about the arrest. It must have just happened. From what I knew of the son, I wasn't surprised. By all accounts, he was bad news. I also wasn't surprised to discover he was Cheyenne O'Rourke's new significant other. The girl had a history of poor decision making and had, in fact, once come close to being arrested for murder herself.

"I don't know what you expect me to do for Sean," I said. "Doesn't he have a lawyer?"

"His dad got him one." She shrugged. "But, like, you know."

"No, Cheyenne, I don't know. Why don't you enlighten me."

She rolled her eyes, making me wonder why I was standing there trying to make sense of her—or rather, Sean's—predicament when I should have been nailing down a lucrative assignment.

But I knew why. I was intrigued. And that wasn't good. When I'm intrigued, things tend to get messy. Heck, when I breathe, things tend to get messy, so I figured I might as well hear her out. Then I could tell her I had no intention of getting involved and be on my way.

I see you smirking. It's very unbecoming and totally uncalled-for. Well, somewhat uncalled-for. Maybe.

Patrick called out, "For cripes sake, Cheyenne, I need you over here."

I looked at the lunch line, which had doubled in the past sixty seconds. The girl's dad had three blenders, two griddles, and the broiler going as he ladled vegetarian chili with one hand and wiped up spilled carrot juice with the other.

"*Yeah, yeah,*" she screeched. "Can't you see I'm *busy*? Gawd!"

"This thing with Sean is none of my business," I told her. "It's his lawyer's job to prove he didn't—"

"Yeah, 'cause he did *such* a good job defending Sean three years ago." Another eye-roll, this one accompanied by a disgusted shake of the head.

No way was I going to ask. I had no business asking. I needed to get out of there, stat, and hightail it to Betsy van Heel's house. I opened my mouth to tell her *sayonara.* "So what happened three years ago?"

Dang! I hate it when that happens.

"The break-ins?" Her expression suggested I was a little slow. "Umm…"

"Okay, burglaries," she said. "Whatev."

I was tempted to tell her that if she kept doing that, her eyeballs would remain permanently rolled up toward the ceiling.

"Okay, I think I'm catching on," I said. "Sean was arrested for burglary three years ago."

"Duh."

"And his dad is hiring the same lawyer who represented him

before," I said, "only it didn't go so well back then."

"The guy's totally useless," Cheyenne said. "Carlos Levine, that's the idiot's name. He didn't, like, get him off or anything."

"Was Sean guilty?" I asked.

"Yeah. So?"

And his lawyer didn't, like, get him off or anything. Life is so unfair.

"You said 'burglaries.' Plural. What are we talking about here?" I asked. "Did he break into homes? Businesses?"

"Homes. Like, three of them," she said. "Well, three that they found out about. But he didn't hurt anyone. He always made sure no one was, like, home."

"He did time, I assume?"

She nodded. "A year. That was before I knew him."

"How old is Sean?" I asked.

"Twenty. So back then he was, uh…" Cheyenne's brow furrowed in deep cogitation.

Twenty minus three. Come on, Cheyenne, I know you can do it. Finally I offered, "Seventeen?"

"Wait," she said. "I'm working it out."

"And he's been clean since then?"

She hesitated. "Depends what you mean by clean."

"Okay, you have to leave this to Mr. Levine." I started to back away. "He knows Sean's legal history, he's in the best position to—"

"No!" She sank her minty-fresh talons into my arm, halting my retreat. "You have to help him. You know about this stuff."

"What stuff would that be?"

"Like, murder and stuff," she said. "That's why they call you the Death Dame."

"Diva," I said.

"What?"

"I'm called the—Never mind. It doesn't make me an expert on murder."

"Just look into it." She dug her nails deeper into my arm, making my knees buckle. "Do some, like, investigating. Sean didn't do it. I mean, sure, he hated his bitch mom for kicking him out of the house and everything. Oh my Gawd, he would not shut up about it. He might've wished she was dead, but that doesn't mean he did it."

"Did he?" I asked. "Wish she was dead?"

"Yeah. So?"

I glanced at the clock again. Betsy van Heel had now been waiting three and a half minutes for me to knock on her door. And I still had to make my way to said door, which would take me another five to seven minutes, depending on the lunchtime traffic. "Okay, okay, I'll do it."

Cheyenne's face lit up. "You'll prove he didn't kill her?"

"I'll look into it. That's all I can promise. Now, give me back my arm."

3

Mummy Dearest

HAPPILY, MY MEETING with Betsy van Heel went great. She didn't seem to notice I was ten minutes late, which didn't surprise me since she turned out to be more than a little flaky.

Right about now you're thinking, Really? The lady wants you to get in touch with someone who's been in the ground for fourteen years and she strikes you as flaky?

Betsy van Heel might be a tad wackadoodle, and I might not personally believe in the mumbo-jumbo she subscribed to, but since she'd decided I was the person who could get through to the late Harvey van Heel, I intended to do this thing right. I'd do my homework, research the heck out of it, and give it my best shot. Only then would I let Betsy fork over the promised thousand bucks.

And just for the record, in the more than two decades I've been Death Diva'ing, I've never cheated a client. In my book, taking advantage of a client's grief, confused state of mind, or, as in this case, nonstandard belief system was tantamount to robbery. It was a matter of conscience, part of a Death Diva code of honor I subscribe to.

That evening I found myself driving through a torrential downpour to meet with yet another prospective client. That's how it is with my strange business, it's the proverbial feast or famine. This one was a woman named Evie Moretti, and she lived in an apartment building I was familiar with, called The Americana. She'd sounded young on the phone that morning, but taciturn. She wouldn't offer much info about the job she wanted me to perform, except to say it involved the missing property of a recently deceased person.

I suggested she might be better off reporting the suspected theft to the cops. She immediately dismissed that idea, at which point I figured it wouldn't hurt to hear her out. Evie informed me she got home from work around six p.m. It was about half past six when I pulled into the building's parking garage and located a vacant guest space.

After Evie buzzed me into the building, I took the elevator to the fourth floor and knocked on the door of apartment 4A. The woman who opened it was indeed young, in her early twenties. She was on the tall side, about five nine, and dressed in a conservative blue skirt suit, her blonde hair pulled back into a neat chignon. She wore simple pearl stud earrings and rimless eyeglasses.

"Ms. Delaney?" she asked

"Please, call me Jane. It's nice to meet you, Ms. Moretti."

I expected her to reciprocate by inviting me to call her Evie, or Evelyn, or what have you. Instead she continued to block the doorway and said, "Would you mind showing me some identification." It was not a question.

My surprise had to be apparent. In all my years as a freelance businessperson, I'd never been asked to prove who I was. "Um… sure, just give me a sec," I mumbled as I rummaged through my briefcase. "Here you go." I shoved one of my business cards at her.

She took it, examined it carefully, turned it over. And stared at me, clearly waiting for something more official. What did she think, that there was some sort of Death Diva international organization, with regional chapters, an annual conference, and holographic photo ID?

Okay, now I was starting to get steamed. First the woman is downright secretive on the phone about what she wants me to do for her, and then she acts like I'm some sort of impostor, just pretending to be *the* Jane Delaney, Death Diva extraordinaire.

I managed to keep my expression more or less neutral as I handed over my driver's license. One of the tougher lessons my line of work has hammered home is the importance of repressing my snarky side in the interest of keeping the larder stocked with Fruity Pebbles and Vienna sausages. The sausages are for Sexy Beast, although he manages to snag his fair share of Fruity Pebbles too.

And yes, I am, too, capable of repressing my snarky side, I just need a really good reason to make the effort. Like avoiding starvation.

As my prospective client peered closely at my license, I noticed that her left ring finger was bare. No Mr. Moretti in the picture, then.

At last she handed it back and stepped aside to wordlessly invite me into her apartment. What, no blood test? No waterboarding? I decided right then that if she demanded a list of references, I'd walk. I mean, I've done work for an impressive proportion of the Crystal Harbor citizenry, leaving the vast majority of those clients more than satisfied with my services. Clearly it was word of mouth that had brought Evie to me in the first place. You'd think that would be good enough.

Her home was furnished traditionally, in assorted variations of beige with little in the way of decoration. I noticed right off if there were no family photographs on display.

She invited me to sit but didn't offer so much as a glass of water. I settled into a Queen Anne wing chair. She sat on the camelback sofa across from me. A manila folder lay on the coffee table between us.

Evie got right down to it. "This is a rather sensitive situation, Jane."

"That describes almost all the assignments I handle, Ms. Moretti. Why don't you tell me what this is about and we'll take it from there. You said some property went missing?"

"That's right." She reached for the folder. "A collection of figurines. Well, 'figurines' isn't really accurate. We're talking about a wide range of collectibles, everything from cheap kitschy stuff to pieces worth thousands." She handed the folder to me.

Inside was a thick stack of eight-by-ten photos. The top one was split into four sections, showing a close-up of a glass paperweight in the shape of peach, from four different angles. I chewed back a smile. Quite the coincidence considering that several hours earlier Cheyenne had coerced me into looking into the Peaches Gillespey murder. This was turning into a peachy day indeed.

Oh, come on. You couldn't see that one coming?

My smile faltered when the next picture showed a lovely little carved marble peach, also from four angles. This was followed by images of a tacky snow globe labeled *Atlanta, the Big Peach!*, with a little plastic peach tree inside it. The glitter sitting at the bottom was pink rather than white, from which I deduced this was in fact a peach-blossom globe. Which made sense because, I mean, how much snow does Atlanta get?

I moved on to the next sheet, containing four shots of an

intricately detailed porcelain peach which appeared to be an antique. The paint was worn in places, and I wouldn't have been surprised to learn it was at least a couple of hundred years old.

I quickly flipped through the rest of the photos. You guessed it, more peach tchotchkes, four dozen at least, of every conceivable material and design. I looked at Evie. "Okay, I have to ask. Are you related to Gertrude 'Peaches' Gillespey?"

"Peaches was my mother. I assumed you knew."

"Well, your name is Moretti, so…"

"Carter Moretti is my dad," Evie said. "He and Mom were in a common-law marriage for twenty-four years."

I suppose *common-law marriage* sounded a little more respectable than *shacked up*. "But they split recently, right?" I asked.

She stiffened. "What does that have to do with anything?"

If this woman was going to be so prickly about every darn thing, I didn't even want to try working with her. I wagged the folder. "I assume this collection belonged to your mother?"

She nodded, frowning.

"And now you don't know where these items are, but you suspect that someone in your family, or someone close to your family, made off with them during the months when your mom was missing. Hence the sensitive nature of the assignment. Am I getting warm, Ms. Moretti?" I figured if I called her Ms. Moretti enough times, eventually she'd get a little embarrassed and ask me to call her by her first name. I mean, I was close to twice her age.

Evie sighed deeply. "It's not that I think someone made off with them. Well, that could be what happened. The thing is, it's my brother. Sean. I suppose you know he was arrested earlier today. They think he killed her. I'm sure everyone knows by now, considering how fast bad news spreads in this town."

I merely nodded, making no mention of Cheyenne and the promise I'd made her to look into the murder. I said, "You think Sean took the peach collection?"

An angry flush suffused her face. "I think he gave them away. Or even threw them away, just to spite me. But someone could very well have simply walked off with them. It wouldn't have been difficult."

"Why?" I asked. "Isn't your mom's home locked up?"

"Sean's living there now. He moved back in as soon as we realized she was really missing. At first we hoped she was just taking a vacation."

"Without telling anyone in the family where she was going?" I asked.

Her expression was weary. "It wouldn't have been the first time. And then after she and dad broke up, she started, um… well, her social life really picked up, and she became even more unpredictable."

"Meaning she was actively dating," I said.

Evie squirmed. "That's one way to put it."

"Was there someone special," I asked, "or was she seeing more than one man?"

"I really don't see what this has to do—"

"Ms. Moretti, if I'm going to take on this assignment, I need some background. Whatever you tell me will remain strictly between the two of us. You won't be reading about it in the *Harbor Herald*, I promise."

I know what you're thinking. You're thinking, Jane, you didn't really need to know about Peaches's sex life. Admit it, you were just curious.

Heck yes, I was curious. But I did indeed have a legitimate

reason to venture down this particular conversational path. Evie had indicated that someone close to Peaches might have swiped her collection. It was entirely possible that someone was a new, possibly untrustworthy, paramour. Before I agreed to take on this assignment, I needed to know what I was dealing with.

Evie avoided my gaze. "Okay, well, the fact is, my mother was enjoying her freedom."

"Meaning she was dating different men and didn't have one exclusive guy." I waited until she confirmed it with a sour nod. Why was Evie so worked up about her newly single mom playing the field? Maybe the whole thing just weirded her out. She struck me as pretty uptight.

I said, "You mentioned that your brother Sean moved *back* into your mom's house after she went missing. So he used to live there with her?"

"Yes, until she kicked him out."

I already knew this from Cheyenne, I just wanted to hear Evie confirm it.

"Why did she do that?" I asked.

"Well, she and Dad had just broken up—"

"Who did the breaking up?" I asked. "Your mom or Carter?"

"Mom did. Well, they were both unhappy, but he probably would've stuck it out if she'd let him. Dad's not one for big changes or rocking the boat."

When she didn't elaborate, I said, "Meaning what?"

Evie sighed. "Meaning she'd been supporting him for twenty-four years and he'd put up with an awful lot from her during that time."

The same could be said for a lot of *wives*. I didn't think it politic to mention it. "So your mom dumps your dad and, what, he moves out of the house? Where did he go?"

"He moved in with his mother, my grandma Audrey," she said.

"Is your grandpa still alive?"

She shook her head. "Grandma's been a widow for years."

"How old is your dad?" I asked.

"Forty-five. Same age my mom was."

Kind of an awkward age to move back in with your elderly mother. "Is it temporary?" I asked. "I mean, is Carter planning to get his own place?"

"He can't, he has no real source of income. I just wish he'd get a job, any job, and stop sponging off Grandma's Social Security, but…" She sighed. "What can I tell you, she still spoils him."

"Okay, well, did your mom kick Sean out at the same time?" I asked.

"Yes, and I didn't blame her one bit. My brother's hard enough to handle when there are two parents in the house. It's a full-time job, believe me. Mom was kind of starting fresh, like I said, and the last thing she needed was a slacker druggie like Sean hanging around and getting in the way."

This was the most sympathetic thing I'd heard her say about her dead mother since we'd started talking. As critical as she was of Peaches, she had even less use for her younger brother. "So I'm guessing Sean moved in with your grandma at the same time your dad did."

Evie made a face. "Grandma Audrey lives in this little two-bedroom house. Sean was sleeping in the basement and making both their lives hell."

"And neither of the men had a job, is that right?" I asked.

"Right."

So it was the women in the family who kept it together,

financially. I could understand why they'd had it up to here with those two layabouts.

"When did all this happen, Ms. Moretti?" I asked. "When did your mom give your dad and your brother the boot?"

"About…" Evie gave it some thought. "Actually, I can tell you exactly when it happened. It was the day before Halloween."

"What precipitated it?" I asked.

"That's not important. Just a stupid argument."

I remained silent, waiting.

Finally she said, "Okay, if you must know, the whole thing started with a disagreement over trick-or-treat candy."

I let my skeptical expression say it all.

Evie raised her hand in a scout's-honor gesture. "Dad wanted to buy the good stuff, the stuff every kid hopes to get in their trick-or-treat sack. You know."

In unison we intoned, "Chocolate." My mouth watered as I imagined tearing into a giant Kit Kat bar. I'd have to swing by the 7-Eleven convenience store on my way home.

"Jane, the thing you have to realize about my mom," Evie said, "is that she was cheap. Oh, not where her own needs and desires were concerned. She never denied herself anything as far as I could tell. But, well, I never knew her to make a charitable donation or lend anyone money, and she was always stingy with dad and Sean and me, always questioning any purchase, demanding to know where every nickel went."

"So the trick-or-treaters would get what?" I asked. "Candy corn?"

"Candy corn would've been a huge step up," she said. "Try Licorice. Taffy. Raisins."

"Yeesh. Well, I suppose there are some kids who like that stuff. Just tell me she didn't hand out…" I could tell from Evie's expression she was way ahead of me. I shook my head and groaned, "No. Oh no…"

She offered a grim nod. "Some years it was all they got. Those damn circus peanuts. She said it was because they're sort of peach-colored."

I shuddered. How had such an unfeeling monster earned her jolly nickname?

The idea that a fight over trick-or-treat candy caused the breakup of Evie's family was as tough to swallow as a handful of marshmallowy circus peanuts, but it was clear I could expect nothing more from her on the subject.

"Okay. Question," I said, as if I hadn't asked a ton of them already. "Did you live with your mom too? I mean, you know, in the recent past."

Evie was already shaking her head. "I haven't lived at home since the summer before my freshman year of college. I knew that once I got out, I'd never move back in with her again. I always made sure to line up summer jobs on campus so I wouldn't have to."

"What do you do for a living, Ms. Moretti?" I asked.

"I'm a sales rep for Conti-Meeker Pharmaceuticals."

So Evie was one of those drug-company salespeople you sometimes see in doctors' offices. I wouldn't have thought she had the personality for sales, but what did I know? She could be a whole different individual when she was chatting up physicians about how her company's hemorrhoid medication is so much better than the competition.

"That sounds interesting," I lied. "Any cool new wonder drugs I should hit up the doctor for at my next physical?"

I expected that lame gag to die the ignoble death it deserved, but Evie sat up a little straighter and locked gazes with me.

"Well, I don't know if you suffer from anxiety or nerves, Jane, but if so, you should know about Zenaproche."

"What?" I said. "No, that's okay, I really don't need—"

"It's a brand-new sedative just coming onto the market," she continued, "with fewer of the side effects associated with alprazolam, diazepam, and lorazepam. Zenaproche is well tolerated at doses of—"

"You know what, Ms. Moretti? I'm good on the, uh, sedative front." I'd take a shot of fine, aged tequila over a pill any day, but I refrained from mentioning that. "So getting back to the matter at hand, let's jump ahead about a month from when Carter and Sean moved out of your mom's house. When's the last time anyone saw Peaches?"

"I can only speak for myself," she said. "I never saw her, or heard from her, after Thanksgiving."

"Did she host it at her house?" I asked.

Evie shook her head. "She wasn't much for family holidays. Oh, she loved to entertain, but on her terms, with her friends. Anyway, we always went to Grandma Audrey's for Thanksgiving."

"Was it just the immediate family? I mean, you know, you and your parents, your brother, and your grandma?"

"No, there were a bunch of aunts, uncles, and cousins," Evie said. "Seventeen of us in all. She pushed together some folding tables and snaked them from the dining room into the living room. That's the way it is every year. Easter and Christmas too."

Good grief. As if poor Grandma Audrey didn't have enough on her hands supporting her freeloading menfolk.

"When did you realize your mom wasn't around?" I asked.

"About a week and a half after Thanksgiving," Evie said. "She hadn't been answering my calls or texts, which in itself wasn't unusual, so I wasn't worried at first. Then her cleaning lady called to ask if Mom had gone on vacation without telling her. I asked my dad if he'd heard from her, and he said no. So we called a few of her friends, and none of them knew where she was. That's when I called her editor."

"Her editor?"

"At *You Know It*, the magazine that published her advice column every month," Evie said. "His name is Gordon something. He said she was behind schedule and he'd been trying to get in touch with her. That's when I really got worried, because Mom never missed a deadline."

"I assume you checked her house," I said.

"Sure," she added. "Mom had so many clothes and pieces of designer luggage, there was no way to tell if she'd packed for a trip. I took the precaution of removing a few things from her house for safekeeping. Her jewelry and mink coat, accumulated mail, and any important paperwork I could find. I mean, there was no telling when she'd be back, and I couldn't keep an eye on the place twenty-four seven."

"That sounds sensible," I said.

"I wish I'd thought to take the peach collection, too," Evie said. "Mom's car was still in the garage. My dad used to drive her to the airport before they split up. We figured if she flew somewhere, she took an Uber or something."

If Peaches's car had been left in the Historical Society's parking lot overnight, someone would have called the cops, and her body would have been discovered shortly after the murder. I wondered if she accepted a ride there from her killer. Of course, it was always possible she drove herself and that the killer returned Peaches's car to her garage after the murder.

"When did you report her missing?" I asked.

"That same day," she said. "She'd been gone for a while at that point, so they got right on it. Not that it did any good. No one had seen her, and there was no record of her traveling or using her credit cards."

And all that time, Peaches had been quietly undergoing natural mummification in the overheated attic of the Crystal Harbor Historical Society. Mommy was becoming a mummy.

"Anyway," Evie said, "Sean moved back into Mom's house the very next day."

"He didn't waste any time," I said.

"No kidding. He did it while I was at work and couldn't stop him. By the time I found out about it, he'd already changed the locks."

Pretty enterprising for someone she'd described as a slacker druggie. Living in Grandma's basement had clearly lost its appeal.

"So who owns the house now?" I asked. "I mean, I'm assuming your mom left a will."

Evie shook her head. "No will. She was one of those geniuses who figure if they don't leave a will or buy life insurance, they'll never die."

"Well, I'm no lawyer," I said, "but I believe that in the absence of a will, you and your brother are supposed to inherit equally. Which means, as far as the house goes, that you two should be able to sell it and split the proceeds."

"Sean has trashed the place so badly," Evie said, "it's probably lost half its value. It's a shame. It's a fine old house and used to be a real showcase. Mom inherited it four years ago after her dad died, but we'd been living there with him since before I was born. Grandpa owned the house outright, but he could no longer afford the utilities and real estate taxes, so Mom had been paying those."

"Sounds like it worked out for everyone." I withdrew a small notebook and pen from my jacket pocket. "What's the address?"

"Fifty-thirteen Rayburn."

I knew the neighborhood. Wide streets lined with mature shade trees and big, stately, well-preserved homes, most of which had been built in the early part of the twentieth century.

"I have to ask," I said, "if Peaches inherited anything else besides the house."

"You mean like cash?" she asked.

I nodded. "Maybe your grandfather left her investments or other valuables?"

"I don't think so. By the time he died, he didn't have much to his name besides the property on Rayburn and its contents. Why?"

I chose my words carefully. "Well, your mom's standard of living was apparently quite comfortable, if not extravagant. She provided for a family of four for many years, traveled extensively, entertained, and was able to maintain a large house in a nice section of Crystal Harbor. Obviously the advice column wasn't her only source of income. Are you aware of any others?"

"I don't see what all of this has to do with—"

"Background," I reminded her. "It could be relevant."

Evie avoided my gaze while she formulated an answer. I already knew she was a private person, but the question needed answering. My gut told me the apparent discrepancy between income and lifestyle could indeed be relevant. Not to the search for her mom's peach collection, necessarily, but to the favor I was doing for Cheyenne. No need to mention that, though, right?

Finally she said, "Well, I know my mother worked before she had me and my brother."

"What kind of work did she do?" I asked.

She'd started fussing with the hem of her suit jacket. Now she caught herself at it and smoothed the material. "She did some modeling, I believe. Mom was very attractive when she was young. Tall and slim, with beautiful long, dark hair."

"You *believe* she did some modeling?" I asked. "You're not sure?"

"No, I'm sure. It's just that I'm, um, trying to remember what kind of modeling exactly. She didn't talk too much about it. Magazine ads, catalogs, that sort of thing."

"Fashion shows?" I asked. "You know, like runway work?"

Evie said, "You know, I think she did do some of that. Commercials, too."

"Did she start modeling right after high school?" I asked.

"Mom dropped out at sixteen. She was smart, but she couldn't stand school. Used to cut class and party any chance she got. Big shock, she failed every subject. All her friends told her that with her looks, she could be a supermodel, so she decided to quit school and take the plunge."

"Wow. Sounds like your mom was…" *Foolhardy. Shortsighted. Delusional.* "Focused. She knew what she wanted and she went after it."

"And that kind of work pays real well," Evie said, "so I guess she was able to save up enough to live on later."

"She must've gotten very good investment advice," I said.

"I'm sure she did." She folded her hands in her lap and looked directly at me. Her body language said, *Move on.*

I don't take my orders from body language. "In that case," I said, "you and Sean will get to split more than the value of the house and its contents. There should be some cash lying around."

She looked confused for a moment, as if the thought of inheriting her mom's modeling money never occurred to her. "Oh. Right. Well, I don't know how much there is left, but yeah, I guess so."

"All right, what do you say we move on," I said, sweetly. "Have you been inside your mother's house since your brother moved back in?"

"Just once." Her expression darkened. "Sean won't let me in, but it turns out Grandma Audrey has a key, so after he was arrested this morning, I went in during my lunch break to check up on the place."

"Is that when you noticed the peach collection is missing?" I asked.

She nodded. "You wouldn't believe the condition of the house, Jane. Garbage everywhere, filthy laundry and takeout containers all over the place. And trust me, you don't even want to know the condition of the bathrooms. I don't think he's opened a window since he's been there. And did I mention the cats? The whole place smells like a litter box."

"I assume you asked your dad if he took the peaches?"

"They don't belong to him," she snapped. "Mom told me the entire collection would be mine someday."

"Fair enough," I said, "but isn't it possible Carter moved it somewhere to, you know, keep it safe?"

"I asked. He says he didn't." Her tight features told me it was a sore subject.

"You mentioned your brother's girlfriend," I said. "We're talking about Cheyenne O'Rourke, right?"

Evie looked surprised. "That's right. I thought you didn't know Sean."

"I don't," I said, "but I know Cheyenne."

"My condolences."

"So when you say it wouldn't be difficult for someone to walk off with the peaches," I said, "you're referring to your brother's, um, lack of diligence?"

"If that's a polite way of saying 'drugged-out stupor,' then yes." Oddly, this stiff young woman seemed less embarrassed by her brother's drug habit than her single mother's love life. She added, "Any one of his lowlife buddies could have swiped my mom's peach collection and Sean probably wouldn't even be aware of it."

I tapped the folder containing the photographs of the collection. "A few of these look like they might be worth something."

She nodded. "Most of them are just silly gewgaws, but she had a few really valuable pieces mixed in with them. Did you see the netsuke?"

"Umm…"

Evie commandeered the folder and flipped through the photos until she found the one she was looking for and handed it to me. This figurine appeared to have been carved from jade and depicted a grasshopper perched on a peach. The carving was exquisitely detailed and really quite lovely and graceful.

"This piece isn't even an inch and a half long," Evie said. "Netsuke is a Japanese art form dating from the seventeenth century. The designs are limitless and they actually had a practical purpose. They were used to help attach little pouches or baskets to men's kimono sashes so they could carry stuff around."

"I'm guessing the kimonos didn't have pockets," I said.

"I guess not," she said. "Anyway, netsukes are incredibly collectible. Mom got this one on a trip to Japan about twenty years ago. A few years later it was appraised at seven thousand dollars. I doubt its value has declined since then. If anything, it's probably increased."

"Seven grand for this tiny thing?" I said. No wonder Evie was eager to get her hands on Peaches's peaches.

"This antique netsuke is probably the most valuable piece in the collection, but there are a few others that are worth quite a lot, as well." She located another photo, this one showing a sleek, almost abstract peach figurine. "A famous ceramic artist created this. He's pretty old, and when he dies, I expect this thing to soar in value, maybe even surpassing the netsuke."

"Did your mom insure the collection?" I asked.

"No," she said. "I mean, there's the usual homeowner's insurance, of course, but she never added a rider for the peaches. At least she photographed them. I guess I should be grateful for that."

"Obviously your mom had been collecting peaches for a long time."

"Since she was a child," Evie said.

"The whole collection could probably fit in a small duffel bag," I said. "So someone could indeed have made off with them while your brother was, um, napping or something. But you also suggested he might have given them away or tossed them out. Why on earth would he do that if the collection is worth so much? Not to mention the sentimental value."

"Sean doesn't make the most rational decisions even when he's sober. And I'll be frank with you, Jane. I know I can speak for my brother when I say that this collection has zero sentimental value for either of us. My mother was not the kind of person to inspire that kind of gooey emotion. The last thing I want is to look at those peaches every day and be reminded of the cold, narcissistic woman who raised me. As soon as I get my hands on that collection, if I ever do, it goes right to an auction house."

I wondered how much therapy that pretty little netsuke could buy. Probably not enough to make a dent in this young woman's mommy issues.

I asked, "How has Sean been supporting himself since he moved out of your grandma's house?"

Evie shook her head in disgust. "She takes him hot food every day, can you believe it?"

"Kind of like a reverse Meals on Wheels, huh?" I said. Someone should teach Grandma Audrey the meaning of the word *enabler*.

"She spoils Sean just like she's always spoiled my dad," Evie said. "She buys in to all my brother's BS about how life is unfair and nothing is ever his fault. He's been working on her to pay his water and electric bills so they don't turn off service."

"Can your grandma afford that?" I asked.

A wave of anger scalded Evie's pale complexion. "No, of course she can't afford it. She's talking about getting a part-time job so she can help him out. The woman is seventy-three, for crying out loud. She's worked her whole life and now she has to deal with this? She won't listen to me, so I'm just trying not to get involved. He knows better than to ask *me* for money."

I opened my briefcase and extracted another business card. This one did not have my name on it. "Ms. Moretti, there's a lawyer here in Crystal Harbor who might be able to help you settle your mom's estate. His name is Sten Jakobsen and he's had a practice here in town forever. He knows his stuff and he'll treat you fairly."

Evie accepted Sten's card. For the first time since I'd been in her presence, I saw her expression soften. "I appreciate this, Jane. I honestly didn't know where to start." She took a deep breath. "Now that you know what's involved, is this something you'd be willing to take on? Tracking down Mom's peach collection? It's not something I can handle on my own, especially with… everything else I have to deal with right now. The funeral and all that."

I wasn't about to tell Evie that I'd already promised to look into her mother's murder, at Cheyenne's insistence. For one thing, it would only muddy the waters, and for another, I intended to do the least amount of "investigating" required to get Cheyenne off my back. The girl seemed to have no inkling that clients actually pay me for my services.

"I'll do my best," I said, "but I need you to understand that I might not be successful."

"I'm prepared for that," she said. "I'd still like to hire you."

"For this type of work I charge an hourly fee plus expenses. We can agree to cap it at whatever upper limit you're comfortable with."

"You'll need a retainer, I assume?" she said. "Some sort of deposit?"

I waved away the offer. "Not in this case." It's not that I thought the hours wouldn't add up. They very well might, depending how much snooping I had to do. However, my gut told me this particular client had no intention of stiffing me.

I pulled a blank work order out of my briefcase, filled in the details of the job, and passed it across to her.

From what I'd already learned about Evie's personality, I would have been shocked if she'd reflexively signed it and passed it back, as so many of my clients did. Sure enough, she spent several minutes reading every single word.

As I watched her pore over the document, I thought about the Big Thing we'd barely touched on: her brother's arrest for the murder of their mother. I told myself that not only did I owe it to Cheyenne to find out what I could, but there was the possibility, however slim, that Sean's guilt or innocence was somehow related to the missing peach collection.

Finally Evie affixed her neat signature to the document and returned it to me. "I'll scan it and email you a copy," I said, and lifted the folder full of photos. "It would help if I had these for reference."

"Of course. Take them," she said. "I have the digital files."

I tucked them into my briefcase, along with the work order. "I need to ask you an uncomfortable question, Ms. Moretti."

Her gaze sharpened. "You want to know if I think Sean did it."

I nodded.

"Do I think he's capable of murder?" she said. "I've asked myself that since he was arrested. Bottom line, I don't know. A few years ago I would've said no, it's impossible. But now, after everything we've been through with him…" She offered a sad shrug.

"Do you happen to know why they arrested him?" I asked. "I mean, what evidence they have?"

She looked uncomfortable. I couldn't blame her. "I don't know all of it," she said. "There was an argument. Well, I'm sure there was more than one. Anyway, on at least one occasion a neighbor heard Sean threaten Mom."

"Threaten her how?" I asked. "With violence?"

Evie took a deep breath. "That's my understanding."

"Did this blowup happen before or after Thanksgiving?" I said. "I assume both Sean and your mom were at your grandma's that day, right?"

She nodded. "Apparently it happened a day or two after Thanksgiving."

"How soon after that did she go missing?"

"I have no way of knowing," Evie said. "I didn't even realize she wasn't around until about ten days later, like I said."

"Thank you for your candor, Ms. Moretti. One more thing. I know your brother did time for burglary."

"Only a year, thanks to this amazing criminal defense attorney Mom hired. Carlos Levine. His fees are astronomical, of course, but he came through. We thought for sure Sean was looking at five years, minimum. Levine will be handling the murder case, too, though I haven't a clue where Dad will find the money to pay him."

Her obdurate expression told me sisterly obligation went only so far. If Sean was counting on her portion of their inheritance to help pay for his defense, he was to be sorely disappointed. Considering his history, I couldn't blame her.

"Is there anyone else you think the police should look at?" I asked.

"I'll tell you what I told the detectives," she said. "My mom was not an easy person to like. She turned offending people into an art form."

"I know her advice column came across that way," I said. "I assumed it was an act, a persona she adopted to sell magazines."

Evie gave me a wry smile. "There was no acting involved, believe me. That was Mom. Well, except that I never knew her to be much of a writer, but she had her editor, Gordon, to whip her column into shape."

"You mentioned she offended a lot of people," I said. "Do you have anyone particular in mind? Who, you know, might have been angry enough to do your mother harm?"

"There's this one guy I mentioned to the detectives," she said. "His name is Burke Fletcher. He became incensed over one of Mom's columns, really went off the rails. Blamed her for wrecking his marriage."

"Did he threaten her?" I asked.

"Not in any way she could prove," she said. "She tried to get an order of protection, but without a certifiable threat, the request was turned down."

"When did this happen?"

"The harassment started in late summer or early fall," she said. "Around the beginning of September, I think. Mom kept hoping he'd get bored and stop."

I said, "What form did this harassment take?"

"Irate emails at first, before she changed her email address. That's when he graduated to online trolling."

"Did he ever show up at her house?"

"If he did, he never made his presence known," Evie said, "but Mom suspected he came by a few times. She had no hard evidence, it was more of a feeling. You know, that she was being watched. Anyway, she finally reported him to the police in late November. Not long before she went missing." Her expression said the timing was suspicious. I had to agree.

I stood. So did Evie. I held out my hand. "If anything else occurs to you that you think I should know, please give me a call, Ms. Moretti."

"Thanks, Jane, I'll do that."

4

Here Comes Tinsel!

"GET A LOAD of this one." Dom tapped his phone and began reading off the screen. "'Dear Peaches, I like eating kibble. One might even say—'"

"Wait, wait." I steered my red Mazda onto the street I'd been looking for, in one of the quaintest old neighborhoods of quaint old Crystal Harbor. "*Kibble?* As in dog food?"

Sexy Beast, who'd spent the short ride staring out the passenger window and excitedly car-whining in my ex-husband's ear, perked up at the mention of "dog" and "food" in the same breath. When his turbocharged nose turned up nothing even remotely Vienna sausagelike, he emitted an eloquent snort. *You have failed me yet again.*

Dom took a moment to scan the "Peaches Preaches" advice column in the online edition of *You Know It* magazine. He shrugged. "Cat kibble, dog kibble, it doesn't say. Could be monkey kibble. Iguana. Ferret. Shall I continue?"

I waved him on as I slowed the car and squinted at house numbers.

"'One might even say I love the stuff,'" Dom read aloud. "'Can't get enough. I keep little bags of it on hand for a quick energy boost in the car and at my desk. Kibble offers complete nutrition and a satisfying crunch. It's my only unorthodox habit if you don't count drinking my morning coffee out of a straw, which in my opinion everyone should do, but haters gotta hate. My girlfriend thinks my preference for kibble is strange and has threatened to break up with me over it. I say she's overreacting. We have a bet going. If I win, she has to buy me the big fifty-pound bag of premium kibble. If she wins, I have to buy her a year's worth of the freeze-dried mealworms she likes to sprinkle on her salad. We agreed to let you decide the winner.' Signed, 'Snack Attack.'"

"Here we are," I announced, "number 5013 Rayburn Street."

Dom's attention shifted to the property, a classic old Queen Anne Victorian painted—no surprise here—pale peach with frothy white trim. A turret, gobs of gingerbread, the whole nine yards. The house itself appeared to be in decent repair. The same could not be said for the ratty-looking lawn, barely visible beneath a carpet of decaying leaves, twigs, and wind-blown litter.

"The place looks deserted." He indicated the dozens of plastic-wrapped newspapers scattered across the brick walkway and the steps leading to the curved wraparound porch, flung there every morning like clockwork from the delivery guy's car. "It's like no one's been here since Peaches went missing, what, four months ago?"

"The son's been living here most of that time. Sean Moretti, age twenty. His sister Evie says he's been trashing the place." I cut the engine. "You know, Dom, you didn't have to come with me. I'm perfectly safe."

"Oh yeah, this fellow here, he'll protect you from a murderer." He hefted seven-pound SB in one hand and examined him from all sides, earning a snort of irritation from both me and my dog.

"I didn't bring SB for protection," I said. "I brought him as a sort of icebreaker."

"Oh. Well, that makes sense," he said. "It's a well-known fact that matricidal maniacs are totally charmed by high-strung little poodles."

"Pay no attention to him, SB. There's nothing wrong with being a little sensitive." I reached into the backseat and grabbed the straw bucket tote that served as Sexy Beast's home away from home. "So what did she say?"

"Who?"

"Peaches!" I said. "How did she respond to Kibble Boy?"

"Oh." He peered at his phone's screen. "She writes, 'Dear Snack: A winner? You expect me to pick a *winner* of your disgusting bet?!?! There are no winners here, you deranged, kibble-chomping freak. And that goes double for your wormy lady friend. I'd suggest you see a shrink, but your revolting breath would knock the poor guy out cold. I'm gagging just writing this. My advice? Switch to pretzels and potato chips, and guzzle mouthwash until it's coming out of your ears. And stay out of the damn pet department.'"

I got Sexy Beast settled in his plushly lined tote and stepped out of the car. The first day of April was cold and breezy, but thankfully, dry. SB and I both squinted against the brilliant late-morning sunshine. "That was kind of tame for Peaches," I said.

Dom nodded as he joined me on the sidewalk. "Maybe she's losing her edge." He winced. "I mean, you know, maybe she *was* losing her edge before she..." He mimed slitting his own throat.

"It was more like..." I mimed strangling myself, eyes and tongue protruding.

Dom stepped closer and murmured, "Uh, you know, he

could be watching us from the house. The son."

"From what I've heard about his relationship with Mummy Dearest, he wouldn't care. Plus, he's probably the one who did the, um…" I did a quick strangle face.

"As if I needed reminding." His venomous scowl proved the point.

I said, "You'd better lighten up before we ring the bell or we'll never get past the front door."

Dom took a deep, calming breath, which had no discernible effect on his frame of mind. "Do you have your spike?"

"My what? Oh." I released a long-suffering sigh and extracted my key ring from the pocket of my suede jacket. Dangling from the ring was a five-inch purple aluminum spike, enhanced with finger grooves down its length. The purpose of the grooves was to provide a secure grip while attacking one's attacker.

Dom had gifted me with the self-defense gizmo a couple of months earlier, no doubt envisioning the padre on the receiving end. Instead I'd used it to help extract myself from an altogether different threat. Since the thing had actually proven its worth in a most impressive way, I now kept it with me at all times.

"Okay?" I wagged the spike in front of his face. "Satisfied?"

"I'd be happier if you also carried a firearm, or at the very least a can of pepper spray, but I guess I should be happy you've at least got this thing."

Sexy Beast responded with a yip of approval. Either that or he was urging us to move our conversation somewhere warm.

I said, "A *firearm*?" I immediately thought of Dom's fiancée, Bonnie Hernandez. Presumably the chief of police carried a firearm, though I'd yet to see it, for which I supposed I should be grateful. I clutched my jacket collar closed, wishing I'd worn a scarf. "First of all, do you have any idea how byzantine the pistol-permitting process is in Suffolk County, New York?"

"You're in a dangerous profession," he said. "You should be able to get a concealed-carry permit."

"A dangerous profession?" I said. "Most of the time I'm organizing funerals and tossing ashes hither and yon. I don't think that qualifies. Plus, from what I hear, the whole permit process could take something like a year or more." He started to speak, but I charged ahead. "Dom, I want you to stop for a moment and imagine me—*me*, Jane Angela Delaney, your ex-wife—walking around with a loaded gun in my purse. Tell me. What's the first thing that just popped into your head?"

He bit his bottom lip. I ignored how adorable and sexy it made him look, because I'd known this man a long time, and that adorable and sexy gesture meant only one thing: He was hiding something or preparing to fib.

I gave him my best narrow-eyed scowl. "Be honest, Dom. I will know if you're lying."

His expression said he knew he was busted. "Okay, so maybe concealed carry isn't the best option. I'm concerned about your safety, Janey. You can't deny you've had some close calls. Can you blame me for being concerned?"

"Tell me."

"Huh? Tell you what?" More lip nibbling. He didn't even realize he was doing it, bless his exasperating little heart.

"You know darn well what," I said. "Whatever popped into your head when you imagined me schlepping a loaded gun."

"It's cold, Janey." Dom put on a show, rubbing his palms together and stamping his feet. Yeah, yeah, it wasn't *that* cold. He nodded toward the house. "Come on, let's get this over with."

I got in his face. "This is not over. I *will* find out." Then I stomped up the walkway and onto the porch, kicking aside every newspaper in my path. SB barked happily at this new game, struggling to escape the tote bag and join in the fun.

I admit I glanced behind me to make sure Dom was bringing up the rear before I rang the doorbell. I'd put on a show of annoyance earlier when he'd insisted on accompanying me for my protection, but between you and me, I was glad he was there.

A minute passed. *Nada.* I murmured, "Maybe he's not home."

"Maybe he's too high to get off the couch." Dom reached past me and stabbed the bell a few more times.

The door was opened by a genial-looking older woman. "Are you selling something? If you're selling something or looking for donations, I'm afraid you're wasting your time here, although I wish you luck. Well, hello there." She stripped off one of her yellow plastic cleaning gloves and reached out to pet Sexy Beast, chuckling at his enthusiastic response. "Oh, what a little darling! What's her name?"

The look I gave my ex said, *See? Sometimes I actually know what I'm doing.*

"His name is Sexy Beast," I said.

"Well, who could argue with that?" She laughed again as SB attempted to crawl out of the tote and climb onto her. "You're just the sexiest little thing I've seen all day, yes you are. Are you a good boy? Are you? Oh, I know you are."

I took a not-so-wild stab. "Mrs. Moretti?"

She looked pleasantly surprised. "Have we met, dear?"

I shook my head. "My name is Jane Delaney. I'm a, um, friend of your granddaughter's. Evie." I indicated Dom. "This is my... another friend. Dom Faso."

Dom offered his nice-to-meet-yous, and Mrs. Moretti said, "Oh, Evie doesn't live here. She has a nice apartment in that… Now, what's that building called again?"

"The Americana," I said. "No, I know she's not here. I came to speak with your grandson. Sean."

"Oh." Her perplexed gaze flicked over us in a way that told me we didn't look like the kind of people Sean generally hung with. She stepped aside. "Well, come on in, then. I'm sure he'll be happy to have visitors."

I myself was sure of no such thing. Before we'd taken one step, Mrs. Moretti waved at someone behind me, hollering, "Good morning, Zak! Isn't it a gorgeous day?"

Reflexively I turned to see who she was addressing. Across the street, a man about my age was hopping out of a red Jeep Wrangler with a couple of plastic bags from The Home Depot. He wore close-fitting, ripped-knee jeans, a suede bomber jacket, and impenetrable sunglasses. The stylishly cut honey-brown hair—close-cropped on the sides, artfully shaggy on top—was the icing on the cool-guy cake, marking him as someone I could more easily picture living in the trendiest section of Brooklyn than the wilds of suburban Long Island.

Zak responded with a perfunctory wave before disappearing into his own home, another grand old Victorian, this one painted sage-green with cream trim. The house and tree-studded lawn appeared neat and well maintained.

Mrs. Moretti led us into the foyer and shut the door. "Such a nice boy, that Zak. A *widower*." She whispered the word, as if dead wives were something shameful and catching. "Kind of quiet, but isn't that the best sort of neighbor? I'm sure he's not one of those who complained to the town about—" she flapped her hand toward the closed front door "—the lawn and all that. I can only do so much, and right now I have my hands full inside. I don't live here myself, of course, I'm just tidying up a bit. Peaches kept the place so nice, but, well, I guess boys will be boys. The police were here yesterday, of course, poking through everything, and that didn't help one bit. Poor Peaches, isn't it just awful what happened to her. Not that we always saw eye to eye, she could be, well, rather opinionated. But isn't it just awful."

I must admit I barely registered every other word. The instant I stepped over the threshold, I slammed up against an invisible wall of Stink. Dom and I exchanged a look. The smell wasn't simply rotting food, or unwashed laundry, or stale kitty litter, or the musty funk of a house closed up for too long, or a couple of other things which I refuse to name and you can't make me. It was all of those, overlaid with the eye-stinging tang of ammonia and pine cleaner. Two cardboard cartons occupied one corner, overflowing with cleaning supplies Mrs. Moretti apparently had brought from her own home.

I struggled to imagine the foyer as it must have looked when Peaches was in residence, with its intricately carved oak banister, cut-crystal chandelier, and tastefully patterned marble floor. A layer of grime coated every surface. The red staircase carpet was a patchwork of mystery stains and cigarette burns, dozens of them. It appeared that Peaches's son and his pals had been using her elegant staircase as an ashtray.

Sexy Beast's sniffer worked overtime, cataloging the various components that comprised The Stink. Never was I happier to be the owner of a puny human schnoz.

Mrs. Moretti indicated the twenty or so bulging black trash bags piled up against one wall of the foyer, alongside several pieces of broken furniture and a couple of rolled-up rugs tied with rope. I tried not to contemplate what might have caused her to conclude those rugs were unsalvageable.

"Garbage pickup is Thursday," she said, "but I know they won't take all this. I'll have to cart it to the dump myself."

Dom and I looked at each other again. *She'll* have to cart it to the dump? What about her grandson? He was the one responsible for the mess. I recalled Evie mentioning that her grandmother was seventy-three—clearly a vigorous seventy-three, but still. Even if Sean was too much of a slacker to help, where was his dad, Carter? Why was he letting his mother take on this monumental job by herself?

I opened my mouth to say something, only to receive an elbow jab from my mind-reading ex. He was right, of course. It was none of my business. I needed to focus on my reason for being there.

Something live bumped my leg and I screamed, leaping back with an athletic agility I didn't know I possessed. Naturally, SB began barking like crazy. Dom lifted him out of the tote to keep him from leaping to my rescue.

"Oh, don't worry, that's just…" Mrs. Moretti squinted at the gray cat that had rubbed against me. "Well, for goodness' sake, I don't know who that is. I don't think I've ever seen that one before." She sighed. "Another mouth to feed."

Another cat, a marmalade, chose that moment to slink out from between a couple of garbage bags, while a black cat with white paws made its leisurely way down the stairs. Through the entrance into the living room I saw two more felines reclining in a patch of sunlight while another daintily picked its way across a debris-strewn console table.

I said, "How many cats does Sean own?"

"None, according to him," Mrs. Moretti said. "And they

didn't belong to his mother, either. She couldn't stand cats. They just started showing up somehow after he moved back in. I swear, every time I come here, there are a few new ones. Not to mention the litters that have been born here. I make sure the poor things don't go hungry, but I really wish I knew how they were getting in. Oh, where are my manners? I have a pot of coffee on. Hazelnut, it's yummy. Can I interest you?"

Dom and I said a quick, "No, thanks," in unison. I didn't even want to think about the condition of the kitchen, or of the bathrooms, which I would need in short order if I had a cup of coffee. For that matter, I already had to pee, but I was determined to hold it in if it killed me.

Right on cue, she said, "Well, those toilets aren't going to unclog themselves," and snapped her cleaning glove back on. "Sean's in the solarium. Just head to the back of the house. You'll find him."

"Thank you, Mrs. Moretti," I said.

"Oh, please, call me Audrey." She hustled through a doorway into another part of the house while Dom and I began to wend our way through the hellscape of this once stately home.

"How long did you say the son's been here?" he asked as we moved into the large living room, or parlor, or whatever it was.

"Almost four months." I concentrated on shallow breathing. The smell was becoming progressively worse the farther we ventured into the house. I was glad to note that Audrey had opened the windows to admit the chilly breeze, though this place was going to need a lot more than a simple airing out.

"How does one guy create this kind of disaster in four months?" Dom said.

"I'm assuming he had help." I nodded toward a mountain of beer cans, liquor bottles, and broken glassware in one corner of the room. It wasn't a stretch to imagine Sean and his buddies drunkenly hurling Peaches's cut-crystal stemware at the walls. The delicate striped wallpaper in that section was now hopelessly stained and torn. "Sean probably turned this place into party central."

A trio of calico kittens scampered among the dozen or so empty pizza boxes piled up under the big bay window. It appeared that someone—as in someone of the human persuasion—had attempted to climb the floor-length peach silk drapes, now half torn from the rods.

I couldn't help but notice piles of cat turds here and there, most notably in the unused fireplace. At least I assumed they'd been deposited by the resident felines, but who knew? If a squadron of feral cats had somehow managed to find refuge in this house during the preceding frigid winter, perhaps other critters had done the same. A multi-hued layer of animal hair blanketed most surfaces.

Dom perused the room as he returned Sexy Beast to the tote bag. "Check it out."

I followed his gaze to a curved antique china cabinet standing on graceful paw feet. The only item on display was the huge striped cat currently perched on top of it, giving itself a lick-bath. The shelves were bare, if one didn't count a smattering of glass shards.

I moved closer to the cabinet, gingerly skirting a sad little puddle that someone, or something, had recently yakked up. The curved glass sides of the cabinet were intact, but the front section of glass—the locked door—had been bashed in.

Dom said, "Are you thinking what I'm—"

"Yep." This was where Peaches's peaches had resided, her four dozen or so figurines of differing worth and aesthetic merit.

On a hunch, I stepped closer to the mound of cans and broken glassware in the corner and peered closely at the debris. I saw nothing remotely peachlike, no trace of the figurines.

"What do you reckon he did with them?" Dom asked.

"That's what I hope to find out. I checked eBay and all the other online sites where stuff like that is sold. None of them showed up." I was hopeful that, wherever the figurines currently were, the collection had been kept together and not split up.

I endeavored to ignore my surroundings as I led the way into the dining room, which—and I know you'll find this hard to believe—had been thoroughly trashed. From several rooms away I heard the sound of a toilet struggling to flush, followed by Audrey hurling cuss words at it. The mildest cuss words in the dictionary, mind you, but the lady was not pleased.

The ruckus reminded my bulging bladder that it was being woefully neglected. *Hello?* it griped. *I hope you aren't planning to sneeze.*

I realized we were nearing our destination when I heard a male voice holler, "Grandma! I need another Coke!" This was followed by irritated mumbling during which the young man called his long-suffering grandmother a foul name.

I stiffened. Sexy Beast growled low in his throat. And okay, yeah, he might have been reacting to the pair of cats who chose that moment to commence a yowling battle over an abandoned hot dog. I prefer to believe SB was outraged at the young man's rudeness and lack of respect for his elders.

My ex, who knew me too well, laid a calming hand on my shoulder.

I hissed, "That kid needs to be taught a lesson."

"Agreed, but it's not in our job description," he whispered. "Focus, Janey."

I sucked in a deep breath and regretted it immediately.

"Let's get this over with." We stepped into the solarium, a circular, sun-washed oasis that was like being inside a goldfish bowl, but in a good way. The walls, back door, and domed ceiling were constructed entirely of glass panels in a curving white framework, offering unimpeded views of the freeform lagoon pool and sprawling lawn, surrounded on all sides by a tall privacy hedge.

The room was furnished in wicker, pale wood, and delicate fabrics, now embedded with grime and cat hair. The many houseplants were, alas, brown and wilted. Obviously they hadn't been watered during the past four months since Peaches's departure. The only exception was a towering yucca tree, its thick trunk crowned by a profusion of long, spiky fronds. I recalled that these evergreens are native to arid regions, and apparently hardy enough to withstand the neglect they'd endured.

Sean Moretti lounged on a delicate wicker chaise, thumbs a blur as he texted on his phone. He had a pasty complexion, frizzy dark brown hair, and a scrawny physique that bespoke an aversion to exercise, aside from the occasional neighborhood break-in. Sean wore black-rimmed eyeglasses and a pretty silk robe adorned with a peach-tree motif.

I looked at Dom. He looked at me. Sean was so intent on his texting, he hadn't noticed our entrance.

I jumped when he yelled, *"Grandma!"* at the top of his lungs. "How long you gonna make me wait for a damn Coke?"

He glanced up and noticed us at last. A dismissive scowl. "I don't have to talk to you."

"Excuse me?" I said.

"Get the hell out of here. You wanna bust my chops, call my lawyer."

"You think we're cops?" Dom asked.

His expression said, *Duh.*

"What about *him*?" I indicated Sexy Beast peeking over the top of his straw tote. "Is he a cop, too?"

Sean spared barely a glance for my adorable pet, which told me everything I needed to know about his character. Not fair, you say? He's allowed to not be a dog person? Maybe so, but something told me Sean Moretti wasn't anything but a Sean Moretti person.

He said, "Whoever you are, I got nothing to say. Get lost. *Grandma! Sometime this year?*"

I tensed. Dom placed a soothing hand on my back—*focus!*—as Audrey hustled into the room with a frosty bottle of Coke. "Sorry, Sean, I was just trying to get that toilet un—"

"What, we suddenly ran out of glasses?" He snatched the bottle out of her hand. "And ice?"

"Well, I'm, I'm just, I'm kind of busy—"

"Yeah, busy wishing you'd never bailed me out." He brought the bottle to his mouth and took a deep swallow.

"Oh, now, Sean, you know that's not true."

"Then why—" a belch that registered 3.4 on the Richter scale "—why are you letting reporters in here? Huh?"

She regarded Dom and me with wide-eyed alarm. "They told me they're friends of Evie's."

"And you just let them in? Of course you did, you dumb—"

"All right, that's enough," Dom barked. "Who do you think you are, talking to your grandmother that way?"

I tugged on his arm. "Um, Dom," I murmured, "what happened to *focusing?*"

He shook me off and got right in Sean's face. "This woman is running herself ragged trying to clean up *your* ungodly mess—"

"Oh, I don't mind," Audrey said. "Sean has enough worries, poor boy."

"—and all you can do is sit there and order her around like she's some *servant*? And why, for the love of God, are you wearing—" he gestured at the silk robe "—*that!*"

"Oh, blame me," Audrey said. "All of Sean's clothes are in the wash, you should have seen the state of them, so I figured he could wear his mother's robe in the meantime. Didn't know we'd be having visitors. Oh! Where's my head? I've got to get his undies into the dryer and start another load." She hurried out of the room.

Just the thought of Sean's undies and the "state of them" triggered my gag reflex. *Focus, Jane!* "Listen," I told him, "we're not reporters. I really am a friend of your sister's."

"Like that's better?" A mottled flush enlivened his vampiric pallor. "Get the hell out. I got no use for that stuck-up b—"

"And Cheyenne," I quickly added. "We're friends of Cheyenne's."

He gave us the once-over, with a dubious frown. "Now I know you're lying."

"Ask her." I nodded toward the phone lying in his lap. "My name is Jane Delaney. She wants me to look into your, um, predicament, see if I can help somehow."

"I got a lawyer," he said.

"I'm more of a… sort of an investigator," I said.

"Cheyenne doesn't have any money."

"No, I'm doing it as a favor," I said, while asking myself why, in the name of all that's holy, I had agreed to it. "We're friends, like I said."

"I didn't do it," Sean said. "I didn't off my mom. End of story."

"Okay, well, let's see if we can't find out a little more." It was clear Sean wasn't going to invite us to sit. I scanned the room and settled on the least objectionable piece of furniture, a blond-wood bench whose filthy cushion was drooping onto the flagstone floor. By unspoken agreement, Dom and I finished the job and tugged it all the way off. The big white cat that had taken up residence on the cushion never budged, riding it to the floor uncomplainingly while yawning and delicately cleaning her face.

After dragging the bench closer to Sean's chaise and settling ourselves on it, I dug SB's halter and leash out of the tote. He'd had enough of being carted around and was eager to explore. That said, the last thing I needed was to lose track of his whereabouts in that nightmarish house, hence the leash. I slid its looped handle around my wrist. Predictably, he went into full play stance in front of the cat—chest down, rump up, a jaunty yip thrown in for good measure. She responded by swishing her tail and growling low in her throat. I pulled him back and shortened the leash. SB isn't good at taking hints, and I could foresee this particular play date ending badly.

While Dom and I did all this, Sean occupied himself by guzzling soda, belching, and texting. "Yeah," he announced, "Cheyenne says she sent you. Woulda been nice to get a heads-up. The stupid—"

"Glad that checked out," I chirped, and produced my little notebook. "So let me ask, since you mentioned your grandmother bailing you out. The judge set your bond at how much?"

"A million bucks." He looked proud of that, the idiot. "But my lawyer got her—it was a lady judge—he got her to lower it to half a mil."

Evie had described Carlos Levine, her brother's defense attorney, as amazing. I now had to agree since, for starters, he'd kept Sean from being remanded to custody, no small feat considering his prior conviction for burglary and generally snotty attitude. And then to get the "lady judge" to cut his bond in half? I knew who I wanted in my corner if I ever found myself facing a murder rap.

Hey, it could happen, and almost did after Irene was killed.

I said, "And your grandma was able to put up the whole amount?"

"Sure, no problem."

I couldn't see Audrey Moretti being able to write the court a check for five hundred grand. "Did she use a bail bondsman?"

"Yeah." He started playing with his phone again. I wanted to ask him to put the thing away, but it was a matter of choosing my battles. The guy seemed not to notice or care that I was doing him a favor.

"And he charged her a nonrefundable fee," I said.

"I guess." A shrug. What did that have to do with him?

The fee would have been in the neighborhood of ten percent. So Audrey was out fifty thou, money she'd never see again whether or not Sean showed up for court. I recalled Evie mentioning that Audrey was considering taking a part-time job to help support her shiftless grandson. It couldn't have been easy for her to scrape together fifty thousand dollars.

I struggled to keep my tone neutral as I asked, "What about collateral?"

Sean's only response was to snicker at something on his phone. In one swift move, Dom stood, grabbed the device, and shoved it into his jeans pocket. Sean objected, of course, in colorful language, and started to rise. Dom shoved him back down and said, "This lady is trying to keep you from spending the rest of your sorry life behind bars—assuming you're as innocent as you claim. In return, you're going to give her your undivided attention and provide complete and polite answers to all her questions. You'll get your phone back when we're through here. Is there anything about what I just said that you don't understand?"

Sean had a smart-ass response all ready to go, I could tell, but something in Dom's expression made him swallow it back down. The men glared at each other as Dom returned to his seat next to me.

"Okay," I said. "Collateral. The bail bondsman would have required—"

"Yeah, yeah," he said. "She put up her house."

That's what I'd assumed. It said something about the inflated real estate values in Crystal Harbor that even Audrey's modest little home—two bedrooms, according to Evie—was sufficient to secure a bond of that size. "You know what that means, right, Sean?"

"It means I get to hang out here instead of jail."

"*It means,*" I said, "the bail bondsman has a lien against your grandmother's house. If you skip out on your court date, she loses her house and you have bounty hunters coming after you."

"Who says I'm gonna skip?"

"I just wanted to make sure you understand the consequences." I strongly suspected I was wasting my breath. "Let's talk about your case. What evidence do the cops have against you?"

"None. It's total BS."

"They must have had some grounds for arrest." When he responded with another shrug, I said, "Didn't a neighbor report an argument between you and your mom? Shortly after Thanksgiving?"

Sean's face twisted into an ugly sneer. "That loser Zak should mind his own business."

Zak was the fellow who lived across the street, the one Audrey had greeted. I said, "Apparently Zak heard you threaten your mom."

"She threatened *me* all the time."

"She did?" I said. "How? What did she say?"

"Always saying she was gonna kick me out, stop supporting me. If I don't 'change my ways.'"

"Change your ways how?" I asked.

"Like get a job," he said. "Or go to college. Or check this out—she said I could join the army. Learn some discipline. I mean, for real?"

What a heartless monster that Peaches was.

"And in the end, she *did* kick me out!" Sean was the picture of aggrieved victimhood. "Me and Dad both. I mean, what kind of person does a thing like that? But I'm back here now, and she can't do a thing about it, can she?"

"So this argument Zak overheard," I said, "when he says you threatened your mom. This was a day or two after Thanksgiving, right?"

"I don't remember," he said.

"Okay, well, where did it take place? Inside the house? Somewhere else?"

"I don't remember." His expression was mulish.

I sighed. "Sean, we've already established that I'm not a member of law enforcement. I'm not trying to trip you up or anything, so just be straight with me."

An exaggerated grimace. "Mom was always bitching at me. And I didn't take crap from her, okay? So yeah, we got into it a few times. But I wouldn't have, like, said I was gonna kill her or anything. If I did, I didn't mean it."

"So you don't recall the specific fight Zak witnessed? Right after Thanksgiving?" I tried to spur his memory. "We're talking the end of November. I believe that's when we got our first snowfall."

"What can I tell you?" he said. "I was probably zoned."

How could you argue with a convenient catch-all excuse like *I was too high to remember?* I wanted to ask him if that was the last time he saw his mother, but what was the point when he couldn't remember when, where, or even *if* that particular altercation took place?

Sexy Beast had been dozing, catlike, in a golden puddle of sunshine on the stone floor. Now he roused himself, stretched luxuriantly, and leapt onto the bench. Dom settled him on his lap.

"So your mom followed through on her threat to kick you out," I said, "but was she ever physically violent or threaten you with violence?"

"What," he said, "turning me out on the streets wasn't enough?"

"You weren't exactly on the streets, though, were you?" I said. "You and your dad moved in with your grandma Audrey."

"Yeah, some picnic that was. Sleeping on a lumpy old pullout sofa in her basement. Plus, Grandma wouldn't let Cheyenne stay over." He rolled his eyes at prudish old Grandma. "I moved back here as soon as I found out Mom was missing for real."

Not for the first time, I wondered what Peaches had been doing in that attic. Was she looking for something? Meeting someone? Had her murderer snuck up on her or was it someone she knew and trusted?

"Okay," I said, "so you don't recall the argument Zak claims he overheard. Even if it happened, that alone isn't enough to get you arrested for murder. What other evidence do the cops have on you?"

"I don't remember too much of what they said."

"Too high again?" I didn't even try to mask my skepticism. How high do you have to be to forget why you've been arrested for murder?

He answered with another shrug and a smarmy little smile.

There was little I could do to help Sean if he wasn't willing to cooperate. I intended to check in with my pal Howie Werker, a local police detective, and try to find out what they actually had on the kid. Once I'd done that, I'd consider my promise to Cheyenne fulfilled, and leave the rest of it in the capable hands of the Amazing Carlos Levine, Esquire.

Sean held out his hand. "Gimme my phone."

"In a minute," I said. "There's something else we need to discuss first."

"Come *on*, dude."

"It'll just take a—"

"No! We're done." He wagged his hand toward Dom. "Give me my damn phone and get the hell out."

Dom withdrew Sean's phone from his pocket. The look I gave him said, *Really? You cave to this little cretin just like that?* I should have known better. Instead of handing it over, he started tapping the screen.

"Wow," Dom said, "twenty-one texts just in the last few minutes. You're a popular guy."

Sean jerked up on the chaise. "Give me that!"

"Your pal Scott's been trying to get ahold of you. Seems he has something for you. It's going to cost more than last time, but it's premium—"

"That's private!" Sean yelled, prompting an answering howl from Sexy Beast. "What you're doing is illegal."

"Is it?" Dom asked mildly as he continued to scroll through Sean's messages. "You'd better call the cops, then, and tell them you didn't give me permission to read these texts from your dealer."

"Hmm," I said. "Buying and using illicit drugs while you're out on bail. Don't the courts frown on that sort of thing?"

"Oh, and here are a bunch of new messages from someone named Tinsel." Dom looked at Sean. "Tinsel? Really? Please tell me she was born on Christmas. Then at least there'd be some justification."

Sean was turning all kinds of interesting colors, but I noticed he didn't try to snatch the phone back. My ex might have been twice his age, but he was easily twice as strong, not to mention bigger and unencumbered by reflex-slowing felonious substances.

I turned to Dom. "What does our girl Tinsel have to say?"

His dark eyebrows rose. "Tinsel is one healthy girl, I'll give you that."

I leaned over to check out the phone display. "Wow. So that's Tinsel. Hey, Sean. Does Cheyenne know Tinsel is sending you nude selfies?"

Sean affected nonchalance. "I can't help it if some random girl has the hots for me. It's not the first time. Doesn't mean I do anything about it."

"Tinsel says you did." Dom scrolled through her texts. "Tinsel says the two of you did a whole bunch of naughty things right here in this room, just yesterday. Why, here's a picture of you and Tinsel on this very bench."

"Eww, really?" I looked at the picture. So glad we'd ditched the cushion. "That Tinsel sure is limber. Tell me, Sean, how did you meet Tinsel?"

"Why do you two keep saying her name so much?" he griped.

"We just like the way it sounds," Dom said. "Tinsel Tinsel Tinsel."

"It sounds shiny," I said. *"Tinsel."*

"Does Cheyenne know Tinsel?" Dom asked.

"Yeah, they're besties." Sean scowled. "Don't tell Cheyenne about this. It's none of her business."

"None of her business?" I said. "I don't know if I can keep you and Tinsel a secret, seeing as Cheyenne is my close personal friend and all."

"Seriously, dude." Sean actually looked worried. "Cheyenne's got a temper. It's not like I planned to cheat or anything. It just happened."

"I hear you, man," Dom said, tapping a picture to enlarge it. "Hard to resist a woman who can do *this*. That Tinsel, I'm telling ya."

"So you won't tell Cheyenne?" Sean said. "Seriously, that girl's crazy jealous. She'll kill me."

"Well, now, here's the thing," Dom said. "It's really up to Jane here, and I sense she's becoming a little impatient with you. Is that a fair assessment, Janey?"

"Why, yes it is, Dom. I'm so miffed at Sean right now, I can't wait to run straight to Cheyenne and tell her all about what he's been up to with her best friend, Tinsel. You know what? Send me some of those adorable pictures of Tinsel in case Cheyenne wants proof."

"Good idea." Dom started forwarding the texts. "Here comes Tinsel!"

"Dude!" Sean cried. "Okay, stop, stop. If I answer your questions, do you promise to keep your mouths shut about Tinsel?"

"That depends," I said. "Are you going to stick to the truth? Because I'm telling you right now, Sean, if you lie to me, or if you give me more of that 'too high to remember' nonsense, Cheyenne gets an earful, and an eyeful, of what you've been up to."

"All right, jeez," he whined. "What do you wanna know?"

Time to get to work on behalf of a *paying* client. "It's about your mother's peach collection," I said.

"Her what?"

"All those figurines," I said, "the little knickknacks and things shaped like peaches that she collected over the years. She kept them in that china cabinet in the living room, right?"

"Oh, that crap," he said. "Yeah, I know what you're talking about. I don't know where that stuff is."

"Are you sure?" Dom said. "Because it looks like someone broke into the china cabinet to get to them."

"What do you care?" he asked. "I thought you were here to help me stay out of jail. Those peach things, they got nothing to do with my mom's murder."

That's what I'd originally assumed, too, but experience had taught me that assumptions can be dangerous.

I said, "Just because the connection isn't obvious at first glance doesn't mean there's no connection. Was that peach collection still in the china cabinet when you moved back here in December?"

Sean got a cagey look. Before he could say a word, I jerked upright and stabbed a finger toward him. "Remember what I said, Sean. One lie, the teeniest, tiniest fib, and you'll be *hoping* they put you behind bars for life."

In case this mental giant failed to catch my meaning, Dom added, "Where Cheyenne can't get to you."

Sean rolled his eyes. "I don't remember if those peach things were there when I moved back, okay? And I don't know what happened to them."

"That's hard to believe," Dom said, "considering you've been living under this roof full-time. And something tells me you don't leave the house much."

"People come by," he said. "It's a big place. I can't keep an eye on everyone all the time."

I said, "So you're telling me that one of your buddies smashed the door of that china cabinet and swiped that whole collection, all fifty or so pieces, and you never knew about it?"

He responded with one of those indolent shrugs I was coming to despise.

"When did you notice they were gone?" I asked.

"Seriously," he said, "who cares? If someone wants all that ugly junk, what's it to me?"

Did he really not know some of those pieces were valuable, or was he counting on me not knowing? It was hard to believe Peaches never bothered to show him the few special pieces or mention their worth. Then again, if she was aware of his fondness for drugs and aversion to gainful employment—and apparently she was—then it might have served her purposes to let him believe it was all a bunch of worthless gewgaws. Why tempt him?

I tried a different tack, softening my tone. "You know, Sean, if you did something with your mom's peach collection, you can tell us."

"Or if you know who has them," Dom added. "It's not like

you're going to get in trouble if you, I don't know, gave them away or whatever."

Whew, what a relief it must be for the young man awaiting trial for murder to know he wouldn't get yelled at for misplacing his mom's tchotchkes.

Sean's expression said we were the biggest dummies he'd ever met. "Why would I get in trouble for getting rid of something that belongs to me? Mom told me she was leaving all those junky peach things to me if she ever kicked the bucket." Sean held out his hand. "Now, gimme my phone and get lost."

5

They'd Never Find Your Body

BLINDING SUNLIGHT GREETED us when we left the house. I inhaled a refreshing lungful of untainted air and was about to unlock the car when Dom moved in close. For a giddy moment I thought he was going in for a smooch—totally inappropriate behavior for a man engaged to be married, of course, but that didn't stop my heart from giving a little kick.

Instead he murmured, "So *both* kids think they're inheriting the peach collection?"

"The result of a memory lapse, I suspect," I whispered. "She promises them to one kid, forgets she did it, and later promises them to the other one. It happens all the time, trust me. I can't tell you how many family squabbles I've been called in to referee, for just this reason." I beeped the car locks and opened the driver's-side door, but didn't get in.

"What?" Dom followed my gaze to the house across the street, the sage-green Victorian.

"That's where Zak lives. The guy who overheard that argument between Sean and Peaches." The smile I gave Dom was equal parts playful and pleading. "Do you have to get right back to the office?"

I knew that as the zillionaire owner of the Janey's Place

health-food empire, my ex didn't *have* to do anything he didn't want to, workwise, but I figured it was polite to ask.

Dom's long-suffering sigh didn't fool me for an instant. He was as intrigued as I was, by both Peaches's murder and Peaches's peaches. "All right, come on," he said, and led the way across the street.

The door sported a whimsical brass knocker shaped like a woman's hand holding a little globe. My triple tap was answered by vigorous barking from inside the house. These were loud, deep, authoritative barks. Doberman? Rottweiler? Sexy Beast, predictably, responded in kind, prompting me to reach into the tote and get a firm grip on him. I heard a muffled command from inside. The other dog quieted and the door swung open.

Zak had shed his suede jacket and now wore a butterscotch-colored pullover with the sleeves pushed up. He didn't ask what we were doing there but simply waited, unsmiling.

I smiled, though, and so did Dom. "Hi," I said. "My name is Jane Delaney and this is Dom Faso. And this little guy is Sexy Beast. You might've seen us going into Peaches's house earlier?" No response. I charged ahead. "Audrey said your name is Zak, I believe?"

He hesitated, and in truth, I couldn't blame him for being cautious. I'm sure he'd seen all manner of lowlifes coming and going at the house across the street during the past four months.

I added, "We're friends of Audrey's granddaughter, Evie." The not-so-hidden subtext being: *We're friends of your dead neighbor's respectable, hardworking daughter, not her good-for-nothing son. See? Don't we look respectable, too?*

A big, shaggy, white dog that was definitely not a Rottweiler was attempting to squirm past his master to check us out. He appeared to be mixed-breed, with blue eyes, cocked ears, and one of those smiling dog faces that seem irresistibly expressive. Right now that smile, along with the enthusiastically wagging tail, was saying, *Cool! New friends! Come on in! Make yourself at home! I'll share my tennis ball with you!*

He and Sexy Beast exchanged a congenial conversation in Dog. This alone told me Zak's pet must be a pretty easygoing fellow, because SB generally had little use for other canines. That said, he'd made significant progress during the past year since I'd become his guardian. Irene hadn't believed in doggie socialization, while I made it a point to regularly expose him to other canines, mostly through long walks around the neighborhood and frequent jaunts to the local dog park.

I couldn't help myself. "Look at that face! Hey there, cutie." To Zak: "May I pet him? Her?"

Even the grumpiest stranger can rarely resist someone loving up his pet. "Him. This is Dylan." He allowed the dog to push past him and receive scritches from me and Dom.

"Are you as musical as your namesake?" Dom asked the friendly pooch.

"He's been known to howl along with my harmonica," Zak said, "but that might be more criticism than accompaniment. Anyway, he's named for Dylan Thomas, the Welsh poet, not Bob Dylan."

"'Do Not Go Gentle Into That Good Night,'" Dom said. "I've always found that poem very moving."

A glimmer of respect softened the other man's features. "I'm Zak Pryce." He and Dom shook.

"Nice to meet you, Zak." I offered my hand, and he shook it. Zak's hand was large and pleasingly rough, as if he was no stranger to manual labor, despite looking like something out of *GQ.*

Now that we were all acquainted, I said, "I hope this isn't too much of an imposition, Zak, but do you mind very much if we come in for a minute? It's about Peaches. I'm helping the family tie up some loose ends and I just have a couple of questions for you."

Clearly he did mind, but how to tactfully refuse to help the family of a murder victim? "I'm kind of busy, but I guess I can spare a couple of minutes."

"Thanks so much," I said, as he stepped aside to let us enter the foyer. "We'll be out of your hair in no time. Oh, what a lovely home." I wasn't lying. Even in the midst of renovations, it was impressive. The original century-old woodwork was in varying stages of refinishing. The place smelled of freshly sanded wood and shellac. Assorted tools and supplies, including a wallpaper steamer, rested on a nearby drop cloth, alongside the Home Depot sacks he'd just brought in.

"I see you're doing some work," Dom said.

"I'll be putting this house on the market as soon as I close on my new place. It'll show better with some sprucing up."

"Oh, you're moving?" I asked. "Where to?"

"Brooklyn," Zak said. "I bought a brownstone."

I chewed back a grin. Brooklyn. I'd called it. "What section?"

"Crown Heights."

Dom said, "I've heard there's a vibrant arts community in Crown Heights. Artists, writers, musicians…"

He was already nodding. "I'm a writer."

"Zak," I said, handing SB's straw tote to Dom, "may I use your bathroom?"

"Of course." If he wondered why I hadn't used the john in the house I'd just left, he was too polite to ask. "There's a powder room down that hall on your left."

When I returned to the foyer, it was vacant. "We're in here," Dom called. I followed his voice to the big, comfortable kitchen, which smelled of fresh paint—a muted robin's-egg blue—and brewing coffee.

My ex sat on a counter stool at the concrete work island while our host produced coffee mugs and milk. So much for Zak being too busy to talk. I sensed Dom and I had passed some test.

Meanwhile Sexy Beast and Dylan raced from room to room, enjoying the butt-sniffing, play-chasing, dominance-establishing stage of early canine friendship.

"—an urban near-future apocalyptic coming-of-age story," Zak was saying, "that draws heavily on Bronze Age mythology. Hittite mainly, but with a dash of Rigvedic thrown in to shake things up."

"Zak's been telling me about the novel he wrote," Dom said as I took the stool next to his. "It sounds fascinating." The subtle wide-eyed look he gave me said Zak's book did not, in fact, sound fascinating at all and please please please make him stop talking about it.

"I adore Rigvedic mythology," I said. "I'd love to hear all about it, Zak. Don't leave anything out."

Dom reached under the counter and pinched my thigh, hard. "Oh, let's not have any spoilers," he said. "Just tell me where I can buy a copy."

"I wish," Zak said, as he set the coffee fixings and a basket containing a selection of herbal teas on the island. "I'm still workshopping the manuscript. It's not quite ready to submit to publishers yet."

"How long have you been working on it?" I asked.

"I started it junior year of college."

So, close to two decades. Well, you can't rush true art.

While Zak poured coffee for himself and me, Dom poked through the basket of teas, finally selecting Nasty Grass Clippings Low Energy Blend. Okay, maybe it was really called Lemon Verbena Sunrise, but I mean, please. Give me strong, black high-test any day. I'm talking about coffee with shoulders. I want a single cup to leave me too jittery to sign my name.

"Does your book have a happy ending?" I asked Zak, who failed to repress a look of disdain. Clearly I'd just revealed myself as a lowbrow mouth-breather, my love of Rigvedic mythology notwithstanding. (I'd have to look that up one of these days.)

"Important fiction isn't about happy endings or satisfied expectations," he said. "Its job is to challenge everything the reader knows about him or herself—"

"So what else do you do?" Dom asked.

Zak frowned. "What, you mean my day job?"

Dom nodded. "Obviously you don't support yourself with your writing. *Yet*," he hastened to add.

"I'm a copywriter." Zak lifted the whistling kettle from the stove and poured boiling water over Dom's tea bag. "Have you ever visited the KrunchWorks website?"

"Can't say that I have," Dom said, "but I'm friends with Norman Butterwick." Dapper nonagenarian Norman, who'd attended my birthday party, owned the KrunchWorks snack-food company. It was the source of his fortune, along with the Easter Buddy brand of egg-dying kits, which his late wife, Maud, had inherited.

"Well," Zak said, "I'm responsible for most of the content on the site, as well as some other advertising materials."

I said, "Sounds like interesting work."

"No, it doesn't." His tone brooked no argument. "I'm

hoping this move to Brooklyn will jump-start a new phase in my life, one driven by creativity rather than the need to chase a paycheck."

At the very least, I thought, maybe the move would help him finish that darn book. "Well, for the record," I said, "I'm a huge KrunchWorks fan. I love everything they make."

There was that flash of contempt again—for KrunchWorks' offerings, I hoped, and not my less-than-refined palate. You might have already noticed I'm no stranger to junk food.

Dom said, "I take it you're not in love with your company's products."

Zak spread his arms. "Do you see any bags of Ched'r Wheelz With X-treme Cheeze! around here? I have no use for the greasy, salty, sugary factory foods those giant companies have deliberately gotten the public addicted to."

Which might explain why we hadn't been offered a cookie to go with our organic, fair-trade (and far too weak) coffee, I mentally harrumphed. And was the turbinado sugar he'd put out really any better for you than regular sugar? *Harrumph harrumph.*

Dom was nodding like a bobblehead at Zak's grumpy pronouncements. "I'm with you on that, man. That stuff is poison."

"Well, it hasn't done me in yet." I turned to Dom. "And you've been known to sneak a few Picante Gigante Tac-O's at my place." Another popular KrunchWorks snack.

Dom chose that moment to change the subject. "So, Zak, are you on vacation this week?" It was a Tuesday, after all.

"No," he said, "I work from home, and my boss doesn't really care which particular hours of the day or night I get the work done as long as it gets done."

"How long have you lived here?" Dom asked.

"My whole life, if you don't count college and a few years after. This was my parents' house, and my mom's parents before them."

I said, "Doesn't it bother you, the thought of this wonderful place not being in the family anymore?"

Zak took a moment to answer, a moment during which I realized I had yet to see this man smile. "I guess it does bother me if I let myself think about it, so I try not to think about it. Anyway, I have no one to leave it to, so what's the use in beating myself up over it?"

Since he kinda sorta went there, I said, "Audrey mentioned that you lost your wife. I'm so sorry."

Dom murmured something appropriate, and Zak nodded his thanks.

"Under the circumstances," I said, "a fresh start in a new place might be just the thing."

His eyebrows pulled together. "It wasn't recent, if that's what you're thinking. My wife's death, I mean."

My face heated. "Oh. I'm sorry. I just assumed…" Way to put your foot in it, Ms. Assumptions Can Be Dangerous.

"Stacey died eleven years ago," he said. Our surprise must have shown, because he added, "I was twenty-seven. We were married for four years."

An awkward silence ensued, which Dom broke by asking, "Did you inherit this house?"

"No, Mom and Dad retired to Florida the year before Stacey died. They sold us the house for a bargain price—which was very generous of them, and the only way we could've afforded it. Before that, we had an apartment in the city."

So Zak and Stacey lived here for a year, more or less, before he became a widower. I was too polite and well brought up (I'll wait till you stop giggling) to ask how Zak's presumably young wife met her maker. The Death Diva had no such qualms. She was dying, pun intended, to come right out and ask point-blank. Fortunately, Polite Jane prevailed and kept our big yap firmly zipped.

Likewise, I refrained from commenting on Zak's statement that he had no one to leave the house to. At thirty-eight years of age, he still had plenty of time to remarry and fill this charming old place with kids. Of course, it was entirely possible he wanted to flee the sad memories the house must hold. But if that was the case, why wait eleven years to make the big move?

Sexy Beast and Dylan, having finally tired themselves out, trotted into the kitchen, shared the water bowl, and collapsed in a heap on the big, cushy dog bed tucked into one corner of the room.

I turned to Zak. "So you and Peaches grew up across the street from each other."

"Well, yeah," he said, "but she was seven years older than me, so we didn't go to school together or anything. We never really socialized."

Dom spoke up. "Even after you moved back here? Carter and the kids were living here with her then. You didn't, I don't know, have each other over for cookouts or anything?"

"What can I tell you?" he said. "We didn't run in the same circles."

"You're both writers, though," I said, "so there's kind of a connection there, right?"

Zak looked at me sharply. "Her advice column and my novel have nothing in common."

Dom kicked me under the counter. I got the message. I was

well on my way to antagonizing Zak when I should be trying to wheedle information out of him.

Focus!

"Well," I said, "it's terribly sad that Peaches's own son was arrested for her murder."

I left that hanging there, hoping for a response from our host. He simply nodded in agreement. Yes, sad indeed.

So much for the subtle approach. "We understand you witnessed an argument between Sean and Peaches," I said. "Shortly after Thanksgiving."

"That's true, unfortunately," he said.

"Where did it take place?"

Zak's frown got even frownier. "Why do you want to know?"

I opted for honesty. Hey, it's been known to happen. "Sean's girlfriend, Cheyenne, is convinced he's innocent. She asked me to do a little investigating and see if I could maybe turn up something the police might've overlooked."

He said, "Something exculpatory, you mean, to try and get him off the hook. Good luck with that."

"Well, obviously that's what she's hoping for," I said, "but she'll have to be satisfied with whatever legitimate facts I turn up."

"You told me you're friends with Evie," Zak said. "Was that just to get through the doorway?"

"Yes." This honesty thing was wearing me down. Before he could kick us out, I added, "I do know Evie, though. No lie. And if I'd told you I was here on behalf of Cheyenne, would you have let me in?"

Zak's look of annoyance was tempered with grudging respect. "So you're, what, a private investigator?"

"No, I have a freelance business assisting clients who've lost loved ones," I said. "I'm sort of a jack-of-all-trades when it comes to the deceased." There really is no logical way to describe what I do. Every time I make the attempt, I'm met with varying degrees of incomprehension on the part of my listener. Zak, however, got it on the first try.

His hazel eyes widened. "You're the Death Diva. I've heard about you."

I spread my arms. "In the flesh."

"You did this weird thing for a friend of mine recently," he said.

"'Weird thing' doesn't really narrow it down," I said. "You'll have to be more specific."

"She wanted you to make some jewelry from her dead sister's hair," Zak said. "Well, not you personally, but apparently you arranged for a jewelry artist to do the work."

"Oh yes, that was for Ruth Neely," I said, and Zak nodded. "She got a bracelet, a ring, and a locket out of it. Believe it or not, that's nowhere near the strangest assignment I've done. Don't ask," I added, not because I didn't want to discuss my most bizarre jobs—well, there were a few I really *didn't* want to discuss—but because I had no wish to get Zak sidetracked.

"So this argument," I said, "between Sean and his mom. Do you remember what day that was?"

"Like I told the detectives," he said, "it was the afternoon of Friday, November twenty-ninth. Around two p.m."

"You have a good memory." What a delight after Sean's slimy evasiveness. "Where did this argument take place?"

"Her front yard," he said. "Well, it started inside the house and spilled over onto the porch. Sean was trying to get away from his mom, and she basically pursued him down the steps and into the yard."

"And you just happened to be outside at that moment and saw what was going on?" I asked.

"I was on a ladder out front, putting up Christmas lights."

Zak didn't strike me as the kind of guy to decorate his house for the holidays. "One of those high-tech displays?" I guessed. "Like where the lights blink in time to music and change colors and all that?"

One side of his mouth quirked. It wasn't a full-on smile, but it was the closest I'd seen. "We're talking full-on retro. Those fat, multicolored lights from the fifties and sixties, the kind my parents had when they were kids. They kept up the tradition when I was little—the house always got blinged out the day after Thanksgiving, like clockwork—and, well, I guess it just doesn't seem like Christmas without them."

"I know what you mean." I offered a half smile. "Childhood traditions are hard to let go of."

"I did Peaches's house every year, too," he said.

"Really? I thought you two didn't know each other that well."

"We didn't, not really," he said, "but the first time she saw me putting up lights—"

"The day after Turkey Day, right?" I grinned, and miracle of miracles, so did he. It turned out Zak Pryce was quite the looker when he smiled.

"That's right," he said. "It was twelve years ago, the first Christmas after Stacy and I moved in. Peaches hurried over and within two minutes managed to wheedle me into putting up her lights too—and then taking them down after New Year's. I've done it every year since."

Dom looked surprised. "What about Carter?"

One eyebrow quirked. "Could you see Carter Moretti up on a ladder, working with electricity?"

"We haven't met him," Dom said. "Kind of hopeless with honey-do tasks, is he?"

"That's one way to put it," Zak said. "Honestly, I didn't mind doing it every year. Not if it kept Carter from shorting out the Northeast power grid."

I wouldn't have expected that kind of neighborly spirit, not to mention holiday sentiment, from someone like slick, artsy Zak. I must admit, I found myself charmed.

Dom was staring at me. Reading my mind, as usual. "So." His tone was brisk. "You were out there on the ladder when you noticed the commotion across the street."

"It would've been impossible *not* to notice," he said.

"They were that loud?" I asked.

"Yelling at the top of their lungs. I would've gone back inside the house to get away from them, but I was stuck up there on that ladder, with an armful of lights I was trying to untangle."

Dom said, "Peaches and Sean must have seen you."

"Oh, I'm sure they did," Zak said, "but they were too worked up to care."

"Were there any other neighbors around?" I asked.

"None near enough to hear."

"Sean's mom had kicked him out of the house about a month before that," I said. "Carter, too."

"Which was good news as far as I was concerned," Zak said. "I'm referring to Sean, not his dad. I have nothing against Carter. Kind of a nebbish, which isn't the worst sort of neighbor to have."

The message being: better a harmless nebbish living across the street than a lazy, drugged-out part-time burglar.

"What were they arguing about?" I asked.

"By the time she chased him outside," he said, "it was basically a lot of name-calling and general invective. They were both dropping f-bombs and worse."

"Did it get physical at any point?"

"Not that I saw. And neither of them was bleeding." He shrugged. "But if words could kill…"

Yeah, about that. "You told the police you heard Sean threaten his mother," I said.

"His exact words?" Zak poured me a second cup of weak coffee. "Quote, 'You better watch your ass, you miserable old slut. I know guys who'd be thrilled to do a Jimmy Hoffa on you, just for the fun of it. All I'd have to do is snap my fingers. They'd never find your body.' End quote."

I wondered how high someone would have to be to forget making a threat like that. "Did you report this conversation to the cops?" I asked. "I mean, you know, at the time it happened."

He shook his head. "Peaches didn't seem to take it seriously, so I saw no reason I should. For all I knew, that could have been the ten millionth time he'd said something like that to her."

Dom said, "Did Peaches threaten Sean in any way?"

"Not that I heard."

Well, she'd already followed through on her threat to kick him out of the house and stop supporting him, and Sean hadn't claimed she'd threatened him with physical violence, at least during his conversation with me.

"When's the last time you saw Peaches?" I said, knowing the cops had no doubt asked the same thing.

"That was the last time," he said. "That fight out on the lawn."

"Did they say anything else that stuck in your mind?"

"Not really, nothing as memorable as that Jimmy Hoffa stuff." Zak drained his coffee mug and placed it in the sink.

"I get the feeling you think the cops arrested the right guy," I said.

"Well, the kid already has a record." He shrugged, as if it wasn't that big a leap from burglary to first-degree murder. "On the other hand, don't they say that nine times out of ten, it's the spouse?"

"Carter?" I mused, leaving aside that he wasn't Peaches's legal spouse. After near a quarter century together, he might as well have been. "The two of them *were* estranged. But didn't I just hear you say he was an okay neighbor? Just a little nebbishy?"

"You know what they say about the quiet ones," Zak said. "But I'm just thinking out loud. I have no reason to think Carter wanted to do Peaches harm."

"While we're on the subject of suspects," I said, "do you know the name Burke Fletcher? Evie mentioned him to me."

"The name sounds familiar," Zak said. "Wait. Is he the stalker?"

"I don't know if his behavior approached the level of stalking," I said. "I assume that if it did, Peaches would have been able to get the order of protection she wanted."

"Right, right." He was nodding now. "Fletcher's that guy who accused her of destroying his marriage. Seems his wife wrote in to the 'Peaches Preaches' column complaining about him, and Peaches advised her to ditch the bum, or words to that effect. So she went ahead and dumped him—"

"Hold up." Dom made the "time out" *T* gesture. "This woman divorces her husband on the basis of a single advice column written by a stranger?"

"Apparently," Zak said. "And they'd been married a long time, too, something like thirty years."

"Wow," I said. "That's pretty extreme."

Dom said, "I'm sure we don't know the whole story."

"Well, apparently he was harassing Peaches, at the very least." I turned to Zak. "How do you know about Fletcher?"

He paused to consider the question. "Peaches told me about him when I was putting up her Christmas lights. The guy really had her rattled."

I was itching to meet Fletcher, to chat with him face-to-face, if for no other reason than to get his version of this strange story. But no, I'd promised myself I'd just toss a few questions Howie's way, and that would be the last of my involvement. No one was paying me to look into Peaches's murder, after all. I had no legitimate reason to pursue it, apart from Cheyenne's conviction that her good-for-nothing boyfriend du jour couldn't possibly have offed the mother he so detested. Having met the boyfriend in question, I failed to share her blind faith in his innocence.

"Listen," Zak said, "maybe you can advise me on something, since you know the family. I don't want to come off as insensitive or grabby or whatever. I mean, it's only been a few days since Peaches was found."

Yeah, by me, I wanted to say. "What's on your mind?"

"Well, she was really grateful to me for doing her lights every year, and she offered me a kind of thank-you gift."

"Oh yeah?" I wondered where this was going.

"She told me that in the event she died," he said, "there was something she wanted me to have. I just don't know how to approach Evie about it. Or if it's too soon."

"I don't know if you realize how thoroughly Sean has trashed that house," I said. "Under the circumstances, I'd say the sooner you act on this bequest, the better. What did she leave you?"

He said, "Have you ever seen her collection of peach figurines?"

6

Cute as the Dickens

"I DON'T KNOW how I'm going to manage without my Joanne." Ken Curran bravely held back tears as he stood at the microphone in front of a packed house at Dawn's Depot.

In my many years as the one and only Death Diva, I'd arranged funerals and memorial services at every sort of establishment you can imagine. This was not the first time the grieving party had chosen a watering hole as the venue in which to honor a departed loved one, but it was a first for this Texas-style saloon and piano bar.

Dawn's Depot had been established fifty-seven years earlier by one Dawn Ann Hammond, a transplant from the Hill Country of central Texas. Finding herself far from her hometown of Gärlichnott, one of the first communities established by the German immigrants who'd settled in the Hill Country, Dawn had longed for the comfortable, noisy, and occasionally rowdy dive bars and roadhouses she'd left behind when she moved north.

The eighty-six-year-old owner was a perpetual presence at Dawn's Depot. Anytime it was open, even for private events like this funeral, she was there, enthroned on a vinyl-upholstered stool near the small wooden stage, a bourbon-filled water glass in her hand.

Dawn was a locally famous Character. (Take my word for it, she'd earned that capital C.) The skinny octogenarian wore her implausibly carroty hair in a neat French twist, which was the only ladylike thing about her if you didn't count the heavy turquoise jewelry that probably weighed more than she did. We're talking elaborate Native American necklaces, earrings, brooches, bracelets, rings, and belt buckles, usually several pieces at once. When it came to her turquoise, Dawn subscribed to the fashion rule that if a little was good, a lot was better. As for clothing, on any given day you'd find her wearing her customary Western pearl-snap shirt, well-worn jeans, and fancy cowboy boots.

Of course, there was always music at Dawn's, provided by either a DJ playing country songs or, more often, a live act onstage. Making arrangements on behalf of my client, Ken Curran, a pudgy, thirty-four-year-old tech-industry executive, I'd booked a popular Texas swing band, who'd take the stage as soon as the weepy part of the funeral was over. At that point the guests, nearly a hundred of them, would begin chowing down on Texas barbecue with all the trimmings, downing pitchers of beer, and kicking up their heels on the scarred wooden dance floor located more or less in the center of the place.

I say *more or less* because Dawn's Depot lacked anything resembling a normal architectural layout. It had been cobbled together all those year ago out of several railroad cars set at odd angles to one another, and at slightly different levels, the off-kilter spaces crammed with an ever-growing assortment of cheesy decorations. Throw in perpetually dim lighting and the disorienting angles of the place—accentuated by strings of blinking lights in a variety of shapes and colors—and navigating your way to the ladies' room in the caboose (don't even get me *started* on the ladies' room in the caboose) could be quite the challenge, depending on your degree of inebriation.

Dawn's Depot was located on the outskirts of snooty, upscale Crystal Harbor. A few years earlier, some of the snootier, more upscale residents decided such a déclassé establishment had no place in their respectable town and attempted to have the property condemned. Thankfully, that plan was quashed through an organized effort led by my dear friends Sophie Halperin and Sten Jakobsen, who managed to secure local landmark status for Dawn's Depot, thus ensuring the survival of a little slice of Texas heaven in one of the most buttoned-up corners of Long Island. So there.

As it happened, Peaches's funeral was being held at the exact same time, across town in an actual church. I'd had nothing to do with those arrangements. Evie had been more than up to the task of giving her mom a proper sendoff, despite the tragic circumstances of her death, not to mention the arrest of her own brother for the murder.

Zak's comment about having inherited Peaches's peaches gnawed at the edges of what passed for my mind. Just how many people thought those darn things belonged to them? More to the point, how many people had she promised them to? It all sounded pretty fishy, though it also sounded like precisely the sort of mean, petty practical joke that mean, petty Peaches would decide to play from beyond the grave.

Of more immediate concern, and I hate to put it in such crass terms (because you know me, I'm never crass), but if it turned out that someone other than Evie was the legitimate owner of her mother's collection, would she still be willing to pay me for trying to locate them? Maybe I should have required a retainer after all.

Some of the funeral-goers there at Dawn's Depot had been able to snag tables, but for most of them, it was standing room only. Though it was high noon, it might as well have been midnight. The place sported few windows, and little light made it through them on this overcast day in early April.

I'd taken up position at the front of the room near Dawn so I could keep an eye on everything and make sure the event ran smoothly. I wore my usual funeral uniform of gray skirt suit, white blouse, fake pearls, and low heels. My friend Maia Armstrong was catering and she was a pro, so I anticipated no problems with the quality or quantity of the vittles. Ned, the grizzled bartender, stood at the ready near the beer taps, and the band was all set to take the stage at my signal. Everything was under control.

You know, that smirk is very unbecoming. Is it so implausible that I, Jane Delaney, might have everything under control?

I glanced at my watch. Ken Curran had been holding forth onstage for close to twenty minutes. Far from winding down, he seemed to be getting himself more worked up by the second.

"I was a mess before Joanne entered my life." He could barely choke out the words. Now he stabbed his finger toward all those acquaintances, relatives, and coworkers who'd heard about the free beer and barbecue. "Some of you know what I'm talking about. I see you nodding."

"Oh, brother," Dawn groused in her gravelly smoker's voice. She took a healthy swig of her bourbon.

It's not that Dawn was without compassion, it's just that her compassion had its limits. And this particular funeral—or, as Ken preferred to call it, "celebration of life"—had bumped right up against those limits. Mine, too, if I was being honest, but the anticipation of the healthy fee he was paying me had a salutary effect on my empathy.

Which was another way of saying, pay me enough and I'll weep crocodile tears for the most unlovable deceased individual.

In this case, the deceased individual reposed in an elegant bronze casket perched atop the baby grand piano on the stage. But, Jane, you might well ask, how on earth could a baby grand piano support a bronze casket? To which I would answer, it's no problem at all when the casket in question is the approximate size of a toaster oven. One of those cheap little toaster ovens you can't reheat a slice of pizza in without folding it up the sides.

For poor dead Joanne, you see, was not a person. She was Ken Curran's emotional-support animal.

Yeah, I know, another animal funeral. You'd think I'd have learned my lesson. Animal funerals have a way of getting out of hand. But this time was different. May I remind you, this time I had everything under control.

"Joanne!" Ken fell on the piano, sobbing, hugging the closed casket. "What will I do without you? How can I go on?"

The guests shuffled nervously, muttering to one another.

Dawn leaned toward me. "That's a lotta carryin' on for a little bug."

"I don't know about 'little,'" I whispered.

The deceased was a Goliath bird-eating tarantula, *Theraphosa blondi*, which was native to South America and just happened to be the world's largest spider. Joanne had a leg span of twelve inches, and her body—the big, scary middle part containing the fangs and venom—was close to five inches long. I provide this information in case you ever find yourself in the market for a, you know, emotional-support bug.

"This ain't nothin'," Dawn rasped. "You come to Texas, I'll

show you tarantulas."

"As big as Joanne?" I asked.

She spread her arms. "Big as a hubcap."

Uh-huh. Dawn might try to claim that everything's bigger in Texas, but I suspected Joanne could gobble up their native tarantulas for lunch—with plenty of room left over for the odd lizard, small mammal, or, yes, bird.

Ken was now wailing in grief and vigorously shaking the casket. "Don't leave me, Joanne! *Don't leave me!*"

According to my heartbroken client, Joanne had recently slowed in her movements and stopped eating, finally croaking on her back with her long, hairy legs in the air. I'd witnessed her reassuring deadness myself before advising Ken that a closed-casket service was the way to go in this particular instance. More, um, dignified.

I wasn't concerned about the bug in the box. Dead is dead. I did, however, keep a wary eye on the very live snake Veronica Sheffield was cuddling, her terrified gaze never straying from Joanne's casket.

Veronica was in her early fifties, elegantly dressed as always, her highlighted chestnut hair neatly styled. Her snake was about eighteen inches long, ringed with bands of red, black, and yellow. Veronica stood not far from the stage, and I noticed that those around her were giving her—or rather, her wriggling companion—plenty of space.

Veronica was one of my most reliable, well-heeled, and eccentric clients—a winning combo as far as the Death Diva was concerned—and I had no intention of alienating her by forbidding her to bring her own emotional-support animal to this funeral. Yes, that's right, Lewis the snake kept his owner from suffering panic attacks when confronted with the myriad things that could be counted on to freak her out. And, you guessed it, spiders were right up there at the top of that list—even, apparently, dead ones. Live snakes, not so much. Hence Lewis's presence during these not-so-solemn proceedings.

And it wasn't as if Dawn were going to object. The crusty Texas native was no stranger to critters that slithered or crawled. I leaned toward her while my client's onstage meltdown entered the howling, clothes-rending stage, and said, "What I want to know is, since when do vermin get to be called by people names like Joanne and Lewis?"

She knocked back the last of her bourbon. "My five ex-husbands all had people names, so where do you draw the line?"

I watched Lewis attempt to slide under Veronica's collar while she patiently discouraged him. "Listen," I said, "I've been wondering what kind of snake that is. Do you happen to know?"

Dawn glanced at Lewis and said, "Looks like a king snake."

"Are they poisonous?" I asked.

"Nah."

I started to heave a gusty sigh until she added, "Course, it could be a coral snake. They look kinda the same."

"And coral snakes are—?"

"Poisonous as hell." Dawn turned and waved to catch the eye of Ned, the bartender. She signaled for a refill.

You might point out that it makes little sense to seek emotional support from a creature that could do you serious damage with one little bite, and you'd be right. But you don't know Veronica Sheffield. This is the woman who hired me to get a hot Irish priest to talk dirty to her dead friend at the local cemetery. It was the first time I'd enlisted Martin in a Death Diva assignment, and he'd played his role almost too well.

So, with Veronica calling the shots, I'd say it was fifty-fifty whether Lewis was a harmless king snake or a venomous coral snake.

I kept a wary eye on my client, who had clambered up onto the piano and was now clutching the little casket to his chest and rocking himself, screaming, "I'll never find another bug like you, Joanne!"

"So, uh, Dawn," I said, "how do we determine which kind of snake Lewis is?"

"You'll find out when he bites you." She guffawed, then quickly pushed her dentures back. "Damn upper plate."

That's when I recalled there's a little rhyming ditty to help tell the difference between the two kinds of snake. It all came down to their red, black, and yellow bands, and which colors were touching. I tried to recall the rhyme.

Let's see… It was something like *Red touches yellow, there's a good fellow. Red touches black, better stand back!* Yeah, that sounded right. I peered at Lewis as he writhed between Veronica's fingers, and was relieved to see a pattern of black, yellow, red, yellow, black. Lewis's red bands abutted only yellow bands, not black.

All righty, then. One less thing to worry about.

Up onstage, Ken fiddled with the latch that held the casket closed. "One last look," he sobbed.

Okay, enough was enough. The time had come to rein in my distraught client. No one needed to see Ken's gigantic, dead bug, least of all nutty, arachnophobic Veronica.

I ascended the three steps to the stage and gently took him by the shoulders. "I think we need to wrap this up," I said, as kindly as I could.

"Help me get this thing open," he wailed, when the stiff latch refused to budge.

"Ken, I know this is hard, but…" I tried in vain to pull him down off the piano. "We owe it to Joanne to let her rest in peace."

"*No!*" He pounded on the box. "I have to see her one last time."

The funeral-goers were restless, and who could blame them? Their patience had been taxed to the limit, and they were more than ready to attack the beer and barbecue.

I tugged on the casket. "Better to remember her as she was, Ken. That's what she would have wanted." Putting my back into it, I managed to wrench the thing out of his grasp, just as the latch gave way and the lid flew open.

The world's biggest spider scrambled out of the casket and up my arm to my shoulder. At this point my memory of the event becomes a bit hazy, as I'm sure you can appreciate. I do recall that Joanne was russet brown in color and weighed as much as a small puppy. Cute as the dickens too.

Just seeing if you're paying attention.

I also recall that I screamed louder and longer than I ever have in my entire life, while staring into the fanged face of my nightmares. For that matter, everyone in the room was vocalizing pretty enthusiastically. Well, except for Veronica, who stood frozen to the spot, gawking in horror at Joanne while clutching Lewis to her chest.

Ken, as you can imagine, was ecstatic. "It's a miracle! Stand still, Jane, so I can grab her."

If I told you I stood perfectly still while a skillet-size spider scampered over my head and under my jacket, would you believe me? I didn't think so. I entertained the assembled throng with my rendition of the tarantula tango, screeching and flailing and finally tumbling off the stage, which Joanne took as her cue to sprint into the crowd. Dang, that thing moved fast!

It was nothing less than pandemonium as the shrieking guests tripped over one another in their attempt to evade the not-so-deceased guest of honor.

Ken launched himself into the melee. "Don't hurt her! Don't step on my Joanne!"

"Lewis!" Veronica came up for air, goggle-eyed, empty-handed. "Where's Lewis? *Where's my snake?"*

Which, as you might have guessed, raised the pandemonium to a whole new level. I couldn't speak for anyone else, but I'd never felt less emotionally supported in my life. I just prayed no one would be trampled as the crowd rushed the exits.

By contrast, Dawn was the picture of serenity. Without rising from her stool or relinquishing her bourbon, she reached over, snatched up the little casket where I'd dropped it, and peered inside.

"Mystery solved." She lifted out what at first I took to be a second tarantula, this one limp and unmoving. "Damn thing was just molting. They can look like goners when they're gettin' ready to wriggle out of their old exoskeletons."

By now only a handful of Ken's closest, and bravest, kinfolk remained. Someone yelled, "There they are!" The group sprang apart, revealing Joanne and Lewis locked in a grotesque death match. Lewis writhed over and around Joanne as she angled for an opportunity to deliver the coup de grace.

Meanwhile their frantic owners threatened each other with lawsuits if anything should happen to their beloved companions. As much as she valued Lewis, Veronica wasn't about to intervene, not if it meant tangling with a tarantula.

I said, "Ken, go ahead and try to separate them. Lewis can't hurt you, he's a harmless king snake."

"Uh-uh-uh, I wouldn't do that, young fella." Dawn had relinquished her seat at last and stood squinting at the combatants. "That there's a coral snake. Chock-full of venom."

Veronica blinked. "It is?"

"No, you're wrong, Dawn," I said. "I'm telling you, it's a king snake. You know the old saying. 'Red touches yellow, there's a good fellow. Red touches black, better stand back.'"

Dawn laughed so hard, her upper plate nearly flew out of her mouth. "It's 'Red touches yellow, *kills a fellow*. Red touches black, friend of Jack.'"

Oops. But I was close, right? I mean, my version rhymed and everything.

Oh, who asked you?

So we were dealing with a poisonous snake after all. Where was an emotional-support mongoose when you needed one? As it turned out, Joanne did just fine on her own. Within seconds, she'd dealt the death blow. We all watched as Lewis went still, paralyzed by his adversary's venom. Joanne seized him by the head and started dragging him toward the dimmer recesses of the saloon. Ken followed close behind, cajoling her to climb back into the casket and let him take her home.

Veronica was less broken up than I would have predicted, which kind of made sense considering she'd just learned that the snake she'd been relying on to keep herself calm and contented was, well, a snake. She made no mention of retrieving his body for a proper funeral, which was just as well since it appeared Joanne had other plans for him.

Dawn clapped me on the back, with surprising force. "I haven't had this much fun since my third husband's girlfriends and me threw him a little surprise party. You can throw a funeral here anytime."

7

It Wouldn't Not Be Fun

THAT EVENING I found myself in yet another venerable gin mill. Murray's Pub had been a Crystal Harbor institution since the late nineteenth century, which meant it had a good seven or eight decades on Dawn's Depot. Murray's wore its age well, the wood paneling, floors, and bar scarred but lovingly maintained, the original gas light fixtures long since wired for electricity. Soft bluegrass music played in the background.

Every Wednesday night Murray's hosted a trivia contest, which could reliably be counted on to pack the house. Not that I was in the mood for another crowded bar after the earlier fiasco at Dawn's, but at least this time I was there as a civilian. In the event the proceedings got out of hand (which was not outside the realm of possibility), the pub's owner, Maxine Baumgartner, was more than capable of handling it. Ditto for the bartender on duty, who just happened to be Martin McAuliffe. The padre lived in a one-bedroom apartment over the bar, which was a pretty sweet commute.

Suffice it to say, by the time I got to Murray's that evening, I was more than ready for some silly fun with a few good friends while tossing back a frosty brewski or two. For the trivia game, I partnered with three of my best pals: Mayor Sophie Halperin and the local police detectives, Howie Werker and Cookie Kaplan. Cookie chose our team name: You Can't Spell Manslaughter Without Laughter.

Maxine—Max to the pub's regulars—was in her early fifties, with a blonde ponytail and a pugnacious attitude. As always, she officiated, calling out the trivia questions, tallying up the scores, and rewarding the winners. Our team came in first, which surprised precisely no one who knew Sophie, the mayor being a bottomless font of arcane knowledge.

Coming in first place meant the four of us got to share a fifty-dollar bar tab, good for food and booze, which we had vowed to consume by the end of the night. Fortunately, Max had a soft spot for cops, and she was fond of Sophie and me, as well, so she had no problem letting the four of us linger after the place emptied out.

We'd claimed a booth near the back. I sat on the outside of the bench next to Sophie. Howie and Cookie sat across from us. The remains of nachos and fried calamari littered the table, along with our nearly empty beer glasses.

"I hope you're still hungry." It was petite and elegant Nina Wallace, stopping by our table on her way out. Nina was an avid baker who never went anywhere without an armload of homemade goodies. It was her one redeeming quality if you didn't count her sense of entitlement and win-at-all-costs campaign style. Oh wait, those last two aren't actually redeeming qualities, are they? Never mind, then.

"These were left over." She deposited a plastic food container filled with assorted yummies at the center of our table. "If I bring them back home, they'll just end up on my hips. So *please* take them."

Nina weighed about a hundred pounds. I'd never hated her

more than at that moment.

"You know, I used to take cookies and brownies to trivia night, but then it finally occurred to me—" she bonked herself on the head and made a *Duh!* face "—that savory things might go better with beer. Not that *I* drink beer, of course, I'm strictly a prosecco girl, but everyone else seems to like it."

"We'll happily accept them," Howie, ever the gentleman, said. He was in his early forties, tall, dark-skinned, and easy on the eyes. "Thanks, Nina."

"You're welcome, Howie." She pointed. "Those long ones are olive, herb, and Parmesan breadsticks. These over here are cheddar scones. There's one Black Forest ham and Gruyère thumbprint pastry left—"

I wished she'd hurry up and leave so I could stuff my mouth, which was watering like a faucet, despite all the snacks I'd already crammed into it that night.

"—and these round ones are pesto pinwheels."

"Those things look amazing," Cookie said. She was a recent hire by the Crystal Harbor Police Department, having been brought on last fall when Bonnie Hernandez was promoted from detective to chief. Tonight Cookie had corralled her curly brown hair into a charmingly disheveled bun. She wore her customary burgundy-framed eyeglasses and funky earrings—little enameled purses this time, one blue and one green.

"Well, they couldn't be easier to make. Email me through the Historical Society and I'll send you the recipe." Nina leaned in close to Cookie and whispered, "You're wearing two different earrings."

"I know." Cookie smiled at her. "It's on purpose."

"Oh!" Nina tittered as if she'd never heard of such a thing. "Well, aren't you brave. I wouldn't have the nerve."

I'd been wondering how long it would take the mayor-elect to detonate her signature backhanded compliment. "Good night, Nina," I said, hoping to push her out the door before she lobbed one in my direction. I was feeling a tad fragile after the failed funeral for an undead tarantula, and I yearned for the comfort of an emotional-support cheddar scone.

My companions echoed my good-night to Nina, all except Sophie, who remained uncharacteristically mute. Nina responded by looking straight through her, the two recent mayoral candidates having not a lot to say to each other.

Martin was wiping down bottles in the speed well behind the bar. "'Bye, Nina. I'm going to steal a couple of those breadsticks."

Max, busy balancing the cash drawer, did not look up. "We're closing up now, Nina. See ya." Once the door had shut behind the other woman, Max said, "Is that slimeball really going to be our mayor? Tell me it's all a bad dream."

"You never know." Sophie wore a mysterious little smile as she selected a pesto pinwheel and admired it from all sides. "Stay tuned."

"*What?*" I twisted in my seat to face her. "What's going on, Sophie? Tell us!"

She tormented us by taking her time masticating the delicacy before washing it down with the last of her beer. "Not much to tell. Town Council's investigating campaign improprieties."

I smacked her shoulder. "How long have you been sitting on this? Why am I just hearing about it now?"

"Figured you were the one that got them looking into it."

"Not me." I snatched up a cheddar scone. "You made me promise I wouldn't kick up a fuss about Nina's dirty tricks, and I kept my word."

"You didn't make *me* promise," Cookie said, "and I gave the Council an earful, let me tell you."

"Me, too," Howie said, as he rooted around in the snack container. "Where's that thumbprint ham thing? Gotcha!"

"Who *didn't* complain about that so-called fair election?" Max shoved her arms into the sleeves of her leather bomber jacket and headed for the door, where she flipped the sign from OPEN to CLOSED. "Night, folks. Martin, you'll lock up."

He gave her a lazy salute as he finished filling a pitcher, which he carried to our table. "Enjoy the last of your winnings, guys," he said as he poured.

Cookie said, "Looks like you intend to enjoy our winnings with us, Martin."

"What gave it away?" He hip-bumped me and squeezed in at the end of the bench.

She tapped her skull. "A seasoned detective like me knows how to read the signs."

"Like that extra beer glass you brought with you," Howie said. "That's what we seasoned detectives call a clue."

The padre raised his glass to them. "The bad guys don't stand a chance with a couple of seasoned detectives like you on the case."

I waved my hand in the air. "I have a question for the seasoned detectives."

Howie pointed a stern finger at me. "We are not discussing the Peaches Gillespey case with you, Jane."

"You don't know what I was going to say."

"No, but I know what it was going to be about," he said. "Drink your beer and let's talk about something else. The poker tournament's coming up. Who do you think's going to win this year?"

Sophie said, "My money's on last year's winner. Even though he's a cheating scoundrel."

"I take exception to that, Mayor." Martin leaned around me to address Sophie. "I'm a reprobate, not a scoundrel, and I cheat only when it's absolutely necessary. Last year it was not absolutely necessary. Talk to me again after this year's tournament."

"Because I didn't even bring up the Gillespey case," I said. "You did, Howie. So obviously you want to talk about it."

Howie turned to his partner. "Isn't Jane doing a good job of not talking about the Gillespey case, Cookie?"

"She sure is, Howie. Gosh, I'm just so darn proud of Jane."

Sophie said, "I hear you guys don't have that much evidence against the son."

And this, in case you were wondering, is what best friends are for.

"It's not going to work, ladies." Howie gestured with his glass. "And you, Mayor, should know better than to try to pump us for information about an ongoing—"

"There's the fight a neighbor overheard," she said. "Sean threatening his mom."

I said, "Yeah, but he didn't say he was going to strangle her. He talked about getting someone to make her vanish, Hoffa-style."

Howie glowered at me. "And you know this how?"

"She did vanish, though, didn't she?" Martin shrugged. "Just for a few months, but still."

"Something else we know," Sophie said, "is that Sean's supposed to inherit half of his mom's estate, whatever that comes to. If you're in the market for a motive."

"Thank you, Mayor," Howie said dryly. "I'll jot that down

in my little notebook."

"So, Jane," Cookie said, "I have to assume you've been talking to Peaches's neighbor across the street since you know about the Jimmy Hoffa comment."

"I might have, you know, bumped into Zak when I went to see Sean."

"What were you thinking, paying a call on Sean?" Howie said. "You have no business talking to that little creep."

"As a matter of fact," I said, "it was business that brought me there. Evie hired me to track down her mother's missing peach collection."

Cookie grimaced. "She collected *peaches*?"

"Not the fruit itself," I said. "Little figurines and knickknacks shaped like peaches. Some of them are worth quite a lot. Apparently someone broke into her china cabinet and made off with them."

I refrained from mentioning my other investigation, the one Cheyenne had literally strong-armed me into. I didn't want to watch Howie have a stroke. And why stir the pot when I had no intention of pursuing it after that night?

"When did this happen?" Howie asked.

"Sean says he has no idea when they went missing," I said, "for whatever that's worth. Evie didn't find out until the day before yesterday when she managed to get into the house."

"Well, she didn't report the theft," Cookie said. "It would've been nice to know, on the off chance it has something to do with the murder."

"Keep us apprised of your progress on this knickknack thing," Howie told me, "but stay away from Sean. He's bad news."

"No problem, I'm done with him," I said, and meant it.

Sophie wasn't finished grilling the detectives. "Did the killer leave fingerprints?"

"I don't know," was Howie's cryptic response. Meaning maybe the cops found fingerprints, and maybe some of them belonged to the killer, and maybe that killer was Sean, and maybe he had no intention of letting Sophie drag the information out of him.

She said, "So then, what other evidence do you have against him?"

The detectives seemed disinclined to answer, so Martin did it for them. "The rope."

Sophie and I were all ears. Cookie just shook her head, with a little smile.

Howie was not smiling. "How do you know about the rope?" he demanded, followed immediately by, "Don't answer that. And don't talk to these two about it."

I didn't waste time wondering how Martin had learned details of the case no one outside the police department was privy to. He had at least one buddy on the force who didn't mind sharing juicy info about ongoing cases. Probably while sucking down a beer or three in this very pub, but that was conjecture on my part.

"Howie," Sophie said, "come on, it's just us here. Tell us about the rope."

Cookie looked at Howie expectantly, which reinforced my impression that she was the easygoing one—in other words, the one to hit up for details. I'd known Howie a long time, and it was no secret he did everything by the book. Or at least tried to.

I turned to the padre. "I assume you're referring to the rope that was used to tie Peaches to that chair in the attic, the yellow nylon rope that you and I observed with our own eyes when we discovered her dead body." I included that last part to remind the detectives that Martin and I were not exactly uninvolved bystanders in this case and that our questions were not driven by ghoulish curiosity.

Well, maybe ten percent ghoulish curiosity and ninety percent legitimate interest. Okay, okay, twenty-eighty.

"So what's Sean's connection to the rope?" Sophie asked.

"My guess?" I said, while Howie treated us to the death stare. "The cops probably found the same kind of rope in his house. Except he was living with his grandma when Peaches was killed."

Martin polished off a breadstick, nodding. "The cops found the exact same kind of rope in Audrey Moretti's basement."

"On a hook in the utility room," Cookie said. "The crime lab will tell us if there's a match." When her partner gaped at her, she added, "What? They already know. Here, have a scone."

"This is what he needs." Sophie lifted the pitcher and topped off Howie's glass. "Drink up, Detective."

"But Carter was living with Audrey, too," I said. "Still is, actually. Which means he had as much access to the rope as Sean did. And don't they say that nine times out of ten it's the spouse?"

"You've been watching too much *Law & Order*," Howie grumbled.

Would you believe this wasn't the first time I'd heard that?

Sophie said, "But think about it. The mother of his children kicks him out after, what, twenty-five years?"

"Twenty-four," I said.

"From what I heard," she said, "Peaches wasn't exactly the maternal type. Carter raised those kids practically single-handedly. Kept house and cooked, too."

"A househusband," Howie said.

"I don't think that's the politically correct way to put it," Cookie said, "but yeah, he doesn't seem to have had any other career that whole time."

"Carter couldn't have been happy to be dumped like that," Sophie said. "So he had motive, too."

Everyone at the table chewed on that awhile. Well, we also chewed on the last of Nina's home-baked snacks, and fought over the crumbs.

Martin said, "You know, no one's mentioned the other person who had access to Audrey's rope." When we all just looked at him, he said, "Audrey. It was her rope."

"Have you met Grandma Audrey?" I asked. "Because I have, and I'm telling you, I just can't see her tying her daughter-in-law, or whatever you want to call her son's long-term girlfriend, to a chair in that hot attic and strangling her with her own scarf."

"Yeah, and that's another thing," Sophie said.

"Of course it is," Howie groaned. "Let's have it."

"The heater was going full blast in that attic," she said. "Obviously either Peaches or her killer turned it on when they went up there."

"And the killer didn't bother to turn it off when he, or she, left," I said.

"It was pretty cold right after Thanksgiving," Cookie said. "I remember it snowed then."

"So that old, uninsulated attic would've been freezing," Sophie said. "Still, why bother to heat the place if you're not planning to hang out for a while? Did she go up there to meet someone?" I assumed she didn't expect an answer. If so, her expectations were fulfilled.

"Okay, I have to mention something," I said.

Howie gestured expansively. "Why hold back now?"

"Now that I'm thinking about that rope... well, I mean, yellow nylon rope isn't exactly uncommon, which is why I didn't think anything of it at the time."

I now had both detectives' full attention. "Where did you see rope like that?" Cookie asked.

"In Zak Pryce's house."

"You were in his *house*?" Howie scowled. "I thought you said you just bumped into him. What does Zak have to do with the knickknacks?"

Quite a lot if he was to be believed. "It's complicated. Can I just tell you about the rope?"

Cookie gave her partner a quelling look, and said, "Go ahead, Jane."

"Well, Zak is renovating his house," I said, "so he has a lot of tools and supplies and stuff lying around. Including yellow nylon rope."

"Same thickness as the rope Peaches was tied with?" Cookie asked.

"Maybe. I mean, it's hard to say, but it looked like the same kind." I shrugged. "It's pretty common, though, right? That kind of rope."

The detectives exchanged an unreadable look. "Yeah, pretty common," Cookie said.

"Zak Pryce is another one you'd do well to keep your distance from," Howie said. "I never did believe his alibi."

"Wait." I shook my head to clear it. "Since when is Zak a suspect?"

He paused with his beer glass halfway to his mouth. "I figured you knew all about the guy."

"And how can he, or anyone, have an alibi for Peaches's murder?" I asked. "We don't know when she died."

"Not Peaches," Sophie said. "Zak's wife. Right, Detective?"

"That's right."

"Happened ten or twelve years ago, as I recall," she continued. "Stacey Pryce drowned in her bathtub."

"I was the first responding officer," Howie said. "Zak claimed he came home and found her that way. It was clear she'd been dead for some time."

"Where did he say he'd been?" I asked.

"Right across the street," Howie said, "with his good pals Peaches Gillespey and Carter Moretti. Said he spent several hours over there that day, drinking gin and tonics and watching tennis. It was early September. The U.S. Open was going on."

"Stacey didn't join them?" I asked.

"Tennis bored her to tears, according to him. She stayed home."

I was shaking my head. "It doesn't make sense. I mean, Zak told me he never socialized with them. Said they didn't run in the same circles. That's the way he put it."

"That was my impression, too," he said. "But Peaches and Carter both vouched for him, claimed he was there most of the day. They said Stacey waved to them from the doorway as Zak crossed the street to their house."

"Didn't they eventually find sedatives in her system?" Sophie asked.

"The tox screen showed Xanax and alcohol. She had a prescription for anxiety, and was known to sometimes mix it with vodka."

"According to the husband?" Cookie said.

Howie gave a bleak nod. "According to the husband. He

said he warned her repeatedly about the dangers, and she kept promising to stop. We spoke to all her friends and relatives, and no one else ever saw her mix pills and booze."

Martin said, "But isn't that the kind of thing only a spouse might know about? I mean, who goes around advertising something like that?"

"In any event," Howie said, "it was finally declared an accidental death. That case has bugged me for eleven years."

It occurred to me that if Stacey's death had been more recent, the toxicology lab might have found Zenaproche, the new sedative Evie was hawking, rather than Xanax in her system.

Vigorous pounding on the door made us all jump. Martin got up and engaged in a short, shouted conversation with the tipsy couple on the other side of the glass. When "Closed!" failed to convince the pair, who could clearly see us sitting in our booth drinking beer, the padre said, "Private party!" and turned his back on the couple, who gave the door one last, frustrated thump before staggering away to locate a bar that would serve them.

"I for one am really enjoying our private party." Cookie raised her glass to the group.

"Can't remember when I've had such a good time," Howie grumped.

Martin sat back down next to me, giving my jeans-clad thigh an affectionate squeeze as he did so. I stopped breathing. Then I figured I'd better start breathing again because it would be awfully embarrassing to collapse in a dead faint and end up with scone crumbs plastered to my face.

"Where were we?" Martin asked.

We were squeezing my thigh. Do it again.

"You know," Sophie said, "if Sean had a motive in the form

of inheritance, then so did Evie."

"And she's no fan of her dead mom," I said.

"Yeah, that came through loud and clear when we interviewed her," Cookie said. "But nothing else raised a red flag, and it's not exactly unheard-of for a mother and daughter not to get along."

"You know," I said, "Audrey Moretti hosted Thanksgiving. The whole family was there."

"I see where you're going with this," Martin said. "Anyone who was present that day could've made off with some of that rope."

"Including Evie," Cookie said.

"Do you know if she got in touch with Sten?" I asked Sophie, who used to be a paralegal in Sten Jakobsen's law office and still seemed to know everything about his practice.

She nodded. "He's tracking down her grandfather's will."

"Audrey's late husband?" I asked.

"No, Peaches's dad," she said, "the one who left her the house when he died four years ago."

"I didn't realize there was an issue regarding his will," I said. "Evie didn't mention it when we spoke."

"She was told he left one," Sophie said, "but she never saw it, and she can't find it in her mom's papers."

"Let me guess," I said. "She thinks Peaches might not have been straight with her about what it said. Like who's supposed to inherit what."

"Doesn't seem like there was a lot of trust in that family," she said. "Also, Sten's helping her apply to the Surrogate's Court to become the administrator of her mother's estate. Of course, that'll take time."

"Speaking of her mother's estate," I said, "where exactly did

Peaches's money come from?"

"What do you mean?" she asked.

"Well, she enjoyed a pretty comfortable standard of living, despite having no regular source of income aside from her advice column. And for sure that couldn't have paid much."

"Maybe she inherited it," Martin said.

I shook my head. "Her dad left her just the house. According to Evie, her mom did some modeling when she was young, and it earned her enough so she never had to work again."

"Huh," Sophie said. "Never knew that."

"Probably because it's not true," I said.

"Evie lied about the modeling?"

"Well, it's not *all* made up," I said. "I researched the heck out of it, and all I could find was a few print ads for a local department store. No fashion shows, as Evie claimed. No commercials or magazine covers or anything else that might've brought in the big bucks. And she was never signed by a major agency."

"So maybe Evie exaggerated," Sophie said, "or maybe Peaches did. To make herself appear more glamorous."

Martin said, "But then, where *did* the money come from?"

I looked at the detectives, who'd remained silent during this exchange. "I know you must've gone over her bank statements after her body was found."

This was too much even for Cookie. "Jane, you know we can't share that kind of information."

"I'm not interested in how much money she had, just where it came from. Like, for instance, did she receive electronic transfers from an investment firm?" Which, if such transfers were regular and substantial, would indicate there was some truth to

Evie's story, after all. "Or maybe you found something more, I don't know, intriguing?"

Not that I expected them to budge, but I had to try, right? Oh, don't tell me you wouldn't have done the same thing.

"Okay, forget about her bank statements," I said. "What about her computer? Any stunning revelations there?"

Something shifted behind Howie's eyes. Cookie shot him a quick glance before lifting her beer glass, only to discover it empty.

"What?" I said. "What surprises did you find in Peaches's computer?"

Sophie was studying them like a lioness studies a lame gazelle. "The surprise is that you didn't find her computer. It's missing, isn't it?"

"Dammit," Howie said.

My jaw unhinged. "Her computer is *missing*? That's big news."

"What about her cell phone?" Sophie asked.

"It must've been in her purse," Cookie said, while pointedly ignoring her glowering partner. "We can't locate that either."

I said, "So the killer made off with both her computer and purse."

"You're assuming the same person has both," Cookie said.

Dang! There I was, making another assumption. I hate it when that happens.

Howie knocked back the last of his beer and plunked his glass on the table. "Time to call it a night."

"I just have one more question," I said.

"No." He started to rise.

"Burke Fletcher."

Howie sat back down and pointed that finger at me again.

"Do not go bothering any more private citizens, Jane."

For the record, the only private citizens I'd "bothered" both happened to be murder suspects. Well, one had kind of been considered a suspect years earlier, before the authorities decided his wife had gotten herself too doped up to stay alive in her own bathtub.

"I have no intention of bothering Mr. Fletcher," I said, although that might have been a lie, considering I was still dying to know how a "Peaches Preaches" column had tanked his marriage. "All I want to know is whether he's on your radar."

"He's on our radar," Cookie said, "in the sense that we know who he is and have spoken with him."

I said, "Back when he was harassing Peaches, you mean? After she reported him in November?"

"No, Fletcher lives in Rego Park," she said, naming a section of Queens located about twenty-five miles west of Crystal Harbor. "A detective with the Hundred Twelfth talked to him back then."

"And before you ask," Howie said, "it's no state secret that we questioned him about Peaches's murder. We questioned a lot of people about Peaches's murder."

Howie was a swell guy and he liked me, but clearly he'd run out of patience. I resigned myself to the fact that I could expect no more information from the detectives.

As it happened, I was wrong.

I helped Martin clear and wipe down the table. He'd moved into the apartment over the pub eight months earlier, yet had never invited me up for the proverbial nightcap. I sensed that invitation was imminent, but it wouldn't happen that night. The padre was too much a gentleman to get frisky in front of the others.

But, Jane, you say, didn't he get frisky during your birthday party when he implied that the two of you were headed upstairs for some hanky-panky? True, but I'm pretty sure everyone knew he was just having fun tweaking me. When and if he finally got around to asking me up to his place, it would have nothing to do with fun.

That didn't come out right. Certainly it wouldn't *not* be fun. Oh, you know what I mean.

Once we were out on the sidewalk in the chilly night air, Martin locked up the pub, bade everyone good night, and unlocked an adjacent door in the building. I watched through the glass panel as he took the stairs two at a time.

Sophie was parked in front of the place, so she was soon on her way. As the detectives and I strolled the half block to where our cars were parked, Howie asked me, "You like dogs, right, Jane? You know anything about a breed called a cheer, cheer something?"

"Something about Mount Etna," Cookie said.

"Cirneco dell'Etna?" I said, correctly pronouncing the first word *cheer-NEH-koh*.

He snapped his fingers. "That's it. This guy Fletcher, he has three Cirnecos."

"Actually," I said, "the plural is Cirnechi. It's a pretty rare breed."

"I guess so," he said. "*I* never heard of it before."

"He showed off their glamour shots," Cookie said. "Nice-looking little dogs."

"Get this," Howie chuckled, as he beeped his car. "The guy's on a dating site for dog lovers. You ever heard of such a thing?"

Why, yes, I thought, with a sly smile. *Yes, I have.*

8

Daddy Issues

"AUDREY, PLEASE DON'T go to any trouble." I sat in her cramped living room, made all the more cramped by a motley assortment of tchotchkes cluttering every horizontal surface. And yes, of course I checked. No peaches. I occupied half of a love seat whose floral chintz upholstery had seen better days.

My hostess was still on her feet. "Since when is it trouble to take some cookies out of a box?" she said. "I have to apologize, dear. I haven't had time lately to do any baking, but the good news is, I still have one box of Girl Scout cookies left."

She'd had time to throw *something* in the oven, though. I tried to identify the mouthwatering aroma that wafted from the kitchen. Baked ziti? Chicken parm?

Audrey had already pressed a cup of coffee into my hands, and I didn't want her scurrying back into the kitchen to arrange Thin Mints on a doily, or to fuss with whatever was in the oven. I wanted her right there where I could have a few words with her before her son appeared. Carter was upstairs in his room, making himself presentable. It was about two in the afternoon. I couldn't help wondering whether he routinely spent the day in his pajamas until and unless a visitor showed up.

I patted the seat next to me. "Please sit down. You deserve a rest." When I'd arrived, she'd been moving heavy furniture to vacuum under it.

"Oh, I'm not tired, dear," she said, but she obediently sat, smoothing the wrinkles out of her lime-green slacks. "I always say, the key to a long life is keeping active. My mother was a dynamo, let me tell you. She lived to a hundred, and that's my goal."

"Something tells me you'll make it. You have a lovely home, by the way," I said, to be polite. Audrey's house was on Tulip Lane, the flower-named streets being the least desirable section of Crystal Harbor.

"Why, thank you. Aren't you sweet. It's not fancy like a lot of homes in this town, but I've been here since I was a young bride of twenty-two, and I couldn't imagine living anywhere else. This place holds too many special memories for me to even consider moving."

Then keep your fingers crossed, Grandma, I wanted to say, *and pray to the patron saint of slacker druggies, 'cause somewhere out there is a bail bondsman with a lien on your little dream house.*

If I were Sean's grandmother, I'd keep him chained up in the basement until his court date.

"Oh, but you should have seen the way those police officers left it." She *tsk*ed.

"You mean after they served the search warrant?" I asked.

"I understand they have a job to do, but do they have to be so harum-scarum about it?"

If they weren't so harum-scarum, they'd risk missing important evidence, such as the yellow nylon rope they'd found in her utility room. I did not point this out.

Several framed family photographs were clustered on the coffee table. A Sears studio portrait of Audrey's grandchildren as adorable toddlers, before Evie developed Stick Up Butt Syndrome, and Sean learned how to sneak into homes that were not his own and help himself to their contents. There were a couple of candid snapshots of the two during their teen years: Evie at the podium during a high school debate tournament; Sean gleefully squirting charcoal lighter on an already flaming grill.

I squinted at a picture of a young couple, before picking it up for a closer look. "Is this Carter and Peaches?"

"Oh yes," Audrey said. "That was taken shortly after they started dating. She was his first serious girlfriend, you know."

In the picture, Carter wore a football uniform, the helmet tucked under his arm. He was a good-looking kid, with green eyes and appealingly shaggy light brown hair. Peaches was nearly as tall as he was, slim and pretty in a fuzzy pink jacket and snug jeans. A gentle breeze lifted her gleaming dark hair. They were grinning, arms around each other's waists, by all appearances in the full blossom of young love.

"How old are they here?" I asked.

"Twenty, both of them. He played football for Fordham." Her proud smile faded. "Unfortunately, he wasn't able to keep his grades up, and, well, there went the football scholarship. He never graduated."

I wanted to ask if his relationship with Peaches had anything to do with his plummeting grades, but I suspected I already knew the answer.

"Her hair was so pretty back then," I said. "Did she have a problem with it later in life?"

"Why, no," she said. "Of course, she started getting it touched up a few years back. Dark hair shows gray so readily, but hers always looked perfect. I guess she was a little vain that way."

I replaced the photo on the coffee table. "Well, but she wore a wig. At least, um, some of the time." *At least, um, while morphing into a human Slim Jim in an overheated attic.*

Audrey looked startled. "Peaches? Never."

"You never saw her with blonde hair?"

"Blonde? I can't even imagine it," Audrey said. "I can always tell when someone's wearing a hairpiece, believe you me, and with Peaches, it was always her natural hair. What made you think she wore a wig?"

"Hey there." It was Carter Moretti, descending the stairs. He wore a teasing smile. "Sounds like I'm missing an exciting conversation."

"Hi, Carter. I'm Jane Delaney." I stood and we shook.

"You're the one that found Peaches." He took a seat in the recliner, tilting it back and elevating his sock-clad feet. His youthful good looks had not survived the onslaught of middle age. The tall body under the sweatpants and flannel shirt had the soft look of an ex-athlete who's forgotten what the inside of a gym looks like. There were bags under his eyes, and his graying hair needed a trim.

"I did, yes," I said. "I'm so sorry for your loss."

He gave a sad shake of the head. "I had no idea… We thought she was on vacation somewhere. At least that's what we hoped, at first."

Audrey said, "Jane was asking if Peaches ever wore wigs. I never saw her in one. Did you?"

He scrubbed a hand over his bristly jaw. "She did wear a wig once in a while. A blonde one. Just for fun, you know?"

"Well, that's news to me." She rose. "I just made coffee. I'll get you a cup."

"Did you remember my soda when you went shopping?" he asked.

She nodded. "I bought four six-packs this morning, so that should hold you awhile. I'm sorry we ran out. I should've noticed we were running low. Would you prefer soda to coffee?"

"That'd be great. Just bring me the bottle." He offered a warm smile. "Thanks, Mom."

Carter might be just as dependent on Audrey as his son was, and just as willing to let her run herself ragged for him, but at least he expressed appreciation. I supposed that counted for something, although the urge to shake some sense into both of them was overpowering.

After Audrey left the room, Carter asked, "So what brings you here, Jane?"

"It's about your wife's—I mean Peaches's collection of peach knickknacks."

"My daughter told me they're missing." He frowned. "Sean should be more careful about who he lets into that house."

"Evie hired me to try and track them down. I'm a kind of investigator. I specialize in…" I paused. How to forestall a long and potentially confusing conversation?

"Stuff that's missing," he said, as if it were obvious.

Sure. That worked. "So anyway, I've been checking in with everyone who might have any information about the collection."

"Well, that was nice of Evie. I guess she knows I can't afford your services."

"When you say it was nice of her to hire me, that's because…?" I suspected I knew where this was going, and I was right.

"Because that collection belongs to me," he said. "Peaches told me that if anything ever happened to her, she wanted me to have it."

In case you haven't been keeping count, that makes four

individuals who were promised—or claimed they were promised—Peaches's peaches. How many more so-called owners were going to materialize before I eventually located those darn things? Because I *would* locate them. It was personal now. Even if I weren't being paid, I wouldn't rest until I'd found them.

But I still really wanted to get paid.

"So you think one of your son's friends stole the collection?" I asked.

He shrugged. "Isn't it obvious?"

"Sometimes it's worth thinking outside the box," I said. "For instance, can you recall anyone who really admired the collection? Like, more than normal?"

"Everyone liked those things. Or said they did. A few of the pieces, yeah, they're kind of nice. Others…" He gave an eloquent shrug.

I offered an impish smile. "What, you're no fan of peach-tree snow globes?"

"Oh no, that one rocks. Takes snow globes to a whole new level. A few of the others, though, like that little Japanese thing? Eh. I can take it or leave it."

"Okay," I said, "but you do know that that little Japanese netsuke is worth a heck of a lot more than the snow globe, right?"

"Sure." Another shrug. "People like that old stuff, and they'll shell out big bucks for it. Doesn't make it better."

No way was I going to tell Carter about the competing claims on his beloved snow globe and the other pieces. I was pretty sure that in the absence of a written bequest, the peach collection, like the rest of Peaches's estate, would be shared equally by her children. Since Carter and Peaches were never legally married, he had no right of inheritance.

Which made me wonder if he might be the one who bashed in that china cabinet and made off with the peaches. I mean, would you be able to resist snatching a bunch of tchotchkes worth somewhere in excess of thirty grand when the alternative was to walk away from a twenty-four-year common-law marriage emptyhanded? Hard to argue with the arithmetic.

I reminded myself that the cops had thoroughly searched this house a few days earlier. If they'd stumbled across something as distinctive as a bunch of knickknacks shaped like peaches, while investigating the murder of someone named Peaches, don't you think Howie and Cookie would have learned about it? Yet the detectives hadn't known of the collection's existence before I mentioned it the previous evening at the pub.

"Obviously I wish you luck in your search," he said. "Anything I can do to help, just ask."

"If anything occurs to you, or if you remember something and don't even know whether it's relevant, I'd appreciate your getting in touch with me." I handed him one of my business cards.

He looked at it. His brow knitted. "Death Diva? I don't get it."

"It's a… well, it's a nickname. That's not important. Just call me if you think of anything." I really needed to get some new cards made up, with a more neutral business name for occasions such as this.

Audrey bustled back in with a plate of cookies and some paper napkins, which she placed on the coffee table, and a bottle of Grampy Deke's Original Black Cherry Soda—*Now with MORE high-fructose corn syrup!*—which she handed to her son.

"Nectar of the gods. Thanks, Mom." Carter took a long swig, and sighed. "We ran out of this stuff a few days ago and I went into withdrawal," he joked.

Audrey resumed her seat. "Carter, don't let me forget I have a lasagna in the oven for Sean. I don't want it to burn."

So that was the source of the divine aroma. He produced his cell phone and tapped the screen. "How long?"

"I should check it in another fifteen minutes."

He did a little more tapping, setting an alarm, I assumed. "You're too good to that boy, Mom."

What about the overgrown boy lazing around in the recliner? She wasn't too good to *him*?

I took a slow, deep breath. *Focus, Jane.*

Audrey turned to face me. "Did you know that Peaches's mother used to be president of the Historical Society?"

"Really?" I said. "When was this?" I reached for a cookie. And yes, they were Thin Mints. Can I read people or what?

"Oh, around thirty-five years ago," she said. "Peaches was a child then, of course. But Linda—that was her mother's name— Linda took her responsibilities very seriously. She spent every afternoon in that old building. I suppose some of the appeal was social. She'd meet her friends for lunch and then they'd spend a few hours on their volunteer activities. Nice not to have to work for a living. That was mean. I shouldn't have said that. Linda died fairly young, poor woman. When Peaches was still a teen."

"Jane doesn't want to hear about all this, Mom," Carter said. "It's boring."

"Not to me," I said. "So Peaches would've been in elementary school when her mom was president of the Historical Society."

"Yes," Audrey said. "She told me she was eight when Linda started having her go directly there after school instead of letting herself into an empty house. She'd sit in her mother's office and do homework or play with some toys she kept there. But her favorite thing was exploring that old attic."

Her words struck me like an electric jolt. My reaction wasn't lost on Audrey, who said, "I know. Isn't it just awful that the place that brought her such joy as a youngster ended up being..." She shivered.

Her tomb.

Carter said, "She showed me that attic when we first started dating. It was kind of special to her. You know, like her own secret hideaway when she was a kid."

"And her mother didn't mind her going up there?" I asked.

"She didn't know," he said. "The Historical Society is in this big old house, with lots of rooms, a basement—"

"I know, I've been there." Too many times to count, including five days earlier for my surprise party.

"Peaches would tell her mom she was walking around the grounds or having a snack in the kitchen or hanging out in the little library they have there. Stuff like that."

"What did she do up there?" I asked.

"Just kinda poked around, like kids do," he said. "It's full of all this old stuff from, I don't know, Civil War times. Earlier even. I think she found her first peach knickknack up there."

"Really? Which one? I've seen pictures of them."

"It's this little porcelain thing," he said. "Some of the paint's worn off. Don't know what she saw in it, except her nickname's always been Peaches, from when she was a baby, so..."

"I remember that figurine," I said. "It looked like a real antique. I'm guessing it might fetch a nice price from a collector."

"Like I said, these folks with lots of money love that old stuff."

"Do you know how she got the nickname?" I asked.

Audrey spoke up. "Linda told me her mother used to admire baby Gertrude's 'peaches and cream' complexion. She started calling her 'Peaches' and it stuck."

I had a hard time picturing irascible Peaches Gillespey as an adorable, rosy-cheeked infant. "So, Carter, what did you think of that attic when she took you up there?"

"To be honest, I didn't see what was so special about it," he said. "Just a dusty old place full of dusty old things. But she was real excited to show it to me, and I was really into her, so I didn't mind."

"What did you do up there?" I asked.

Carter's gaze flicked to his mom, just for an instant, but long enough to make me regret having asked. He colored slightly as he said, "Nothing really. Just looked around and left."

Yeesh. Doing it in that spooky, cobwebby old attic? I can't imagine it was any less spooky or cobwebby a quarter century earlier when this romantic tryst took place. A testament to young love, I supposed. Not to mention young hormones. I hoped for their sake it hadn't been winter. Or summer, for that matter. The place must be an oven in August.

"Do you mind if I ask you two a very personal question?" I said. "Feel free to tell me it's none of my business."

"I have a pretty thick skin," Carter said, "after all the questions the cops asked. Shoot."

"Do you think they arrested the right person?" I figured it sounded better than *Did your son kill his mother?*

And yeah, I know what I said about stopping my investigation into Sean's guilt or innocence. Are you always so literal?

Audrey stiffened. "They certainly did *not* arrest the right person. Sean had nothing to do with it."

"I wish we could know that for sure," Carter said.

Angry color suffused her face. She stabbed a finger at her chest. "Well, *I* know it for sure. My grandson is not a murderer. And I don't want to hear again how he's not really my grandson."

Carter's gaze flashed on me. "Save this for later, Mom. We don't need to—"

"I don't care what any stupid DNA test says. You are the only father that child has ever known. You raised him, for heaven's sake. And I'm his only grandmother. So don't you dare tell me he's not our blood."

Whoa. Good time to keep my mouth shut and blend into the woodwork.

Carter sat straight up, to the clanking accompaniment of the recliner's internal workings. "Those DNA tests weren't my idea, but I can't say I'm sorry I finally found out."

"Well, you should be sorry." Her eyes glistened. "If you'd never found out, then you and Peaches wouldn't have split up."

"Is that what this is about?" he demanded. "Are you sick of having me under your roof? Eating your food? Driving your car? I couldn't have stayed in that house after Peaches died, anyway. It belongs to the kids, not me. You know that."

"They would've let you live there."

Fat chance, I thought. That house was bound to go on the market as soon as Evie could get it into salable condition.

"Live there with Sean?" he said. "Are you kidding me? You know what that kid's like. Peaches had some control over him 'cause she held the purse strings. It's been years since he listened to me."

"I just want things back the way they were." Audrey grabbed

a paper napkin and dabbed her eyes. "What was Evie thinking, making you all take those tests?"

"She didn't *make* anyone do anything," he said. "It was a present for the family. She thought it would be fun for us to run our DNA."

"Well, all she did was open can of worms, and now you don't love your own children anymore."

"Don't say that." Carter looked away. I noticed he did not deny her accusation.

Audrey closed her eyes for a long moment, as if struggling to regain control, then shot me a mortified look. "I'm so sorry, Jane. You shouldn't have had to hear all that."

"No apology necessary." I placed my hand on hers and gave it a little squeeze. "In my line of work I often witness altercations of a personal nature. You have my word that nothing I see or hear will leave these four walls." Which was true unless I learned information about a crime, in which case all bets were off.

"Are you a psychologist, dear?" she asked.

Carter answered for me. "Jane finds stuff that's gone missing. Evie hired her to look for Peaches's knickknacks. You know, the ones shaped like peaches? Some lowlife made off with them."

"Oh, I know." Audrey shook her head in disgust. "You should see what they did to that fine old china cabinet."

"When heirlooms end up lost or stolen," I said, "it inevitably leads to finger-pointing and accusations. I can't tell you how many times I've had to break up outright brawls." This had the added benefit of not being a lie.

"So family squabbles are nothing new to you," she said. "I suppose that makes me feel a little less embarrassed."

"No need to feel embarrassed," I assured her. No need to

stop sharing juicy details either. I had to keep them talking.

I said, "I take it Evie surprised the family with a gift of genealogy tests from one of those DNA companies."

"Last fall." Audrey looked at her son for confirmation. "October, was it?"

"We spat in those little tubes back in September," he said, "and sent them in. Me, Sean, and Evie. It took a few weeks."

"Peaches refused to participate," she told me, with a meaningful look.

"She didn't want *any* of us to do it," he said. "The whole thing was stupid, she said, a waste of money. She was really mad about it. I didn't figure out why till the results came back at the end of October."

"I'm guessing they showed you aren't Sean's biological father," I said.

He nodded miserably. "Evie's either. Those kids were fathered by two different guys."

Sean's last argument with his mother, the one Zak had witnessed, had occurred a few weeks after Sean found out he wasn't related to Carter. Not only had he threatened Peaches's life, he'd called her "you miserable old slut." The vile insult now took on new meaning. As did Evie's judgmental attitude about her mother's love life.

Audrey's features were pinched, her expression harder than I'd ever seen it. "Peaches herself probably didn't know who got her pregnant either time. But she knew it wasn't Carter. I'd bet my life on it."

Her son did not disagree. "For twenty-four years she lets me think I'm the only one. She lets me raise those kids as my own. I did everything. Took them to school, the doctor, all their activities. Dried their tears. Read them bedtime stories."

"But don't you see?" Audrey said. "*That's* what makes you their father, not some, some invisible bits of DNA. Peaches did a terrible thing, deceiving you that way, deceiving all of us. And I have no doubt she's answering for it at this very moment. But your children are innocent. And they *are* your children, Carter."

"It's not so easy to—"

The alarm on his phone trilled. He shut it off, and Audrey got up and headed into the kitchen to check on Sean's lasagna.

"That must have been some scene in your house," I said, "when those DNA tests came back."

"I'll never forget it. It was the day before Halloween. Sean and me got emails with a link to the results. They tell you where your ancestors came from, you know? Says I'm mainly Italian and German, no surprise."

"And Sean?" I asked.

"No Italian or German in him," he said. "Like, zero. Which I knew had to be a mistake, right? I mean, they did say he's part Irish and English, which is from his mom, but then there's this big old chunk of Russian, and get this, three percent Native American. I mean, Russian? Native American? So I knew this had to be wrong."

"Did you ask Peaches about it?"

"Sure. She gets all hot under the collar, says they mixed up his spit with someone else's. Says I told you not to bother with this nonsense."

"And you believed her?" I asked.

"Yeah," he said. "Figured it was a waste of money, like she said. Wasn't until Evie got involved that we realized what's what."

"I assume she got her results at around the same time."

He nodded. "Only, she was a little better at figuring out the site. She showed us how you find your relatives on it. And guess what. Me and Evie? Not related. Me and Sean? Ditto."

"What about Evie and Sean?" I asked.

"Turns out they're half siblings," he said, "based on how much DNA they share, which is twenty-five percent. I know for a fact they got the same mother."

"But different fathers. And neither of them is you. That must've come as quite a shock."

"Ya think?"

"Did Peaches continue to deny it?" I asked.

"She tried to, but Evie wasn't having it. She forced her to admit the truth. Anyone else that did what she did, they'd be groveling, begging our forgiveness. Not Peaches, no sirree. She was just angry that her little secret wasn't so secret anymore."

"So she kicked you out," I said. "You and Sean."

He nodded, his face contorted in outrage. "She acted like *we* were the ones that did something wrong, can you believe it? Cut me off without a dime, just like that. After promising me I don't know how many times that we'd always be together, that she'd support me for the rest of my life. And to top it off, Sean was now a hundred percent my responsibility. She wanted nothing more to do with either of us."

"*Your* responsibility? Even though it had just been scientifically proven that he did not spring from your loins?"

"Doesn't matter," he said. "Peaches knew my mom would never let me just cut him loose."

What I thought but didn't say was that Sean was not a kid anymore and should be his own responsibility at this point. As should his father, for that matter. What would the two of them do when Audrey was no longer around to take care of them? I couldn't see Evie supporting them, cleaning and cooking for them, and making sure they don't run out of their favorite sodas.

"Evie told me her mother had started dating," I said.

"*Started* dating?" He snorted. "You're assuming she ever stopped."

"Do you happen to know whether there was anyone special? Or did she, you know, play the field?" Before he could respond with a nasty comment, I added, "It's always possible that one of her, um, new friends might have made off with the peach collection."

"They could've been lined up outside her bedroom, taking tickets and waiting their turn, for all I know. I stopped caring after she gave me the boot."

"So you would have been willing to stay with Peaches," I asked, "even knowing how she'd deceived you?"

He spread his arms, indicating his current living situation. "It's not like I had a lot of options."

"Can I ask why the two of you never got married?" I said.

"I wanted to from the get-go," he said. "Peaches didn't believe in marriage. She was a… a free spirit, I guess you'd say. Eventually I realized there was more to it than that."

"What do you mean?"

"She wanted to keep me poor and dependent on her," he said. "Wanted to make sure I never had a legal right to anything that was hers, even after she was dead."

"How did the kids react to the news that you're not their biological dad?" I asked.

"Sean's relieved to find out he's not related to a loser like me."

Lovely. "What about Evie?"

"She kept hammering away at her mother, demanding to know who her real dad is. If Peaches knew, she took it to her grave." He glanced toward the entrance to the kitchen and lowered his voice. "Mom keeps saying *I'm* their real dad, in the ways that count, you know? But I gotta be honest, I'm having a hard time with it."

"That's understandable, Carter. You've had quite an emotional blow. I have a feeling that with time, you'll come to see it your mom's way," I said, with more conviction than I felt.

From the kitchen, Audrey called, "More coffee, Jane?"

"Oh, no thanks, Audrey. I'm good."

She came back in and parked herself next to me once more. "Sorry that took so long. I decided to put a couple of chickens in to roast. There's just enough room for them in Sean's freezer. Ever since that boy was little, he could never resist Grandma's roast chicken, with my 'secret spices.'"

"No problem," I said. "Carter and I have just been chatting."

I thought about Evie's version of her parents' breakup versus what I'd just learned from Carter and his mother. The only point of intersection in the two stories was the date: October 30. Carter and Peaches might indeed have argued about trick-or-treat candy that day, as she'd claimed, but the conflict that tore them apart was far more painful and destructive.

Evie had deliberately misled me. If it had been a onetime thing, I'd have let it slide, considering she was such a private person and that we were dealing with a particularly scandalous family secret. But there was also that tall tale about her mom's incredibly lucrative modeling career. How many other lies had Evie fed me?

And where *had* Peaches's money come from?

"Peaches was an attractive woman," I said. "I understand she was a model at one time."

"Only for a little while," Carter said, "after she quit school."

"Yeah? I have this image of her as a glamorous supermodel."

"Nah, it was nothing like that. A few clothing ads."

Audrey turned to her son. "I believe she gave it up by the time you two met. Isn't that right?"

"Uh-huh." He kept his gaze on the cookie he was reaching for.

I adopted a teasing tone of voice. "So she didn't make the kind of outrageous fortunes you hear about?"

"I wish," he said, before cramming the whole cookie into his mouth.

"Well, but at least she had her advice column," I said. "'Peaches Preaches.' That's pretty glamorous, too. I'll bet she made a nice living from that."

Audrey said, "Oh, she didn't start writing that column until just a few years ago."

"Eleven years," Carter said.

"Has it been that long?" she said. "It really is true what they say. The older you get, the faster time flies."

"And that magazine didn't pay her that much, believe me," he said. "She did it mainly for the attention. Same reason she got involved in modeling."

"Well, that's surprising," I said, "considering her comfortable standard of living. Of course, it's none of my business where she got her money."

As those words left my lips, I kept my eyes on Carter, who suddenly found his empty soda bottle of absorbing interest. His mother broke the silence.

"It's no big secret," Audrey said. "Peaches inherited a nice little bundle from her father. She told me so."

"But didn't her father die just four years ago?" I asked.

Meaning how did she support herself and her family during the decades before that?

"You know," Carter said, "I think her old man was giving her money every year while he was still alive. For tax reasons or something. She never really explained the ins and outs, but it was enough for us to live on, so I wasn't about to complain." His chuckle sounded strained.

"Well, I never knew that," Audrey said, "but I guess it makes sense. It must be nice to just have money handed to you like that."

Evie had told me that not only did her grandfather die with no assets beyond his house, but that Peaches had been paying the upkeep on the house the entire time her family had lived there with him—more than twenty years. In other words, Peaches was helping to support her father, not the other way around. Which one was telling the truth, Carter or Evie?

The heavenly smell of roast chicken began crowding out eau de lasagna, sparking a mental debate of momentous consequence. Where to order takeout tonight? The Italian place or the chicken place?

"Okay, this might seem like it's coming out of left field," I said, "and the connection might not be obvious at first, but trust me, it pertains to Peaches's missing knickknacks. Both of you know the neighbor across the street there on Rayburn, right?"

"Of course," Audrey said. "That nice boy Zak Pryce. He's a *widower*." Was she capable of saying the word without whispering?

"It's about him being a widower, as a matter of fact," I said. "His wife died eleven years ago. She drowned in her bathtub."

"That poor girl," Audrey said. "I remember when it happened. Awful, just awful. Carter, you must recall it better than I do. You lived right across the street from them, for heaven's sake."

"Sure." Her son gave a dismissive shrug. "Stuff like that doesn't happen every day."

I said, "Oh, I'm sure Carter remembers it better than he's letting on. After all, he and Peaches provided Zak's alibi."

Audrey's eyes grew round. "Alibi? What does she mean, Carter?"

He looked like he wanted to slink upstairs and change back into his jammies. "It's no big deal," he said. "The cops asked Zak where he was when Stacey drowned, and he told them he was at our place, watching tennis. We backed him up, is all."

"Why didn't you ever tell me about this?" she said.

"'Cause it's no big deal, like I said. The guy needed an alibi and we gave him one."

She pressed a hand to her heart. I'll admit I was content to sit back and observe while Audrey did the heavy lifting in this conversation. "You lied to protect him?"

"No. You're twisting my words. I never said we lied. Jeez, Mom."

Okay, you got me. There was, in fact, no connection between Stacey Pryce's death and Peaches's missing knickknacks. I just told them that to justify my snooping. I felt terrible about the fib and braced myself for a lightning strike.

There. Now, may I continue?

Audrey said, "But I thought you told me Zak was just a neighbor, that you just waved to each other." She helpfully demonstrated by giving a little wave.

Carter was getting antsy. "Yeah, and the one time we decide to be nice and invite him over, his wife croaks on him. So much for getting chummy with the neighbors."

"I suppose." His mother wore a troubled frown.

"Now, see, you're getting yourself worked up, I can tell," he said. "Why do you think we never mentioned it, Mom? 'Cause we knew how you get."

"They decided it was an accident, though, right?" she said.

"That's right, just a tragic accident." Carter wagged his empty soda bottle at her. "I could use another one of these next time you get up."

9

Lather, Rinse, Repeat

SO ABOUT THAT dog lovers' dating site. Obviously Howie considered the very idea laughably bizarre, as if anyone who sought a relationship based on a mutual devotion to their pets had to be, well, more than a little desperate. Whereas to me it seemed like a perfectly reasonable and totally not desperate thing to do. Can you guess why? Oh, come on, guess.

Yep, I'd been a member of dog-loving-singles.com since the previous summer, after concluding that the men in my life were far less reliable companions than man's—make that woman's—best friend. I'd ended up suspending my membership a few weeks later, after suffering through a handful of the Worst Dates Ever. After Howie's offhand comment about Burke Fletcher, however, I reactivated it and started noodling around on the site, hunting my quarry.

For security reasons, members don't post using their actual names. They choose silly usernames that say something about themselves. There's a subtle art to this, which I belatedly discovered after signing on as *Sexy_Beast's_Mama*. What can I tell you? I was new to this whole computer dating thing. When I finally connected the shockingly salacious invitations I was receiving with my unwittingly salacious username, I wised up and changed it to *Doggie_ Style*.

Just kidding. My fellow dog lovers now know me as *Must_Love_Poodles*. Fortunately, members don't have to rely on usernames alone. The site lets us filter results by geographical location and (drumroll, please) dog breed. You'll never guess how many members of dog-loving-singles.com live in Rego Park *and* own three Cirnechi dell'Etna.

Okay, you guessed right. Needless to say, I lost no time setting up a date with the one and only gentleman who satisfied both those criteria. *I_Didn't_Name_Them* was the proud human guardian of Lather, Rinse, and Repeat. Yeah, guardian. Using the term *owner* will get you banned from the site.

The pictures Burke had posted showed smallish dogs that looked a little like greyhounds, but with tan coats and large, upright ears. The dogs were handsome specimens, as was their owner. For some reason, this came as a surprise, partly because of his age—I knew him to be in his early sixties—and partly because he was, well, a stalker. Maybe. I still wasn't clear on that. Perhaps even a murderer. At the very least he'd harassed Peaches and scared her enough to try for an order of protection.

Burke's photo showed a fit older guy with an appealingly craggy face, light gray eyes, and thick salt-and-pepper hair cut in an attractive spiky style.

We exchanged cordial messages in which we arranged to meet for lunch at a café in Roslyn, a village situated approximately halfway between Crystal Harbor and Rego Park. The weather lady promised one of those unseasonably warm early April days that are downright intoxicating after a long, frigid winter—an ideal day to enjoy the café's dog-friendly outdoor patio.

Before my face-to-face meeting with Burke Fletcher, I had a

little homework to do. A quick online search in the "Peaches Preaches" archives turned up the particular column that had marked the beginning of the end of his marriage.

Dear Peaches,

I can't believe I'm writing to you, but I'm at my wits' end and don't know where else to turn. I've been married for thirty-one years to a man so mean and controlling, I can't believe I've put up with him this long.

He's verbally abusive. He doesn't let me take a job outside the house. I'm not allowed to visit my family or friends. I'm a virtual prisoner in my own home. Lately he's been trying to get me hooked on drugs.

There's no telling what he's going to do next. I'm honestly afraid for my life. Please help me.

It was signed "Prisoner of Love." This is how Peaches responded:

Dear Prisoner,

Please help you? Yeah, right, that'll happen. There's only one person who can help you, you whiny little doormat, and that's you. You can't believe you've put up with him for so long? Well, I can. You're just another sniveling complainer who refuses to take responsibility for her life.

Since you seem to need step-by-step instructions, here they are:

Step 1. Divorce him.

There is no Step 2. Just jettison that controlling bastard from your life and file that blighted marriage under Better Late Than Never.

And good luck being a grownup for the first time in your namby-pamby life.

It was trademark Peaches, all right. I'd read plenty of her columns, but I must admit, none had made me cringe the way this one did. In part it was because I knew how it turned out—Burke's wife actually did leave him, on the recommendation of a stranger—but also because, let's face it, her letter to Peaches was pretty alarming.

I left the house early so I could get to the café before Burke did, watch for his arrival, and make a run for it if he looked like a homicidal maniac.

Thank you for the reminder. Yes, I'm well aware that homicidal maniacs tend to look like regular folks until it's too late. I've met my share of them, in case you've forgotten. Would it hurt you to indulge my delusions, just this once?

I hadn't mentioned this so-called date to either my ex or the padre, not wanting to put up with their so-called rational objections. And after all, I'd be meeting Burke in an open-air eatery in full view of the staff and other diners, and I still had the so-called self-defense spike Dom had given me, so I was so-called safe, right?

And for the record, I was no longer trying to convince myself that my poking and prying was all about those pesky peach tchotchkes. But I mean, what was I supposed to do when faced with the irresistible opportunity to chat up a guy who'd clearly had it in for the murder victim? And yeah, I know Howie and Cookie already interviewed him, but who knew what he might let slip when he had his guard down?

The café's hostess escorted me through the charming restaurant and onto its charming patio. It might have been the first warm, sunny day of spring, but it was also a weekday, so only a handful of the dozen or so tables were occupied. The other diners wore business attire and were unaccompanied by pets, so I assumed they worked in the area.

Even though I'd arrived a good fifteen minutes before our scheduled meeting time, wouldn't you know it, there was Burke, comfortably seated at a table on the far end with a direct line of sight to the doorway. His canine trio lounged at his feet, gnawing on the homemade dog biscuits the restaurant provided its canine customers.

Well, dang. The guy was one step ahead of me already.

My date stood as I approached, prompting his dogs to do the same. He wore a dark blue linen shirt, open at the collar, and neat khakis. "Lovely to meet you, Jane. I'm Burke." Instead of shaking my hand, he placed a chaste kiss on my cheek.

I mumbled some words which I can only hope were appropriate to the situation, because the second surprising thing about Burke Fletcher, apart from his good looks, was his British accent.

A totally distracting combination, and so not fair. At least he was a lot older than I, but for the life of me, as his appreciative silver-gray gaze took me in, I couldn't remember why that was supposed to matter.

"And here's Sexy Beast, in the flesh," he said.

SB rode in the straw tote hanging on my shoulder, drawing the attention of Burke's dogs. They rose onto their hind legs to get a better look, and smell, of the newcomer, while going to amusing lengths to avoid placing their paws on me. So Burke might indeed be a homicidal maniac, but at least he knew how to train his pets.

For his part, Sexy Beast commenced the shrill whining that signaled his distress at being confronted by other dogs, but found it impossible to maintain his anxiety in the face of all that doggie love. *There are dogs here! But they're super friendly! I'm conflicted!*

"Please, have a seat, Jane. Let me help you with that." He relieved me of the tote. "This whole area is fenced, so there's no need of a leash, unless you want to use one, of course. Don't worry about the lads. They're just eager to make friends."

I examined our surroundings and saw that both the patio and an adjoining lawn were indeed contained within a tall wooden fence. The lawn appeared to be a kind of mini dog park, complete with bowls of water and a poop-bag station. Satisfied that there were no toy-poodle-sized gaps in the enclosure, I lifted Sexy Beast out of his tote and deposited him on the wooden deck, to the tail-wagging excitement of Burke's "lads." The gang ran off to explore their new playground.

We suspended conversation while examining the menus, finally settling on personal-size brick-oven pizzas: pepperoni, soppressata, and Italian sausage for me; roasted mushrooms, cipollini onions, and smoked mozzarella for Burke. He already had a glass of soda in front of him, ginger ale by the looks of it, so I asked for iced coffee (with my usual two shots of espresso) in lieu of the pinot grigio I'd planned to order.

After our waiter—a young actor type named Aaron—had collected our menus and left, Burke said, "Tell me about yourself, Jane. What do you do for a living?"

I've learned that when bending the truth, it's best to avoid turning it into a pretzel, in part because it's not always easy to remember some random fib you told, but also because it's impossible to sound knowledgeable about a subject when you know absolutely nothing about that subject. For this reason I chose not to tell Burke I was an astrophysicist or a belly dancer or principal bassoon with the New York Philharmonic.

Taking a cue from my conversation with Carter and Audrey the day before, I said, "I'm an investigator, specializing in locating missing objects."

Without skipping a beat, he said, "Do you work for an insurance company?"

"Um, no, I'm freelance." Thinking fast, I added, "But insurance companies sometimes hire me. If they, you know, suspect a fraudulent claim." I looked around. Where was Aaron with my wine? Then I remembered. I'd ordered amped-up iced coffee. The perfect choice for soothing the nerves.

"Fascinating," he said. "What are you currently working on?"

How had I lost control of the conversation so quickly? "Oh, it's a lot more boring than it sounds. What do you do, Burke?"

"I'm a dialect coach." He smiled at my baffled expression. "The short explanation is that I train actors to do accents, although there's more to it than that. I help opera singers enunciate unfamiliar languages. I've even worked with a couple of comedians on celebrity impressions."

"Wow. Unlike my job, yours really does sound fascinating," I said. "Which brings me to the obvious question. Is *your* accent on the up and up?"

His smile broadened. "Born and bred in Manchester. I moved to New York in my late twenties, with every intention of returning to England after a few years. But then I got married, and Ellen had no desire to leave the States, so here I am."

The truth? I'd already known about Burke's unusual occupation and some other basic details, having Googled him the night before. Clearly I hadn't dug deep enough, though. His British origins had eluded me.

Aaron appeared with my iced coffee. I stirred in cream and three sugars, then added a fourth, because it's a well-known fact that sugar has a calming effect.

"How long have you been divorced?" I asked.

"Full disclosure." The smile was now history. Burke looked every inch his age as he explained, "Ellen and I are separated. I've become resigned to the fact that there will be no reconciliation. The time has come for me to move on with my life. So you should know that my divorce is not yet final, if that's a deal breaker for you."

"It's not." In the face of this man's undisguised pain, I was suddenly ashamed of my subterfuge. "I've been divorced for eighteen years."

His eyebrows rose. "I can only assume you were a child bride."

"I was twenty-one when we got married. Also when we split up eight months later. I just turned forty."

"I'm surprised you never remarried," he said.

"What can I tell you?" I said. "I never found the right guy."

That's what happens when you spend your entire adult life mooning over the one that got away. At least that pitiful phase of my life was behind me.

"Can I ask why you divorced so quickly?" When I hesitated, he added, "If I'm being impertinent, you can tell me to shut up."

"No, it's all right," I said. "I wanted children. I assumed he did, too. That's a conversation we probably should've had before the wedding."

"Never assume," Burke said. Watching me bite back a smile, he said, "What?"

"It's just that I've been doing too much of that lately. Making assumptions."

"Dangerous habit," he said.

"Don't I know it."

The corners of his eyes crinkled, and I thought, *Holy cow, am I on a date?*

I gave myself a mental kick in the butt. *Focus, darn it!* Burke had just handed me the opening I needed. If he could be impertinent, so could I.

"So what about you?" I asked. "You were married a long time. What caused the breakup?"

His direct gaze never wavered. "My mental and physical abuse of my wife."

I stared at him, speechless. My nape prickled.

I couldn't bolt out of there without Sexy Beast. Where was he? My gaze zeroed in on the grassy dog park where he was play-wrestling with his new pals. How long would it take me to sprint over there, snatch him up, and jump the fence? Okay, awkwardly clamber over the fence in my cute little pencil skirt and three-inch heels.

"Why so quiet, Jane?" The accent I'd thought so sexy moments earlier now sounded like Anthony Hopkins' portrayal of Hannibal Lecter in *Silence of the Lambs*.

Where was that darn tote bag? I whipped my head around, finally spying it under the table, just out of arm's reach. A lot of good Dom's stupid self-defense spike did me zipped into an interior compartment of that thing, under a pile of assorted doggie paraphernalia.

"Where's your sense of curiosity?" he asked. "Don't you

want all the gory details?"

"If this is your idea of a joke," I said, "you'll notice I'm not laughing."

"It's no joke, as you very well know."

I opened my mouth to tell him I had no idea what he was talking about, but one look at those steely gray eyes made me shut it again.

"I see you've decided not to prolong the charade," he said. "That's to your credit, I suppose."

My mouth felt dry as sand. I took a long gulp of my iced coffee. "When did you figure out this isn't a real date?"

"Call me suspicious," he said, "but when this attractive young woman suddenly popped up on the dating site and expressed interest in meeting me, my antennae twitched—and not in a good way. Recent events being what they were, I decided it would behoove me to find out everything I could about *Must_Love_Poodles.*"

"But all you had to go on was..." I paused, thinking it through.

"Your photo, dog breed, and geographical location."

"I was careful not to be too specific about my location," I said.

"Clever Death Diva," he said. "You used Suffolk County, knowing Crystal Harbor would set off alarm bells, being Peaches Gillespey's hometown. But why engage in that kind of subterfuge if you have nothing to hide? Sadly for you, I'm no slouch when it comes to online research. I deduced who you were even before we shared first names in our messages."

Talk about underestimating your enemy. "Then why did you agree to meet me?" I asked.

"To find out why you targeted me, and get you to back off. I didn't kill that horrid woman, but if I had, well…" He spread his arms, indicating the romantic "first date" I'd engineered. "This was a very foolish thing for you to do."

Don't you hate it when coldblooded killers are right? Not that I knew for certain he was a coldblooded killer, but nothing he'd said or done so far had convinced me otherwise, his protestations of innocence notwithstanding.

"You're not the only person I targeted, if you want to call it that," I said. "The fact is, I've recently spoken with several people who were in Peaches's, um, orbit."

"After meeting with them under false pretenses?" he asked.

What was I supposed to say to that? *No, you're the only one I pulled this kind of stunt on. Please don't kill me.*

I said, "You must know I'm the one who found her body."

"I do know that," he said, "and I can't help but wonder what you were doing in that attic—a place so desolate, no one had set foot up there during the entire winter."

Howie and Cookie wondered the same thing. Sometimes the truth really is the best answer. "There was a crowded party going on in the building," I said. "My birthday party, in fact. A friend and I were looking for a quiet place to talk."

"The friend being Martin McAuliffe."

A little zing of fear shot through me as I wondered how much this man knew about my private life. "Anyway," I said, "seeing Peaches like that… I mean, it's not as if I've never seen a dead body. In my line of work, it comes with the territory. But this was different."

"Because this time it was so richly deserved?"

I was saved from having to respond by Aaron, who told us our pizzas would be right out and did I want another double-shot iced coffee. For some reason, I said yes, despite the army of ants stampeding under my skin, plucking my nerves like banjo strings.

Burke declined a refill of his ginger ale. He watched Aaron walk away before continuing. "What you're trying to say is that viewing Peaches's mummified husk had a profound effect on you and that you feel compelled to find out what happened to her. Well, we all know *what* happened to her. The question is *who*."

"Um…" Did I dare agree with that statement, when Burke himself might be the *who*? "I'm not trying to conduct my own investigation, if that's what you're getting at. The police have this case well in hand. They've even made an arrest."

"The loathsome son. I take it you're not convinced." He cast his gaze toward the dog park, where the restaurant hostess was dispensing dog treats and sidestepping something in the grass. "I see I have a bit of tidying up to do before I leave."

Because heaven forbid the man who quite possibly tied Peaches Gillespey to a chair and strangled her with her own scarf should fail to clean up after his pets.

He turned that icy gaze on me once more. "If you're not conducting your own murder investigation, as you claim, then why are you talking to people who were connected to Peaches?"

"Believe it or not, Burke, I actually have a legit excuse. Her daughter hired me to locate some items that have gone missing."

"What sort of items?" he asked.

I couldn't see what harm it would do to tell him. "Peaches had a collection of figurines and whatnot, and all of them are shaped like… Are you going to make me say it?"

"Apples?" He frowned in deep cogitation. "Grapes? Bananas? No? Well then, I can't imagine."

"She collected them since she was a girl," I said.

"How unutterably banal," he said. "And what do some

peach-shaped gewgaws have to do with me? Make it good. I always enjoy a little light fiction."

"Sorry, you're getting the truth," I said. "This gewgaw thing has nothing whatsoever to do with you. You were right when you said I feel compelled to look into Peaches's murder. The cops might not consider you a suspect, but there's still that 'person of interest' thing. I saw an opportunity to meet you and I jumped at it. End of story."

"Not that you're *investigating* or anything."

"So about the loathsome son," I said. "Sean Moretti. You're right. I'm not convinced he did it, but I'm not ruling it out, either."

"The detectives there in Crystal Harbor, particularly your friend Howard Werker, seem to believe the young man went straight from introductory burglary to graduate-level matricide and skipped all the classes in between."

"It could happen," I said. "Just like someone could go straight from spousal abuse to premeditated murder, with a little stalking thrown in because hey, why not."

Burke stared at me for long moments during which I forced myself to stare right back.

Yeah, I know, but since I couldn't undo my boneheaded decision to meet the guy under "false pretenses," I figured I might as well at least try to squeeze a little information out of him. He was fully aware I was doing it and would either play along or garrote me with a dog leash. I perceived virtually no middle ground between those two options.

Aaron chose that moment to reappear with our food. He placed the pizzas in front of us and swapped out my empty iced-coffee glass for a full one. Was there anything else he could get us? No? Enjoy!

Under normal circumstances, I'd dive headlong into a meal that looked and smelled so amazing. All that beautiful sausage and pepperoni. My stomach, however, had other plans. It squeezed into an even tighter ball and said, *Nah, I'm good.*

The dogs appeared at our feet as if by magic. They sat without being commanded, licking their lips and staring fixedly at our meals. The sausage would have been too spicy for Sexy Beast, so I cut a small piece of cheesy crust and gave it to him. His three companions carefully tracked my movements before returning their attention to their owner.

"Lads, you know better than to beg at the table," Burke said. "Don't let someone else's bad habits rub off on you."

I had an overwhelming desire to grab the nearest leash and garrote *him.*

"Off with you." He pointed to the dog park. "Go."

His dogs hesitated, looking from Burke to me, as if expecting me to invite the wrath of their possibly homicidal owner by feeding them at the table. I was just defiant enough to say, "Don't worry, Sexy Beast, I'll bring home a doggie bag."

He actually knew what those two words meant, having been the happy recipient of countless doggie bags over the years, so with one last wistful sigh, he trotted off. Lather, Rinse, and Repeat moped along behind him, casting longing glances back at our table.

I'd half expected a refined fellow like Burke to attack his pizza with a knife and fork, which would have allowed me a glimmer of superiority. Apparently he'd been a New Yorker too long to commit that particular regional faux pas. He picked up the first slice and made all gone with it in short order.

I said, "I have to ask how your dogs got their names."

He blotted his mouth with his napkin. "Ellen named them.

She has a quirky sense of humor."

"Let me guess," I said. "She's a hairdresser."

"No," he said, "she's a woodworker. But one of the first things we noticed about our new puppies—they're litter-mates, by the way—was that they love bath time."

"I'll bet you get some funny looks when you call them by name in public."

"Most people assume I'm giving them bizarre commands. Rinse! Repeat! Now I must ask you. How did Sexy Beast get his name?"

"His first owner loved movies. *Sexy Beast* was one of her favorites."

"I've never seen it," he said. "I shall remedy that posthaste. Is there something wrong with your meal, Jane? You've barely touched it."

As if he weren't well aware of the reason for my sudden loss of appetite. "I'm too tense to eat, Burke. You make me nervous."

My candor seemed to catch him off guard. "That was not my intention."

Like hell it wasn't. His casual mention of my "friends" Martin and Howie was no doubt intended to rattle me. I hated that it was working.

"Don't worry," I said, "I won't starve. Let's get back to our previous discussion. Before the food came."

"Ah yes," he said. "You seemed to be accusing me of stalking, spousal abuse, and murder."

"Wrong," I said. "My statement did not rise to the level of accusation. If anything, you accused *yourself* of spousal abuse. 'My mental and physical abuse of my wife,' I believe is how you put it."

"I thought it was clear I was referring to Ellen's unfounded accusations of abuse," he said. "I know you must have read her letter to Peaches, the one that started all the trouble."

"I did," I said, "and I found it disturbing."

"My wife is very bright but emotionally unstable, Jane. I recognized the signs early in our marriage."

How convenient. A loony wife whose word couldn't be trusted. "Did you get her help?" I asked.

"Of course. I hoped that with appropriate medical treatment and psychotherapy, she would improve, and indeed she did enjoy long stretches—weeks, sometimes months at a time— when she seemed perfectly normal. Unfortunately, it never lasted. It's the reason we never had children."

I said, "Has she ever been hospitalized?"

"No." His tone was firm. "The specialists I've consulted assure me Ellen's not a danger to herself or those around her. Over the years I developed strategies—coping mechanisms, I suppose you'd call them. Ways of getting through the rough patches with a minimum of trauma. I moved my office into our house so I could see clients there and spend more time with Ellen."

"It must take real commitment—" I winced at my poor word choice. "I mean, it can't be easy to care for someone with that kind of condition for so long. Some people would question why you stayed with her."

Burke's gaze was steady. "I love my wife very much, Jane. It's not a burden to care for someone when you can't imagine life without her. And as I said, Ellen has many good days when no one would guess anything is amiss. Or rather, she did before we separated. Now..." He gave a sad shake of the head.

"She claimed you didn't let her have a job," I said.

"Ellen couldn't possibly hold down an outside job. She'd tell you so herself during those interludes when she was thinking clearly. After a number of disastrous attempts, I encouraged her to concentrate on the activities that brought her joy."

"You said she's a woodworker?" I said.

"She designs and constructs birdhouses. Well, she used to." He produced his phone, tapped the screen, and handed it to me. "This is her Instagram."

I scrolled through the pictures. "Oh, these are gorgeous." And they were. Each birdhouse was more elaborate and whimsical than the last.

"Most of those have been sold."

"Oh. So it's more than just a hobby," I said.

"I converted the garage into her woodworking studio," he said. "Then on the weekends we did the craft-fair circuit. I also helped her with online sales through her website. She had repeat customers and was justifiably proud of what she'd accomplished. All that ended after she moved out."

"Where is she living now?" I handed back his phone.

He scowled. "In Connecticut, with her sister, Trish. I like to think Trish means well, but her brand of help creates more problems than it solves."

"How so?" I asked.

"Trish believes in alternative treatments for every sort of ailment, no matter how serious. Dietary supplements. Healing crystals. Essential oils. It's all about auras and chakras, that sort of rubbish. She rejects medical science, particularly psychiatry. The doctors are trying to cheat people, you see, keep them sick. It's all a dark conspiracy."

I thought I saw where this was going. "Does Ellen's treatment plan include physician-prescribed medications?"

"It did when she was still seeing a physician. You will recall she mentioned drugs in her letter to Peaches. That I was trying to push them on her, something like that. Sometimes when Ellen was having a good stretch, she'd decide she no longer needed her meds, and then I'd have to monitor her carefully to make sure she kept taking them. When she was having a bad day, my gentle reminders were often interpreted as verbal abuse. That was Trish's influence."

"And now?" I said.

"For the past half year Ellen's sister has been 'healing' her with her voodoo treatments. She refuses to let me visit, which is ironic considering Ellen's letter to Peaches had accused *me* of keeping her from her friends and family. Which was never the case, of course."

"I take it Ellen is no longer doing her woodworking?" I said.

"Correct, and she hasn't done a craft fair since the summer. Even her website has been shut down."

"Isn't there anything you can do? Legally?" I asked. "I mean, if her proper medication is being withheld."

"Ellen is considered capable of making her own health-care decisions," he said. "There's nothing I can do for the woman I love, short of kidnapping her. Meanwhile I lie awake at night heartsick over what she's going through. I know Ellen, I know how confused and frightened she becomes, not only when she's off her meds but when the two of us are separated for even a short time."

Burke sounded so sincere, and yet I had to remind myself he could be spinning a tale for his own criminal purposes. I couldn't discount the possibility that he'd mistreated his wife and that she'd finally managed to extricate herself from a living nightmare.

Absently I picked up a slice of pizza and bit off a chunk.

Heaven. I wiped my mouth and said, "You say you're still devoted to your wife, and yet you joined a dating site."

"It's called going through the motions." His expression was bleak. "Yes, I joined the site, but I've yet to go on a date."

"A *real* date, you mean." As opposed to our phony-baloney date.

"I should, though," he said. "It's been seven months. All my efforts to see Ellen, to even open a dialogue, have been rejected. The only communication we have is through our lawyers. It's time I accepted that our marriage is over."

"I have to admit I was put off by Peaches's response to Ellen's letter," I said. "I mean, on the one hand it was typical Peaches, but I can't help thinking she might have handled it in a more constructive way."

"I'll tell you who *did* handle it in a more constructive way," he said. "The other advice columns Ellen wrote in to."

My eyes widened. "There were others?"

"Two that I know of. One of them, she wrote to about three years ago, the other a little over a year ago, both times during one of her low points."

"Similar content each time?" I asked. "I mean, the same sort of complaints?"

He nodded. "Almost exactly the same letter she sent to Peaches. I only learned about them after the fact. Ellen has her own computer and cell phone, of course, and access to the Internet."

"How did those other advice columns respond to her plea for help?" I asked.

"By actually trying to help her," he said. "The first columnist happened to be an actual psychologist. She exchanged a couple of emails with Ellen, then spoke with her on the phone to make sure she really was okay. By that time Ellen was doing better and was able to explain the situation and thank the woman for checking up on her. The second time was a bit more fraught, but it all worked out."

"What happened?" I asked.

"This columnist also emailed Ellen, but she was too depressed to respond. So the man—he was an ethicist by training—contacted the police, who paid us a visit at home. Unfortunately, Ellen was suffering through a particularly bad patch, and she stuck to her accusations. So it was a bit of a kerfuffle, as you can imagine, but the officers handled it in a professional manner, and in the end it was all sorted out."

"That's not the only run-in you've had with the cops," I said.

"I wouldn't categorize any of the encounters as run-ins," he said, "but yes, there have been a few. Fortunately, they've all ended satisfactorily."

Which meant one of two things: Either Burke was indeed the dutiful husband and all-around nice guy he presented to the world, or he was a sociopath with a really good act. A dog-loving Dr. Lecter.

"Well, let's see," I said. "The cops talked to you back in November after Peaches told them you'd been stalking her. Which, coincidentally, was shortly before she died." I picked up another slice of pizza. I had to remember not to clean my plate. I'd promised Sexy Beast a doggie bag, and the greedy little poodle wasn't likely to forget it. "And then our Crystal Harbor detectives interviewed you a few days ago," I continued, "because the victim of your stalking had turned up as a shriveled corpse. So I guess they figured, you know, another chat couldn't hurt."

"Okay, a tad judgmental," he said, "but accurate as far as it goes."

"What?" I said around a mouthful of pizza. "It's judgmental to say you were stalking her?"

"There's a difference between stalking and harassing. And make no mistake, I bloody well did harass that woman, every chance I got."

"So you admit it."

"Let me back up," he said. "After Ellen decided to follow through on Peaches's divorce edict, I immediately emailed Peaches. I explained the situation and asked her to help defuse the crisis she'd created with her irresponsible advice. I appealed to her better nature, in other words. Sadly, that only works with someone who possesses a better nature."

"No one who knew Peaches has ever accused her of having one of those," I said.

"It soon became clear she had no intention of trying to make things right. Eventually she changed her email address."

"What did you do then?" I asked.

"I contacted her editor at *You Know It* magazine," he said. "The publisher, too. They ignored me. So I showed up at their offices. They had security escort me out of the building."

"So you did do some stalking."

"It's called trying to have a meeting," he said. "They had no interest in hearing me out. Peaches's column was a rich source of advertising revenue for the magazine. To them, she was a cash cow. They don't care about real people or the lives they're ruining. I realized I could expect no help from anyone involved. That's when the gloves came off."

"I know you did your share of online trolling," I said.

"If you want to call it that. I was convinced that if I could generate enough outrage on social media, it would force Peaches, or the magazine, to do something. Apologize. Issue a retraction. Something."

"Obviously it didn't work," I said.

"My pain, and my wife's, were viewed as just another source of entertainment, particularly by Peaches's dedicated fans."

"Did you threaten her?" I asked.

"I know we just met, Jane," he said, "but do I strike you as the kind of dim-witted git who'd put an actual threat in writing?"

"Okay then, did you ever speak with Peaches?" I asked.

"Not in person, but I did manage to procure her phone number," he said, "which she promptly changed, naturally. We had one conversation."

"And?"

"And what? Did I threaten her verbally? Knowing she couldn't prove it?" He wore a pleasantly neutral expression meant to give nothing away while at the same time telling me everything I needed to know.

I hope you won't judge me too harshly if I admit I found it hard to blame him.

Yet isn't that how sociopaths operate? Manipulating everyone around them while remaining blissfully unencumbered by a pesky conscience?

"What else did you and Peaches chat about?" I asked.

"I tried to find out the name of her ghost." He lifted his last slice of pizza. "No luck."

"Wait, her…? Did you say 'ghost'?"

"As in ghostwriter." Watching my jaw drop, he said, "I didn't realize it either until I read the emails she sent me. They could have been written by a child, one who lacked even a rudimentary grasp of grammar, punctuation, and spelling."

"Well, but people are never as careful in email as they'd be in, say, a business letter."

"This went well beyond simple carelessness," he said. "Her writing was a disorganized mess, barely coherent. Granted, the 'Peaches Preaches' column wasn't exactly high literature, but trust me, this woman wasn't capable of producing even that."

I recalled Evie saying that her mother wasn't a very good writer. "She had an editor, though," I said. "Isn't it his job to whip her writing into shape?"

"The most gifted editor in the world couldn't have turned Peaches's prose into anything publishable. The only option would have been a complete rewrite."

"Meaning a ghostwriter," I said. "Hired by the magazine, do you think?"

"I suppose it's possible," he said, "but why would they go to such lengths? If Peaches had been a celebrity, then yes, I could see it, but she was far from a household name when her column debuted."

"So you're thinking, what, that she hired her own ghostwriter?" I asked. "And that *You Know It* never knew it?"

"It's the only explanation that fits," Burke said. "I reckoned if I could get her to tell me who actually wrote the column that destroyed my marriage, I might be able to persuade that person to intervene on my behalf."

"I'm guessing she refused to admit she used a ghostwriter."

"Not that I expected her to," he said, "but it was worth a try."

"But what about the nasty tone of her column?" I said. "From what I understand, that was pure Peaches."

"All that means is that the ghost was someone she knew. Or more to the point, someone who knew *her* and was capable of writing 'advice' that reflected her malignant personality. What?" He was suddenly alert, watching my expression. "Do you know someone who fits that description?"

"I might, but…" I shook my head. "It doesn't make sense."

"What doesn't make sense is semiliterate Peaches Gillespey penning the columns that bore her name," he said. "Who is this person?"

"I'm probably wrong. No, I'm definitely wrong. Forget it."

Burke placed his napkin on the table and signaled the waiter for the check before returning his attention to me. "Ellen is my life, Jane. If I've lost her for good, then little else matters. If you know something that can help me get through to her, it would be a grave mistake to withhold it. Please do not underestimate me."

10

Pork Rinds for Everybody!

SO THAT WAS a threat, right? It felt like a threat, but it wasn't, you know, blatant or anything. And he said it with that sexy-scary accent, so how was a girl supposed to process something like that?

I was still fretting over Burke's words the next evening while preparing for a séance in the home of my new client, Betsy van Heel. It was Betsy who'd hired me to get in touch with her dead husband, Harvey. She'd offered a thousand bucks if I made a sincere effort, and an astounding twenty grand if Harvey actually decided to interrupt his fourteen-year dirt nap to pop in and say howdy.

I'd tried to explain that this sort of thing wasn't in my skill set, but Betsy had insisted I give it a try, having thrown away an ungodly sum of money on con men and women over the years. I might not be a professional medium, in other words, but I was a professional Death Diva with a reputation for honesty and integrity, and that was good enough for her.

In the end, I'd agreed to take the assignment, on one condition. I required Betsy to sign a written statement declaring that no matter the outcome of our séance—whether Harvey deigned to finally make an appearance or remained his old, elusive self—she would never spend another dime trying to communicate with him. I even went with her to have the paper notarized, thinking it might make her take it more seriously.

Of course, if she decided to break her promise, there wasn't a darn thing I could do about it. Her reliance on fakes and charlatans was a kind of addiction, and in the end only she could kick the habit. I hoped our signed "contract" would give her a shove in the right direction.

So this was (fingers crossed) my client's last hurrah when it came to summoning poor dead Harvey, and I was determined to give it my best shot. While it's true I'm a confirmed skeptic when it comes to all things supernatural, I do acknowledge the existence of unexplained phenomena. I don't claim to have all the answers, and I respect the efforts of those who struggle to fill in the blanks. Communing with the spirits via séances has a long, albeit sketchy, history, and during the past five days since accepting the job, I'd made it my business to learn the right way to go about it.

And lest you accuse *me* of bilking a grieving widow: The Death Diva code of honor—aka my conscience—would never permit me to take unfair advantage of a client. Not once did I consider trying to bamboozle her out of that twenty grand.

In any event, by the time I found myself setting up in Betsy's home office, I'd put in so many hours on preparation, I felt like I'd already earned my thousand bucks. Or I should say, my five hundred. I needed a partner for this job, and Martin was the natural choice since we'd worked together before, so I'd be splitting the fee with him. Unfortunately, the various props I'd purchased to give the séance an authentic feel took another big bite out of my take-home.

I suppose I could have omitted the props, but cutting

corners would have made me feel like one of those frauds who'd taken advantage of Betsy for so long. So in the end, this assignment had turned out less lucrative than I'd hoped. So what? I wasn't missing any meals.

Betsy had declared that the séance must be performed in her home since that was where Harvey had lived and where his spirit, or ghost (not the writing kind), or whatever you want to call it, would naturally hang out. I'd chosen her home office for several reasons: It was closed off from the rest of the house, meaning fewer distractions; it used to be Harvey's man cave, meaning he might be drawn to the space; and it was already furnished with a round table, a holdover from the poker games he'd once hosted there. One of the first things I'd learned about chatting up spirits is that a round table is de rigueur.

I'd had the bright idea of asking Betsy what her late husband's favorite color was, thinking that would be a good choice for the tablecloth.

Plaid. His favorite color was plaid. Seems Harvey wore an awful lot of plaid. Not wanting to get into a verbal tussle with my client regarding the definition of *color*, I went out and bought a plaid tablecloth, which I'd placed on the poker table, along with several objects that had held special meaning for him: A Romeo y Julieta cigar, lovingly propped in Harvey's favorite ashtray, which he'd filched from the MGM Grand in Vegas in 1999. His well-used DVD of *Dumb and Dumber*. A can of Miller Lite. A bag of pork rinds. A bottle of Frank's RedHot sauce (to flavor the pork rinds, natch). A framed, autographed photo of Sylvester Stallone. The collar and tags once worn by Harvey's favorite beagle, who was named for his favorite actor. See above.

To these I added three snow-white pillar candles, which I

arranged in the center of the table, around a crystal ball. Seems spirits are attracted to the heat and light candles emit—a cozy break from the damp chill of the grave. I didn't have any particular plans for the crystal ball, but it had looked so darn cool sitting there in the occult shop I'd visited in Manhattan, I couldn't resist.

I heard the doorbell ring, followed by Betsy's voice greeting Martin. That was another thing I'd learned about séances, that you need at least three people. I'd been planning to act as medium, but Betsy had insisted only a man would do, the better to summon a male spirit. I suspected she was inventing a lot of these rules on the fly, but I was afraid that if I ignored her preferences, she might decide the thing hadn't been done right, a perfect excuse to go back on her promise to stop spending money on crooks.

Betsy appeared in the doorway, breathless with excitement. She was pushing seventy, but tell that to her coal-black hair, worn in a severely angled bob. She wore the black sheath dress and matching jacket she'd bought for Harvey's funeral fourteen years earlier. It was her séance outfit, meant somehow to entice her husband's ghost to pull up a chair and take a load off.

"Jane!" she said. "Prince Phineas Windex is here!"

"Who?"

Martin swept past her into the room. "I am Prince Phanaeus Vindex," he corrected her, in a bizarre accent that was equal parts Eastern European and hillbilly—Boris Karloff meets Dolly Parton. Dialect coach Burke Fletcher would have thrown up his hands in defeat. The prince wore an enormous, multicolored turban, embellished with gold tassels.

I groaned. "What on earth—"

"Madam," he said, lifting Betsy's hand, "it will be my

incalculable pleasure to open a door to the spirit world for you this evening." Bending low, he brushed his lips against the back of her hand, her cue to giggle like a besotted schoolgirl. "I will serve as translator, if you will, interpreting and clarifying communication between the numinous realm of our departed loved ones and our own earth-bound existence. This I will accomplish thanks to my highly attuned psychic abilities, while you two lovely ladies support my efforts with your innate feminine energy."

Oh, brother. "Um, Betsy," I said, "we're going to need a small bowl of water. And let me ask you, did Harvey ever wear jewelry of any kind?"

"He had a diamond pinky ring," she said. "He wore it all the time."

"An object that personally significant might help to draw him to us," I said. "Do you still have it?"

"Of course. It's in my little safe upstairs. It might take me a few minutes."

"That's okay," I said. "No rush."

Once my client was out of earshot, I got in Martin's face. "What do you think you're doing? This was not part of the plan. That ridiculous accent, and, and…" I gestured toward the turban, which suddenly looked disturbingly familiar. My eyes narrowed. "Is that Irene's wall hanging? From the dining room?"

He abandoned the accent. "Looks better on me, don't you think?"

Irene had brought the antique silk tapestry back from Morocco about fifteen years earlier. Since then, it had hung undisturbed in her dining room, which, of course, was now *my* dining room. And since Martin lets himself into my place anytime he feels like it, Irene's exquisite wall hanging was now perched atop his noggin.

My attention had been so fixated on the turban, I only belatedly noticed the rest of his costume: black silk pajamas and a red velvet smoking jacket.

"Hugh Hefner's ghost called," I said. "He wants his outfit back."

The padre adjusted the lapels of the jacket, which appeared vintage. "You don't recognize this?"

"Is that a trick question?"

"It belonged to my grandfather," he said. "It wasn't doing anyone any good in that trunk in your attic. And I know he would've wanted me to have it."

If Arthur McAuliffe, Irene's husband and Martin's paternal grandfather, was indeed the jacket's original owner, then I had to agree with the padre. Arthur and his first wife, Anne, had adored their grandson, once they learned of his existence eleven years after his birth. That's how long their middle son, Hugh, a married deacon, managed to keep his bastard son a secret.

A few years later, Irene set her sights on Arthur, broke up his marriage to Anne, ended up inheriting Anne's dream house, and—because Irene was big on adding insult to injury—bequeathed it to a poodle upon her death. Martin was understandably bitter about the whole thing.

The padre eyed my gray skirt suit. "A little underdressed, no?" As if *I* were the one dressed inappropriately. As if he weren't well aware that this boring gray suit was my all-purpose Death Diva uniform.

"What's with the prince thing?" I asked. "Do I even want to know what that stupid name means?"

"Probably not." He lifted the cigar and sniffed it. "Sounds real aristocratic, though, don't you think? Our client was impressed, and that's what matters. This is just the thing to complete my outfit. What do you think?" He clamped the cigar between his teeth and struck a pose.

"I think you need to switch to a pipe, Hef. And leave the props alone." I plucked the cigar from his mouth and replaced it on the purloined ashtray. "I know I'm going to hate myself for asking, but how *did* you come up with that name?"

"*Phanaeus vindex* is the scientific name for the noble dung beetle," he said. "Are you hating yourself yet?"

"Whatever possessed me to involve you in this assignment? You do remember what we discussed, right, Padre? This is going to be a straight-up, by-the-book séance. No funny stuff, no trickery, no *Harvey*. Betsy gets the good-faith effort I promised her, and we get the thousand bucks we earned. Period."

"Okay, I've been thinking about that."

"No."

"Hear me out." He peeked through the doorway to make sure we weren't about to be interrupted. "I came up with some great ideas, Jane. Got my timing down and everything. This'll work or my name isn't Prince Phanaeus Vindex."

"No." I crossed my arms. "End of discussion."

"I brought everything I'll need, and you can't even tell." He spread his arms, making me wonder what he'd concealed beneath Grandpa Arthur's loose-fitting smoking jacket. "Don't you even want to know—"

"We've been over this," I said. "We are not going to take advantage of our gullible, grieving client."

"Is it taking advantage to give her what she wants more than anything in the world?" he asked. "Betsy has spent years trying to connect with her dead husband."

"Yeah," I said, "and spent tons of cash on it, too."

"So what's another twenty grand?"

Normally I found the padre's impish smile pretty darn irresistible, but now, in conjunction with the outlandish getup? Suffice it to say, I resisted.

"She's rich," he added. "She'll never miss it."

"Let me be perfectly clear, Martin." My expression was as serious as he'd ever seen it. "If you pull something during this séance, I will lose all respect for you."

His face fell, a clear indication that I'd hit him where it hurts. Which should have cheered me, since it meant he valued my good opinion and hated the thought of disappointing me.

Oh, who am I kidding? It did cheer me, though I took pains to maintain my stern expression.

"I wasn't really going to do it," he griped.

"I know." I patted his velvet-clad arm. "You're better than that." This particular armor-piercing round found its target, judging by the padre's pitiful moan.

What's that you say? I was having altogether too much fun at Martin's expense? Are you seriously suggesting he didn't have it coming?

Betsy's approaching footfalls put an end to our little tête-à-tête. "Here we are," she said. "A bowl of water and Harvey's ring."

I thanked her and set both items on the table, along with a small cloth sack I extracted from my purse. Since electronic devices can interfere with psychic energy or some such baloney, I made certain all cell phones had been deposited outside the room, then lit the candles and turned off the lights. Candlelight reflected off the crystal ball and the big, showy diamond in Harvey's gold pinky ring.

Next I lit a stick of incense (a "magick resin blend," heavy on the balderdash) and invited Betsy and Prince Dung Beetle to help me cleanse the space by circling the room clockwise and letting the fragrant smoke infiltrate all corners.

After I tucked the incense into its little holder, the three of us sat and held hands, creating an unbroken circle around the table. The padre was to my left, Betsy to my right. We took several slow, deep breaths, which would have been more relaxing if I hadn't been trying to stifle an incense-induced sneeze.

I'd coached Martin on his role, and I could only hope he'd taken the rest of my instructions more seriously than he had the "don't cheat the client" part.

"We will begin with a group chant," he intoned, in that preposterous accent, "meant to center my metaphysical energy and to invite Harvey to join us here this evening. Listen carefully to the following words and repeat them with me. 'Dear Dead Harvey, we have gifts for you, although it's stuff you used to own, so not really *gift* gifts, but anyway, follow the light down to us—or up, no judgment—and let us know what's on your mind.'"

Needless to say, this so-called chant bore little resemblance to the one I'd hammered into his head. Betsy seemed a mite confused, but she obediently repeated his words in unison with the two of us.

"Are you here with us, Harvey?" he said. "Are you trying to reach us? Give us a sign. Try moving something on the table, just a little, so we know you're here. Maybe give the water in that bowl a little jiggle."

We sat very still for a full minute, staring at the bowl, and would you believe it? Nada. Bupkes. Zilch.

I know. Amazing, right?

"Or how about this, Harvey?" Martin said. "Try making a

sound. Tap the table or something."

Crickets.

No problem, I'd come prepared for a little downtime. "We can release one another's hands now," I said. Reaching for the small cloth sack, I untied its drawstring and emptied the contents—a complete set of one hundred wooden Scrabble tiles—onto the tablecloth in front of Martin.

Now Betsy really looked confused. "We're going to play Scrabble?"

"Not exactly," Martin said. He pulled one of the candles closer so we could all make out the letters printed on the tiles and busied himself turning them right side up. First he arranged some of them to spell out YES, NO, and MAYBE, forming a triangle with the three words. He arranged the rest in several rows in alphabetical order, giving each tile its own space. He used just one of each letter, replacing the spares in the sack.

I produced a little pendulum from my pocket, essentially an upside-down teardrop carved from pale moonstone. It was about two inches long and hung from a slim chain ending in a bead. You wouldn't believe the variety of pendulums offered by the occult shop. Or maybe you would. It was all new to me.

I handed the little device to the padre. "Betsy, I assume you're familiar with Ouija boards. You've probably come across them in séances."

"Oh yes, they're very popular with mediums," she said. "I wanted so badly to believe it was Harvey pushing that little gizmo around the board, spelling out messages from beyond. I'm ashamed by how easily they fooled me."

"Well, that's all behind you," I assured her, hoping it was true. "I did bring a Ouija board, and we could use it if you want, but I think it's time for a different approach, don't you? You told me Harvey's favorite game was Scrabble. It occurred to me he might be more inclined to communicate with Scrabble tiles."

Martin suspended the pendulum over the tiles. "We're hoping he'll answer our questions by pointing to various words and letters with this." He demonstrated by swinging the pendulum.

Betsy gasped. "That's brilliant!"

I wondered how brilliant she'd consider it when her husband's ghost declined to do any pointing. I reminded myself that when it came to this particular séance, it truly was the effort that counted, rather than the results.

"Harvey," Martin said, "if you're here, please move the pendulum. Just give it a little nudge."

We waited. The thing just hung there.

The padre's princely accent never wavered as he said, "Harvey, your loving wife Betsy wants you to know how much she misses you and wants to connect with you. She selected these gifts because she knew how much they meant to you." He lifted the ring. "I understand you wore this every day. Pretty spiffy." He set it down and wagged the cigar. "Been a while since you had one of these, huh, buddy? You must miss it." The can of beer came next. "Bet you could put away a few of these in your time, am I right?"

He set down the beer and reached for the bag of pork rinds, only to recoil the instant his fingers touched it. Betsy and I were instantly alert.

"What?" I said.

"It's nothing. A little static electricity."

The room suddenly felt warmer, making me wish I'd removed my suit jacket before commencing the séance. Could it be a hot flash? Could they be starting already? The icing on the childless, middle-aged cake.

Not to be defeated by a bag of pork rinds, Martin snatched it up and held it aloft. "Your favorite snack, huh, Harvey? Did you—*Whoa!*" He dropped the bag.

"More static electricity?" I asked.

"No, it uh… it moved."

"The bag?" Betsy's eyes were round.

Belatedly he remembered his phony-baloney accent. "Like someone was trying to grab it."

I sent Martin a pointed look, but his attention wasn't on me. He was staring nervously at the bag of pork rinds.

I was more hurt than angry. He'd lied to me. Yessed me. Well, I'd deal with him later. In the meantime, I needed to wrest control of this séance before Betsy got her hopes too high.

"Here, let me." I lifted the bag and tore open the top of it, the better to entice the late Harvey van Heel. In the next instant, the bag flew out of my hand, scattering the crunchy, lightweight snacks all over the table.

Betsy's eyes were now huge. "Did you do that on purpose, Jane?"

"Um, no. The bag slipped from my fingers. Sorry."

That was my story and I was sticking to it. It certainly hadn't been yanked out of my grasp, even if that's what it felt like. Because I was the only one touching it, so that was impossible. Right?

The look Martin gave me probably appeared entirely neutral to our client, but I could tell my excuse hadn't fooled him.

I was wondering how to get this thing back on track when the silence was interrupted by a soft sound, like someone sniffing a few times. I looked at my companions. They looked at me. Okay, it was the heating system. That had to be what we heard.

The padre took up the pendulum once more and held it over the little Scrabble tiles. "Harvey, we sense your presence here with us this evening."

Dang! I wish he hadn't said that. Betsy looked so excited, so hopeful. How to backpedal and let her down easy?

She looked around the room. "Harvey! Speak to me, sweetheart. Are you happy on the other side?"

The pendulum abruptly jerked back and forth a few times, as if someone were batting it around. Martin stiffened, then gave me a barely perceptible shake of the head, as if to say, *I didn't do that.*

We heard another sound then, a gentle scraping, and watched in astonishment as a couple of the pork rinds bounced a little on the tablecloth.

How the heck was Martin doing that? Because it was the only explanation. Whatever tricks he literally had up his sleeve, he'd decided to put into action, despite his seeming change of heart.

The water in the bowl started to move. It wasn't the subtle quiver we were supposed to be on the lookout for, but a series of small, rhythmic splashes that left the tablecloth damp, and the three of us staring in openmouthed astonishment.

If Harvey was indeed messing with all this stuff, then I have to say, he was a pretty clumsy ghost. I wondered if he'd been that way in life.

I gave myself a mental whack. *Harvey isn't here. Ghosts aren't real. Jeez, Jane.*

Enough was enough. I held out my hand to the padre, who seemed downright relieved to relinquish the pendulum.

I suspended it over the yes/no/maybe tiles. "Beloved spirit," I said, "if you really are here with us, please answer Betsy's question. Are you happy where you are now?"

Nothing happened at first, and I was on the verge of abandoning the whole Scrabble thing when a subtle tingling sensation shimmered through me from head to toe. No doubt it was the result of nerves, as was the abrupt feeling that I was no longer alone. I'm not referring to Martin and Betsy. It was as if some other entity had chosen that moment to invade my personal space in a big way.

I swallowed hard. This is what happens, I told myself, when a rational, clear-thinking individual messes around with this occult claptrap. It had a way of infecting your brain and turning you dopey. I was determined to resist it, as much for my client's sake as my own.

Just then, the pendulum began to move, swinging in the direction of the YES tiles.

"He's happy!" Betsy crowed. "Harvey's happy on the other side."

So much for taking control of the séance.

Could my breaths have moved the little pendulum? My random muscle twitches? Could the thing be that sensitive? I closed my eyes and took a deep, calming breath, then another. After a few moments I felt centered, but that weird tingle never left. Then someone licked my left cheek.

My eyes snapped open. "Padre! I mean, Prince! What do you think you're doing?" My hand flew to my cheek, which felt dry and unlicked.

Martin looked surprised. "What?"

"You know darn well what."

Betsy said, "Prince Windex didn't move a muscle, Jane. He's been sitting still this whole time. What happened?"

I didn't want to say, because why would the ghost of her

deceased spouse lick my cheek? And if it *was* Harvey, had his breath been so stinky in life? That more than anything convinced me the cheek licker couldn't have been Martin.

I took a deep breath, held the pendulum as steady as I could manage, and asked, "Beloved spirit, are you Harvey van Heel?"

NO.

Betsy gasped. "That can't be right."

I said, "Who are you? What's your name?"

The pendulum swung toward the *S* tile. We watched as it moved on to *Y*, then *L*.

"Cousin Sylvie has some nerve," Betsy fumed, "trying to make amends at this late date. *I haven't forgotten the green-bean-casserole incident, Sylvie! So you can just zip it!*"

The pendulum did not, however, spell out *Sylvie*. We watched, stunned, as it spelled out *Sylvester*.

Martin squinted at the framed photo. "Stallone? Isn't he still alive?"

"No, it's *Sylvester!*" Betsy grabbed the dog collar and jingled the tags. "*Our* Sylvester."

I looked at my companions. "We summoned a beagle?" I'd read about deceased pets channeling their doggy thoughts through a human medium. The problem is, I didn't believe in that stuff. No, really.

"Harvey used to sneak Sylvester those awful pork rinds," she said, "even though it gave him such bad gas. The dog, not Harvey. Well, him, too. Anyway, that silly dog just loved those things."

I asked, "When did Sylvester, um…"

"Cross the Rainbow Bridge?" she said. "Fifteen years ago. A year before Harvey passed."

I said, "Sylvester, are you with your daddy Harvey now?"

YES.

"My time will come," Betsy told her dead pooch. "Take good care of Daddy until I get there."

My eyes were starting to mist. I swallowed down the lump in my throat and said, "Are you a good boy, Sylvester?"

MAYBE.

"There's no maybe about it." Betsy was shedding real tears now, and I had to fight to keep from joining her. "You're the best boy, Sylvester. Daddy and I love you so much, and we know you love us."

I said, "Prince Windex, um, Vindex, do you have anything you'd like to ask Sylvester?"

It might have been a trick of the candlelight, but I could swear the padre was a little choked up, too. He cleared his throat. "No, I'm good."

I said, "Sylvester, if you happen to come across three little poodles named Annie Hall, Dr. Strangelove, and Jaws, would you tell them hi from Janey?"

YES.

"Oh, and one more thing," I said. "Your mommy has been trying to talk to your daddy ever since he crossed over into the spirit world, but she's going to stop now. She still loves him very much, but it's time for her to move on with her life. We know your daddy would agree with that decision. Will you give him that message for her?"

YES.

11

No More Dates of Any Kind

DON'T WORRY, I refused to accept Betsy's twenty grand, even though she went so far as to shove the check into my purse when she thought I wasn't looking. As I tore it in half, I gently explained that summoning Sylvester wasn't part of our deal. I'd done my best to communicate with her late husband, as promised, but in the end, my best hadn't been enough.

Martin and I walked away with the smaller, fair fee and a host of unanswered questions. For her part, Betsy believed she'd gotten the bargain of a lifetime, and maybe she had. Or maybe the three of us had experienced a type of group hysteria that, once begun, fed on itself until we were convinced we'd had a conversation with a dead dog.

You'll be happy to learn I no longer suspected the padre of going back on his word. He was as flabbergasted by Sylvester's spectral visitation as I was. In the end we agreed to chalk it up to that group-hysteria thing. Just don't question me too closely about it.

The next day at noon I was at the Historical Society again, this time to attend an actual planning meeting for the town's upcoming annual poker tournament, as opposed to the fake meeting Sophie had concocted to lure me to my birthday party just over a week ago.

The brunch meeting had concluded a few minutes earlier, but Sophie and I were in no hurry to abandon the nineteenth-century elegance that was the Historical Society's drawing room. We lingered, kicking off our shoes and curling up on either end of an antique mahogany sofa upholstered in silver-gray and taupe striped silk jacquard.

We sipped the dregs from a pitcher of mimosas and nibbled the last of a platter of pastries, made by guess who. Well, Nina Wallace was the president of the Historical Society, after all, until she formally took up her duties as mayor in a few weeks. Thankfully, she and the other committee members had departed after the meeting, leaving me and my best bud to catch up in private.

"Without question, Nina is the devil incarnate," Sophie said, admiring the treat she was about to stuff into her piehole, "but there's no denying she makes a mean blondie."

"You think she's aware the Town Council is investigating election irregularities?" I asked.

"Oh, she's aware, all right. The accusations are totally baseless, don't you know. Just her enemies—yeah, that's what she called them, her *enemies*—trying to make trouble for her. She'll be vindicated in the end blah blah blah."

"Whereas in reality…" I prompted.

"In reality," she said, "they've found evidence of vote buying and ballot tampering. For starters."

"For real? I thought we were dealing with run-of-the-mill dirty tricks. Nasty but legal. Her usual MO."

"What can I say?" Sophie drained her glass and poured us both another. "Nina's aiming for the big leagues. Next stop, national politics."

"Heaven forbid," I said. "Okay, I can definitely see Nina buying votes. But how was she able to tamper with ballots?"

"By sending her flying monkeys into the local senior center and nursing home to distribute absentee ballots, help voters fill them out, and then turn them in for counting. Would you believe it, not a single one of those votes went to me. Seems all those old folks want Nina to be their next mayor. Even my aunt Millie and my cousin Irving."

I clucked my tongue. "What's the world coming to when you can't count on the support of your own family?"

"Can you stand another intriguing tidbit?" she asked. "One that has nothing to do with the election?"

"Oh, I don't know, Sophie." I split the last blondie in half and shared it with her. "You know me. When have I ever been interested in intriguing tidbits?"

"It's about Peaches," she said, and smiled at my sudden alertness. "Well, you know I always have my feelers out."

"What have you learned from your vast network of spies and correspondents?" I asked.

"Don't get too excited," she said. "It's not much. Only that a glass soda bottle was found at the scene."

"In the attic?" I said. "I never saw a bottle. Of course, I was so rattled by the sight of Peaches's mummified corpse, I wasn't really paying attention to anything else. Plus it was dark up there."

"It had fallen off the desk and rolled into a corner," she said, "so I'm not surprised you didn't notice it."

"How do they know it wasn't lying there for years?" I asked.

"Whatever brand it was, apparently the bottle had been redesigned not too long ago," Sophie said. "This was the new design, and the lab people could tell the dried residue inside was only a few months old."

"What was the brand?" I asked.

She shrugged. "Couldn't find that out. Or the flavor."

"So either Peaches or her killer brought a bottle of soda up there with them," I said. "Maybe it got knocked off the desk during a struggle."

"Do you know whether Peaches drank soda?" she asked.

"No idea. Sean does, though. I saw him drinking Coke out of a glass bottle."

"Hmm." Sophie frowned. "One more thing linking him to his mother's murder, *if* it was a bottle of Coke they found."

"Well, but most people don't stick to just one kind of soda."

"No," she said, "but they usually have a preference. What about Evie? You met her, right?"

"She didn't drink anything when I was with her," I said, "but she bought some kind of soda at the beach yesterday. Her dad's definitely a soda drinker. Black cherry."

"And her grandma?" Sophie said. "Audrey? I'm thinking of people who also had access to the kind of rope Peaches was tied with."

"Again, I can't say. I didn't see her drink anything. For what it's worth, she's far from Peaches's biggest fan." I'd already told Sophie, not just about my excursion to Long Beach the day before, but about the whole DNA mess and how Peaches had deceived Carter and her kids about their paternity. She'd promised to keep it to herself.

"What about the neighbor? That Zak fellow." Obviously she was running through her mental list of suspects.

"I think I can state with confidence that Zak Pryce doesn't drink soda," I said. "He's all about healthy eating. There's someone else, though. Remember the guy I asked Howie about? Burke Fletcher?"

"The one who blamed Peaches for wrecking his marriage?"

"Yep," I said. "He drinks ginger ale."

"Which you know because…?"

I hated it when Sophie looked at me that way. "Because I might have, you know, met him," I said.

"Are you *trying* to get yourself murdered, Jane? What's your plan? To visit every suspect in turn until one of them says, Hey, you know what? Yeah, I did it. Here." She presented her wrists for handcuffing. "Take me in."

"I didn't go to his *house*, Sophie. Jeez, give me some credit. It was a date. We met at a restaurant."

"A *date*? Oh, that's okay, then," she said, dryly.

I told her how I'd connected with him via the dog lovers' dating site and gave her a brief rundown of our conversation, including Burke's insistence that semiliterate Peaches Gillespey had been incapable of writing her "Peaches Preaches" advice column.

"Who does he think wrote it, then?" she asked.

"He has no idea," I said, "but I do. Zak is a writer, and he lives right across the street from Peaches. Pretty convenient, wouldn't you say?"

"Is he a real writer," Sophie asked, "or some unappreciated genius who's convinced he's the next Hemingway?"

"Both, actually. He's been working on a novel for a million years, but his day job is copywriter for KrunchWorks. Meaning he actually gets paid to string words together. So he has to have *some* talent."

"I don't know." She was shaking her head. "It's kind of flimsy."

"No question," I said, "but it gets a little less flimsy when you consider that the first 'Peaches Preaches' column was published eleven years ago, in November—a mere two months after Zak's wife, Stacey, died."

"That still gets a big 'so what' from me."

"Let's say Burke is correct and that Peaches couldn't write to save her life." I winced. "You know what I mean. Don't you think it's interesting that her first column appeared shortly after Peaches and Carter provided Zak with an alibi for his wife's supposedly accidental death?"

"Okay, when you put it like that, it's... yeah, it's interesting," she conceded, then sat up straight. "Do not go doing anything about it."

"You sound like Howie."

"That's because we're both kind of fond of you and don't want you to end up like Peaches," she said. "Stay away from Zak. And Burke, too. No more doggy dates. No more dates of any kind. Lock yourself in your house and don't let anyone in."

"Martin doesn't need a key," I pointed out. "He comes and goes as he pleases."

She waved that off. "Oh, he's okay."

"Not everyone in this town would agree with you," I said.

"I'm still the damn mayor of this burg, and I say he's okay." She set her empty glass on the coffee table. "Listen, before I go, there's another fun tidbit you might be interested in. It's about Evie. Now, don't go spreading this around or Sten will never talk to me again."

"Ooh, this is going to be good," I said.

"Well, you know Sten's been trying to track down her grandfather's will. Peaches's dad."

"Right," I said. "It wasn't with any of her mom's papers."

"He found the lawyer who drafted it," she said. "Good news, the guy held on to the original. And get this. Turns out Evie's grandfather left that big house on Rayburn to *her*, not to her mom."

"Wait a minute," I said. "Are you telling me Peaches lied about inheriting her dad's house four years ago? It was supposed to go to Evie all along?"

"That about sums it up," she said. "Don't know why you're so surprised. It's not like it's the worst lie she ever told her family."

That would be the Big Fib about Evie's and Sean's biological fathers.

"So then, what did he leave to Peaches?" I asked.

Sophie made the universal *zero* sign with her thumb and forefinger. "Quote, 'To my daughter, Gertrude Violet Gillespey, I leave nothing, for reasons well known to her.'"

12

A Good First Impression

I WAS STILL thinking about Evie a couple of hours later as Sexy Beast and I took a leisurely stroll around our neighborhood on this mild Sunday afternoon. I was proud of SB. His social skills were improving. He actually managed to have civilized butt-sniffing interactions with two other canines during our walk. For some reason, though, he still barked like a maniac at Buttercup, the scary-looking pit bull who lived around the corner. For her part, Buttercup always responded with a slightly wounded expression, as if to say, *Hey, man, can't we all just sniff butts and get along?*

I owed Evie a report on my progress in locating her mom's peach collection. Which is to say, I owed her the disappointing news that so far, I'd come up empty. It wasn't for lack of effort. Besides poring over all the online retail and auction sites, I'd visited countless pawnshops, antiques stores, flea markets, estate sales, auctions houses, and tag sales. I'd spoken with a bunch of appraisers who dealt in collectibles, as well as Peaches's friends, neighbors, and relatives.

I was beginning to worry that the entire collection had been trashed, though I couldn't imagine what would motivate someone to do such a thing—aside from justifiable hatred of

Peaches, so yeah, maybe. A more likely scenario was that Peaches's peaches had been transported somewhere far, far away where I had no hope of locating or retrieving them.

I had to admit it might just be time to call it quits, though I hated the idea of giving up. I meant what I said before. At this point it was personal. I needed to know what had happened to those darn things.

Of course, I supposed I could try to locate them using my newfound psychic abilities. Don't worry, I wasn't that far gone yet. After that séance, just the thought of playing a round of Scrabble made me break into a cold sweat.

Back at the house, I sucked down a bottle of orange soda while Sexy Beast lapped up some water and settled down in his bucket bed for a well-earned snooze. I checked the time—almost three p.m.—and searched the contacts in my phone for Evie's number, intending to update her. My finger hovered over the green Send button.

One thing I've always demanded from my clients is honesty. In return, they know they can count on my discretion. I'm like a lawyer or doctor that way. I can't do a proper job for a client who's being evasive or dancing around uncomfortable subjects. Or, let's face it, outright lying as Evie had done. The more I thought about it, the more indignant I became.

I tucked the phone into my purse and grabbed my car keys. The drive from my place to the Americana apartment building took fourteen minutes. I parked in the same guest spot my Mazda had occupied six days earlier when we had our initial meeting. The difference was, back then she'd been expecting me. I rode the elevator to the fourth floor and knocked on the door of 4A.

After a few moments I heard a barely audible scuff on the

other side. I leaned over and stared directly into the peephole. *Yeah, it's me. Surprise!* Seconds ticked by as I sensed her internal debate.

The door rattled under my fist. *Bang! Bang! Bang!* "I know you're in there, Evie. Open up." Nothing. I turned to look down the vacant hallway. "Sorry about the ruckus, ma'am," I said, to no one. "I'm Evie Moretti's parole officer. She missed a couple of appointments, so she might be going back to prison—"

The door swung open. Evie wore a lavender chenille bathrobe and a look of alarm as she leaned into the hallway to see which of her nosy neighbors I was telling scurrilous lies to. I pushed my way into her apartment while she was still figuring it out. Good grief, that was embarrassingly easy.

Her straight, blonde hair was unbrushed, her makeup half done. A can of hairspray and an electric curling wand protruded from a pocket of her robe. "What are you doing here, Jane? Why didn't you call first?"

And give you time to invent more lies? "I was in the neighborhood. Figured it was a good time to get caught up, Evie." To hell with *Ms. Moretti*, I was irked. I made myself comfortable on her sofa, adjusting the throw pillows for good lumbar support, then said, "Mind if I sit?"

"I just, I don't have time for this right now. I'm on my way out."

"Hot date?" I asked.

She colored slightly. Either she did indeed have a hot date or the whole idea of men and women and dating and sex made her uncomfortable. Judging by her attitude regarding her mom's social life, I thought I knew which of those options we were dealing with.

That wasn't my problem. I wasn't her shrink, I was the

damn Death Diva and I was there for some answers.

"It's none of your business what my plans are." Evie stalked to her apartment door and opened it. "Now, I happen to be busy, so please leave and give me proper notice when you would like to schedule a meeting." She seemed even more uptight than usual, and that's saying something.

I leaned back and crossed my legs, settling in. I offered a negligent wave. "You go ahead and finish getting ready. Meanwhile we can chat."

Her eyes widened in outrage, and I sensed her trying to decide how much trouble it was worth to throw me out. At last she said, "Suit yourself, but make it quick. I only have a few minutes."

She exited the living room and disappeared into her bedroom, slamming the door behind her. Immediately I jumped up and raced over to her desk, which occupied one corner of the room. Her open laptop computer displayed her screen saver, a glamour shot of that new sedative she'd told me about: Zenaproche. The photo showed a couple of white oval tablets artfully positioned next to a labeled prescription bottle, with a soothing, unfocused background. A company girl all the way, our Evie.

"I'm afraid I've made little headway in locating your mother's collection," I said, loud enough for her to hear me through the closed door. Meanwhile I pulled open a desk drawer, swiftly perused the contents—legal pads, folders, and enough spare tape, staples, and paper clips to last five years—and moved on to the one under it.

"That's terribly disappointing," she called. "I assumed you'd have it all wrapped up by now."

Assumptions are dangerous, I mentally chastised, as I riffled through credit cards, her passport, and bills awaiting payment. "You have to prepare yourself for the possibility that the collection is irretrievable," I said, and yanked open the bottom drawer. More bills. At least that's what the stack of paperwork appeared to be at first glance. When I looked closer, I let out a gasp.

Belatedly I realized Evie had said something. "Sorry," I said, as I snatched up the top document. "I didn't catch that."

"I said, that's entirely unacceptable." She sounded really irritated. "My mother wanted me to have that collection. It's part of my inheritance. It didn't just disappear into thin air."

The document I was looking at was a bank statement—*Peaches's* bank statement, representing the most recent activity in her checking account. I could tell it had been printed out from Evie's computer rather than snail-mailed. I scanned the paper with laserlike intensity while I told Evie, "Turns out it might *not* be part of your inheritance, after all."

"What does that mean?" she called. "I know what she told me."

"Yeah, well," I said, "seems she might have told a few other folks the same thing."

The statement showed very little activity for March, not surprising considering that Peaches had been in no condition to do any banking. The only debit was an automatic monthly payment for newspaper delivery. I recalled the papers piling up on her lawn, unread.

There was one direct transfer of $3,650 from *In No Time* magazine, representing a fraction of the amount required to maintain her lifestyle. Other than that and a little interest income, I saw no deposits of any sort, yet the balance at the end of the month was over eighty thousand smackers.

Carter had told me that Peaches's father had given her money during his lifetime and had left her a bundle upon his death. I'd questioned Sophie about it the day before, and learned that both claims were false. The old man had relied on Social Security to help him squeak by during his final years, and died with no assets aside from his house. I wondered if Peaches had lied to Carter about the source of her money, just as she'd lied about so much else.

So then, where *did* her money come from? I must have asked myself that question a hundred times during the past week.

"Who told you that Mom promised the peaches to them?" Evie demanded. "Never mind, I can guess who. My brother for starters. That's just the sort of thing he'd do. Not that he gives a darn about the collection, but I couldn't see him passing up a chance to cheat me out of what's rightfully mine."

While she griped, I gave the bank statements for December through February a quick once-over. The exact same activity as March, which is to say, almost none. "Your dad also claims he's supposed to get the collection," I said. "Plus your mom's neighbor Zak Pryce."

"Zak?" she laughed. "This is getting ridiculous. If they don't have written proof, their claims mean nothing."

"Well," I said, "in the absence of a will, I would think you and your brother would have to split the peach collection, if it ever turns up."

She didn't respond to that. I glanced at the closed door to her bedroom, willing it to remain shut for at least another minute or two. I flipped to Peaches's bank statement for November, when she'd still been alive, and was immediately struck by how different it looked from the more recent ones. There were multiple withdrawals and debits, unsurprising for an active household, plus the same modest payment from the magazine for her advice column. What *was* surprising was a cash deposit of forty-one thousand dollars.

A cursory peek at the rest of the statements, which went back a full year, revealed the same cash deposit, the same forty-one grand, landing in her account every single month. Whatever the source of that money, it dried up when Peaches did. This despite the fact that for four months, no one knew she was dead.

I said, "If you want me to keep looking for the collection, I can do that, Evie. But it might make more sense—and I'm thinking of your wallet here—for us to settle up now."

I'd searched all the desk drawers except for one, the wide knee drawer under the desktop. I pulled it open, expecting to find pens, scissors, and other assorted office junk. Instead I stood gaping at a second laptop computer, this one adorned with a pretty holographic sticker in the shape of a peach.

The hinges of Evie's bedroom door squeaked. In one smooth movement I closed the drawer and swiveled to stare out the nearby window, as if transfixed by the view of the day care center across the street.

Evie's gaze ricocheted off the sofa and around the room until she spied me at the window. Her freshly mascaraed eyes narrowed in suspicion. I noticed she'd replaced her eyeglasses with contact lenses, and managed to coax her hair into a mass of sleek waves. She wore a sedately patterned wrap dress and a long, oatmeal-colored cardigan. Her simple shoulder bag was black.

I offered a cheerful wave. "Just stretching my legs, Evie. Where are we going?"

"We'll take up this discussion another time." She plucked her keys from a hook and held the door open for me. As I exited her apartment, she added, "Let me think about how to proceed regarding the peach collection, Jane. Meanwhile please don't add any more hours to your invoice."

I assured her that was no problem. I told her how much she owed and asked her to let me know when she'd come to a decision. We rode the elevator in strained silence and separated in the parking garage, Evie heading toward her blue Camry while I got behind the wheel of my red Mazda. Not once did she glance at my vehicle, for which I was grateful. It would make the next part easier.

Well, of course I was going to follow her. What did you think? My snooping in her desk had only added to the list of unanswered questions.

As Evie passed me on her way out of the parking garage, I took note of her license plate. I let two cars get between us before pulling out of the garage and following at a distance, sticking with her as she made a couple of turns that took her out of Crystal Harbor. I had a hunch she was heading for the Northern State Parkway, but in which direction, west toward New York City or east toward, well, points east?

Luckily for me, Evie Moretti was a careful, responsible driver, who never exceeded the speed limit and always telegraphed her intentions via her turn signal. West, it was, and I took care not to follow too closely as we picked up speed on the six-lane highway. Traffic was light, so it was a fairly simple matter to keep her in my sights as she changed lanes.

Were we going to Manhattan? I hoped not. I hated driving in Manhattan. I needn't have worried. After a few minutes she headed south on the Meadowbrook Parkway. I expected her to exit the parkway at some point, but we just kept going, and going some more, until we were practically in the Atlantic Ocean.

Finally she exited onto the Loop Parkway and headed west, toward the City of Long Beach, which occupies a skinny barrier island immediately south of Long Island. I tailed her for another ten minutes as she made her way to the beach and parked near the boardwalk. I chose a spot some distance away and quickly swapped out the suede jacket I was wearing for a plain gray hoodie I kept in my trunk for emergencies. I was grateful I also kept sunglasses in the car.

Well, this was a kind of emergency, right? For sure I needed to keep Evie from recognizing me while I figured out what she was doing down here and why it made her so jittery.

I watched her make her way up the long ramp to the two-mile-long, elevated boardwalk, which ran parallel to the shoreline about a hundred yards away. It was too early in the season for swimmers, sunbathers, and volleyball tournaments. Nevertheless, the mild temperatures, hovering around seventy degrees Fahrenheit, had coaxed many locals into coming out to enjoy a sunny Sunday afternoon at the beach.

The center lane of the wide wooden boardwalk was reserved for bicyclists, the two outer lanes for pedestrians of all stripes, from families out for a casual stroll to runners. The edge of the boardwalk facing the sea was studded with shore-facing benches and a metal railing. Hotels, apartment houses, and concession stands lined the other side.

The briny breeze whipped my hair around my face, prompting me to tuck it under my hood and tie the drawstring. Between the hood and my dark glasses, I doubted Evie would spot me in the crowd even if she turned around to look behind her. Which she didn't do. She kept walking, seemingly with a specific destination in mind.

I expected her to enter a hotel or apartment building, at

which point I'd have little choice but to cash it in and go home. The only other option would be to skulk around outside in case she and whoever she was meeting eventually appeared. Then what?

While I pondered this, Evie's steps slowed, then stopped in front of a seafood joint called Dagne's Clam Bar. I halted about twenty feet away. She stared at the eatery for a few moments, and I waited for her to enter. Instead she turned to look at the bench situated directly across the boardwalk from it.

A man sat on the bench, his back to us. He was significantly older than Evie, judging by his graying temples. He wore jeans and a maroon pullover and appeared relaxed, one arm thrown over the back of the bench as he watched a couple of kids play with their dog at the water's edge.

I watched Evie wipe her palms on her cardigan. I watched her take a deep breath. I watched her cross the boardwalk toward him, staring so fixedly at the back of his head that she nearly got mowed down by a bicycle. Finally she rounded the bench and greeted him.

The man stood and removed his sunglasses. He smiled, prompting Evie to do the same. Then he pulled her close and wrapped her in a bear hug. She hesitated a moment before reciprocating. I couldn't see her face, which was buried in his shoulder, but I saw his face, saw the emotion he didn't even try to hide.

I know what you're thinking. You're wondering if I noticed a physical resemblance between the two. Did she have his eyes, his nose? Honestly, I was too far away for that kind of scrutiny, but based on body language alone, I can tell you that one thought crowded out all others.

This is Evie's biological father.

You might very well say, But, Jane, couldn't that man be her uncle or some other relative? Maybe an old friend or former teacher?

He could be, but he wasn't. I felt it in my bones.

Between the crowd and the breeze and my hoodie, I didn't have a prayer of overhearing their conversation from where I stood pretending to study the menu in the window of the clam bar. And I didn't dare creep closer.

The breeze was doing a number on Evie's hair. She kept pushing it off her face, finally resorting to clutching it in a fist while the two of them conversed. This, after all that work with her curling wand.

Because it's important to make a good first impression, right? If I was correct about the identity of her companion, that first impression should have been made twenty-three years earlier when she was a newborn.

After a few minutes they rose and started strolling the boardwalk, still chatting. I followed at a discreet distance as they made their way to the Shoregasboard: an asphalt lot ringed with colorful food trucks selling everything from seafood and burgers to tacos and Cuban food. I watched them decide on the kosher deli truck, where they bought thick pastrami sandwiches, coleslaw, and drinks: some kind of soda in a cup for Evie, and a bottle of iced tea for her maybe-dad. My stomach squealed. I hadn't put anything in it since those blondies several hours earlier, and that pastrami was calling to me.

They sat at one of the picnic tables located in the middle of the Shoregasboard and continued their conversation while chowing down. Meanwhile I strolled the perimeter, taking care to keep out of Evie's line of sight. I did manage to snap some pictures of her companion, while making it appear I was more interested in the fancifully decorated food trucks behind him.

Finally they finished eating, tossed their trash, and shared a lingering hug. The man kissed her cheek. Even at a distance I detected the sheen of moisture in his brown eyes as they parted. She stood watching him as he wove around the trucks and disappeared from sight.

Evie started toward me on her way back to the boardwalk, which was the most direct route to her car. She didn't notice me, but then she seemed oblivious to everyone and everything around her.

I removed my sunglasses as she approached, and pushed my hood down. I could have been one of the potted trees studding the Shoregasboard for all the impression my sudden appearance made. She was about to pass right by me, her gaze focused inward.

"Evie," I said.

It took a couple of seconds for the word to register and for her to notice me. At last I saw the reaction I'd been attempting, up until this point, to avoid. Her jaw dropped and she blurted, *"What the hell!"*

"Enough lies," I said. "It's time for you to come clean."

13

Who's Your Daddy?

"SO WHAT'S HIS NAME?" I asked. "Your biological father."

We were back on the boardwalk, walking along the beach side. "I don't know what you're—"

"Don't even start," I said. "I meant what I said, Evie. I've had enough of your lies. And I know all about the DNA tests. Carter told me."

She flushed. "Dad had no right to share that outside the family."

"Your parents' split had nothing to do with a fight over Halloween candy," I said, "and everything to do with the fact that your dad had spent half his life raising children who, unbeknownst to him, had been fathered by other men."

"I made up that stuff about the candy," she said, "because the real reason was none of your business."

"Why did you give your family those DNA kits?" I asked.

She took a deep breath. "I always suspected my mom was cheating on my dad, possibly for the whole time they'd been together. I don't look anything like him, and neither does Sean. So I thought, what the heck, let's find out. I told them it would just be this fun family activity."

"A fun family activity your mom wanted no part of."

"Which only reinforced my suspicions," she said. "Anyway, this man you saw me talking to, he's not my… he's not who you think he is. He's just an old friend."

"Well, you and your 'old friend' look an awful lot alike." This was, in fact, true, as I'd discovered after snapping those photos of him. I steered her to the railing, produced my phone, found the best shot, and zoomed in for a detailed close-up. "You have your mother's height and nose, but this man's eyes, for sure. His face shape, too. See?"

I watched conflicting emotions duke it out as she studied the picture. She didn't try to deny the resemblance. Finally she said, "Why do you care about this? I hired you to find my mother's collection, not to snoop into my family's private affairs."

Affairs being the appropriate word, considering what Peaches had been up to while in a supposedly committed long-term relationship. "You've been withholding information from the police," I said, "information that could very well be pertinent to their investigation into your mother's death."

"The identity of my biological father has no bearing on the case."

I said, "That's for the authorities to determine," when what I wanted to say was, *Like hell it doesn't.*

I didn't mention that I'd already gotten Howie and Cookie up to speed on the whole DNA drama. It was the first they'd heard that Carter shared no blood with the children he'd raised. He'd neglected to mention it to the detectives during his interview. Neither had Evie, Sean, or Audrey. Everyone was keeping mum about the family disgrace.

Watching Evie struggle to keep her wind-whipped hair out of her face, I dug around in the pockets of my hoodie and came up with two wrapped mints, some tissues, a lip balm, a concert stub from three years earlier, assorted change, a safety pin, a bracelet with a broken clasp—so that's where that thing had gotten to!—and a hair elastic, which I handed her. "Here."

She accepted it with muttered thanks and faced into the wind to corral her hair into a ponytail.

This was a pretty sensitive conversation to have in the midst of so many strangers. I pointed to a nearby ramp which led to the beach. "Come on."

I could tell Evie would have preferred going straight home, but the only response she offered was a pointed sigh as she followed me down the ramp. I suspected she wanted to ascertain what else I knew, since clearly I was on to her lies.

At the foot of the ramp she removed her plain black flats while I shucked off my sneakers and socks, then rolled up the bottoms of my jeans a few inches. We took off barefoot across the cool, white sand toward the shoreline.

Telling Evie it was time for her to come clean was one thing. Making it happen was another. Since she was so fond of lies, I decided to offer a whopper. "By the way, Carter also told me where your mom's money really came from, so you can drop all that supermodel nonsense."

She looked cagey. "What did Dad tell you?"

What Carter had actually told me was another big, fat lie: that Peaches had been supported by her father, who then left her a pile of cash when he died four years ago. Since both Evie and her dad felt the need to fib about how Peaches had supported herself, I figured it must be something embarrassing, illegal, or both.

"I can understand why you exaggerated your mom's modeling career," I said. "The truth is so much more, shall we say, disreputable."

Evie wore a worried little frown. Nevertheless, she said, "Dad would never have confided in you. Not about that. You're bluffing."

We'd reached the smooth, wet sand close to the water's edge, and paused to watch a couple of seagulls bicker over the remains of an ice cream cone someone had dropped. Waves rolled ashore with soothing regularity.

"Forty-one grand in cash," I said. "Every month, like clockwork."

Evie gaped at me. "How do you know about that money?"

"Didn't I just say? Your dad told me all about it. Also you forget, I'm a trained investigator." And yeah, that's two more Jane Delaney fibs if you're keeping count. For the record, I'm not a real investigator, and I have no formal training in, well, anything.

I could almost see the gears turning in her head. "Well, even if Dad collected those payments every month and took them to the bank," she said, "that doesn't mean he knows… everything. He wasn't directly involved in anything underhanded. Certainly he never said anything to me about it."

"Because he was trying to protect you from the truth," I said. "Trust me. He knows it all. And now so do I."

Evie's words were revealing. *Even if Dad collected those payments every month.* Which told me we were talking about multiple cash payments that added up to forty-one grand, and also that Carter acted as bagman, collecting and then depositing the money into Peaches's bank account. But I still didn't know how many people were paying her, or for what.

We started walking on the wet, pebble-studded sand, letting cute little baby waves roll over our feet while scurrying out of reach of their big brothers. A pair of barefoot runners, an older couple, offered friendly greetings as they jogged past.

Evie appeared lost in thought. At last she said, "Dad was always doing that. Trying to protect us. He was—*is*—a good father. I just wish he'd been more, I don't know, assertive. He let Mom treat him like crap. And it didn't stop when they broke up. You should've seen her at Thanksgiving, viciously insulting him, belittling him in front of everybody. It's like she was determined to deny him the slightest shred of dignity."

"I'm glad to see you still consider Carter your real father," I said.

She looked at me sharply. "Of course he's my real father. This whole thing with David doesn't change that. I just needed… I needed to know. To meet him."

David. So I had the first name, at least.

We'd reached a rocky jetty, which sheltered little tide pools studded with barnacles. Evie selected a rock to sit on, while I climbed up onto the jetty, awkwardly stepping from rock to rock. Funny, this had been a lot easier when I was a kid.

"Did you find David through the DNA site?" I asked.

"Yes, but not that first one," she said. "There are several sites where you can run your DNA, so after I found out I'm not related to my dad, I registered on the others."

"To maximize your chance of finding the man who fathered you," I said.

She nodded. "And I finally did, just a couple of days ago. We exchanged a few emails and agreed to meet here."

"What's his last name?" I asked. When this was met with silence, I added, "You know I can find out, Evie."

I must have done a good job of making her think so, because she sighed and said, "Waldmann. David Waldmann. He's an orthopedic surgeon in the city."

"Does David have a family?" I asked.

She nodded. "That's why he was willing to pay Mom all those years. To keep his wife and kids from finding out."

My heart banged so hard, I nearly took a header off the jetty.

Was the wind messing with my hearing? Had Evie just admitted her biological dad was one of the people Carter had been collecting cash from every month?

Gingerly I retraced my steps across the rocks to the safety of the sand. "So David knew about you all along?" I said. "He knew his, um, relationship with your mom had produced a daughter?"

She shook her head. "Oh no, he had no idea before we found each other on the DNA site. My existence came as a complete surprise."

So then, what the heck was the hush money for? I couldn't ask outright, since I'd led Evie to believe that Trained Investigator Jane Delaney was all-knowing.

I sat next to her. "I'm curious. How did you find out about the rest of it?" Whatever *the rest of it* was.

"Well," she said, "after we realized Mom was missing, Dad and I went to check on her house."

"Right," I said. "You told me you collected her valuables and documents for safekeeping."

She shot me a quick look. "Her laptop, too."

Really? You don't say. "And this was shortly after Thanksgiving?" I said.

"December ninth. It was a Monday. I left work early, picked Dad up at Grandma's, and drove over to the house. The place was a little stuffy, but everything was in order. Not like now." She grimaced.

"Does your dad know you have your mom's computer?" I asked.

"No," she said. "He didn't see me take it. I shoved it into this small suitcase along with her papers and mail."

"Obviously you found something intriguing on it." In addition to Peaches's most recent bank statements, which Evie had printed out.

"The first thing I did," she said, "was look for any hint about where she might have gone. You know, airline charges, hotel reservations."

"And you didn't consider it a major red flag when none of that turned up?" I asked.

"Not really," she said. "If she was traveling with a friend, he might've taken care of the arrangements."

He, huh? I had to remind myself she could be making all this up. I was no stranger to Evie's on-again-off-again relationship with the truth.

"You didn't stop there, though, did you?" I said. "By that time, you already knew Carter wasn't your biological dad. It's only natural you'd search your mom's computer for clues to his identity."

"Well, sure," she said. "It's why I took it, if I'm being honest."

Now she was being honest? "By then you'd already spat in all those little tubes, hoping the guy who'd fathered you was doing the same thing."

"It wasn't all spitting," she said, as if that mattered. "A couple of those DNA companies ask for cheek swabs. I'd already sent my samples to them by the time I got ahold of Mom's laptop, but the results weren't back yet."

"What did you find on her computer?" I asked.

"Not the name of my biological father. That would have been too easy. But I wouldn't say I came up empty in the potential-dad department. If anything, I got more than I bargained for. I found her spreadsheet."

Spreadsheet? I don't care how active your sex life is, who keeps track of it on a spreadsheet?

"Well, that must have been eye-opening," I said.

"Understatement of the year. Once I realized what I was looking at... well, you can imagine my shock." Evie frowned into middle distance, as if picturing the salacious spreadsheet. "It was all there, in neat rows and columns. The men's names, dates, all of it. Plus a section for notes. Almost like a journal."

"How many names?" I asked.

"A lot," she said. "A little over a hundred."

I struggled to school my expression. That sure was a lot of spreadsheet entries. My, ahem, entries would fit on a Post-it. One of those really tiny ones. "What else was on there besides names and dates?" I asked.

"Well, payment information, of course," she said.

Ah. Now we were getting somewhere. I had to tread lightly. "How far back do the payments go?" I asked.

"Twenty-seven years," she said. "You know."

I nodded as if I did indeed know. "Sure. Of course. Going back to when your mom was..." I did some quick arithmetic. "Eighteen?"

Evie nodded. "When *I* was eighteen I was packing for college and daydreaming about meeting a nice boy there."

"While at the same age, your mom was..." I lifted one eyebrow and nodded, as if to say, *We both know what your mom was up to.*

"Having sex for money," she said.

Her words socked me in the gut. I averted my gaze for a moment, as if contemplating the breaking waves. Could it be true? Had Peaches been a…

Prostitute?

When I felt in control of my features, I looked back at Evie, who was eyeing me closely. Too closely. She said, "You told me you knew about it."

"Well, sure, I knew about the prostitution," I said, as offhandedly as I could manage. "I didn't realize she documented her, um, activities on a spreadsheet."

"My mom was an organized person," she said, as if that explained it. "She had separate columns for everything. Like 'incalls' and 'outcalls.' Do you know what those terms mean?" When I shook my head, she said, "Neither did I until I looked them up. 'Incall' means the client goes to the call girl. 'Outcall' means she goes to him. She had a lot of repeat customers. All the appointments were made through an escort agency."

Well, at least Peaches had been a supposedly higher class of prostitute. She hadn't walked the streets, if that counted for anything. Evie's disgusted expression told me it made no difference to her. Streetwalker or escort, a whore was a whore.

"She even had two separate columns for the different kinds of payments," she said.

"You mean like cash or credit?" I said.

She scowled. "That's not funny."

I hadn't realized I'd made a joke. What else could she be referring to except different levels of payments for different varieties of services? Eww. I didn't want to know.

Her tone was bitter. "I suppose I should be grateful that she stopped selling her body when she got pregnant with me."

"You aren't?" I said. "Grateful?"

"I might be if it meant she went straight," she said, "but we both know that didn't happen. I'd thought nothing could be more devastating than learning my mother had been a prostitute. But she didn't stop there, did she?"

Sometimes I actually know when to keep my mouth shut. No, really. This happened to be one of those rare instances.

She squeezed her eyes shut, still struggling to come to grips with hard truths she'd learned four months earlier when she'd stumbled across the infamous spreadsheet. Apparently prostitution wasn't the only criminal activity Peaches kept detailed notes about.

I'd let Evie believe I knew all about it, but that's not why I reached over to stroke her back. It was an automatic response to a fellow human in pain. I handed her a tissue and watched her dab at her moist eyes.

"Sorry," she said.

"No apologies necessary."

"I, um…" She cleared her throat. "I guess I'm still waiting for the shock to wear off. In a way, I called it, back when I was a kid. Not that it's uncommon to grow up with a love-hate attitude about your family. You know what I mean. 'No one else's family is as weird as mine.'"

"That's true," I admitted with a smile.

"I grew up ashamed that my folks weren't married," she said. "I thought it was the worst thing in the world. I begged Mom to 'do the right thing,' I guess you'd say. She was the stubborn one, not him."

"A lot of people have unmarried parents nowadays," I said. "It's become a lot more accepted."

"Then your circle of friends widens," she said, "and you meet someone whose family is seriously messed up, and you start to think, gee, maybe mine isn't so weird after all. You begin to gain, I don't know, maturity. You stop demanding perfection."

I hadn't expected this level of wisdom from uptight Evie Moretti. "I think most of us go through that," I said.

"Yeah, well, I'd give anything to turn back the clock," she said, "when the worst thing about my family was no marriage certificate. Then my idiot brother gave us a new worst thing when he decided to break into our neighbors' homes and spent a year in prison."

"Your family isn't the only one with a black sheep," I said.

"Well, the next part's all on me," she said, with a self-deprecating sigh. "I just *had* to act on my suspicions that my dad wasn't my dad. If I'd let it alone, if I hadn't bought those DNA kits, Mom and Dad wouldn't have split up. I wouldn't have gone snooping in my mom's computer to find out who my biological dad is. I wouldn't have learned about the prostitution, or the blackmail that came after."

Ah. So we *were* talking about hush money, only it had nothing to do with an out-of-wedlock child. David Waldmann hadn't been paying Peaches all those years to keep quiet about Evie. Until two days ago, he hadn't known Evie existed. Which meant he must have been paying Peaches to keep quiet about him hiring a prostitute. And apparently he wasn't the only one.

Two spreadsheet columns, Evie had said, for two kinds of payments: one for prostitution and the other for blackmail. First you pay the call girl to do things with you, then afterward you pay her to keep quiet about the things she did with you.

Evie said, "Maybe Mom would still be alive if I hadn't started the DNA thing."

"How do you figure?" I asked.

"Sean was so angry at Mom after he found out Dad wasn't, you know, his biological dad," she said. "I mean, my brother hadn't gotten along with Mom for a long time, but he was really out of control after that. Started picking fights all the time, throwing her infidelity in her face, calling her a… well, a slut.”

I thought of the argument Zak had overheard. *You miserable old slut.* “Did Sean try to find out the identity of his—”

“No.” Evie shook her head. “He wouldn’t even know how to go about it, and I don’t think he really cares who fathered him, only that Mom cheated on Dad. By that time it was regular, garden-variety cheating, because the prostitution stopped before I was born. Sean still doesn’t know about that, and I have no intention of telling him. If Dad decides to, that’s up to him, but I doubt he’ll do it, because my brother’s such a loose cannon.”

“So you think Sean was angry enough to kill your mother?” I asked.

“When you throw drugs into the mix?” she said. “I hate to say it, but yes.”

I stood. “Let’s walk, Evie. I don’t know about you, but my butt’s growing numb on this cold rock.” We resumed our trek up the beach. I said, “I know your mother was receiving forty-one K a month, but I’m fuzzy on how many former clients she was blackmailing. Your dad wasn’t specific.”

“There were six men,” she said, “all paying different amounts. David was paying her five thousand a month.”

“For how long?” I asked.

“Twenty-three years,” she said. “He was her last regular client. She never told him he got her pregnant. I guess you could call it a very underhanded way of extracting child support.”

“So when you and David connected on the DNA site,” I said, “did he realize you were Peaches’s daughter?”

“Not until I told him,” she said. “The name Moretti meant nothing to him. At first he assumed I was the result of some one-night stand in his youth. He didn’t know the name Peaches

Gillespey either. Mom used a made-up name when she worked for the escort service—Layla Bissett."

"And the other five guys?" I said. "How much were they paying her?"

"Between one thousand and eleven thousand a month," she said, "depending on their ability to pay and degree of desperation. Mom was very good at reading people and exploiting their weaknesses. She thoroughly researched their private and professional lives, knew just which former clients to target."

"What I don't get is why they paid at all," I said. "Wouldn't it have just been her word against theirs?"

"Dad didn't tell you about the videos she secretly recorded?"

I winced. "I guess that would do it. Where are those videos now?"

"On her computer," she said. "And no, I didn't watch them." And risk viewing the moment of her conception? I'd say she'd made the right call.

"If I could go back in time and talk to my teenage self," Evie said, "I'd assure her that in fact she had it right. No one else's family *was* as weird as hers."

"So help me get clear on the timeline," I said. "Your mom did a little modeling starting at age sixteen, right? Then at eighteen she switched to, um, escort work—"

"Sex work." Evie kicked a pile of dried seaweed. "Call it what it is. And you skipped an important part, Jane. The sugar daddy."

"Oh. Right. How could I forget about the sugar daddy?"

"Modeling wasn't the dream career Mom thought it would be," she said, "and this rich old guy—she calls him 'Number One' in the spreadsheet—he's taken with her looks and he sets her up in this swanky Manhattan apartment and supports her for about eight months. Then Number One has a stroke and his kids give her the boot."

"So then, the sex work started…" I prompted.

"The sex work started soon after," she said. "I'm guessing the sugar daddy was like a gateway drug. She was a call girl for about a year and a half before she met my dad."

"Your grandma told me they were both twenty at the time?" I said.

"Yep. My dad was… well, he was inexperienced," she said. "His buddies hired Mom for him as a birthday gift. I'm guessing he didn't tell you that part."

"Um, no. So then, he was actually one of her—"

"Clients," Evie said. "That's right. They fell in love, and she promised to be faithful. No more sex work."

"While in reality…" I said.

"While in reality, she didn't stop. She did reduce her, uh, workload, but she continued to see a few regular clients on the sly for two more years, until she got pregnant with me. Of course, Dad had no idea, not until we got the DNA results. I'm sure that to this day, he hasn't seen that spreadsheet. He's not the most computer-savvy person, plus she had everything locked down with passwords. I found where she kept those."

"Since you took your mom's computer back in December," I said, "the cops didn't find it when they searched her house the day they arrested Sean. I'm guessing that when they talked to you, they asked if you knew where it was."

Evie shrugged, without looking at me. So I wasn't the only one she'd been lying to. I had to wonder whether she seriously considered the contents of Peaches's computer irrelevant to the murder investigation, or whether she had another reason to withhold it from the police.

I said, "The detectives must have reviewed your mother's bank records. Did they ask you where that forty-one K a month came from?"

"I told them I didn't know," she said.

Good grief. Had she been straight with Howie and Cookie about anything?

"It must have occurred to you," I said, "that every one of your mother's blackmail victims is a potential murder suspect. How do you know one of them didn't get fed up with shelling out hush money all those years and decide to end it for good? The police need to know about those men, Evie. They need that computer."

She was shaking her head before I finished speaking. "If one of them was going to kill her, they wouldn't have waited decades to do it. The police have the right person—my brother. My mom's background, the sex work and the blackmail, it's awful, but it's in the past, and it has no bearing on what happened to her."

"At least consider—"

"No." She stopped walking and speared me with a hard look. "It's *private family business*, Jane. I have no intention of making our shame public. That's final."

Well, I'd done my best. I'd given her a chance to come clean on her own, to turn over Peaches's laptop to the detectives and share what she knew. Evie might be counting on the fact that I'd once promised to keep everything she told me confidential. It pained me to have to violate a client's privacy, but it would pain me more to keep mum about information critical to a murder investigation.

I'd phone Howie as soon as I got back to my car. Scratch

that. I'd phone Cookie, since her grumpy partner would doubtless give me a hard time for involving myself in police business. That's how he'd see it, when all I was trying to do was share pertinent information I'd come across, as any good citizen should. Detective Howard Werker needed to lighten up.

We continued slogging across the sand toward the boardwalk. "I hate to admit it," Evie said, "but it'll be a relief when they convict Sean and put him away. Then I can start to put this whole horrible thing behind me."

I'd never before heard someone yearn for the day a family member would be sent to prison for murder. I wondered if she'd convinced herself he was guilty so she would no longer have to deal with the stress of the murder investigation.

"Meanwhile," she added, "at least I now have the legal right to kick him out of Mom's house and start to undo the damage he's done. I still think of it as Mom's house, but I found out it actually belongs to me."

This was another *You don't say* moment. With Evie, I was either pretending to know something I didn't, or pretending not to know something I did. There seemed to be no middle ground. I pasted on a quizzical expression. "The house is yours? I thought you and Sean would have to split it."

"It turns out my grandfather left it to me, not Mom," she said. "She tossed out his will and told everyone the house was hers. Mr. Jakobsen managed to locate the original will. He's done a terrific job for me, Jane, with that and other stuff. Thank you for recommending him."

"You're welcome," I said. "I'm glad Sten was able to help you. If I may ask, why do you think your grandfather disinherited your mother? I mean, I'm just assuming she didn't inherit anything from him."

To my daughter, Gertrude Violet Gillespey, I leave nothing, for reasons well known to her.

"That's right," Evie said. "Grandpa had no financial assets to speak of, but he did have the house and its contents, which included some fine furniture, antiques, and artwork. He left all that to me. She didn't get so much as a spoon."

"Even after she paid the upkeep on the house all those years?" I said.

"Grandpa made no secret of the fact that he disapproved of Mom's 'lifestyle choices.' Most people assume he meant her living in sin with my dad, but that never seemed to bother him. He was always nice to me and Sean, and to Dad, too. But he was cold toward my mom. I never could figure out why, and Mom wouldn't talk about it. What do I think now? I think he knew about the sex work."

"I can see how that particular lifestyle choice might disappoint a parent," I said. "Good luck getting the house in shape. I suppose this means your brother will have to move back in with your grandma and your dad."

She sighed. "Poor Grandma. She should kick the both of them out and let them fend for themselves for once."

We'd reached the ramp to the boardwalk. I halted there, and so did Evie. "Listen," I said, "I have a question that might seem a little, well, odd. It's about the day your neighbor Zak Pryce's wife died."

"Oh yes, what a nightmare," Evie said. "I liked Stacey. She was always so nice to me. She took me out for my first mani-pedi when I turned twelve. My mom would never have done anything like that with me. Two months later, Stacey was gone."

"Zak was at your house that day, watching tennis on TV with your folks," I said. "That's what he told the police, and your mom and dad corroborated it. So the thing I'm wondering is, did you happen to see him at the house that day?"

"No. That was a school day," she said, "the first Friday of the school year, in fact. We had our first Mathletes meeting that afternoon. I remember I came home near dinnertime, and Sean—he was nine then—he couldn't wait to tell me what happened across the street, like it was the most exciting thing ever. Like something on TV."

"I guess the police had already talked to your mom and dad by then," I said.

Evie nodded. "Stacey had already been... well, they'd already taken her away. The detectives were still over at Zak's place, but all the emergency personnel were gone by the time I got home."

"So Zak used to do stuff with your folks?" I asked.

"No, not really," she said. "Well, not at all, as far as I knew. But I guess that day was an exception. It's too bad. If he'd been home, Stacey might still be alive. They might have kids now. It's too sad to think about."

"Thanks." We put on our shoes and started up the ramp. "I was just afraid you and your brother might have been traumatized by the, um, incident."

"Well, coming home to the terrible news was bad enough," she said. "Sean was around when the whole thing went down, but like I said, he found it entertaining. That's how he's always been, since he was in diapers. A little hoodlum."

We'd reached the boardwalk, and I was about to take my leave of Evie when the opening bars of "Tequila" sounded from my phone. I almost dumped the call, but then I saw it was from Martin. He was more of a texter than a caller, so I figured it might be important.

I held up a finger. "One second, Evie. I apologize, I have to take this." I answered the phone with, "Make it fast, Padre."

"The crime lab got results on the residue in the soda bottle they found with Peaches," he said. Obviously he'd been chatting with his cop buddy again.

"And…?" I said, while Evie politely waited for me to wrap up my call.

"And they found a sedative in the bottle," he said. "A lot of it. Someone spiked Peaches's soda."

My nape prickled. "Do they know what brand? Specifically?"

"I haven't been able to find that out," he said, "but I'm working on it. Could be anything. Dr. Pepper, Mountain Dew—"

"Not that. The, um, other," I said.

"Oh, you mean the sedative. Yeah, it's a new one. Never heard of it before. It's called Zenaproche."

14

Apathy and Stultifying Torpor

WELL, THAT WAS AWKWARD, standing there with Evie at the very moment I learned that Peaches's killer had apparently drugged her before doing the deed. And what had been the murderer's drug of choice? Why, none other than Zenaproche, the new sedative that dedicated pharmaceutical rep Evie Moretti had been hawking.

You'd be proud of me. My facial expression didn't change one iota as I took in Martin's surprising news. Well, maybe one iota. Okay, more like three or four iotas if we're getting technical. Fortunately, I don't think she noticed.

I called Detective Cookie Kaplan as soon as I got home and filled her in on everything I'd learned from, and about, Evie Moretti. We talked about Peaches's purloined computer, the prostitution and blackmail spreadsheet (positively *brimming* with new suspects), biological dad David Waldmann, and Evie's connection to Zenaproche.

Cookie didn't press me on how I'd learned the crime lab had found a sedative in the soda bottle. Well, not too hard, anyway. She was well aware that both Sophie and Martin somehow had access to sources of classified information, and there wasn't a darn thing she or Howie could do about it. And since neither the mayor nor the padre—nor yours truly for that matter—tended to broadcast sensitive information all over town, Cookie probably figured she had more important battles to fight.

"But what about the fact that no drugs were found in Peaches's system?" Cookie asked. "No Zenaproche, nothing."

I hesitated too long.

"Great," she said. "You didn't know about that till I told you."

"Look at it this way," I said. "I'd have found out soon enough. We both know that."

"You and your pals are out of control," she said, but the complaint was tinged with admiration.

"So what does it mean that the sedative in the bottle wasn't found inside Peaches?" I asked. "That someone tried to drug her and failed?"

"Well," Cookie said, "the soda bottle was found on the floor, so maybe it got knocked over before she had a chance to drink it."

"And they're certain the bottle is connected to the murder?" I asked.

"The lab says the timing checks out," she said, "so yeah, we're going on the assumption it's connected."

THE NEXT MORNING I took Sexy Beast to the groomer's. Back when Irene had owned him, she'd indulged his aversion to shampoo and clippers, essentially turning the poor little guy into a matted hairball on legs. Once I became his guardian, SB started getting his curls coiffed on a regular basis. He now looked and smelled like the pampered little lapdog he was born to be.

Rocky was the most sought-after groomer in Crystal Harbor and beyond. Not only did he do an exceptional job on all manner of canines and felines, but he had a sweet, patient personality that instantly put all animals at ease, including animals of the human persuasion. If Rocky had a last name, no one knew what it was. He was like a Hollywood celebrity that way, or one of his four-legged clients.

Minnie Shapiro was behind the desk when I carried Sexy Beast into Rocky's salon, charmingly decorated in a laissez-faire bohemian style, with an eclectic mix of colors, patterns, and textures that shouldn't have worked together yet somehow did. Minnie was a hundred ten years old. Okay, I don't know how old she actually was, but I've often wondered how many of the town's Prohibition-era speakeasies she'd frequented back in the day.

Minnie paused her yoga practice to greet us. "Well, hello there, you sexy little beast."

"Thanks, Minnie." I struck a pinup-girl pose." You're not so bad yourself."

"SB," she said, "how do you put up with this one?"

He snorted as if to say, *I tried driving her out into the country, but she keeps finding her way back.*

"The usual?" she asked, meaning the kind of cut I preferred for Sexy Beast's apricot coat.

"Yep," I said. "Clean face and feet, short all over the body, fluffy topknot." No pompons for my beloved pet, thank you very much. Leave the froufrou for the show dogs. As for the topknot, I always suspected Rocky practiced on Minnie's own neatly rounded tuft of dandelion fluff.

The door to the inner sanctum opened and Rocky emerged. He was around fifty, but the only hint of middle age was his neatly trimmed salt-and-pepper hair. We should all be so slim and fit at the half-century mark.

He said, "Well, if it isn't my favorite toy poodle."

"What about your favorite Death Diva?" I said.

He pretended to look around. "Is she here?"

I mock-pouted. "I'm feeling very unloved today. First Minnie and now you."

"I *pay* Minnie to be mean. Makes me seem absolutely adorable by comparison." He took in my jeans and dark green (stretched-out but comfy) sweater. "Is that what you're wearing?"

This line had been a running joke between us since the previous summer when I'd found myself on detestable Miranda Daniels's detestable TV program, *Ramrod News*, wearing nothing but some va-va-voom undies I'd been trying on, over my own drab granny panties. Did I mention this incident occurred in a lingerie store? My good pal Rocky never lets me forget the humiliation.

Well, isn't that what good pals are for?

"SB," I said, "you have my permission to pee on his leg."

"As if he would ever." He took Sexy Beast from me and played kissy-face with him for a bit, before turning him over to Minnie for scritches and a treat. "Jane, can I have a word?" He led me across the room to an overstuffed, zebra-patterned love seat out of earshot of his nosy receptionist.

I'd never known Rocky to look uncomfortable, but he looked uncomfortable now as we settled on the love seat. I said, "Did someone die?"

"Oh, it's nothing, you know, *terrible*, it's just something Ian mentioned." Ian was Rocky's boyfriend. "You know he and

Bonnie are good friends, right? I mean, you might even know this news already, only it just happened, so probably not."

I thought of Bonnie's antipathy toward Martin, her desire to apprehend him in the commission of some felony or other so she could have the pleasure of sending him away for a good long stretch. Had she gotten lucky? Had the padre gotten careless? I wiped my damp palms on my jeans. "Okay, let's have it."

"Well," he said, "and I mean, I have no idea whether you even care at this point, because you are so *over* Dom. You are still over him, right?"

I allowed myself a sigh of relief. It wasn't about Martin. "Rocky, are you trying to tell me Dom and Bonnie have set the wedding date?" I asked. "Because as far as I'm concerned, it's about time."

"That's just it," he said. "There's not going to *be* a wedding. Not between Dom and Bonnie, anyway. She has a *new man*."

My gasp was loud enough to make Minnie look up from her Warrior Pose, and Sexy Beast to look up from his Napping Pose on the little zebra-patterned dog bed that was a miniature replica of our love seat.

"No!" I blurted. "I mean, sure, they broke up for a little while last summer, but as far as I know, there was never anyone else."

"Well, there is now," Rocky said. "His name is Clay something, and he's a, I don't know, something in finance. Or insurance. Something *boring* anyway."

"I appreciate the heads-up," I said, "but if you're expecting me to drop my 'over him' act and snatch Dom up now that he's single, then make yourself comfortable, 'cause you're in for a good long wait. Meaning yes, I am well and truly over him."

"I'm relieved to hear it, Jane," he said. "You wasted too

much time mooning over that man. Not that I have anything against Dom. He's a great guy, but he's not *the* guy for you."

"I must say, though, this is a surprise. I really thought it was going to work out between the two of them."

"Okay," he said, "I have to tell you what else Ian said. He's about ninety-nine percent sure the breakup was mostly about *you*."

"*Me?*" I said. "Rocky, you know there's nothing between Dom and me."

"*I* know that," he said, "and I'm pretty sure Bonnie knows it, too. But she also knows Dom is still hung up on you."

"Sure he is," I scoffed. "That's why he went through those two other wives after we divorced, and had three kids with them. Because he's still hung up on me."

"Maybe he wasn't always," he said, "but he is now. At least, that's what Bonnie thinks. Ian said she would never have given that finance guy a second *look* if she thought she could make Dom forget about you."

The door to the shop opened and Zak Pryce entered, accompanied by Dylan. The big, white mutt made a beeline for Sexy Beast, their exuberant greetings marked by, yes, Downward Dog Pose as they invited each other to play. The dogs' excitement over reuniting made me consider, not for the first time, getting a second pooch to keep SB company.

Zak was still the epitome of Brooklyn chic in slim black jeans, a black V-neck tee, a subtly striped wool scarf, and a charcoal-gray cardigan that appeared hand-knitted. The two of us exchanged greetings, and Minnie signed Dylan in.

"All right," Rocky said, rising, "I'd better get busy or I'll have a regular dog pageant on my hands. Come on, guys, let's go get *gorgeous*."

Sexy Beast and Dylan happily followed their groomer into the mysterious place where the magic happened. The door closed behind them.

Behind her desk, Minnie assumed the one-legged Tree Pose and said, "You two know the drill. It's gonna be a while. I'll text you when they're ready."

I was still seated. Zak turned to leave, but I caught his eye and patted the cushion next to me, wordlessly inviting him to set a spell. I hadn't clapped eyes on Peaches's neighbor since Dom and I knocked on his door nearly a week earlier, and I was hoping he might shed light on a Big Question that had been nagging me for several days.

Yeah, I know what Sophie said about keeping my distance from Zak. And okay, so she wasn't wrong, but no way was I going to squander an opportunity like this. And just like when I had my "date" with Burke, we were in a commercial establishment with plenty of foot traffic. Plus we were under the watchful eye of a hundred-ten-year-old yogi. So, uh, safe, right?

He hesitated, so I said, "Come on, Zak, keep me company for a bit."

Fortunately for me, he was too well brought up to refuse. "Okay, but just for a minute." He sat next to me. "I'm on a deadline."

The KrunchWorks website could wait. "I'm glad we ran into each other," I said. "I've been thinking about you."

This earned a wary look, as well it might. He probably thought I was coming on to him. Part of me wondered what would happen if I failed to disabuse him of that notion. Not that I was interested, but it was fun to speculate. There was no denying Zak Pryce was easy on the eyes.

I mentally debated how to work my way around to the Big

Question, then recalled how well bald-faced lies had worked for me with Evie the day before. Why mess with success?

"So listen." I glanced around and lowered my voice, for effect. We were far enough from Minnie to avoid being overheard. "I really shouldn't be telling you this, but I like you and I thought you deserved to be warned."

He frowned. "Warned about what?"

"Well, I'm friends with our police detectives here in Crystal Harbor," I said. "Howie Werker and Cookie Kaplan. I know they spoke with you after Peaches's body was found."

"They spoke with all the neighbors," he said. "It's not like they singled me out."

"Oh, I know that. It's just that Howie and Cookie sometimes let things slip when we're shooting the breeze, and…" I looked away, as if conflicted. "You know what? Forget I said anything. I really shouldn't be telling you this. So how are the renovations going? Think you'll be able to put the house on the market soon?"

He turned to face me squarely. "Never mind the house, Jane. What did you want to warn me about?"

I made a show of biting my lip and sighing. Finally I said, "Okay. They know you ghostwrote Peaches's advice column."

His expression never altered, but a slight flicker of his eyelids gave him away. "That's preposterous. Her kind of writing and mine have nothing in common."

"Yeah, you said that before, but Howie and Cookie know you wrote it." I shrugged. "You seem like a nice guy. I just wanted to prepare you."

He stared at me another few moments, then turned and directed his stony gaze out the front window. Finally he said, "It was that bastard at the magazine. The editor. Gordon. He must've told the cops."

"Gordon knew you were writing Peaches's column?" I said.

"Not while she was still alive," he said. "The magazine had no idea she wasn't writing it herself."

"When did they find out?"

"After her body was discovered," he said. "I immediately contacted Gordon and told him I'd been writing the column all along—I had my notes and drafts to prove it—and that I wanted to keep writing it."

"Wouldn't it be a little weird for a man to be writing under Peaches's name?" I asked.

"Trust me," he said, "I want nothing to do with 'Peaches Preaches.' The new advice column is called 'Dear Dylan.' It launched online three days ago and will appear in the print edition once it gains in popularity."

"Congratulations," I said. "You named the column after your dog. Cute."

"Well, I certainly couldn't use my real name," he said. "The tone of 'Dear Dylan' is a hundred eighty degrees from the column I wrote for Peaches, but it's still nothing I'd want associated with my literary work."

Heaven forbid. "I have to ask if you have any specialized background that qualifies you to give personal advice to strangers," I said. "Like a psych degree or whatever."

Zak's smile was more than a little condescending. "As if I need some official-looking piece of paper to do this. Do you have any idea what kind of observational skills it takes to tackle the kind of novel I'm writing? The sheer degree of empathy? You forget, Jane, I'm a lifelong student of the human condition."

"Yeah, I, uh, forgot about the empathy thing."

"It works the other way, too," he said. "Writing this advice column—writing it the right way, that is, not Peaches's way—is giving a boost to my book. It's inspired me to add a character who's an advice columnist. He suffers from ennui, always solving the problems of others while his own life is marked by apathy and stultifying torpor."

Not unlike what I was experiencing at that very moment. "I'm curious as to how Peaches got that gig in the first place," I said. "From what I understand, she was a terrible writer."

"That's true," he said, "but she was a genius at self-promotion. She met Gordon at a party eleven years ago. He mentioned that the magazine was looking to start an advice column, and she said what a coincidence, I'm looking to write one. Which, of course, was BS, but he was taken with her lacerating wit and invited her to submit sample pieces."

"Which she got you to write for her," I said.

He nodded. "Gordon must've known what the public wanted, because 'Peaches Preaches' had tons of fans right from the start. I had no choice but to answer their letters in the most obnoxious way possible," he said.

"As if Peaches herself were answering them," I said. "What were the logistics? I mean, did you two email the letters to each other?"

"No, it was strictly old-school," he said. "She was afraid of leaving an electronic paper trail. She'd decide which readers' letters she wanted answered and leave copies of them in my mailbox. I'd leave the finished work in *her* mailbox. Then she'd retype it on her computer and submit it to the magazine."

"I'm guessing she withheld payment until she was completely satisfied with your work," I said.

Bingo. There was that telltale eyelid flicker. "That's right."

"I'm curious," I said. "Did she pay you by the piece—you

know, for every published letter—or was it by the hour, or what?"

The flicker turned into a tic. "By the piece," he said.

"Oh. So for every 'Peaches Preaches' letter you answered," I said, "she promised you all over again that she'd stick by the false alibi she and Carter provided you eleven years ago."

He stiffened in alarm. "I honestly have no idea what you're talking about."

"Sure you do, Zak. Peaches blackmailed you for eleven years. The deal went like this. She and Carter tell the cops you were at their place when you wife drowned in the bathtub, and in return, you write that horrible advice column for Peaches until death do you part. Did I leave anything out?"

Zak's disdainful chuckle would have been more effective without the madly twitching eyelid. "That's just... Wow, what a story. You should be the one writing novels, Jane. Peaches *hired* me to ghostwrite her column. As in she paid me money. And Peaches and Carter told the police I was at their place that day because I *was* at their place that day. I can't imagine where you got this blackmail nonsense."

"From Carter," I said, and watched his forced grin fade. "Well, he told my detective friends and they told me."

Yeah, I get that you can no longer keep track of the lies. I kinda lost count myself. But hey, they were for a good cause, right? I mean, cops are legally permitted to lie to suspects, so why not me?

Okay, I don't really want to know why not me, so you can just keep that to yourself. Sheesh. Where was I?

Some of the color leeched out of Zak's handsome face. "I—I don't... I mean, he wouldn't..."

"Carter cracked under questioning," I said. "He was no

match for the detectives. It happens all the time."

Zak raked his fingers through his hair. If anything, his fashionable do looked even more fashionable after being abused. "All those years writing that disgusting column, only to have that buffoon turn around and…" He shook his head as if struggling to comprehend his coconspirator's betrayal.

"What happened that day, Zak?" I asked. "The day Stacey died."

He took a deep breath. "I was home that day, writing. Around ten in the morning, Stacey told me she was going upstairs to take a bath. I didn't pay much attention at the time. I tend to get totally absorbed in my story and sort of block everything else out."

"Did Stacey have a job?" I asked.

"Sure," he said. "She was an editorial assistant at a publishing house. I met her at a writers' conference. It was a Friday, but she had the day off."

"You told the detectives that Stacey sometimes abused prescription drugs," I said.

He nodded, his expression grim. "They told me later that she had Xanax and alcohol in her system. She promised me she stopped, and I believed her. After she died, I kept replaying her words in my head, when she said she was going up to take a bath. I should've paid more attention. Was her speech slurred? Did her eyes look glassy? I never even looked up from the computer. I was too damn preoccupied."

"When did it first occur to you that something was wrong?" I asked.

"It was hours later," he said. "I'd been glued to my chair the whole time, working on my book. When I finally dragged myself away from it, I was stiff all over, not to mention famished. When

I realized it was after two in the afternoon, I was annoyed that Stacey hadn't come to get me for lunch We'd planned to go out for sushi."

"And then what?" I asked quietly, though I had no desire to hear it.

Zak looked older than his thirty-eight years, and immensely sad. "I found her… I found her in the tub. The water was cold. She was cold."

"What did you do?" I asked.

"I ran for my phone and punched in nine-one-one, but I didn't press Send. I knew the police would take one look and jump to the wrong conclusion."

"That you killed her," I said.

He nodded numbly. "Stacey was gone and there was nothing I could do about it. I kept thinking about spending the rest of my life in prison for something I didn't do. I was shaking so hard, I couldn't fill my lungs. The panic was… It was paralyzing."

"How did Peaches and Carter get involved?" I asked.

"I had no idea what to do," he said. "All I knew was that I needed help. I kind of stumbled out of the house, and I saw Carter across the street, sweeping his front porch. There was no one else around. He smiled and waved at me, but I must've looked like, well, like a zombie, because he dropped his broom and jogged over to me. I was kind of incoherent, I guess. He brought me into his house, and he and Peaches managed to get the story out of me."

"But they didn't call nine-one-one right away, did they?" I said.

He shook his head. "Peaches went over to my place to… to see for herself. It seemed to take forever, but she was probably gone a couple of minutes. When she came back, she was all business. I was to go back home and call it in, but first the three of us needed to get our story straight."

"What did you think she meant by that?" I asked.

"I didn't know at first," he said. "I was just so relieved that someone else was taking charge and seemed to have a plan."

"Was it like I said? You agreed to ghostwrite her new advice column, and in exchange, they told the cops you were with them all day?"

"That's it in a nutshell," he said. "It was blackmail, pure and simple. And I went along with it. The state I was in, I'd have agreed to practically anything that would keep me out of prison. What makes it worse is that I know Peaches and Carter thought I was guilty as hell. They thought I murdered my wife, and they still concocted this fake alibi. Well, Peaches did the concocting. She drilled Carter on the story until she was confident he had it down and wouldn't mess up under questioning."

"So you started writing her 'Peaches Preaches' column," I said.

His features tightened in revulsion. "God, how I loathed it. I was kind of optimistic at first. Shows you how delusional I was."

"Optimistic how?"

"I actually thought," he said, "that if I made Peaches's advice column as offensive as possible—nasty, mean-spirited, wholly devoid of any redeeming value—that it would die an ignoble death and I could stop writing it."

"Instead, it became wildly popular." I thought but didn't say, *So much for your vaunted knowledge of human nature.*

"The only way I could bring myself to keep doing it," he said, "was by forcing myself to forget that those were real people writing in for advice. Real people with real problems."

"Real people like Ellen Fletcher," I said. Where was all that empathy when Burke's wife reached out for help?

He closed his eyes for a moment as the memory stabbed him. "Her letter had me worried. She might've been in real trouble. I told Peaches we needed to contact her, to find out what was going on. Peaches wouldn't hear of it. She demanded that I write a truly outrageous response, one that would fire up her readership. If it stimulated controversy, so much the better."

"I want you to know just how destructive that decision was," I said. Without providing too much detail or revealing how I'd come by the information, I told him about Ellen Fletcher's emotional problems and how his response to her plea for help had caused her to abandon a loving husband, a stable home life, and the medical support she needed.

I shared this with Zak despite the fact that I still didn't know how much of Burke Fletcher's story to believe. I had a point to make. Zak was not off the hook, no matter how much he tried to blame the malignant tone of "Peaches Preaches" on the woman who'd blackmailed him into writing it.

"If you got that information from her husband," Zak said, "then take it with a grain of salt."

"What do you mean?"

"Burke Fletcher's a dangerous guy," he said. "He threatened Peaches's life. On the phone."

I kind of knew that already. Burke had danced around the subject, but it was pretty clear he'd threatened her. "If he did," I said, "maybe it's because he was frustrated beyond reason by how much damage your so-called advice had done."

"And maybe Ellen's claims were true," he said, "and Fletcher is an abusive husband. In any event, after he threatened Peaches, she told me it was my fault that she was in danger, even though she forced me to answer Ellen's letter the way I did."

"What did Peaches want?" I asked. "She must've wanted something."

"She demanded I ghostwrite this self-help book she wanted to publish," he said. "It would have the same trademark malignant tone as the letters, of course. Either I write the book or she goes back on our deal and tells the cops I admitted to killing Stacey."

The threat had teeth, even if Stacey's death had indeed been accidental and Zak had nothing to do with it. Howie Werker had harbored suspicions about the young widower's guilt for eleven years. He'd probably love nothing more than to reopen the case.

"And there's no statute of limitations on murder," Zak added. "So she really had me over a barrel. I had to agree to it."

"When did this conversation take place?" I asked.

"At the end of November."

Right before Peaches went missing.

"I'm assuming the statute of limitations has run out on Peaches and Carter's crime of providing a false alibi," I said. "They can no longer be charged for that since it was so long ago. That is, Carter can no longer be charged."

"Meanwhile," he said, "if the cops find out about the self-help book, the pressure she put on me to write it, they'll think I'm the one who killed her. I never should've told you about the book."

"They already consider you a suspect," I lied, "because of how she blackmailed you for eleven years. They're just waiting until they have enough evidence to charge you. For both murders."

"Stacey's death was an accident," he snapped. "And I didn't

kill Peaches. Not that I didn't fantasize about wringing her miserable neck, but I didn't do it. That's not who I am."

Perhaps not, but at the very least, he was a guy who, on discovering his wife dead, made sure to cover his own sorry ass before calling 911. A guy who lied to the police. A guy who used his writing talent to demean and belittle the people who wrote in to Peaches, asking for help. My sympathy had limits.

"Then you have to go to the detectives," I said. "Tell them exactly what happened the day Stacey died."

"No matter what I do," he said, "it's going to look bad for me. The blackmail turns me into a prime suspect. Unless Peaches was blackmailing a bunch of other people that I don't know about."

Funny you should mention…

"And it wouldn't hurt to take a lawyer with you," I said.

He took a deep breath. "I'll think about it."

"Don't think too long, Zak," I said. "Don't wait until they bring you in. You need to get in front of this."

15

Lusting in Her Heart

"I'M MIRANDA DANIELS and this is *Ramrod News*, where the truth comes to live free."

Okay, I admit it, I was watching the pathetic not-really-news show, against my better judgment. I was curious about how the media was treating the murder investigation, and *Ramrod News* was, sad to say, an influential media outlet. Millions of viewers tuned in every evening to hear Miranda hold forth on the most titillating, controversial, and/or incendiary current events.

Ramrod News was the television equivalent of "Peaches Preaches": inflammatory, mean-spirited entertainment catering to the lowest common denominator.

Sexy Beast and I were cozily ensconced on the family room's enormous, horseshoe-shaped ivory leather sofa, which faced a flat-screen TV the size of Rhode Island. The sofa was made cozier still by plentiful accent pillows and throws in shades of rose, slate blue, and pale green. I had not chosen the sofa, the TV, or any of my house's other insanely expensive furnishings. Everything was as Irene McAuliffe had left it since I certainly couldn't afford to replace anything. Fortunately for me, Irene—or more likely, her decorator—had excellent taste.

Miranda's face—overly made-up, crowned by a stiff

platinum-blonde coiffure—dominated the television screen as she yowled into the camera. "It's been nine days since beloved advice columnist Peaches Gillespey was found *murdered*. Not just murdered, but *bound, strangled,* and left in an abandoned attic until her body had completely *mummified*, like something out of King Tut's time!"

"Sorry to subject you to this, SB," I said. "We'll stand it as long as we can, okay?"

The look he gave me said he'd put up with Miranda for a few minutes, but there better be a Vienna sausage with his name on it when this horror was over.

"And are the Keystone Kops there in Crystal Harbor doing *anything*?" Miranda squawked. "Oh, they made an arrest, sure. Peaches's son, Sean Moretti, is out on bail."

This was accompanied by video of Sean exiting the courthouse after his bail hearing, during which the "lady judge" had reduced his bond from a million bucks to half that. He was grinning like he'd won the lottery, complete with celebratory fist pumps—not the best look when your mother has been murdered and you're presumed guilty—while his attorney growled something into his ear and tried to pull him away from the cameras.

This was my first glimpse of the Amazing Carlos Levine, Esquire, and I must say, I was not disappointed. Evie had told me he was more than competent. She'd neglected to add he was a tasty treat for the eyes. Close to my age, lean and impeccably attired, with neatly trimmed dark hair and a serious, handsome face. Yum.

Miranda, meanwhile, continued to harangue her viewers. "Talk about lazy police work. 'Let's just arrest Mr. Obvious and call it a day.' Now, don't get me wrong. This Sean character is no prize. He's done time for burglary, which is how he feeds his raging drug habit."

Raging? He wasn't an addict as far as I knew, just a lazy stoner with a larcenous bent.

"Guess why the cops arrested him," Miranda went on. "This is priceless. They arrested this twenty-year-old kid for murder because someone heard him arguing with his mom. That's it! That's all they have on him!"

Well, it wasn't *all* they had. Miranda must not have gotten the memo about the matchy-matchy rope found in Grandma Audrey's basement. The rope that looked just like the kind used to bind Peaches to that chair in the attic, and which Sean had easy access to. Clearly, the padre's source of classified information was more reliable than Miranda's.

She had more to say on this subject. "You show me a kid that age who *doesn't* fight with his—"

I clicked the remote and switched to *The Romano Files*, starring the combative Leonora Romano, an aspiring TV chef who'd settled for a quasi-news show in the same sensationalist mold as *Ramrod News*. The two programs aired on different channels in the same time slot and competed for viewers every weekday evening at six.

I knew Lee Romano, having had multiple run-ins with her during the past half year or so. Recently I'd heard that *The Romano Files* had begun edging out the long-running *Ramrod News*, which I considered a positive development. Not that I liked Lee, but I had a kind of grudging respect for her skills as an investigative journalist. I guess you could say she was the lesser of two evils.

Both Miranda and Lee had contacted me after the story broke, angling for exclusive insider info and begging for an on-air appearance by Crystal Harbor's notorious Death Diva, who'd stumbled across Peaches Gillespey's shriveled carcass while engaged in her gruesome line of work. Take my word for it, that's definitely how they'd spin it.

Both ladies (yeah, I'm being generous) got to hear me utter the phrase "cold day in hell," but they were nothing if not tenacious, so I knew I hadn't heard the last from them.

"—and Peaches was a successful, self-made woman," Lee was saying, "who knew what she wanted and went after it with laserlike intensity, becoming the most talked-about advice columnist of our time."

Lee Romano was fifty but looked closer to my age, having recently morphed from doughy and dumpy to sleek and sexy, thanks to talented surgeons and an experienced image consultant. Like Miranda, Lee was a bottle blonde, but her shoulder-length tresses were a rich honey hue, styled to softly frame her face, in stark contrast to Miranda's stiff white-blonde helmet.

"Peaches was no pushover," Lee continued. "This was a woman with a survivor's mind-set. She'd have put up a fight, believe you me. Her killer would have walked away bruised and scratched, at the very least. Probably walking funny, too, if you catch my drift. Did the police even bother to look into that? To find out whether anyone in the victim's circle of acquaintances looked like they'd been in a fight around the time she was killed?"

I must admit, that thought hadn't occurred to me. It was a valid point. If Peaches's murderer had succeeded in getting her to drink the soda laced with Zenaproche, she would have been easier to handle, meaning easier to kill. However, the drug was not found in her system. Without the assistance of a sedative, I assumed it would have taken a strong person—someone stronger than Peaches, in any event—to subdue her and tie her to that chair.

There I went again, making assumptions. *Stop it, Jane!*

Without warning, another possibility walloped me in the solar plexus. Maybe Peaches hadn't been killed by someone stronger. Maybe she'd been killed by *two* someones of average strength, whose combined efforts overpowered her. My mind began playing with potential suspects as if they were puzzle pieces, sliding them around and pairing them up.

So absorbed was I by this mental exercise that when the doorbell rang, I yelped and clutched my chest. Sexy Beast launched himself off the sofa and sprinted out of the family room, through the adjacent living room, and into the foyer so he could give the big double doors what-for, defending his territory and his alpha female with his imposing seven-pound bulk.

I followed him and opened the doors to find Dom standing on the front porch, holding a crystal vase crammed with tulips, my favorite flower. They were in my favorite tulip colors, too: cream, pale pink, peach, and butter yellow.

"Thank you, Dom. These are gorgeous." I accepted the vase as he entered the foyer, a space far too grand for the likes of my self-effacing pet and me, with its two-story ceiling, macassar ebony floors, and curving staircase. "What's the occasion?"

"Do I need an occasion?" He kissed me on the cheek. He smelled good. Dom always smelled good.

History had taught me that my ex did not, in fact, need an occasion. Very simply, an offering of tulips from Dom signaled that he was in courtship mode.

SB, never one to forget his self-imposed position at the bottom of the pack, groveled before our visitor, tail tucked, awaiting whatever crumbs of affection Dom might deign to bestow. This embarrassing display was rewarded, as always, with hugs and warm praise for my needy little pet.

As we took the two steps down from the elegant living room to the user-friendly family room, Dom's gaze zeroed in on the TV, where Lee Romano was still yammering about the murder and police incompetence. He asked, "Why would you willingly subject yourself to this garbage?"

I set the vase on the coffee table and picked up the remote. "Adios, Lee." The television went blessedly silent. "Have a seat, Dom. Beer? Something harder?"

"Nothing for me, thanks." He arranged pillows in one corner of the sofa and relaxed back against them. Pinning me with what can only be called a come-hither look, he beckoned me to sit on his lap.

Sexy Beast obediently answered the summons, leaping onto Dom and tucking himself against him. To his credit, Dom just laughed and gave the selfish critter more love, while I chose a spot on the sofa that was neither suggestively close nor insultingly far from my ex. At least I hoped I wasn't sending either of those messages.

With a final affectionate pat, he started to lift SB off his lap.

"No," I said, "let him be. He hasn't seen you in a while."

"He saw me just a few days ago." He studied me for a few moments, then said, "You heard."

"If you mean do I know that you and Bonnie broke up," I said, "then yes, I found out this morning."

"Who told you?" he asked.

"It doesn't matter," I said. "You know how news travels in this town."

"So then, you also know Bonnie has someone else," he said.

"I'm sorry, Dom. That's rough. Has she been seeing him long?"

"She and Clay have known each other for years, platonically," he said. "It's the old story. They didn't plan on falling in love, their feelings crept up on them, et cetera, et cetera. If Bonnie's to be believed, they didn't get serious until after she broke it off with me."

Which was his polite way of saying his fiancée had refrained from sleeping with Clay while she was engaged to Dom. If anything, such self-control, while admirable, probably heightened her attraction to her new fella. Nothing stirs the blood, after all, like lusting in your heart.

Not that I know what it's like to lust in your heart, but I've, you know, been told.

"Anyway," he said, "it's over between Bonnie and me."

"Not to be insensitive, Dom," I said, "but I've heard that before."

"I know you have, Janey, and I don't blame you for being skeptical. But believe me, it's over. Even if Bonnie calls it quits with Clay, it'll make no difference. We're done."

"I heard something else," I said. "I heard that Bonnie thinks you're hung up on me. That she wouldn't have gotten involved with Clay if she thought you were over me."

Dom was silent for long moments. Finally he said, "Didn't you ever wonder why Bonnie and I never set a wedding date?"

Only all the time. "It's none of my business," I said.

His knowing expression reminded me he could still read my mind.

"Okay, for what it's worth, Dom," I said, "all of Crystal Harbor has been wondering why you guys didn't set a date. All anyone could figure is that one of you had cold feet. And honestly? I don't think it was Bonnie."

I recalled seeing her in the local bookstore a few months earlier, checking out the wedding-planning section. This was going to be Dom's fourth marriage, but her first, and she'd been as excited as any prospective bride.

"I wouldn't call it cold feet," he said. "I mean, I've tied the knot a few times. It's not like I was nervous or anything. It just… didn't feel right with Bonnie."

"It felt different than with the others? With Lana and Meryl?" I asked, naming Mrs. Faso Numbers Two and Three.

"That's just it," he said. "It felt the *same* as it did with them. It felt wrong. I didn't realize the feeling for what it was back then, when I was preparing to marry Lana, and then Meryl. I was too, I don't know, too impatient, too wrapped up in the newness of the relationship. Too in love with love, I guess."

Too desperate to find someone to spend his life with, more likely. Dom Faso never could stand to be alone for long. "Well, better late than never," I said. "I mean, at least now you know how it's *not* supposed to feel."

"I know how it's supposed to feel, too." His words were so raw, so heartfelt, there was no denying their sincerity. "It's supposed to feel like it did with you and me. It was right back then, *we* were right back then, and we blew it. *I* blew it."

"We were so young," I said, "so inexperienced. It was all so *new*. You can't look back at how we were then and say, that's how it's supposed to feel now. Mature love doesn't feel like that."

"Speak for yourself." Dom straightened, much to SB's annoyance, and reached over to squeeze my hand. "I feel it now, the same as I did then. The bone-deep need to spend the rest of my life with you. The certainty that it's meant to be. You feel it, too. Or you would if you'd just let yourself. I love you, Janey."

Hot tears scalded my eyes. I had to look away, had to fight to keep them from falling. For eighteen years I'd fantasized about hearing my ex-husband utter those words again.

When I could speak, I said, "You're… You're reeling from the breakup with Bonnie. You're confused."

"Don't." He seized me and pulled me onto his lap, causing SB to grumble something about fickle alpha males and stalk to the other end of the sofa. Dom held me tight to keep me from bolting. "Don't minimize my feelings. I've never been less confused."

I offered a watery chuckle. "I'm glad one of us knows what's going on."

"Marry me, Janey," he said. "Marry me and make babies with me. It's not too late to do it right."

Babies. The very thought made my aging ovaries grab their little walkers and dance a jig.

"I don't expect an immediate answer," he said. "Take your time, take as long as you need. I'll be waiting. And this time I really will wait. You have my word."

It was a reference to the previous summer when newly unattached Dom had promised me several weeks to give him an answer and then turned around and gotten re-engaged to Bonnie days later.

Something told me he intended to bring the same dogged determination and single-minded focus to wooing me that he'd brought to building the Janey's Place health-food empire. If so, I was in for quite a siege. I'd be lying if I claimed I didn't find the prospect immensely flattering.

I recognized the look in his eyes. He was getting ready to kiss me. If I let him, it would be a signal, one I didn't know whether I was prepared to send at this juncture.

Then again, I had no doubt that kiss would be amazing.

Then again, there was something to be said for not making it too easy for him.

Then again, there was Martin, standing right next to us.

"What the hell!" Dom blurted.

"Are you two crazy kids up for some Buffalo chicken pizza?" The padre plopped down on the sofa. "Good thing I got a whole pie. Plenty for everybody."

Sexy Beast greeted him enthusiastically. Even he had failed to hear Martin pick the lock on my back door and slip silently into my house—with a pizza. Not just any pizza, but my all-time favorite kind of pizza. The aroma drifted in from the kitchen, teasing my nostrils and making my stomach whine. Meanwhile I resisted the urge to spring guiltily off my ex-husband's lap.

Dom looked mad enough to punch something—the something in question being the padre's handsome face. Instead he turned to me and muttered, "I'm going to buy you the most sophisticated, cutting-edge security system available."

"I have it. It doesn't stop him. You want some pizza?" I peeled his arms from around me and rose as gracefully as I could manage.

"No, I don't want any damn pizza." He got to his feet and confronted the interloper. "Get out, McAuliffe."

I said, "Dom—"

"If you're not gone in thirty seconds," Dom said, "I'm calling the cops. It's called breaking and entering. That's a felony, my friend."

"Nah," Martin said, "it's a misdemeanor. It's only a felony if I make off with, say—" he bench-pressed Sexy Beast, who yipped happily "—this expensive purebred animal."

"It's a crime either way." Dom produced his phone and started to tap in 911. "You've broken into this house for the last time."

I snatched the phone away from him and pressed the red End button. "Knock it off, Dom."

"But—"

"This is my house, remember?" I said. "I get to say who's here legally and who's not."

"He *broke in*," Dom said, not unreasonably. "With *lock picks*."

"How do you know she didn't give me a key?" Martin asked, with a mischievous smile.

I wheeled on him. "You are not helping."

"You gave him a *key*?" Dom said.

"No, but you know what? If I decide to give him a key, that will be my business. I'm going to eat that pizza." I stomped out of the family room, with SB close on my heels. "You two idiots can go hungry."

My ex decided to make some kind of grand statement by storming out of the house. Martin joined me in the breakfast room, where I'd flipped back the lid on the pizza box and stood admiring the cheesy, chickeny deliciousness within.

I grabbed a slice and started to chow down while he set out a couple of plates. Not only had the padre brought me my favorite kind of pizza, he'd procured it from my favorite little mom-and-pop pizza joint. I mean, Dom's offering of my favorite flower was nice and all, but you can't eat tulips. Well, maybe you can, but they sure as heck didn't taste like this.

"Beer?" he asked.

"Soda."

He poured me a glass of orange soda and popped the cap on

a bottle of beer, whereupon we settled in at the round breakfast table and inhaled our first slice before uttering another word. I mean, priorities.

I cut off a few small pieces—avoiding the spicy Buffalo sauce—and deposited them in Sexy Beast's bowl. He made fast work of the treat and begged for more. My singsongy "All gone" let him know that that was all he could expect for now and he'd have to content himself with kibble. He didn't like it, but he knew the drill, and was soon snoring in his bucket bed.

The padre took a breather, and a long pull of his beer. "He's not going to give up, you know."

"I know." I didn't need to bring him up to speed on the Dom-Bonnie front. He probably knew about the breakup before they did.

He affected a casual tone, which didn't fool me for an instant. "You told me you're over him."

He was referring to our conversation in the Historical Society's attic, before we got sidetracked by the creepily preserved mortal remains of Gertrude "Peaches" Gillespey.

"I am over him." I detached another slice from the pie.

"Does he know that?" he asked. "Because judging by the cozy scene I walked in on, I'm guessing the answer is no."

"Well, you know what, Padre? I was just about to tell him when you interrupted us." This happened to be true. No, really.

"You were sitting on his lap," he said. "We men are simple. We tend to take that sort of thing as encouragement."

I set down my slice. "Okay, the lap-sitting was not my idea. He just—No. I do not owe you an explanation. Read into the lap thing what you will. I don't care." I snatched up the slice and bit off a great big chunk. It tasted like indignation.

We ate in silence for a couple of minutes during which I

sensed that Martin regretted tipping his hand. That was how he'd see it, anyway. For the longest time he'd taken pains to avoid any hint that he cared. It was no great mystery as to why. He thought I was still pining for Dom, and he had no wish to be anyone's consolation prize. Well, I *was* still pining for Dom back when I first met the padre. Things change.

Before I could consider how best to demonstrate precisely how much this particular thing had changed, he said, "I have some news about the rope."

I chewed fast and swallowed. "What? Tell me."

"The crime lab made microscopic comparisons and determined that the rope used to tie Peaches to that chair came from the length of rope found in Audrey Moretti's basement. The cut ends even match up."

"Wow," I said. "This is major."

"It did not match the rope from Zak Pryce's house," he said. "Turns out they're not even the same thickness."

"Okay, so who had access to Audrey's rope?" I said. "There's Audrey herself, of course. Plus both Sean and Carter, who were living with her."

"Evie must have visited her on occasion," Martin said. "And for sure she was there on Thanksgiving, which was shortly before Peaches was murdered."

"It would have been easy for her to slip down to the basement," I said, "cut off a piece of rope, and shove it into her purse."

"So it's looking more and more like Peaches was killed by a family member," he said.

"What else did your secret contact in the Crystal Harbor PD tell you?"

"Who says I have just one?" he said.

"Quit showing off. Let's have it." I nibbled on a piece of crust.

"I told you I was trying to find out what kind of soda it was," he said. "I finally hit pay dirt."

"Please don't say Coke. I mean, Sean drinks Coke, but so do about a gazillion other people, so that doesn't exactly narrow down the list of suspects."

He said, "You know anyone who drinks black cherry soda?" I could tell he didn't expect a positive response. One look at my face, however, and he straightened. "Who?"

"Carter," I said, feeling a little stunned. "When I was over at Audrey's the other day, I saw him drink black cherry soda straight from the bottle."

"Did you catch the brand?" he asked.

"Something old-timey," I said. "Grandpa Dan's?"

"Could it have been Grampy Deke's?" he said.

"That's it! Grampy Deke's Original Black Cherry Soda."

"Well, that's what they found in the attic," Martin said. "A nearly empty bottle of Grampy Deke's."

"With just enough residue to test it and find that sedative," I said. "Zenaproche."

"Talk about narrowing down the suspect list," he said.

"Well, kind of," I said, "but don't forget, the whole family had access to that brand of soda, because Audrey keeps it in the house. And we don't know whether the killer actually drinks the stuff or just used it to try and drug Peaches."

"We know Sean's a Coke drinker," he said, "but maybe Evie shares her dad's love of Grampy Deke's."

"It's possible. I did see her drinking soda at the beach. Don't know what kind 'cause it was in a cup. But anyway, she's a soda drinker, for what it's worth." I lifted my glass as if to say, *Join the club.*

"The thing is," he said, "the cops were on the lookout for that particular brand of soda when they searched Audrey's house. Peaches's house, too. They didn't find any."

"I remember Audrey apologizing to Carter for having run out of it," I said. "She'd just gone shopping that morning and laid in several six-packs."

"So that's why the cops didn't make a connection," Martin said.

I said, "Do you think they asked—" but was interrupted by my phone's "Tequila" ring tone. I didn't recognize the number but tapped the green Answer button anyway, prepared to hang up if it was one of those annoying spammy robocalls. "Hello?"

"How's it going, Jane?"

"Not bad, Howie," I said. "I almost didn't pick up. But then I thought: And risk missing out on an amazing deal to lower my credit-card rates?"

He chuckled. "Yeah, I'm calling from a loaner. I'm not near my phone at the moment. Long story. I wanted to run something past you, get your take on it."

"About what?" I asked.

"About Peaches Gillespey, what else?" he said.

"You feeling okay, Howie?" I asked. "Do you have a fever? Maybe a devastating brain injury?" Since when did closemouthed Detective Howard Werker willingly talk to me about an ongoing investigation?

"You want to hear this or not?" he said. "I just thought you might have a fresh perspective on something that's been bugging me, but if you'd rather be kept out of the loop—"

"No, I'm thrilled to be kept in the loop, for once," I said. "Honored even. Listen, Martin's here. You mind if I put you on speaker or is this for my ears only?"

"Like you wouldn't blab to him the moment you hung up," he said. "Sure, no reason he can't hear this. I think I can count on you two not to spread it around."

I pressed the phone's Speaker button, and Martin and Howie greeted each other.

"So listen," Howie said, "I've been giving a lot of thought to Peaches's advice column."

"'Peaches Preaches,'" I said.

"Right. I always assumed she wrote it herself," he said. "I guess everyone did."

Martin said, "She didn't?" I'd been about to fill him in on that, and more, when Howie called.

I said, "Turns out she was a lousy writer. Beyond lousy. Even her daughter, Evie, acknowledged it."

I wasn't about to reveal that it was Burke Fletcher who'd alerted me to Peaches's semiliterate state. Howie didn't know I'd met the man, and I wanted to keep it that way. And, too, I had no desire for Martin to learn that I'd gone all by my lonesome—if you didn't count a small, neurotic poodle—to meet with the person who might very well have strangled Peaches Gillespey in that attic.

"I know you've been talking to a bunch of people about the murder," Howie said. "Don't bother denying it. You must hear things they'd never tell me or Cookie."

"You know I do, Howie," I said, "and haven't I been sharing everything I learn with you two? I mean, just yesterday I told Cookie all about Peaches's history of prostitution and blackmail. Plus Evie's connection to Zenaproche."

"Whoa." Martin's eyebrows rose. "Prostitution? Blackmail? Seriously?"

I turned to the padre. "Yeah, a lot of stuff's been

happening." I mouthed, *I'll tell you later.*

"The reason I'm calling," Howie said, "is to find out if you have any idea who might have ghostwritten Peaches's column."

I sighed, disappointed. "I guess he didn't contact you, then."

"Who?" He sounded suddenly alert.

"Zak," I said. "I spoke with him this morning. Now, don't scold me. I ran into him at the dog groomer's. It's not like I sought him out or anything. Turns out you were right not to buy his alibi back then, for his wife's death. It was total BS. Not that he's necessarily guilty. He says he didn't do it, that it was the Xanax and booze she'd—"

"Wait, back up. Just so we're clear, we're talking about Zak…" Howie waited for me to fill in the last name.

"For real?" I said. "I was kidding about the brain injury. Now I'm not so sure. Zak *Pryce*? Lives across the street from Peaches? Writing the not-so-great American novel? *That* Zak?"

"I knew who you meant," he said, "I just needed you to confirm the full name. For official purposes."

Martin and I shared a silent communication. It went something like this:

So that was weird, right?

Yep. Weird.

"Proceed," Howie said. "What is Zak Pryce's connection to Peaches's column?"

"He wrote it," I said, "from the very beginning. Peaches was blackmailing him, too, but not like the others, the former callgirl clients. They were paying cash. The way it worked with Zak was, Peaches and Carter provided a false alibi for him eleven years ago, and in return, he had to ghostwrite her advice column in perpetuity. He couldn't stand doing it."

"And he said he was going to contact me?" he asked.

"Not in so many words, but I encouraged him to," I said, "and I really thought… well, I figured if he was going to come clean, he'd have done it today. By now he's probably talked himself out of it."

The padre said, "But what incentive did he have to do that? Besides his statement to you, which he could deny."

"Zak might have, um, gotten the idea that the cops already know about the false alibi," I said, "and how Peaches blackmailed him. And that they're just waiting until they have enough evidence to arrest him."

"I'd call that incentive." Martin offered an approving smile for my subterfuge, which accelerated my pulse just the tiniest bit. Or maybe a little more than that. He added, "It's a double whammy. The false alibi and blackmail implicate him in both his wife's murder—well, possible murder—and Peaches's."

"So, Howie," I said. "Think you can stand another intriguing nugget of information?"

"Wait, let me brace myself," he said. "Okay, I'm ready."

"When you interviewed Carter, you must have asked him if he drank black cherry soda. You know, since a bottle of it was found at the scene, laced with Zenaproche." Without giving him a chance to demand how I knew about the black cherry soda, I said, "If he told you he doesn't drink it, he lied. He's addicted to it, according to him. Drinks it all the time, but he ran out of it before you guys searched his house, so you might not know that. You're welcome."

"That *is* an intriguing nugget, Jane," Howie said. "Glad I called."

We said our goodbyes and hung up, whereupon the padre and I set about annihilating the rest of that Buffalo chicken pie. We didn't succeed, both of us calling it quits after a measly three slices.

I washed down the last bite with a slug of orange soda. "I don't know how I feel about this, Padre."

"I know what you mean." He leaned back and patted his flat belly. "I can't put it away like I used to, either."

"No, I mean about Zak," I said. "I really don't think he killed Peaches."

"The evidence points more to a family member, it's true," he said, "but don't forget, the guy's had eleven years to build up resentment. No way was Peaches going to let him stop writing that column."

"Plus she was demanding he ghostwrite a self-help book for her," I said. "It must have felt like she'd always have her talons in him. Still, I don't really feel it, you know?"

Martin got to his feet. "We're going to pay this guy Zak a visit."

"What," I said. "Now?"

"Why not now?" he said. "See if we can't persuade him to go to the cops on his own. It's not too late. Plus you've piqued my curiosity. I want to meet this guy."

"Shouldn't we call first?" I asked.

"And give him a chance to put us off?" he said.

He was right, of course. Ambushing Zak at his home had worked for me before. Of course, I'd had Sexy Beast with me then.

No sense departing from a winning strategy.

16

Another Mouth to Feed

THE SUN HAD set while Martin and I were having dinner. Only the faintest smear of violet lightened the western sky as we took off in my Mazda. On the way to Zak's place, I filled Martin in on all the juicy stuff I'd learned from Evie the day before, as promised.

As usual, Zak was initially standoffish when he answered the door, but the padre scored brownie points by loving up his goofily friendly dog, Dylan. And after all, my own little canine companion is pretty darn irresistible, so within seconds we were standing in his foyer, admiring the fresh wallpaper and gleaming woodwork.

"Wow." I set Sexy Beast on the floor and unhooked his leash so he could pal around with his friend. "You've made a lot of progress in a few days, Zak. It looks great."

"Thanks," he said. "The realtor will be here tomorrow to have a look around and settle on an asking price."

Martin indicated the newly refinished floor we stood on, satiny pale wood with an intricate parquet border. "Is this maple?"

Zak nodded. "You have a good eye. Would you like to look around?"

We took him up on his offer and spent the next half hour touring the stately old Victorian, which, like the one across the street, had stood in that spot for more than a hundred years. I couldn't help thinking this was how these venerable homes were meant to be maintained, with love and respect. I became angry all over again as I recalled how thoroughly Sean Moretti had trashed his mother's house. Then I reminded myself that Evie now owned it and would soon evict him. She could be counted on to restore the place to its former majesty.

That is, unless she ended up doing time for murder.

We ended the tour back in the foyer, where we'd started. Dylan had helped to show us around, with SB bringing up the rear. Now the big white dog shoved a moist toy into Martin's hand, a plush, realistically rendered duck. The padre obediently hurled it down the adjacent hallway, to the delight of the dogs, who dashed after their fuzzy prey and presented it for more rounds of fetch. The padre was happy to comply.

"Do you have a dog?" Zak asked him.

"Nope." He threw the toy again and watched Dylan and Sexy Beast take off. "I'd love to adopt a big fellow like this, but I live in a small apartment. It'll have to wait."

A mental picture materialized, unbidden: Martin playing fetch with a big dog on my property's five acres. Martin possessing an actual key to my house. Martin and I sharing dinner every evening. And more provocatively, breakfast every morning.

Zak's voice jolted me back to the here and now. "So what brought you here, Jane? You said you had something to tell me?"

"I just wanted to reinforce what I told you this morning, Zak. You need to go to the detectives, tell them everything you told me. You're not doing yourself any favors by waiting for them to bring you in."

He waved aside my concern. "Done. I met with them both today, not long after I spoke with you at the groomer's. Before Rocky finished working on Dylan, in fact."

"Wait. No." I glanced at the padre, who appeared just as befuddled. Zak must be lying, just trying to get me off his back. "I have to tell you, I just spoke with Howie Werker, and he hasn't heard from you. So if you—"

"Well, that's just not true." Zak frowned in consternation. "I called my cousin Karen right away—she's a lawyer—and we met Werker and Kaplan at the station around noon. I told them everything. I don't know why Werker would tell you otherwise, unless he considers our meeting confidential or something."

Zak sounded sincere, yet how to reconcile this information with what Howie had told me not an hour before? Very simply, I couldn't. According to Howie, he'd had no idea Zak had been Peaches's ghostwriter, and he hadn't heard from him.

I'd never known Howie to lie to me. Of course, I'd never known him to be confused or forgetful, either, as he'd seemed during our conversation. For instance, it had apparently slipped his mind that just yesterday, I'd provided valuable information about the case. And that business about needing me to say Zak's last name, "for official purposes"? Either Howie, who possessed one of the sharpest minds I knew, was suffering from sudden early-onset dementia or—

Or that wasn't Howie on the phone.

Now that I thought about it, the call hadn't even come from Howie's phone. The caller had claimed to be using a "loaner"— in reality, probably a burner phone that couldn't be traced.

I looked at Martin and saw he'd arrived at a similar conclusion. Dylan, toy in mouth, repeatedly nudged the padre's hand, finally resorting to a frustrated huff. Distractedly Martin grabbed the duck, its fluff now wetly matted, and tossed it. The toy bounced off the edge of the hallway entrance. The look both dogs gave him could only be interpreted as, *You're losing your touch, buddy.*

I said, "All right, um… I must've misheard Howie, then. I'm glad you, you know, decided to meet with them, Zak. Sorry to bother you."

We said our goodbyes, collected SB, and stepped onto the big wraparound porch, warmly illuminated by several hanging lamps. Once the door had closed after us, Martin steered me away from the nearby windows and whispered, "So who was that on the phone?"

I'd been thinking about that. "There's only one person I know who could do such a spot-on impersonation of Howie. Burke Fletcher."

"I don't know anything about the guy," he said, "except what Howie and Cookie said when you mentioned his name at the pub. Fletcher lives in Rego Park and they questioned him because he harassed Peaches at some point."

"I met him," I said. "Don't ask me how."

Martin's expression said he would comply. For now. "So what makes you think he could pull off a stunt like that phone call?"

"Burke is a dialect coach," I whispered. "He trains comedians to do impersonations. And for sure he's familiar with Howie's voice and speech patterns. I mean, the detectives questioned him after Peaches's body was discovered."

"So Fletcher was trying to find out who ghostwrote her advice column," he said. "Why?"

"Because his wife, Ellen, wrote in to the column

complaining about Burke, and Peaches's answer broke up their marriage."

"And he called you because…" he prompted.

"Because I kind of, you know, let it slip that I might know who her ghost was," I said. "He knew I was never going to tell him, so he pretended to be Howie to get the name out of me."

"I've got to hand it to him," Martin said. "It worked."

"Don't remind me," I said. "Now he's going to come after Zak."

"You mean…?" He mimed strangulation.

"No," I said, "at least I don't think so. He wants to get Zak, as the writer of the horrible so-called advice, to intervene with his wife. To try and save his marriage."

"That doesn't sound so bad."

"You haven't met Burke," I said. "He's a scary guy. Maybe."

"That's what most sensible people say about me. What are you doing?" he whispered, as I shifted SB in my arms and reached for the whimsical globe-in-hand door knocker.

"I have to warn him."

First came Dylan's deep, commanding barks, then the door swung open, revealing a frowning Zak Pryce.

"I just need to, um, warn you about something," I said.

Dylan tried to squeeze past him to greet us all over again. His owner told him to sit, and he did, while still managing to scoot closer to us.

I said, "Okay, so the thing is, you and I talked about Burke Fletcher this morning, remember? I know you consider him dangerous."

"What about him?" Zak asked.

"He, um, he might have figured out that you ghostwrote 'Peaches Preaches,'" I said.

Zak stared at me as this sank in. His voice was flat as he said, "And how would he have figured out something like that?"

I took a deep breath, preparing to fess up.

"Listen, man," Martin said, "it was me. Jane told me in confidence, and like an idiot, I let Fletcher trick me into telling him."

"Padre," I said, "you don't have to—"

"I just wanted to give you a heads-up," he said, "because I think he might be planning to pay you a visit."

Zak gazed down the dark street as he processed this unwelcome information. Finally he said, "Got it," and shut the door in our faces.

Martin and I descended the porch steps and crossed the street to my red Mazda, which I'd parked in front of Peaches's house.

"So that was fun," he said. "What do you want to do now? Get a root canal? Walk barefoot on some Legos?"

"Why did you do that, Padre?" I asked him, over the roof of my car. "I'm a big girl. You don't have to take the blame for my stupid mistakes."

"Maybe I like taking the blame for your stupid mistakes." The corners of his blue eyes crinkled. "Even though, and I know you'll concur, this particular mistake was so monumentally stupid, it put all your other stupid mistakes to shame. And that's saying something. Because you've been known to pull some world-class doozies, am I right?"

I sighed in frustration. Okay, it might have been mock frustration. Between you and me, I was kind of thrilled by the padre's gallantry, though I can't say I was completely surprised. It's not as if this was the first time Martin had performed a selfless act on my behalf.

Something besides Zak's safety was gnawing at me. "You know," I said, "assuming that actually was Burke on the phone…"

Martin finished the thought. "He now knows more about the murder investigation than anyone aside from the cops. Well, and us."

"We sure fed him a lot of information. Which is to say, *I* did." I grimaced, thinking about how many classified details I'd unwittingly supplied during that phone conversation. To a suspect.

"For what it's worth," he said, "the guy really did sound exactly like Howie. But I agree. It wasn't Howie."

I beeped the car. "As soon as I get home, I'll call him and tell him what hap—"

That's when we heard it. An agonized scream—loud, prolonged, and coming from the direction of Peaches's backyard.

We sprinted around the side of the house and behind it, while the anguished screams grew ever more shrill and frantic. I thought it sounded like a male voice, but I couldn't be sure.

As I ran, I groped in my jacket pocket for the self-defense spike Dom had given me. Maybe I should have listened to him and applied for a handgun permit, after all.

The shrieks were coming from the domed, circular solarium, which was unlit, impenetrable darkness cloaking whatever horror awaited us inside. The moon had not yet risen. Weak starlight glinted off the glass structure and its door, which stood wide-open.

When we were a few feet away, Martin halted my progress with a stiff arm. My heart was a battering ram as I watched him cautiously approach the doorway, switch on the tiny flashlight he always carried, and shine it around inside.

"Who's here?" he asked.

The screams turned to hoarse cries of *"Help me! Get this thing off me!"* It was a male voice.

I crept closer, clutching SB to my chest, trying without success to make out the action inside as the flashlight's beam skittered around.

Before Martin could finish asking, "Where's the light switch?" the room lit up.

Sean Moretti stood at the other end of the solarium, near the entrance to the dining room, his hand on the wall switch. He wore a T-shirt decorated with a cannabis leaf—yeah, yeah, Sean, we know you're a fan—and striped boxers. "What the hell's going on down here?" he demanded. "I was on level four of Viking Legionnaire Bloodbath."

He seemed not to notice that his father, Carter Moretti, was lying faceup on the stone floor, pinned by the big potted yucca tree, which had toppled onto him. When I say *pinned*, I mean it in the literal sense. The tree's crown of stiff, swordlike fronds had pierced his face, arms, and torso, and his struggles were only making it worse.

I joined the padre inside the solarium and, after securing SB's leash under a chair leg, assisted him in trying to lift the heavy tree off of Carter, whose caterwauling continued unabated. I yelped as one of the razor-sharp leaves bayonetted my arm, slicing right through my brand-new white denim jacket. Dang, that *hurt*. No wonder Carter was screaming his head off.

"Careful, Jane, those things are like daggers." Martin had been slashed a couple of times himself. "Grab the trunk lower down where it's bare. Sean, give us a hand here."

Sean ignored the request, instead padding barefoot through the scattered soil to examine an object lying next to the tree's white, cubical planter, now tipped onto its side. I didn't pay much attention to him, preoccupied as I was by trying to free his dad from the killer yucca.

"Whoa," Sean said, as he examined his find. "No way."

With a final, backbreaking effort, Martin and I managed to lift the tree off of Carter, whose shrieks gained fresh urgency as the lacerating leaves were yanked from his myriad wounds. The muscles in my arms and shoulders howled as we dropped the tree to the floor next to him. Carter looked like a knife thrower's assistant—if the knife thrower in question was really out of practice. And drunk.

In the next instant, an enraged Sean was shoving something in his father's face. "What are you doing with this, Dad? Huh? I recognize it. It's *Mom's.*"

The object he'd found was a purse, I now saw. A large, beige, hobo-style bag adorned with the Gucci monogram pattern. As we watched, Sean upended the purse and dumped its contents onto Carter, who flinched as Peaches's wallet bounced off his nose. Her cell phone and keys fell on his chest, along with a pair of sunglasses. A lipstick rolled onto the floor.

A blister pack of pills landed next to Carter, a manufacturer's sample by the looks of it. The card was labeled *Zenaproche*, and all ten plastic blisters were empty, the pills having been pushed through the foil backing.

Sean's normally pasty complexion had turned crimson by the time a coiled length of yellow nylon rope tumbled out of the purse. Spittle flew from his lips as he said, "You did it, didn't you? You killed Mom!"

"Sean, I…" Carter mewled. "Let me explain."

The yelling got Sexy Beast riled up. He strained at his leash, barking, until I freed his leash from the chair leg and picked him up.

The last item to drop from Peaches's purse was a folded hunting knife. Martin lunged for it, but the fallen tree tripped him up. In one swift movement, Sean snatched up the knife, opened it, and pressed the four-inch blade to Carter's throat.

"You were trying to frame me, Dad, admit it," he growled. "You were going to plant this stuff here and then what, call in a tip to the cops?"

I eyed the tree's tipped-over planter and the small spade lying next to it, and realized that Carter had, in fact, tried to literally plant the evidence, by burying it in the soil supporting the tree—in the pitch dark while his son was occupied upstairs with his video game. His digging must have unbalanced the yucca, which took its revenge in a most painful manner.

I knew the padre was itching to overpower Sean and disarm him, but he couldn't risk it. It would take about half a second for the kid to slit Carter's throat. I had a feeling he'd do it even if Martin and I simply bolted for the door.

Something crashed to the floor with a wet splat. All eyes turned toward the dining room entrance, where a stunned Audrey Moretti stood taking in the scene. A large plastic food container lay upended at her feet, having disgorged about a gallon of what looked, and smelled, like New England clam chowder.

"Carter?" she said. "Is it true what Sean said?"

"Aw, hell." Carter angled his head to more fully expose his throat. "Do me a favor, son, get it over with."

One might have expected the matriarch of the family to try and defuse the situation. One would have been wrong.

"You tried to *frame* your own son for murder?" She stalked over to Carter, glaring down at him while making not the slightest effort to pacify her knife-wielding grandson. Nor did I witness the slightest hint of concern for her son's injuries. "You were supposed to *burn* this evidence, Carter. Isn't that what I said? What did I say about the purse and the rope and all that?"

"You said to burn it," Carter whimpered.

She crossed her arms. "And did you do as I said? Did you burn it?"

"Mom…"

"Answer me!" she barked.

"Okay, no," he said. "But I had a good reason. I figured that stuff might come in handy."

"Yeah." Sean yanked on Carter's hair, making him wince. "Handy for making your son take the rap for your crime. The cops barely had enough evidence to charge me. Because *hello*, I didn't do it. I would've walked, no problem. But if they found all this crap here?"

"Blame your grandma. If she hadn't opened her big yap to *that one*—" Carter cut his eyes toward me "—and told her all about the DNA and how I'm not your real dad, then her cop buddies wouldn't have called me back in for questioning. They wouldn't have decided I'm all of a sudden a suspect. And then I wouldn't have had to, you know, do what I did tonight."

Audrey rolled her eyes. "It's always the mother's fault."

SB growled low in his throat. I followed his gaze and saw a cat slink into the room, drawn by the irresistible aroma of homemade clam chowder. It started lapping up the creamy soup and was soon joined by two buddies.

I said, "Listen, Sean, the best thing you can do is to let us call the cops. You haven't done anything you can't take back, not yet, and I know you don't want to."

"Oh yeah?" At that moment Sean Moretti appeared fully capable of murder. "There's nothing I want more right now than to slit this loser's throat with Grandpa Gillespey's hunting knife and watch him bleed out. You gonna tell me he doesn't deserve it?"

Martin said, "He deserves to spend the rest of his life in prison. You caught him hiding evidence, Sean. We witnessed it. You're a hero, man."

"Shut up," Sean said. "You're just trying to confuse me. I can't think with all the yapping."

Audrey tossed her hand toward the padre and me. "What are those two doing here, anyway?"

Sean shrugged. "Who knows?"

As if he hadn't witnessed us laboriously heaving that lethal yucca tree off of his dad. I said, "We heard the, uh, commotion and rushed over to help."

Sean nodded toward the wooden bench Dom and I had occupied nearly a week earlier. "Sit over there till I figure out what to do with you."

I didn't like the sound of that, but since his knife never strayed from his father's throat, we obediently sat, with the downed yucca tree forming a kind of barrier between us and the others. SB wanted to be let down to explore, but I kept him on my lap.

I noticed that all the wicker furniture in the room had been cleaned and the cushions replaced. The dead plants were gone, the glass was spotless, and the stone floor scrubbed. Considering the events of the last few minutes, Audrey probably regretted the effort she'd invested on that last part.

Her gaze flicked between the rope and us, as if calculating whether there was enough to tie us with. I felt the padre tense. While it was true both of us wanted Carter's carotids to remain intact, there was no way we were going to sit still and let Audrey tie us up. Once we were helpless, what was to stop Sean from doing us in, as well?

"Why'd you do it, Dad? That's what I want to know." Sean punctuated this question with a tiny jab from the tip of the knife.

Carter stiffened, though no blood was drawn. "I—I didn't—It was self-defense."

His son uttered a ripe curse. "You tied her to a chair and strangled her. How is that self-defense?"

"Take that knife away and let me sit up," Carter said. "I'll explain—"

Sean pressed the knife blade more firmly against his father's throat, but only after flipping it over so he was using the blunt side. Carter didn't know that, though. He yipped in terror and said, "Okay, okay. The thing you have to understand is that *she* tried to kill *me*. It's why she lured me up to that disgusting old attic."

I looked at the padre. He looked at me, his skeptical expression mirroring mine. SB's eloquent snort said it all.

Audrey, however, appeared unsurprised by this statement. She settled herself on a pretty wicker armchair, *tsk*ing at the clam chowder staining the legs of her bright pink slacks.

"You're lying," Sean said. "She already dumped you. Why would she try to off you, too?"

"Well, there's something you don't know about your mother." Carter swallowed hard, his Adam's apple bobbing. "Now, don't get upset and, um, do something rash. I swear what I'm about to tell you is true. Peaches… well, she wasn't always what you might call an upstanding citizen."

"I know she was a hooker when she was young," Sean said.

Audrey leapt out of her seat. *"What?"*

"And I know about the customers she blackmailed, too," he continued. "I hacked her computer when I was, like, ten. Who cares?"

"*I* care!" his grandmother said. "Carter, how long have you known about this?"

"Uh… it doesn't matter," he mumbled. "It was way, way in the past. And she was a high-class call girl, not a hooker. There's a difference."

Sean laughed. "Check it out, Grandma. Dad was one of her customers. That's how they met."

Audrey took a moment to let that sink in, then dropped back onto the chair. "She seemed like such a nice girl when you two started going out."

"Yeah, well, that 'nice girl' promised me she stopped selling her body when we got serious," Carter said. "And I believed her."

"At least she was getting paid for it," Sean said, "so I mean, good for her. But then she started giving it away and turned into your basic slut."

"Don't talk about your mother that way," Carter said.

"Really, dude?" Sean wiggled the knife.

Audrey said, "And blackmail on top of all that? So then, the money from her father…"

"There was no money from her father," Carter said. "The old man didn't have anything but the house. We lived on the, uh, the other."

I said, "The detectives must have asked you where her money came from."

"I told them Peaches took care of the finances and that as far as I knew, it was all from her dad. I acted like I had no clue—a total dummy."

What a stretch, I thought. *And they fell for it?*

"Meanwhile," he said, "I was collecting these blackmail payments every month."

"Even after she died?" I asked.

"Sure," he said. "I mean, no one knew she was dead. The guys kept coughing up the cash, right on schedule."

Sean grinned. "Suckers."

Audrey frowned. "How much money did you receive from these men while you were living with me?"

"Well, that first month, November," he said, "after Peaches kicked me out, she collected it herself, so it went right into her bank account. But then after she was dead, before anybody *knew* she was dead, I started making the collections again. Only, I didn't deposit the cash. I kept it. No way are those guys gonna keep paying now that she's gone. I guess you could say I killed the golden goose."

"How much?" Audrey demanded.

"Forty-one grand a month," he said meekly. "A hundred sixty-four thousand total."

His mother flushed a deep red. "Where was that money when you were eating my food, Carter? Sponging off my Social Security? Where was it when I wiped out my retirement savings to bail out your son?"

"He's not really my—"

"You didn't think I could have used some of that money?" Her eyes bulged in outrage.

"It would've drawn attention, don't you see?" he said. "If I started throwing money around. I was gonna share it with you once things cooled down."

Sean said, "Once *I* got locked up for a murder *you* did, you mean. You weren't gonna share that money with Grandma. You were gonna disappear. That was your bug-out cash."

"I swear, Mom," Carter whined. "I was gonna pay you back and then some. I still will if I can somehow get out of this." He cut his eyes toward Martin and me. The hairs on my nape stood up and shook their little fists at him.

"Where's that money now?" Sean asked.

"Lose the knife and we can talk about it," Carter said.

His son's response was to nick him again, this time hard enough to produce a tiny bead of blood. Carter sucked in a breath, but his obdurate expression said he had no intention of revealing the location of the cash.

I kept surreptitiously glancing outside, hoping to spy a cop or two, hoping one of the neighbors had heard Carter's screams and called 911. Barring immediate rescue, I figured our best bet was to try and keep the three generations of Morettis talking as long as possible.

"Answer my question," Sean said. "How'd Mom end up dead?"

"Remember Thanksgiving?" Carter asked. "How mean she was to me? How she ran me down in front of all the relatives?"

Sean cackled. "That was awesome. One thing about Mom, she really knew how to stick it to someone."

Audrey sat up straight. "Well, that particular someone was your father. She should've shown more respect."

"News flash, Grandma," Sean said. "This loser's not my father. And if he was any kind of real man, he'd never have let his woman run around on him."

Said the young man who was cheating with his girlfriend's bestie. I sensed a double standard at work here. And no, I did not point that out, much as I was itching to.

"Okay, so anyway," Carter said, "I was really steamed, and I took Peaches aside before dessert and told her she better start paying me support, and keep paying me, or I was gonna tell everybody about the prostitution and blackmail. Including the cops."

In other words, he'd decided to blackmail the shrewd, experienced blackmailer who had at least thirty IQ points on him. What could possibly go wrong?

"Lemme guess," Sean said. "She laughed in your face."

"Yeah, she did," he said, "at first. But then when she's getting ready to leave, she takes me out to the back porch and says the only reason she was so bitchy was 'cause she's been missing me so much, and my threat was the 'wake-up call' she needed to get her head on straight. She tells me she's sorry for everything and wants me back."

"Why didn't you tell me about this at the time?" Audrey asked.

"Because Peaches said not to. She wanted her and me to do something first, something romantic that we did just once, years ago when we were first dating. She wanted us to meet in the Historical Society attic the next night and, um, you know… 'rekindle the magic.'"

"Gross, dude," Sean said.

"But it has to be like the first time, she says. Totally secret. No one can know, no one can see us go in. She told me to meet her at the building at two a.m., and exactly where to park my car—a few blocks away behind a vacant store. Also she made me promise to wear a disguise, just in case anyone saw me. You know, fake mustache, hat, glasses."

Sean snorted in derision. "Dork."

"Yeah, well, I didn't do it," he said. "And I caught hell from Peaches for that, but I couldn't see the point. I mean, it was two a.m. in the morning, for crying out loud. Why all the sneaking around? We weren't kids anymore. Well, except that we *were* kind of breaking into the building in the middle of the night."

Martin spoke up. "How did you get in?"

"Peaches's mom used to be president of the Historical Society," he said. "When Peaches was a teenager, she snuck off with the keys and made copies. Mrs. Gillespey never knew."

I said, "Did Peaches wear a disguise that night?"

"Yeah, she had on these sunglasses," he said, meaning the ones that had fallen from her purse onto his chest. "I mean, sunglasses in the middle of the night? 'Cause there's nothing weird about that, right? And a blonde wig."

"A wig!" Audrey stabbed a finger toward her son. "You never told me about any wig. You were supposed to take everything of hers out of that attic, in case it could lead the authorities to you. You didn't think that included a *disguise*?"

"I panicked and forgot about the wig, all right?" he said.

"Just like you panicked and forgot to take the bottle of soda with you," she said.

"It rolled onto the floor. Come on, Mom, it was disgusting up there. And dark. What did you want me to do, get down on my hands and knees and grope around for it?"

"Yes! Yes, you should have gotten down on your hands and knees and found the darn thing. I suppose I should be grateful you at least told me about it, so when the detectives asked if we drink black cherry soda, I knew to say no, and to make sure you did the same." She scowled at me. "So that's why you were asking about a wig, Jane. Because when you found Peaches, she was wearing one."

What could I do except nod and say, "That's right, Audrey. I didn't realize it was a, um, disguise."

"Once we got inside the building," Carter said, "I told Peaches she should go ahead and take off the wig, but she said she wanted to leave it on. Fine with me. I figured it was some kind of kinky sex thing."

"Dude!" Sean barked.

So it was okay for him to call his mom a slut, but any suggestion that his parents had a sex life was gross. Got it.

"Sorry," Carter said. "Anyway, I wanted our date to be real romantic, so I brought all this stuff with me. Champagne, scented candles, chocolate-dipped strawberries. Peaches always liked fancy stuff like that. I was thinking it was gonna be magical, a new beginning, like she said. But I gotta tell you, the place was just plain nasty. Not even a decent place to sit, much less, well…"

I thought of the two rusted iron bedsteads I'd seen up there, with their filthy bedding. I suspected that attic had been just as grotty a quarter century earlier, but back then, Peaches and Carter had been a couple of horny kids barely out of their teens, living with their parents, and willing to put up with a lot for the sake of privacy.

"There was this plug-in radiator up there," he added, "and I turned that on because I was freezing my—I was really cold."

I said, "I'm guessing that when you left the attic, you forgot to turn it off."

Carter started to nod until the presence of the knife blade reminded him that wasn't a good idea. "Didn't realize it until they said Peaches got all, you know, mummified. Because of the dry heat."

"It was a blessing in disguise," Audrey said, "him leaving that radiator on. I was thinking that after a week or so, she was going to start to stink, and if it was noticeable in the rest of the building, then someone would go up there to investigate. But Carter's forgetfulness paid off, for once. It bought some time, anyway. Not that it made any difference in the long run."

I didn't like the way she was looking at Martin and me, and wondered if there might be a gun somewhere in the house. That was Grandpa Gillespey's hunting knife Sean was threatening his dad with, so it was possible the old man had kept a rifle or shotgun in the house. For that matter, I wouldn't have been surprised to learn that Peaches herself had owned a weapon.

I decided in that instant that if Audrey left the room for any reason, we'd hightail it out of there, call 911, and hope Sean's self-protective instinct would override his desire for revenge. After all, killing his father in cold blood would result in an extended, possibly permanent, return to the slammer.

Feline growls and hisses drew my attention to the dining room entrance, where five cats now laid claim to the puddle of clam chowder.

Martin said, "So, Carter, you brought the champagne and all that, but who brought the black cherry soda?"

"Peaches," he said. "Who do you think? I was happy at first, you know, that she cared enough to bring my favorite drink. She insisted on popping the cap for me. Later I realized she did that so I wouldn't notice the cap was a little loose."

"Because she'd already opened it?" the padre said.

"Yeah. So she could add her extra-special secret ingredient." Carter groped at his side for the empty sample pack of Zenaproche, which he wagged. "She must've dissolved all of these in that bottle. Probably figured the soda would kill the taste. She figured wrong. I took one sip and said jeez, must be a bad batch. She said, nah, nah, try a little more, I'll bet it's this musty old place messing with your taste buds. Then she pretended to take a sip and said it tasted fine to her."

"Where did Peaches get the Zenaproche?" I asked.

"From Evie," he said. "That's her job, hawking drugs to doctors so they'll prescribe them. She gave some samples of those pills to her mom, hoping they'd, you know, calm her down. Worked like a charm, huh?"

"I've, like, *begged* Evie for samples," Sean griped. "But would she ever?"

"So what happened then?" Martin asked. "After you realized something was wrong with the soda?"

"Well, we argued about it, 'cause she just wouldn't let it go, you know? You're being silly, she says, drink the damn soda. I go, you're so sure nothing's wrong with it, drink it yourself. Only, when I tip the bottle to her mouth, she blocks it with her hand and I lose my grip and it rolls into a corner."

"Peaches couldn't have been happy about that," I said.

"She says, you idiot, I went to all that trouble, and for what. *You* went to all that trouble? I say. Who brought the champagne and chocolate-covered strawberries? Which, by the way, she never touched. I'm just saying."

"Like it would kill her to eat one strawberry," Audrey said. With no irony whatsoever.

"So I'm ready to book it out of there," Carter said, "but I just can't get over how weird Peaches is acting, even for her. I mean, that she even thought a date in that disgusting place would be a good idea. And then her freak-out over the soda. It began to dawn on me that something wasn't right."

Oh, now *it began to dawn on you*, I thought. "So what did you do?"

"I grabbed her purse and looked inside," he said.

"She must have tried to stop you," I said.

"Sure, for all the good it did her. I might not be playing football for Fordham anymore, but there's still plenty of muscle under here." He patted his soft midsection.

"What did you find in her purse?" Martin asked.

"The stuff you see here, basically. The empty pill pack, the rope, and, uh, this knife. Son, do you think you could just ease up—" He broke off as Sean did the opposite of easing up. "No? Okay, doesn't hurt to ask, right?"

"So her plan was to do what?" I said. "Sedate you so you couldn't fight back and then…?"

Audrey said, "Isn't it obvious? She was going to tie him up and then stab him or slit his throat or something. To keep him from squealing to the cops about her blackmail scheme. Not that I knew anything about the blackmail until tonight. All Carter told me was that Peaches went nuts and tried to kill him for no reason."

"Once I found her, you know, murder supplies," Carter said, "she really did go nuts. Tried to grab the knife and stab me. But like I said, she was no match for me, physically. Which is how come she tried to get me to drink that soda with the Zeenapoche… Zennapooch…"

"Zenaproche," Martin said.

"Yeah, that stuff," Carter said. "The names they give these drugs, jeez. So at that point, all I want is to get out of there, but she's fighting like crazy to keep me from leaving."

Sean said, "She knew you'd go straight to the cops about the blackmail."

"I wouldn't have, though," Carter said. "I was bluffing the whole time. I mean, I was involved too deep in that scheme for too many years. If I'd turned her in, I'd have gone down right along with her."

Not necessarily, I thought. If he had a good lawyer—the well-favored Carlos Levine, Esquire, sprang to mind—then perhaps Carter's cooperation with the authorities could have resulted in a favorable plea deal on the bribery charges.

"Peaches was totally out of control," he continued. "Punching, kicking. She even picked up this old fireplace poker and went after me with that."

Martin and I exchanged a look. He'd used that same poker to lift Peaches's wig when we'd thought it was a small, elegantly coiffed animal perched on her face.

"Finally I managed to get her onto this chair," he said, "and tie her to it with the rope she brought. All I wanted was for her to calm down enough to listen to me, so I could tell her I wasn't really gonna turn her in. But she never backed down. There she is, tied up, completely helpless, and she's slicing me to ribbons with that nasty mouth of hers. Going on about how stupid I am, how gullible, how I'm not a real man. It was ten times worse than at Thanksgiving."

"Ouch," Sean said.

"Peaches always knew how to push my buttons," Carter said, "and boy, did she push them that night. I felt myself losing control, but she never let up for a second, wouldn't give me even that long to catch my breath. She was wearing this silk scarf around her neck, and I tried to push the material into her mouth. Like a gag, you know? She bit my hand. Hard."

Even knowing where this story was heading, Sean snickered. I'd never hated him more.

"Before I knew what was happening," Carter continued, "I was twisting that scarf tight around her neck, just trying to get her to shut up." He paused, his chest pumping as if he'd run the hundred-yard dash. "It was her fault. You see that, right? She tried to kill me, and then, then she just would not shut up."

No one spoke for a full minute. We all just sat there avoiding one another's eyes. Finally I said, "Audrey, how did you get involved?"

"Well, Carter called me from the attic," she said, "in a panic. He told me what happened. Not all the details, mind you, but the gist."

"You must have been shocked," I said.

"In a way," she said, "I was half expecting something terrible to happen. If you'd known Peaches, you'd understand. I'm not saying I'm glad she's dead, but I'm grateful things didn't go her way."

"What did you do when he called you?" I asked. "I know you told him not to leave anything up there that she brought with her."

Audrey nodded. "And to wipe the place down for fingerprints. Also to search her pockets for anything that could lead the authorities to him. We checked Peaches's garage and saw that her car was there. I assume she walked to the Historical Society—it's about two and a half, three miles from here. A taxi would have been too risky, considering what she had planned. I made Carter stay home and out of sight for a couple of weeks until his bruises healed."

I recalled Lee Romano's words from her TV show that evening. *Her killer would have walked away bruised and scratched, at the very least.* She was right.

Martin said, "What I want to know is, why did you leave Peaches in the attic? Why not move the body to some remote location? Bury it in the woods or something?"

"That sounds good in theory," Audrey said, "but when you think about it, there were too many risks involved, too many places where trace evidence could be shed. With the sophisticated forensic tools the police have? It would have been like leaving a trail of breadcrumbs from that attic all the way to the disposal site."

"Let me guess," I said. "You're a fan of those true-crime shows."

"Well, they're certainly a lot more entertaining and educational than most of the garbage that's on TV nowadays," she said. "And as for leaving Peaches in a remote location, that attic kind of fit the bill. No one ever went up there, and since her body didn't decompose in the usual way, who knows how long she would have remained undiscovered? If you two hadn't gone up there for your own little romantic getaway—"

"It wasn't like that," I said. "We were just looking for a quiet place to… Aw, forget it."

"Peaches chose that attic because she knew how isolated it was," Audrey said. She took pains to make sure no one saw either of them enter the building. And obviously she planned to leave Carter's body up there. She certainly couldn't have moved him by herself."

"So her plan worked," Martin said, "only, not in the way she envisioned."

Without warning, Sexy Beast gave a sharp, imperious bark and catapulted himself off my lap, bounding gazelle-like over the fallen yucca tree trunk and across Carter's supine form.

SB's abrupt flight startled everyone, including Sean, who jerked backward and watched the small dog sprint toward the dining room entrance.

It was all the invitation Martin needed. He sprang off the bench, leaping over the yucca obstacle course to tackle Sean. The young man howled in pain as the padre slammed his knife hand into the stone floor, dislodging his grip on the weapon. Within seconds, he'd flipped Sean onto his stomach and secured his wrists with the yellow rope.

Audrey started to rise, until Martin snarled, "Sit down!" After a moment's hesitation, she obeyed, her expression resigned. Carter didn't even attempt to sit up but simply lay there, weak with relief. I pulled my phone out of my pocket and called 911.

As for Sexy Beast, some affronts were simply too much to bear. He'd tolerated the chowder-loving cats, just barely, but his patience had its limits. And those limits were currently being tested by the biggest raccoon I'd ever seen. We're talking forty pounds, easy.

The cats appeared well acquainted with this hefty fellow, who'd no doubt spent the winter bulking up on the cat food Audrey had been putting out, not to mention the odd half-eaten sandwich and bowl of cereal Sean had left lying around. The felines ate alongside the masked bandit, paying it no mind as it selected the choicest morsels of clam and potato, shoving each tidbit into its mouth with its delicate little hands and chewing with loud smacking noises.

Sexy Beast made a show of scolding the newcomer, for all the good it did him. The big guy probably thought my precious poodle was a cat with a glandular disorder.

"Well, for goodness' sake," Audrey said, "I don't think I've ever seen that one before." She sighed. "Another mouth to feed."

17

A Slot Machine in Church

ELLEN FLETCHER TAPPED her phone. "Who wants to hear the last 'Peaches Preaches' letter ever published?"

Martin made a face. "Please. I'm eating."

I produced a dramatic groan, but I must admit, my curiosity was piqued. And if it didn't bother Ellen to read it, who was I to object to hearing it?

Burke gave his wife an indulgent smile. "All right, darling," he said, in that charming British accent which no longer put me in mind of a cannibalistic serial killer, "but after this, let's agree never to utter that horrid woman's name again."

"Fine with me." Like her husband, Ellen was in her early sixties. She was petite, with lively brown eyes and long, light brown hair streaked with gray.

The four of us occupied a round, blond-wood table in the Janey's Place vegetarian café, next to the big picture windows looking out onto Main Street, Crystal Harbor's quaint shopping district. I sat between Martin and Burke, and across from Ellen. We were the only customers in the place. It was about eight p.m. on a Wednesday in early May, one month after the Attack of the Killer Yucca.

In the two or three minutes before the cops had responded

to my 911 call that night, Martin had a short, pointed conversation with the Morettis. Apparently he saw little point in Sean being arrested along with his dad and grandma. He offered to untie Sean's wrists and cast him as the hero of the evening's strange drama, the brave soul who'd thwarted Carter's plan to plant evidence and subvert the murder investigation.

Audrey, unsurprisingly, was more than happy to go along with this version of events—anything to protect her beloved, misunderstood grandson. For his part, Carter grudgingly agreed not to mention the unpleasantness involving his son, his throat, and Grandpa Gillespey's hunting knife, once it was made clear it would be his word against that of everyone else present. Well, except for the dog, the cats, and Jabba the Raccoon, and they were too busy licking the floor clean to squeal to the cops.

And yes, failure to mention the knife thing meant I was officially lying to the police, but it was a lie of omission, so not that bad, right?

Evie had kicked her brother out of the family home and was in the process of restoring it to its previous elegance. This meant Sean was once again living with his father and grandmother, who'd both been released on bail. Carter had confessed to killing Peaches, yet on the advice of his attorney, Carlos Levine, had pleaded not guilty. Apparently you can do that. I had little doubt he'd be convicted. Audrey had been charged as an accessory after the fact.

A determination to move out of his grandmother's basement had prompted Sean to get his first ever honest-to-God job. He was now a busboy at The Harbor Room, a local restaurant and Crystal Harbor institution dating from the 1840s. Amazingly, he'd managed to hold the job for three weeks now and was making noises about wanting to become a waiter. That aspiration wouldn't be realized at The Harbor Room, which only hired experienced servers. But if Sean worked hard and stayed out of trouble, he could probably learn on the job at one of the chain restaurants. I was pleasantly surprised to discover he had some ambition. I hoped it would last.

As for the $164,000 in blackmail bucks Carter had collected from Peaches's former clients during the previous few months, it was anyone's guess as to where he'd stashed it. I imagined him fantasizing about the day in some distant future when he'd be a free man and could make use of his bug-out cash, as Sean had called it. So much for paying his mom back for all her sacrifices.

And yes, Ellen and Burke Fletcher were now back together. Imagine my relief when it turned out Burke had nothing to do with Peaches's death and that therefore I had not inadvertently provided her murderer with sensitive information about the investigation. Burke readily admitted to impersonating Howie on the phone. The only thing he cared about, as it happened, was the identity of Peaches's ghostwriter. Once he had that, he lost no time contacting Zak and making his case.

Zak was skeptical at first that Burke was the concerned, loving husband he made himself out to be, but his conscience wouldn't let him ignore the role he'd played in driving the couple apart. Zak managed to visit Ellen at a time when her sister, Trish, wasn't home, and found her to be desperately unhappy. Would you believe it? All those crystals and herbs had failed to cure her.

Ellen missed her husband and dreaded the upcoming divorce, but was in such an emotional black hole that she was helpless to halt its progress. Zak managed to arrange a meeting between Ellen and Burke, which led to their reconciliation. Happily, Ellen was now back in her own home and receiving the treatment she needed. When I'd first met her, she'd offered heartfelt thanks for the role I'd played in helping to reunite her with her husband.

Seeing them together, observing how they doted on each other, I'd come to realize their relationship was in no way one-sided. Burke needed Ellen in his life as much as she needed him.

Ellen brought up the online edition of *You Know It* magazine on her phone. "By popular demand, 'Peaches Preaches,' the final chapter. 'Dear Peaches,'" she read, "'My friend Arnie knows I'm always short on cash, so he told me about this ad firm called Headboards that pays people to have their clients' advertising logos tattooed onto their foreheads.'"

"Wait," I said. "No."

Ellen turned her phone toward me so I could see she wasn't making it up.

"Good grief," I said. "Continue."

"'The pay was supposed to be pretty good,'" she read, "'and it turned out Headboards was looking for someone to advertise my favorite brand of beer, so I figured it was meant to be. The truth is, I was kind of proud to be associated with Schnook Brewing, even in this small way. The company's founder, Augustus Schnook, died in 1903, but I like to think he was looking down from heaven and giving me a big thumbs-up when I showed the tattoo artist what I wanted. At that moment, I'd never felt more like a Schnook.'"

"I've gotta say, the guy knows his beer," Martin said. "That Schnook IPA is just the thing on a hot summer day."

"I'm a fan of Schnook wheat beer," Burke said.

"Nobody cares, gentlemen," I said. "Let the lady finish."

"Thank you, Jane," Ellen said. "Where was I? Ah yes. 'So I get my forehead tattooed, and I have to say, it looks great. The

Schnook logo, in all caps and full color, with the clinking beer steins and everything. I was so proud, I walked right into the Headboards headquarters, thinking I'm going to walk out with a nice, fat check, right? Imagine my surprise when they tell me the tattoo was supposed to be one of those temporary ones. Like a decal that washes off.'"

"Wait, you can get tattoos that, like, wash off?" It was Cheyenne O'Rourke, who'd clomped over to our table in her five-inch platform pumps with a water pitcher.

Cheyenne's neck sported two permanent tattoos: the name *Brian* on one side and *Sean* on the other, both names now overlaid with big *X*'s, which were themselves executed in permanent tattoo ink. Which meant Sean, unlike the tattoo bearing his name, had been a fleeting part of Cheyenne's life. Did she even remember pleading with me to help prove his innocence? Oh well, she had plenty of forehead space left for the next boyfriend.

Thoughts of my promise to Cheyenne brought to mind my failed quest on behalf of Evie Moretti, an actual paying client. I'd wanted so badly to find that collection of peach tchotchkes, I'd *needed* to find them, and I'd failed. For me, those peaches would forever be The One That Got Away.

"Cheyenne," I said, "I'm still waiting for my cauliflower-crust pizza." I figured it couldn't hurt to give it a try, since Janey's Place didn't serve regular pizza.

"You ordered pizza?" she said.

"Yes, and everyone else got their food twenty minutes ago. This is the third time I've reminded you."

I'd insisted the others not wait for me. Ellen had eaten half her veggie lettuce wraps, Burke was almost done with his Thai coconut vegetable curry, and Martin had finished his black bean and rice burrito.

Ellen said, "Miss, can I get a box for my leftovers?"

"Jeez, one thing at a time," Cheyenne griped. "Lemme get her tofu teriyaki first." She clomped off before I could correct her, and without refilling our water glasses.

Martin said, "Why doesn't Dom fire that girl?"

"Because he's a nice guy." I used to consider that one of my ex's more charming traits. "How does the letter end, Ellen?"

"'The company refuses to pay me,'" she read, "'and now I have this permanent advertisement on my face, and I can't afford to have it removed. My girlfriend left me, my dog won't let me near him, and I lost my job as a cashier at the educational toy store. I mean, I like Schnook beer and everything, but I'm in a real pickle here and I don't know what to do.' Signed, 'Schnook for Life.'"

"And the response?" Burke washed down a forkful of curry with a sip of green lemonade, which was normal lemonade blended with spinach, cucumber, and who knew what other ungodly substances. I had to look away.

"'Dear Schnook,'" Ellen read, "'I could suggest you grow bangs. Maybe develop a signature look, like a cowboy hat. Or a bandana headband. Or a hardhat. But those would only be temporary solutions, when what you need is something as permanent as the preposterous facial art you've saddled yourself with for the rest of your days. I'm guessing this isn't the first moronically self-destructive life choice you've made, and for sure it won't be the last. With that in mind, there's only one thing to do, and that is to embrace your brainlessness and go all out with the ink. Do you like Cheetos with your beer? Have that logo tattooed onto your left cheek. What about Skittles? That one goes on the right side. And think about all the other fleshy real estate you can sacrifice to the cause. I hear freak shows are a thing again. There's your new career. Now, excuse me while I pop open a nice, frosty bottle of Schnook Pale Ale and try to forget that half-wits like you have the right to vote.'"

I lifted my water glass. "To Peaches. She was one of a kind."

We clinked glasses. Burke said, "I hope Satan has a strong constitution."

"And a hot fire," Ellen added.

"Shouldn't we be toasting Zak?" Martin said. "He's the one who wrote that column."

"Peaches had to approve everything," I reminded him. "She rejected any answers that had a spark of human decency."

"He has his own advice column now, though," he said.

Burke shook his head. "The magazine canceled it."

"Why?" I asked.

"Too much human decency," he said. "The very opposite of what the readers want. Or what they'd come to expect, at any rate."

Burke and Ellen had become friends with Zak, who'd received multiple offers for his Crystal Harbor house, which was now in contract. He'd just moved to the Brooklyn brownstone he'd purchased, located about a half hour from the Fletchers' home in Queens. The handcrafted birdhouse Ellen had presented him with as a housewarming gift was a replica of the poet Dylan Thomas's green-painted writing shed. Zak had gratefully taken her up on her offer to help decorate his new home.

After Zak met with the detectives and came clean about the events surrounding his wife, Stacey's, death, Howie revisited the original files, spoke to other officers familiar with the case, and concluded that the original finding of accidental death was, in fact, legitimate. He no longer harbored suspicions that Zak had something to do with it.

I'd sensed that Zak suffered pangs of guilt for not having saved Stacey. More recently, though, he seemed like a happier, more centered person. It was as if, by helping Ellen, he'd found a measure of redemption.

"Speaking of human decency," Ellen said, "I saw on the news that your town's mayoral election was overturned."

"That was some scandal," Burke said. "Tampering with ballots. *Buying* votes. In quaint, affluent Crystal Harbor, no less."

"Nina Wallace has always specialized in dirty tricks," I said. "She upped her game in this election and it backfired. The Town Council voted to reinstate Sophie Halperin, who received the majority of for-real votes. Sophie's been great for this town. I wish we could make her mayor for life."

Ellen peered under the table. "What's that you have there, Martin? You've been shopping at Beatrice & Daughters?" Which was an upscale baby store there on Main Street.

Sheepishly he lifted the small, cream-colored shopping bag adorned with the silver Beatrice & Daughters logo. "I know it's a little early. The baby's not coming till the fall, but, well…" He parted the froth of silver tissue paper sticking out of the bag and displayed his purchase, a little, white stuffed lamb.

"Are you going to be a daddy?" she asked.

"A grandpa." He passed the lamb to me so I could admire its adorableness. "My daughter, Lexie, is due in September."

"You're a young grandpa," she said.

"I was a teen dad." His expression softened fractionally as I handed back the toy, telling me he saw through my struggle to suppress the onslaught of emotion.

My eyes stung, and I knew if I tried to speak, the words would catch in my throat. Martin reached under the table, found my hand, and squeezed it. And didn't let go. Had anything in my life ever felt so comforting? His touch smoothed out the sharp, relentless yearning for a child of my own, made it something I could hold, examine from all angles, and tuck back into its dark corner of my psyche.

Ellen made us promise to let her know when the baby arrived. Interestingly, she addressed us as if we were a couple, although I knew I'd introduced Martin as my "friend."

Burke put down his fork. "I'm just going to come right out and say this."

"Uh-oh," Ellen said. "That's the scariest sentence in the English language, coming from my husband."

"I just might have some information the police would be interested in," he said, "only I'd prefer not to explain to them how I came by it."

I frowned. "Information regarding Peaches's murder?"

"Naturally."

"But that was solved, remember?" I said. "What could they need to know at this point that they don't already know?"

"The location of what I have to assume is evidence," he said.

"More evidence?" I said. "Um, how did you come by this information, if I might ask?"

"Oh brother." Ellen addressed me. "This is a wild guess, but you probably don't want him to answer that."

"Nonsense," he said. "We're all friends here. Jane, do you remember when you accused me of stalking Peaches, and I denied it? Well, I didn't come right out and deny it, but certainly I led you to believe my actions never went further than harassment."

"Yes, I remember," I said.

"I lied." Burke blotted his mouth with his napkin. "I stalked that witch from the get-go. Whenever I wasn't with a client, I could usually be found watching her house or following her to various locations. Well, except that I *wouldn't* be found doing these things because as it turned out, I was quite good at it. Perhaps I missed my calling. I should have been a spy."

Ellen's smile was crooked. "What am I going to do with you, Burke?"

"Anything your heart desires, darling." He lifted her hand and kissed it. "I am forever at your service."

Martin asked, "What did you hope to gain by stalking Peaches?"

"Anything I could use as leverage to get her to undo the damage she'd inflicted on Ellen and our marriage," he said. "I reckoned I'd know it when I saw it."

So Carter hadn't been the only one looking to blackmail the blackmailer. "I'm guessing you came up empty," I said.

"Sadly, yes, although it all came out right in the end, thanks to Zak. Something else happened, though, something intriguing. It was Friday, the twenty-first of March. Well, technically Saturday the twenty-second since it was nearly three in the morning."

"That was a week before Peaches's body was discovered," I said.

"That's right," he said. "She'd been missing for nearly four months. I'd stopped watching her house, of course, but occasionally I'd drive out to Audrey Moretti's place and see what Carter was up to. I suppose I hoped he'd slip up and reveal something useful. Of the two of them, he was definitely the weak link."

"You spied on him in the middle of the night?" Martin asked. "Man, that's dedication."

"'Obsession' would be more accurate. What else did I have to do?" His gentle gaze settled on his wife. "I didn't have one decent night's sleep the entire time Ellen was gone."

"Same here," she said.

"So what was Carter up to at three in the morning?" Martin asked.

"He got into his car and drove off," Burke said, "so naturally I followed him."

"Where to?" I asked. *Please don't say—*

"The Historical Society."

He said it! "No no no no no." I raised my palms as if that would make him take back his words. The thought of Carter creeping up to that attic in the middle of the night to check on the progress of his victim's mummification was more than I could stomach.

Speaking of stomach…

I peered toward the food-service counter. Cheyenne was nowhere to be seen. At that point I'd have settled for the tofu slop she'd mentioned.

"For heaven's sake," Ellen said, "I hope you don't mean he returned to the scene of the crime."

"Not exactly," her husband said. "He never went into the building."

Well, that was something. "What did he do, then?" I asked.

"I assume you know the Historical Society sits on seven acres," he said. "There are gardens, a pond, and a thatched-roof children's cottage."

"Children's cottage?" Ellen said.

I explained, "The wealthy farmer who built the two-hundred-year-old stone house that the Historical Society now occupies also built this pretty little play house for his kids. Well, it's not that little. A single room, maybe twenty by twenty feet. The inside is like a miniature nineteenth-century home, furnished with child-size furniture and toys. It's some distance from the main building."

"It sounds delightful," Ellen said. "I'd love to explore it."

"Unfortunately," I said, "it's not open to the public. They keep it locked. There are lots of windows, though, so you can view the interior. I like to imagine the children and their nanny spending hours playing in there."

"Carter never suspected I was following him," Burke said, "first by car, then on foot. There was a half-moon, which provided just enough light for me to see him remove something from the trunk of his car and make his way across the property to the cottage. He let himself in, though I haven't a clue where he got the key."

"Peaches had all the Historical Society keys," Martin said, "from when her mom was the president. It's how she and Carter got into the building the night he killed her."

"Ah," Burke said, "mystery solved. Once he was inside, I approached the cottage and peeked through a window. He was using one of those lantern-type flashlights that illuminates the entire room."

Martin snorted. "Amateur."

"Did you get a good look at the object he took out of his trunk?" I asked. "Did it look like a woman's handbag? Beige, with the Gucci logo all over it?"

"No, it was a white plastic grocery sack," he said. "I couldn't see what was in it, though it stands to reason it's connected to the murder. Otherwise, why go to such lengths to conceal it?"

"What did he do with the sack?" I asked.

"First he reached up inside the fireplace chimney," Burke said, "and pulled a black backpack out of it."

"Out of the *chimney*?" Ellen said.

"Not a bad hiding spot," Martin said.

"I agree," Burke said. "The cottage is kept locked, and that fireplace probably hasn't been used in well over a century, so there's little chance of the backpack being discovered. Carter put the grocery bag inside it and replaced it in the chimney."

"We have no way of knowing whether the backpack is still there," Martin said. "He might have moved it before he was arrested."

"I can't call in this tip," Burke said, "even using someone else's voice. The detectives are on to that. And I have no desire to field inconvenient questions on the subject of stalking. But, Jane, you could tell your pal Howie about an anonymous tip you received."

"Why did you wait so long to bring this up?" I asked.

"Because I assumed the police would have checked the cottage already, that Carter would have told them about it. Have you heard of evidence being retrieved from there?" he asked. When I shook my head, he said, "Nor have I, and I'm beginning to think that whatever is in that chimney, it's going to remain up there until that backpack rots and its contents drop into the fireplace."

A FEW MINUTES LATER, we paid for our food—Cheyenne

tried to charge me for both the pizza and the tofu slop, though I'd been served neither—and said our goodbyes, with promises to get together soon. It was after nine p.m. and fully dark.

Martin had driven us there in his 1966 candy-apple-red Mustang convertible. A sexy ride for a sexy man. I produced my phone while he was still pulling out of his parking spot on the street, and started to call Howie.

He reached over and snatched the phone out of my hand.

"Why'd you do that?" I demanded.

"You don't have to call him right away. An hour won't make any difference."

"Wait a minute." It dawned on me that he wasn't driving toward my house. He was driving toward—

"*No*, Padre." I tried without success to retrieve my phone, prompting him to slide it into the back pocket of his jeans, with a silky little smile. What would he do if I actually thrust my hand in there and felt around for it?

Probably drive off the road, so not a good idea.

"We are not going to that cottage. We don't even have a key—" I broke off with a snort. "Look who I'm talking to." As if Martin McAuliffe needed a key to open any locked door.

"You worry too much," he said.

"This is a police matter. It's not something for us to mess around with."

"I like messing around." The padre's expression said he wasn't talking about police matters.

"Stop that," I said.

"Stop what?" All innocence.

"You know very well what. Come on, Padre. Burke only told us about this because he trusted us to bring it straight to Howie."

"Yeah," he said, "as an 'anonymous tip.' As if an experienced detective like Howie Werker isn't going to immediately connect the dots to Peaches's presumptive stalker."

"He can connect the dots any way he wants," I said. "I don't have to verify his conclusions."

"You know Howie," he said. "He's by the book. No way is he going to tell us what's in that backpack. Aren't you even a little bit curious?"

I was rabidly curious, but I was also a responsible citizen. Most of the time. "I know we're both thinking the same thing."

"The blackmail money," he said.

I sighed in defeat. "One little peek, Padre. If there's even anything in that chimney. Carter might have cleaned it out. Then we put it back, get the heck out of there, and call Howie."

MARTIN SLID THE little lock-pick set back into his pocket and flicked on his tiny flashlight as we stepped over the threshold of the children's cottage. The closed-up space exuded a stale perfume, an amalgam of old wood, dust, and a hint of mildew. The ceiling was beamed, the multipaned windows flanked by floral drapes. An oval braided rug covered much of the plank flooring.

Martin's flashlight beam swept the room, revealing a pint-size table and chairs, doll bed, Windsor chair, and rocking horse. The table was set for a little girl's tea party. Stuffed animals and books occupied the window seat tucked into a bay window. An antique clock and assorted toys and figurines crowded the wooden fireplace mantel. Several unburnt logs perched on the fireplace grate, awaiting a match. I suspected these particular logs had been waiting for that match for decades.

Six weeks earlier we'd found ourselves in a similar situation, furtively scoping out an unfamiliar, sealed-up room in the dark. I'd take this children's cottage over that gross attic any day. The absence of a leathery human corpse tied to a chair was icing on the cake.

Martin didn't waste any time. He knelt on the stone hearth, leaned over the logs, and aimed his light up the chimney.

"Do you see anything?" I asked.

"I think so, but I can't be sure. I'm at a bad angle. Here." He handed me the flashlight, then grabbed both ends of the metal grate and lifted it, logs and all, setting it out of the way.

He scooted into the fireplace and reached up into the chimney. After a bit of groping, he gave a couple of sharp tugs. A backpack fell onto his lap in a puff of black soot.

"Wow," I said.

"Wow," he said.

I lifted the bag and set it on the rug as the padre extricated himself from the fireplace. "You do the honors," I said.

He unzipped the backpack and shone the flashlight into it. Inside were several white grocery bags. He retrieved the top one and upended it over the rug. Green folding money rained down, a deluge of twenties, fifties, and C-notes.

"It's nice to be right once in a while." I pulled out the other three bags. Each seemed to hold about the same amount of cash.

"I'm guessing this all adds up to a hundred sixty-four grand," Martin said.

"Unless he held on to some of it." I sat back on my heels and admired the bounty as the flashlight beam danced over it. I'd never seen so much cash in one place.

"Wouldn't it be nice…" he said.

"Don't even think it." I started shoveling the bills back into the grocery sack.

"I wasn't," he said. "I wouldn't. I'm just saying it's a nice haul. A simple observation."

I preferred to believe that if I weren't with him, Martin would be content to make the "simple observation" and return the cash to its hidey-hole. It irked me that I couldn't be one hundred percent certain of that, given that I knew little of his background, and what I did know was less than reassuring.

We got the money packed up. The padre scooted back into the fireplace and prepared to shove the backpack into place. He hesitated, squinting up into the chimney.

"What?" I said.

"I could be wrong, but… Give me the flashlight." He aimed the beam, squinted some more, then reached up so far his shoulder disappeared. He grimaced. "I can't…"

"Is there something else up there?" I asked.

"Yeah, but it's too high up." He gave up for the moment and shone the light around the immediate vicinity. "No poker?"

"How about this?" A rustic hearth broom leaned against the mantel, one of those old-timey handmade ones that nowadays are mostly for show.

"That's probably what he used to shove the thing up there. Hold the light for me." He poked the wooden broom handle into the chimney, peering upward, while I aimed the flashlight as best I could. "I don't want to push it farther up. If I can just…"

He worked at it for several minutes, repositioning himself a couple of times. "Okay, I think I can reach it now." Up went the arm again, high, higher… Just when I thought he was going to crawl right up the chimney, he cried, "Got it!"

He yanked hard, two, three, four times. Finally the stubborn thing tumbled into the fireplace. It turned out to be a zippered tote bag. Its coating of inky soot failed to conceal the distinctive Gucci pattern.

I dragged it onto the hearth. It was significantly heavier than the backpack. "Think this could be more cash?"

"Only if he was skimming off the top every time he collected the blackmail money," Martin said. "For twenty-four years."

"He wouldn't have dared," I said. "Something tells me Peaches would have noticed if so much as a nickel went missing."

"Good point. So…" He gestured to the bag. "I believe it's your turn."

I pulled the zipper and aimed the flashlight into the bag. And saw what appeared to be a bundle of rags. "Here goes." I reached inside and retrieved a small object swaddled in a kitchen towel. I unwrapped it and sat looking at a cheap plastic snow globe bearing the label *Atlanta, the Big Peach!* I shook the water-filled globe and watched pink glitter fly around the tiny peach tree glued to the base.

"Okay…" Martin's tone told me he was beginning to doubt Carter's sanity.

"This is one of them! One of Peaches's peaches!" I'd told him about the collection I'd expended so much effort trying to locate.

"Seriously? This little, um…?"

"'Worthless piece of junk' is the term you're groping for," I said. "Most of them are a lot nicer. Not to mention more valuable."

Martin helped me unwrap the collection. Some of the pieces were swathed in kitchen towels, some in washcloths, and some in layers of paper towel.

"Check out this little thing," he said, holding the netsuke between thumb and forefinger and examining it with the flashlight. "It's so intricate."

Seeing the jade carving in person, the exquisitely rendered grasshopper perched on a peach, I finally comprehended how it could fetch upwards of seven thousand dollars.

I peeled back a wad of paper towels to reveal a wooden box in the shape of a peach.

"Whoa, is that blood?" He pointed out dark stains on the paper towels.

"Carter bashed in the locked glass door of Peaches's china cabinet to get to these," I said. "I guess it didn't want to give up the goods."

"Well, if there's any doubt who swiped them," he said, "the cops could always run the DNA."

"More DNA," I said. "Carter will be thrilled."

We counted fifty-two peach figurines, crafted of every possible material, including stone, wood, brass, ceramic, melamine, silver, crystal, porcelain, papier-mâché, and several others I failed to identify.

"Let's get this stuff back up there." The padre wrapped a peach-shaped glass Christmas tree ornament in a washcloth.

Within minutes we had the peaches rewrapped and zipped into their tote. Martin laboriously forced the bag back up the chimney, with the assistance of the broom handle. He shoved the money bag after it, then replaced the logs in the fireplace. Standing, he slapped his palms against his soot-stained jeans.

"All that's left for you to do now," he said, "is to call Howie and report your 'anonymous tip.'"

"Let's get well away from here first." I pointed the flashlight at him. "What are you doing?"

Martin was positioning something on the fireplace mantel, carefully placing it between a segmented wooden doll and a cast-iron fire wagon, complete with a pair of horses and a little driver in a helmet.

"No!" I said. "Padre, no! You have to put that back."

The peach-tree snow globe looked glaringly out of place among the antique playthings clustered on the mantel.

"I'm not hauling that bag back down the chimney." He stood back to admire his handiwork. "That's a job for Crystal Harbor's finest."

"You can't leave that thing here," I said. "They'll know we got to the peaches first. It'll compromise the, whaddayacallit, chain of evidence."

"First of all, do you really think the cops care about the peaches? And trust me, no one's going to notice this little thing." He shook the snow globe, set it back down, and watched the glitter settle.

"You're insane." I tossed my hand at it. "How could anyone fail to notice that flashy trinket among all these dull antiques? It's like a slot machine in church. It *screams* at you."

"Have I ever told you you worry too much?"

"But—"

"No one staring through these windows will even know what they're looking at," he said, "except for you and me. It'll be something special just for us."

"People come in here to dust and whatever," I said.

"Yeah, and they'll see what they expect to see. And if someone does notice it, they'll think someone else higher up the food chain put it there, and they won't dare to question it."

"What about Evie?" I said. "She knows every peach in that

collection. She'll notice it's missing."

"You just called it a worthless piece of junk," he said. "She'll assume her dad hung on to it."

The little growly noise I made sounded an awful lot like Sexy Beast. As much as I hated to admit it, he was probably right.

The padre turned me to face him. He commandeered the flashlight, switched it off, and pocketed it. "Don't look at the snow globe, Jane. It'll only upset you." Moonlight spilled through the windows, silvering the Lilliputian furnishings and turning Martin's face into a mysterious, shadowed landscape.

I couldn't help but notice we were standing very close. As in, his arms were around me, and my front was touching his front. That kind of close.

"I won't," I breathed. "I won't look at it." I closed my eyes, to demonstrate how good I was at not looking.

I felt his breath first, the lovely, warm sweetness of it. Then his lips touched my lips, so gently at first I couldn't be sure. Then I was sure and it was a good thing he was holding me up, because my choice was simple. I could either stand on my own or I could lose myself to the sheer dizzying perfection of that kiss.

And I mean, a girl has to have her priorities.

About the Author

Pamela Burford comes from a funny family. You may take that any way you want. She was raised in a household that valued laughter above all, so of course the first thing she looked for in a husband was a sense of humor. Is it any wonder their grown kids are into stand-up comedy and improv? Oh, and here's another fun fact: Pamela's identical twin sister, Patricia Ryan, aka P.B. Ryan, is also a published novelist. Patricia is the Good Twin, and yeah, Pamela knows what that makes her. But hey, Evil Twins have more fun!

It should come as no surprise that everything Pamela writes is infused with her own quirky brand of humor, from her feel-good contemporary romance and romantic suspense novels to her popular Jane Delaney mystery series, featuring snarky "Death Diva" Jane, her canine sidekick Sexy Beast, and a fun love-triangle subplot. Pamela's own beloved poodle, Murray, wants you to know that any similarities between himself and neurotic, high-strung Sexy Beast are purely coincidental.

Pamela is the proud founder and past president of Long Island Romance Writers. Her books have won awards and sold millions of copies, but what excites her most is hearing from readers. Swing by and say hi at pamelaburford.com.